THE SINGLE WIFE

A NOVEL

MELISSA HILL

Fully revised and updated US edition, 2021.
Original UK edition published as 'Never Say Never' by Random House, UK.
© Little Blue Books, 2021.

The right of Melissa Hill to be identified as the Author of the Work has been
asserted by her in accordance with the Copyright, Designs and Patents Act 1988.

PROLOGUE

Man Plans – God Laughs.

It was the gang's last summer together before going their separate ways after uni, and given the conversation, Robin couldn't help but recall that old Yiddish proverb.

"Andrew will be our sports hero obviously," Amanda declared, positioning herself comfortably against her boyfriend's broad chest as she pushed a fair curl away from her pretty face.

Kate rolled her eyes. "You worked overtime on the crystal ball for that one," she muttered caustically. He was already set to sign with a rugby club post-graduation, so it wasn't exactly a reach.

Amanda gave her a withering look. "And you'll end up in politics lecturing us all - as usual."

There'd never been any love lost between those two, Robin thought, and neither bothered to hide it either.

"So what about you, babe?" Andrew returned the attention to the one who craved it the most. "What'll you be?"

"Famous of course," Amanda tittered. "A huge name in music or modelling ... or make it big on TV. Dunno, I haven't decided yet."

"Well, it's worth a shot at least?"

Realising she was outnumbered, Kate held her hands up in mock surrender. "OK, OK, whatever," she groaned. "I still think it's crazy – who's to say we'll even *want* to see one another in the future. To say nothing of tempting fate."

"Ah, don't be so negative. Are you in or not?"

"I'm in."

"Good stuff," Olivia sat back on her heels, eager to start organising. "So we'll meet up where ...?"

"Why not here?" Leah gestured toward the lake.

"Grand. Same spot by the water, so. But when?"

"Oh late afternoon I think, so some of us can get a bit of shopping in beforehand," Amanda suggested airily.

"I think she meant *when* – as in what year?"

"Oh OK, maybe a decade or so – or is that too long?"

"Not feckin' long enough," Kate muttered under her breath.

"So ..." Olivia pronounced solemnly, warming to the theme. "Soon we graduate out into the big bad world to do our own thing. Chances are some of us will stay in touch, chances are some of us ... won't." She gave a sideways glance at Amanda and Kate. "Still, for the sake of our friendship and everything we've shared, all of us agree to reunite here in ... five years?" She checked the date on her watch. "Same time, same place."

"To our last - and next - summer!" Leah raised her glass in a toast and the others duly followed, their expressions joyous with the promise of things to come.

All with the exception of Kate, who still looked sceptical. The others glared at her expectantly.

"OK, OK, I'll go along with it now, but trust me, these things *never* work out," she muttered with a shake of her head, though her eyes twinkled as she grudgingly raised her drink too. "To say nothing of tempting fate. But hey, nobody ever listens to me ..."

ONE

SIX YEARS LATER

Robin stood awkwardly in front of the security guard. Her heart hammered as he ordered her to hold out her arms. She did so, crucifixion-style. He began to pat her down quickly and impersonally and she wondered why she always felt so guilty.

Ben stood on the other side laughing, having just sailed through like every other time.

But even if she did manage to get by without incident, the guards nearly always spot-frisked her anyway. With her shoulder-length auburn hair and light complexion, she looked as Irish as the next woman, so why did JFK airport security always peg her as a potential terrorist?

Inquisition over, she joined Ben on the other side.

He shook his head. "Every, single, time," he joked. "Now come on, better get going."

Robin quickened her step and the two hastened towards their departure gate. They'd been lucky to reach the airport in the time they did with Friday afternoon traffic across Manhattan beggaring belief.

She had lived in NYC for all this time and still couldn't get used to the unrelenting traffic. Luckily the cab driver had driven like a man possessed to get them to the airport in time.

"Have you got the boarding cards?" she asked Ben.

"Me? I thought you had them," he replied seriously, though she knew by the mischievous glint in his eyes that he was only teasing. Hopefully.

"Not the time, Ben," she scolded. "Not when this plane is about to take off."

"Ah, they'd never leave without us."

At the gate, they duly produced their Irish passports.

"Yeah it *is* me, really," her boyfriend joked trying to lighten the tone. "Sure I *know* I'm miles better looking in real life but there you go."

But there wasn't the slightest response to his attempts at friendly humour and the man eventually handed back their passports without comment.

"Jaysus," he said to Robin on the way down the gangway. "Do none of these guys have a sense of humour anymore? It's only a short hop down the road."

Robin was really looking forward to this. She and Ben hadn't had a break away in ages. OK, it was only a few days in Washington, but she was really looking forward to her first visit to the capital. Manhattan could be claustrophobic and things had been so hectic at work lately that they could both do with the breather.

Still, she felt an automatic sense of discomfort as she handed over her boarding card inside the aircraft door.

"Straight down on the left-hand side – 10B and C," the stewardess informed them pleasantly.

She and Ben made their way slowly down the aisle, bumping past people shifting their luggage about and trying to get settled.

Robin reached Row 10 and was about to take her seat and let Ben stow their bags overhead as was their routine, when a familiar scent hit her nostrils. Instantly, she turned around and motioned for him to follow her back up the aisle.

"What is it, hon?" he asked but with a quick glance at the seats directly behind, he soon saw what was bothering her.

"You sit down – I'll talk to them," Robin looked around for a stewardess.

"Are you sure? I'll come with you if –"

"No, I don't want to make a fuss," she said grimacing.

Seeing a stewardess approach from the other end of the plane, Robin waylaid her. Trying to keep her tone low so as not to be overheard by anyone in the immediate vicinity, she quickly outlined the issue.

"Let me look into that, ma'am," the woman said, a little warily, "but as you can see the aircraft is almost fully boarded – it may be difficult to reassign seating."

"Look," Robin said softly, trying her best to sound reasonable, "Please understand that I'm not blaming you, but I did make the request ahead of time and was assured ..." She trailed off, spotting a woman seated in the row next to them blatantly trying to eavesdrop. "If you could just maybe take another look at the seating arrangements, I would really appreciate it. Or perhaps we could just move seats altogether?" She smiled graciously hoping her polite approach would work.

"I'll see what I can do," the stewardess said, heading for the top of the aisle.

Robin felt all eyes on her as she stood there waiting for the other woman's return, and despite her protestation that she could deal with the matter herself, she was relieved when Ben joined her.

"What's happening? Are they going to move them?"

"We'll soon find out," she said, seeing the stewardess approach. But by her expression, Robin knew immediately that her request had been ignored. Again.

"I'm afraid not, ma'am," the stewardess confirmed apologetically. "I don't know what happened. Obviously, reservations didn't pass your request to check in. And since this is such a small aircraft ..." She trailed off as if to imply that in such a cramped space, what difference could it make?

"I don't believe this," Ben interjected hotly. "It's the same thing every time we fly with you lot – how come AA can get it done, Delta can get it done, but your crowd –"

"Calm down," Robin soothed, though she was just as frustrated.

"How about I talk to the passengers in question?"

Robin hated the way people looked at her like she was a raving hypochondriac – the way the stewardess was looking at her now. But she wasn't just looking for attention or special treatment. She only wished that were the case.

"That's all we can do, I suppose," she said wearily, but one look at Ben as they followed the stewardess back down towards their seats, told her that he was fit to burst. She kept her distance as they approached the passengers seated behind Row 10.

"Excuse me," the stewardess said pleasantly to a middle-aged woman accompanied by what looked to be her husband and young son. "So sorry to inconvenience you, but could I request that your son put his snack away for the duration of this flight? Or if maybe we could move you to another seat near the front ..."

"Whaddya mean?" The woman's eyes narrowed. "With my kidneys, I need to be close by the girls' room. Anyway, what's the problem? National Security mean no one's allowed to eat anymore either?"

"That's not the case at all, ma'am," said the stewardess soothingly. "We'll be serving refreshments once airborne and some complimentary snacks too, so if you could –"

"They better be complimentary – and not at those darn New York prices..." the woman's husband interjected. "Anyway, the engine hasn't even started and my boy here is hungry." He glared at the stewardess. "I don't see any sign around here saying you shouldn't eat when you're hungry." With that, he reached forward and took a packet of nuts from his seat-pouch.

"I'm making a polite request for you to please put those away, sir," the stewardess repeated her plea. "I appreciate your confusion but we have a passenger with a medical condition seated in front of you today."

The man leaned forward and looked up at Ben. "What - you addicted to junk food or somethin'?"

"No but my girlfriend has a nut allergy," he announced irritably.

"Ben calm down," Robin said mortified, as everyone in the immediate vicinity turned to look. Sensing an escalation, another stewardess moved towards them.

"Well, I ain't offering her no nuts am I?" the man asked, puzzled.

"That's not it," Ben explained. "She's hypersensitive."

"Ain't my fault if people can't control themselves," the man went on, unmoved. "I paid my fare same as everyone else and nobody's gonna tell me what I can and can't do." As if to prove his point, he tore open the bag and put a handful of peanuts in his mouth, while Robin moved back, terror-stricken.

"Please sir, we need to take off. Again, I'm really sorry for the inconvenience but –"

"Hey," he said, raising his voice and looking nastily at the stewardess. "Me and my family ain't had nuthin' to eat since this morning and we're *hungry*. We're not movin' and I ain't puttin' away no peanuts, my wife ain't puttin' away no peanuts, and my son ain't puttin' away no peanuts for some stuck-up Park Avenue Princess. So there." He sat back and his wife looked on approvingly, satisfied that her husband was the right man to put these troublesome city-slickers in their place.

But then she looked up at Robin and seemed to recognise the terror in her eyes. "We didn't mean any harm," the wife said to her, and then to the stewardess. "But my boy here, he gets antsy when he's hungry and so does Max. We don't mean any harm. And with my kidneys, we really can't move seats."

"That's OK ma'am, but we really need to take off now. So if you and your husband could just put those away, there shouldn't be any issue."

"Or if you lot had just assigned a nut-free zone as requested, there wouldn't *be* an issue in the first place," Ben seethed. "But you just don't care, do you? You just pack in as many idiots are you can fit – who cares?"His annoyance was in full flight now, which is more than could be said for the rest of the passengers on Flight 81268. "It's unacceptable and I won't have it."

Then to Robin's horror, he opened the overhead locker and removed their luggage. "Come on, hon we're going,"

"What?"

"Sir, if you could just –"

"I said, we're going. Forget it. You can bet this is the last time I fly with this godforsaken airline."

Robin looked from Ben to the stewardess, to the peanut crunchers and back to her boyfriend again, but at that stage she didn't care where they went as long as it was away from all the staring, the pointing, the whispered remarks.

Providing a nut-free zone was at the discretion of the airlines, so truly Ben had no right to be so hard on them. But she suspected he was weary of the fact that her (life-threatening) allergy could be so all-pervading.

"Really sir, there's no need ..." The voice of the stewardess trailed off as she realised that Ben wasn't to be placated.

Sitting in the taxi from the airport back to their Lower East Side apartment, and yet another weekend ruined, Robin smarted with embarrassment.

"I made it clear when I made the reservation, really I did," she said, looking miserably at him and trying to convince herself more than Ben.

He took her hand in his. "It was my decision to get off that plane. There'll be other weekends, and anyway, it's not your fault."

But of course it was her fault, Robin knew. It was *always* her fault.

TWO

Leah took a deep breath – a very, very deep breath. This was easily the most terrifying experience of her life. She had done many frightening things over the years – bungee jumping in France, white-water rafting in Belgium, not to mention going through the very scary motions of setting up a business – but this, this was the most terrifying of all.

The night before, she hadn't been able to sleep with nerves and had spent much of the night in her kitchen experimenting with new recipes. It hadn't been a wasted night either to be fair, as she'd come up with a raspberry and white chocolate truffle combo that was absolutely delicious – *Berrylicious* actually, which was exactly what she intended to name the new creation.

She took another deep breath and sat for a few moments more in her little Fiesta before getting out.

You can do this, she told herself. You can do it. Unfortunately, the message wasn't being relayed to the butterflies in her stomach.

Despite her student ambitions to become a pastry chef, Leah found that time abroad after her degree had unexpectedly led her catering career in a different direction.

Eager to further her knowledge and experience, she had spent a few years in France working under the stewardship of a renowned Belgian dessert chef and chocolatier. Her own speciality at college had been pastries and desserts, but working alongside such an artisan and master of his work, Leah unexpectedly fell in love with the intricate handmade chocolatier craft.

To hone her growing skills, she spent a further eighteen months away in Brussels and while there approached with gusto the challenge of marrying delicious flavour combos with the finest chocolate.

By the time the initial apprenticeship was over and her own skills were polished to perfection, Leah was hooked on the artistry of chocolate-making. There was no doubt in her mind as to where she wanted to go with her career, and when she returned to Ireland she immediately set about going into the confectionery trade.

At the time of her return a couple of years before, the country was still in the throes of an economic boom and, following a huge leap of faith (and an equally huge start-up loan), Leah began her own specialised handmade chocolate company.

She named the business Elysium, Greek for 'a condition of ideal happiness', which she felt went some way towards doing justice to her stuff.

While the handmade chocolate business was a thriving Irish trade, there was little in the way of high-end artisan gift options. Thanks to her time in Belgium, she decided that the packaging and presentation should be equally as important as the chocolates themselves. Her signature use of rich purple and gold ornate boxes, covered in beaded silk and wrapped in delicate muslin, soon became hugely popular with card-and-gift stores and tourist retailers.

It was true what they said about finding something you loved and never working a day again she thought, because she adored her job.

Josh, her boyfriend, often complained that she worked way too hard, but as far as she was concerned it was the best job in the world.

Recently she and Josh had set up home together in a one-bed rented apartment on Dublin's Southside. Their relationship was going great, the business was going great, Leah was six months away from her thirtieth birthday and life was great.

But, she thought finally getting out of the car, if she could just get today over and done with, life would be even better. As Josh had pointed out before leaving for work that morning, all she could do was her best.

Unfortunately, Leah knew from experience that her best would probably not be enough.

She jogged up the steps and into the building, her dark pony-tail swinging as she went. She felt strange wearing her hair like that outside of the kitchen, always thinking that the style looked particularly childish on her, probably because of her huge brown eyes and round face.

The ponytail had been Olivia's suggestion – apparently, it never failed. And since the ponytail trick had worked for her best friend, Leah was prepared to take her word for it. She was prepared to try *anything* if it helped her through today's ordeal.

She gave the rather dour-looking receptionist a friendly smile. "Leah Reid," she said by way of announcement when the other woman didn't reciprocate. "My appointment's at ten."

From the receptionist's eventual curt nod to somewhere behind her, she deduced that she should take a seat on one of the plastic chairs lined up along the wall. She sat back, and despite herself began nervously wringing her hands together. Then she stopped herself, realising that at a time like this, greasy, sweating palms were exactly what she didn't need.

She picked up a magazine and was about to check her horoscope when she realised that that particular issue was almost three months out of date. She turned instead to the problem pages. Troublesome spouses and illicit affairs were always in vogue.

"Ms Reid?" She looked up, startled, to see a small, middle-aged man with a clipboard and more importantly, what seemed like a kindly face, looking questioningly at her.

Leah stood up, relieved. This guy looked like a bit of a pussy-cat. Maybe this mightn't be such a disaster after all.

"Great day, isn't it?" she babbled as she followed him inside the office, habitually falling back on the great Irish conversation starter. Well, it was either that or the Dublin traffic and Leah could hardly start moaning about that with him, could she?

Two minutes into the room and all her hopes about this guy being a pussy-cat were cruelly dashed. He asked to see her driver's licence and, when Leah handed it to him, recoiled as if he'd been burnt.

"Out of its sleeve, please," he ordered, his expression po-faced as she obliged. Yikes. Seemed she'd already got off to a bad start.

Nonetheless, she steeled herself and tried to act confident – but not too confident – as he began the questioning. The first one was actually quite simple for her, something about the correct situation in which you should dip your headlights.

"Oh, I never drive at night," she answered pleasantly, "so that doesn't apply."

He looked at her. "Can you answer the question please, Ms Reid?"

Leah thought for a second. "Well, when another car is coming towards *you* I suppose, otherwise you'd blind him. Not that it makes any difference, people just tend to blind you anyway, which is exactly why I avoid driving at night."

He said nothing and went straight on to the next question, this one about the right of way on roundabouts. She was pleased – this was one she knew very well.

"When you approach a roundabout, you automatically have right of way."

He looked at her. "Explain further?"

"Well, when you approach a roundabout and you're not planning to go round it and you just want to go straight through it, then you are automatically free to do so."

By his face, she wondered if she had said something wrong. But no, roundabouts were her *thing*, the one situation where she was completely confident she was in the right.

The problem was other drivers who didn't know how to use it properly and Leah thought wearily, there was always one. She hadn't the heart to beep her horn at the poor eejits (usually men) who didn't know what they were doing, but the problem was *they* always honked at *her*.

A few minutes later it was time for the main event, and she trotted out of the building, leading him to where she had parked the car.

To her surprise, he asked her to walk around it, ostensibly checking for broken mirrors and lights etc, and refused to entertain Leah's protests that of course everything worked fine, wasn't the car only two years old?

Then he mortified her by asking her to recite the Fiesta's registration. Why would anyone need to know *that*, Leah thought when if she had forgotten where she'd parked, it could easily be found by pressing the alarm on her keys and following the sound? She knew it was a two-year-old Dublin registration but that was about it.

Would something that simple mean a fail, she worried now, as she moved up a gear and drove towards the main street.

She had just about remembered to put up her 'L' plates beforehand, Olivia having reminded her that not displaying her learner plates would mean an instant fail and likely revocation of her provisional driver's permit. It had taken her close to an hour to find a place that stocked the bloody things, and nearly another trying to stick them to the windscreen.

Leah cast a quick glance at the test official in the passenger seat, being careful not to swing her ponytail too much – the more elaborate swings, Olivia warned her, were only for checking her mirrors. He was marking boxes and as far as she could see, wasn't watching her driving at all.

A bit rude, she thought. All these months she'd been dreading taking her official driver's test – for the *third* time – and hardly sleeping the last few days thinking about it, and then your man couldn't even be bothered to assess her....

Leah looked up and quickly slammed on the brakes when she realised she had just been about to drive right through a zebra crossing – with of course the obligatory Hollywood movie mother and buggy directly in her path. Yikes. She gripped the steering wheel and smiled beatifically at the tester.

"Nice reaction time, eh?" she said, a little unnerved by her forthrightness. It must be the adrenaline making her giddy, she thought, checking her rear-view mirror before moving off again.

The roads were crazy this afternoon – traffic was crawling at a snail's pace and it was as though the entire population of Dublin knew Leah was sitting her driving test and were out to make things hard for her.

Take this person, she thought, spying a woman in one of those huge SUVs coming towards her, on her way back from the school run, a determined look on her face that suggested she wasn't going to stop for anyone. As she came closer it became even clearer that this particular woman *wasn't* going to stop or give way to anyone, Leah included.

She mentally recited the rules of the road. The other driver's side of the road was obstructed by parked cars and Leah's was clear. Which meant she had the right of way, didn't it? It meant that she was perfectly entitled to keep going, and the other driver had to stay out of *her* way didn't it? Right, so she would keep going and Madam would just have to wait until the road was clear.

So Leah did keep going and ... oh blast her, Madam kept going too. They were getting closer, each eyeing the other, neither willing to give an inch, until finally, in sheer desperation, Leah edged up on the kerb and onto the path. While Madam drove past with a face on her that would sink the *Titanic* and not a wave, a nod of thanks ... nothing.

She steered to her right and the Fiesta's two wheels toppled none-too-gently back down onto the road again.

Her heart pounded. Blast it, blast it, blast it ... would your man see that as initiative? She wasn't sure. Though, nobody was supposed to drive on the path, surely? There was nothing in the rulebook, mind you, but ... she groaned inwardly, just wishing she could open the door and tell the bloody tester to feck off for himself.

This was *not* going well. First, she'd been a bit vague on the questions, then she couldn't remember the Fiesta's registration, not to mention the close call with the zebra crossing ... and now this. Was there anything else that could go wrong at this stage? Anything at all?

Ah sure she might as well keep going and just hope for the best.

But, no sooner had Leah made her brave decision to push on through, one of the 'L' plates she had so painstakingly positioned on the windscreen earlier, came unstuck and plopped into her lap.

Well. She'd definitely failed it now, hadn't she?

The look of pure horror – or was it terror – on the driving tester's face quickly answered Leah's unspoken question.

THREE

Olivia was cleaning the bathroom and wondering how Leah was getting on when the phone rang.

"I'm really sorry to disturb you like this," she heard her manager say with genuine regret, "and if I could have avoided phoning you I would, but if we don't operate soon, the poor little mite could die."

Her insides tightened. "Oh Alma, no – what's happened? Which one?"

"He's just been brought in. By the looks of things he was run over, then some kind-hearted soul," Alma added with heavy irony, "tossed him into the ditch to die. I don't know how long he's held on but he was found by someone this morning out walking their dog." Her voice softened. "I don't even know if we can save him but –"

"I'll be there in ten minutes," Olivia said decisively. On call or not, the very least she could do was try. She put the phone down, grabbed a coat from the cupboard under the stairs and hastened back into the living-room.

"Let's get your coat on, pet," she announced to her daughter.

A qualified veterinary surgeon, she worked part-time at an

animal shelter within driving distance from Lakeview, the village in which she and her four-year-old daughter now lived.

Less than an hour's drive from Dublin, Lakeview was very much a quintessential summer tourist town with locally owned pubs, shops and a gorgeous café along one short main street.

Olivia had moved there to be closer to her parents who'd retired to the sleepy little village years before, and she lived in Cherrywood Green, a small mature estate on the other side of town.

She hated having to drag Ellie the eight or so miles to the shelter but there was no time to call on her mother to babysit. Ellie normally loved 'helping out' with the animals but with such an emergency neither Alma nor Olivia would be able to humour her this time.

"It's not Angel is it, Mummy?" her daughter asked, her eyes wide as Olivia helped her into her coat. An elderly abandoned dachshund, Angel had been at the centre for sixteen months, and the little dog and Ellie had formed a bond within seconds of setting eyes upon one another.

Olivia knew that Ellie would have mixed feelings should poor Angel ever be re-homed. As would Olivia herself. Every dog, cat, pony and ferret had a special place in the hearts of all the employees and volunteers of Paws & Tails Refuge Centre.

"No, this little guy was just brought in," she explained, closing the front door behind them and hurrying her towards the car. "Alma thinks he was hit by a car."

It wouldn't be the first or indeed the last hit-and-run victim upon which Olivia had operated. She'd been working at the centre for years, having gone there not long after she and Peter had bought a house close by, originally intending to spend some time there before something better came along.

But she'd loved it so much she'd stayed, though once Ellie had come along, she'd reduced her hours and now worked only a three-day week and occasional emergencies when the full-time vet was unavailable. This was one of those times.

"You'll save him, Mummy, I know you will," Ellie said, her tone revealing utmost confidence. "You always do."

Pulling out onto the road, Olivia bit her lip, and marvelled at the blind and innocent trust of four-year-olds. Because she knew well that, for all her talents, she hadn't been able to use them when it mattered the most.

There had been an emergency that day too she recalled sadly, her mind travelling right back to that evening five years ago.

If only that poor Lab hadn't swallowed a chicken bone and needed an emergency operation to remove it.

If only she'd been home when she said she'd be.

If only, if only, if only ...

IT HAD all gone wrong from the second she arrived at work that morning. Unusually for Olivia she'd reached the centre ten minutes late – and although she wasn't sure of it at the time, she'd been late for a very good reason.

A short visit to her doctor at lunchtime confirmed her early morning suspicions and from then on in, she might as well have been on a different planet.

Alma noticed it immediately.

"Well, spit it out," the centre manager challenged Olivia soon after helping her administer worming tablets to a particularly skittish Alsatian.

"Spit what out?" she laughed, trying desperately to keep her news to herself but annoyed with herself for being so transparent. An open book, Peter always called her, and he was right. She could rarely keep a secret or her feelings from anyone. Her open face and particularly her wide, expressive blue eyes always gave her away.

"Whatever it is that's got you beaming like a Cheshire cat all afternoon," Alma teased. "Although being married to a hunk like yours would probably be enough," she added with a wink.

"Nothing," Olivia said, unable to stop grinning and unwilling to look Alma in the eye. "I'm just in a good mood today, that's all."

Just then the telephone rang, and as their budget couldn't stretch to a full-time volunteer and Olivia was closest to the door, she went out to answer it. "Paws & Tails."

"Hey love," Olivia heard Peter's familiar voice and she grinned even more broadly.

"Hey yourself," she replied, although she was dying to blurt it out there and then. "What's up?"

"Nothing really, just checking that you're definitely on the eight to four shift today? You're not on a split or anything?"

"Nope – I'm out of here by four. Do you want me to pick up something on the way?"

"No, no – just checking. I might even be home before you yet – depends on how things go here."

She could tell by her husband's weary tone that he was up to his tonsils – again. She hoped Peter would get away from the hospital that bit earlier today, not just because she had something to tell him, but also because he was working way too hard. He hadn't been himself lately, and tended to be tired and a little moody; the stress of working all those hours taking its toll.

"Did you get yourself seen yet?" she asked him. "About those palpitations you had last week?" Olivia didn't want him taking any chances. In a hospital, he was in the best place possible to get himself checked out. It was probably fine, but still –

"It's nothing," he replied, a little testily, and she thought she'd better just let him get back to work. The sooner he did that, the sooner he'd be home.

"Well, take it easy love, and I'll see you this evening."

"Talk to you later."

Most definitely she thought, smiling softly to herself as she put the phone down. Hopefully, he *would* be home before her, because this particular evening they had plenty to talk about.

She glanced up at the clock. Time for a quick afternoon tea break. Olivia didn't normally bother with tea breaks, viewing them as a surefire way to unhinge her attempts at keeping her figure. Still, her tummy was rumbling, she'd had very little for lunch and, in fairness, she wouldn't have to worry about her keeping her figure for too much longer. And starving herself surely wasn't good for the baby.

Olivia's heart leapt. She was actually having a baby. Weird but it still wasn't quite real to her, not until she told him. Even though the doctor had congratulated her and given her a due date, to Olivia it couldn't be true, it wouldn't be real until she told Peter.

After three years of marriage and two years of trying, it finally happened. Had *actually* happened. She was pregnant. He would be ecstatic.

She mentally hugged herself as she tried to imagine what their baby would look like. The doctor had told her to come back in a few weeks for the first ultrasound and she couldn't wait to see Peter's face when they heard the heartbeat for the very first time.

The next hour passed without event and Olivia managed to get through a much overdue pile of paperwork. She sat back in her chair and yawned.

Just then Susan, one of the centre's many volunteers, rushed into the office. "Bit of an emergency – someone's just brought in a poor Lab – he's going into convulsions ..."

Olivia leapt into action and twenty minutes later her hands were buried deep in the dog's abdomen, trying to remove dangerously sharp pieces of bone that had most likely come from a cooked chicken.

Judging by his condition, he was most likely a starving stray that had come across the chicken carcass in someone's refuse and unable to believe his luck, had gone through it with relish and amazing speed. But now the poor thing could lose his life because of it. Shards of bone had punctured his stomach and upper colon and Olivia knew that he was lucky to have been discovered at all.

At last, the extractions were done and she completed the final phases of surgery. Then she looked up at the clock, eyes widening as she caught sight of the time.

It was after ... *five.*

"Blast it, I didn't realise the time. I told Peter I'd be leaving at four!"

"Go on, off with you," said Alma. "I'll finish up here. And sorry – I didn't notice either –"

Olivia hastily cleaned herself up. Then she rang Peter but only got his answer service. Perhaps he was still driving ... She tried the house but got the answering machine. In her haste to get to work that morning, she'd left her phone on the kitchen table, so if Peter thought she'd already left and was trying to contact her on that he wouldn't be able to.

Finally, she left the centre and hurried to her car.

Some twenty minutes later, after battling maddening traffic, she drove into their housing estate; her heart plunging towards her stomach in horror as she saw the ambulance parked nearby.

A small group was standing around on the path outside her house, their faces grave as they saw her car approach.

Among them was her mother, her face stricken as she turned towards her. Her next-door neighbour, Cora and new neighbour, Deirdre with her little boy. Alex, Olivia remembered his name was, and then wondered why all this stupid trivia was running through her mind.

It was a delaying tactic, she thought, simply a delaying tactic. Because one look at her mother's face and she knew that something terrible had happened.

Her body was wracked with fear, her movements almost

zombie-like, she got out of the car and rushed to her mother. "What's going on, Mum?" she asked, her voice shaking. What are you doing here? Where's ...?"

For a long moment, Eva didn't answer; she just continued to stare at her daughter, her expression a mixture of sorrow and pity. Instantly Olivia felt her stomach twist. Oh no, please no ...

"Mum? Where's Peter?" This time her voice was barely a whisper.

"Oh God – " Eva reach for her, her eyes brimming with tears. "Love ... he's ... it was ..." She shook her head from side to side, unable to find the right words.

"Mum I asked you a question!" Olivia cried.

Eva's eyes brimmed with tears, and she shook her head. "I'm so sorry, love," she whispered hoarsely. "He didn't ... make it."

"What – what do you mean?" Olivia barely got the words out. Her mind whirled. "Were you here when – who – ?"

"I only just arrived – Cora from next door phoned me. She couldn't get you at work or on your phone. That new neighbour of yours Deirdre, she –"

Olivia's heart stopped then as right behind her mother, she spotted the paramedics lifting something – *someone* – into the ambulance on a stretcher.

A covered stretcher.

With a cry, she made to run towards the ambulance, but somehow Eva stopped her. "There's no point, love," she said, holding her daughter in her arms. "Nothing you could have done. He's gone."

"No ..." Olivia's words were barely a whisper, and it was as though all the breath had somehow departed from her lungs, all the blood had left her body. She felt as though she was no longer part of herself, as if she were somehow floating outside it.

"There was nothing any of us could do, pet," her mother continued sorrowfully. "By the time the ambulance got here, it was too late – we were *all* too late." She tightened her embrace. "I'm so sorry, love."

"But how ... what ... what happened?" Olivia's legs had turned to jelly and she began to sway.

"They're not fully sure yet, they tried to revive him but it was too far gone. Look, you need to sit down. Let's go... let's go next door to Cora's, OK?"

Shell-shocked and stricken Olivia let her mother lead her away. A million and one emotions coursed through her, but strangely at that moment, she could only make sense of one. "I should have been there..." she blurted hoarsely, overwhelmed with remorse.

"There's no point in saying that, love. There was nothing anyone could have done."

But that wasn't true, and she knew it. Everyone else might have been helpless but *she* would have known what to do. She always did.

FOUR

What's worse, Olivia thought now as she and her little daughter drove home, having successfully operated on the hit-and-run victim – today was her and Peter's wedding anniversary.

It was inevitable that she would think about him, but for Ellie's sake, she had to try not to let it upset her.

She let them both in the door of the modest semi-detached house in Lakeview they'd moved to not long after Ellie was born. It had been a difficult time, trying to raise a new baby on her own so soon after, but Olivia thanked the heavens every day that at least the grief and stress hadn't affected her pregnancy.

Ellie was all she had now, and while her mum, Peter's parents, and good friends were great, Olivia still felt lonely sometimes.

Without Peter, it was like part of her was missing. The two of them had been together so long, had thought they'd be together forever, and then one moment of forgetfulness – of *stupidity* – had taken him away from her.

Everyone kept telling her it wasn't her fault that she'd been late back. Yes, maybe she couldn't have saved him ... but now she would never know, would she? And for a very long time the guilt had almost been harder than the grief.

Still, that was close to five years ago, and except for significant anniversaries or birthdays, Olivia was getting on with it. She had good friends, a nice house close to her parents in a lovely village and of course she had her daughter, her pride and joy.

She made herself and Ellie a small snack.

"Mum, can I do some painting afterwards?" the little girl asked.

"Yes but only if you stay in the kitchen this time," she said, ruffling her fair curls. Her hair was way too long and fly away, but Olivia couldn't bring herself to cut it and part with those beautiful little ringlets just yet.

Later she had just finished cleaning the bath when she heard her phone. She stood up, red-faced from exertion and went to hunt for it.

She didn't recognise the number, but that was nothing new. She hated bloody mobile phones and truly only kept one so she could be contacted by work, or to keep in touch with her mother while she had Ellie.

"Nailed it," the text said.

Olivia smiled. Leah had taken her driving test this morning and, by some miracle must have passed and thus finally surrendered her learner's permit.

Must have changed her phone number again too. Her friend was forever losing her stuff and had changed her number four times this year alone, which was why it was a question of 'pick a number – any number' when you wanted to get Leah on the phone.

"I don't believe it," Olivia wrote back, meaning it. Her friend's driving was ... suspect, to say the least. *"Celebrating tonight so?"* she enquired, thinking that Josh would surely take her out somewhere.

"Definitely. Though need a wingman. Fancy it?"

So Josh must be working late or something. Olivia thought

about it. At that moment, a few drinks and a chat with Leah sounded wonderful.

It was brilliant to have her back in Ireland after her Belgian stint, and although Olivia had made lots of friends over the years, there were none like those who knew you best. With Leah, she never had to avoid the subject of Peter or answer awkward questions about her single status. Not that it was anyone else's business, but she only felt comfortable talking about Peter to those who knew him too. And considering the day that was in it, she could do with some cheering up.

Despite the fact that she hated leaving her, she knew she could ask her mother to look after Ellie, who adored being spoiled by her grandmother.

Eva would be delighted too, she was always on at Olivia to get out and about more. She knew her mum would like her to move on and try to meet someone else. She saw Leah and hunky Josh for the odd drink, but it had been ages - months actually - since she and her friend had been out on the town on their own.

"Will check how land lies and get back to you," she texted again slowly and then using her fixed line phone, dialled her mother's number.

"Would you mind looking after Ellie for a few hours this evening? Leah passed her driving test and wants me to meet her for a drink to celebrate. I can drop her off on my way."

"She ... passed it?" Eva, who knew Leah well, sounded surprised. "Did she bribe yer man?"

"I'd imagine it was something like that or else he was so terrified he just wanted to get it over with," Olivia joked.

"Ha. But of course, I'll take Ellie. We'll be here all evening so drop her over whenever you want."

"Thanks Mum."

"And be sure and enjoy yourselves and don't worry about coming back early," Eva soothed. "It's a Friday night, after all."

"Don't worry, Mum, we're a bit ould for the Temple Bar thing – well, I am anyway," she added wryly, trying to remember the last time she was on a rip-roaring night out in the city.

"Just take your time and enjoy it – that's all I'm saying," Eva said. "Ellie will be fine with me and your dad."

"*Celebrations good to go,*" she messaged her friend then. "*Say where and when ...*"

It was a few minutes before Leah replied. "*Fantastic. Searson's around six? Champers on me.*"

Champers? She really *was* going all out tonight. Well, Olivia didn't care what they drank, she was just looking forward to getting together with her friend for what would undoubtedly be a ... lively evening.

LEAH'S PHONE rang just as she was putting the key in the front door of her apartment.

"Eva," she answered warmly, seeing the number displayed on the screen. "How are you?"

"I'm good," Olivia's mother said cheerily. "Olivia told me about the driving test and I'm thrilled for you. I just wanted to say enjoy yourselves tonight, but also make sure my daughter does too and –"

"Thrilled?" Leah interrupted, startled. "Eva I failed again - miserably. There's nothing to be thrilled about."

"What? But why on earth did you tell Olivia you passed?"

She frowned, confused. "I haven't spoken to Olivia since last night when she rang to wish me good luck, but good luck must have gone on holiday." She rolled her eyes. "What on earth would make her think I'd passed?"

"But she said the two of you were going out for a celebratory outing in Dublin tonight. She wanted to know if I could take Ellie. She wouldn't have made it up, surely?"

"Eva I've been on a different planet most of today, but I'm one hundred per cent positive that I did not ask Olivia to come to Dublin tonight." Although it sounded good, now that she thought about it. She could do with drowning her sorrows. "Where did she say she was meeting me?"

"She didn't mention that. But I'm a little concerned now. I know Olivia is a grown woman and can do what she pleases, but why would she lie about meeting you?"

"Maybe she has a mystery man on the go?" Leah said dramatically, although she dismissed the thought as soon as she said it.

Olivia wouldn't have a secret lover; her friend wouldn't have a lover full-stop. Peter had been the love of her life and the only man she had ever wanted.

Still, it was all a bit ... strange. Olivia was straight as a die and didn't do things like that - lie to her mother or go off and leave her daughter without good reason.

Something was up, Leah knew.

And while she had no idea what was going on, she just hoped for Olivia's sake that her friend knew what she was doing.

FIVE

Robin slung her bag over her shoulder and headed north on Broadway.

Already the air was thick with humidity that she reckoned only seasoned New Yorkers could tolerate. She still hadn't gotten used to the mild spring temperatures, let alone the choking heat of summer. She'd just left the air-conditioned cool of the office for the day, but already her face was red and perspiring and her cotton shirt super-glued to her chest and back.

It wasn't about to get any easier she thought wryly, as she reached Wall St Station and began to descend the steps. The subway was tough going at the best of times, so on a day like today she would be lucky to take in a breath of air, let alone a fresh one.

She was just about to insert her travel pass into the barrier, when her phone rang. Two seconds later and she would have been out of range in the tunnels. She glanced at the caller display and was disappointed when she spotted who it was.

"Hey," she said, her tone flat. A call at this time of day usually meant that Ben was working late – something that lately was happening more often than not, and another reason why that planned trip to Washington would have been such a welcome break.

It was a pity because on an evening like this it would have been nice to throw open the loft's cast iron windows and eat dinner while watching the world go by.

Like Robin, Ben loved to take advantage of the good weather – a result, she thought, of their Irish childhoods when a fine summer's day was a rare event and treated as such.

"It's little Kirsty – she's had an attack and Sarah's had to take her to the hospital."

"Aw, poor thing, is she very bad?" Ben's four-year-old niece suffered from chronic asthma.

"Bad enough, according to Sarah. She forgot to use her inhaler again. They've put her on the nebuliser."

"She's in St Vincent's?"

"Yeah, same as last time."

"OK, I'll meet you there. Does Sarah need anything?" She knew Ben's poor sister would be up the walls.

"Just some peace of mind," he answered grimly. "But Brian's away, so I left work early and promised her I'd go to their place to pick up a couple of things. I'm on my way from there now, so I'll see you soon, OK?"

Sarah and her husband Brian lived about an hour's drive away in New Jersey.

The hospital was close by, so rather than risk the stifling heat of the subway, Robin decided to walk. Still with the choking dead air of the city, by the time she reached the hospital she was so short of breath herself, she could only imagine how poor Kirsty was feeling.

"Thanks for coming – again," Sarah greeted when Robin entered the ward, and she noticed that she had lost an awful lot of weight since she'd last seen her.

She gave her a warm hug before turning to Kirsty, who looked frail and even tinier in the hospital bed. Although thankfully Robin noticed, she was off the nebuliser. She held one hand behind her back.

"Hey there, look who followed me here to see you!"

Kirsty grinned and her eyes lit up when Robin produced a small alligator beanie toy. She had picked it up at a bodega on her way, and while she knew the fearsome-looking alligator probably wasn't the best choice for a four-year-old, she was loath to get something stuffed or furry, in case it would exacerbate her asthma.

The little girl hugged her none-too-cute new alligator toy and grinned at Robin who felt guilty that these days the only time they saw Kirsty seemed to be when she was ill. But because they both worked long hours, Robin as a financial controller for Wall Street, and Ben a graphic-design firm on Lexington, they tended to just chill out at weekends.

Lately, Ben was taking on some additional freelance work in the hope that they could move out of Manhattan and get a place in the suburbs.

"It's either that, or go home," he had said one evening over a pizza, and the wineglass Robin was holding had almost cracked in her hand.

"Back home – to Dublin?" she said, her heart in her mouth as she waited for him to clarify. She had no intention of moving back – not now, not ever. She loved her life in New York. And up until then she'd thought Ben felt the same way.

"It would be nice though, wouldn't it?" he said, his dark eyes shining. "A complete change of lifestyle, something slow and easier than all this mad rushing around."

What was it about the Irish abroad that made them see 'the old country' through rose-tinted glasses? It was as though Dublin had never moved into the twenty-first century and everyone was still working at a snail's pace and travelling along boreens on horses and carts.

Robin spoke to Leah regularly, and from what she could make out, Dublin was booming. Everything was notoriously expensive, and they had introduced some kind of mad tram service, which meant that neither man nor motor could get around the city without sitting in painfully slow traffic.

"But what would you do?" she asked, wondering if Ben was being serious or if it was just wishful but harmless thinking. "I mean, would you seriously contemplate giving up your job – after working so hard to get where you are?"

"Work isn't everything," he said meaningfully.

Thankfully the waitress arrived with their pizza and the moment passed.

Now, as Robin studied Sarah's tired and anxious expression while she softly stroked her daughter's hand, she wondered how anyone could do it.

So much worry, so much anguish – what was it that made people want to put themselves through all that? She adored Kirsty – in fact, Robin adored most children and, funnily enough, they seemed drawn to her in return – but she knew for sure that she herself would not make a good mother.

She just didn't have it in her.

"How's she doing?" The arrival of the paediatrician inter-rupted Robin's thoughts and she moved away from Kirsty's bed to give the doctor some room. He scanned the little girl's medical chart. "This has been her third visit in five months you know," he pointed out sternly. "Hasn't she been using her inhaler?"

The implied accusation was obvious to Robin and indeed poor Sarah, who looked ashamed. Though surely it was impos-sible to teach a child as young as Kirsty the importance of her inhaler. She was barely four years old, for goodness' sake. And Robin could safely assume that her mother didn't enjoy having to rush her to a hospital an hour away, or paying steep bills for the use of the ventilator. But the way the doctor was talking, it was as though Sarah or indeed Kirsty, were being purposefully neglectful.

She made a mental note there and then to give Ben's sister more help. The very least she and Ben could do was to babysit the odd weekend and give Sarah and Brian some time to themselves. It would do them, and indeed Kirsty, some good to let someone else share the load.

Yes, Robin thought – seeing Kirsty's expression light up as Ben entered the room – that is exactly what they would do.

Though hopefully he wouldn't get the wrong idea and start thinking it was some kind of sign that she was ready for motherhood. Well, she would just have to nip that firmly in the bud.

Robin wouldn't be ready for anything like that for a long time to come. If ever.

SIX

When five thirty came and went and there was still no sign of Leah, Olivia wasn't unduly concerned. Her friend was notorious for timekeeping. But then her phone beeped.

"Where are you?"

"Where? I've been here for the last half-hour," Olivia replied.

"U r late."

"No, I'm here – waiting on you."

She looked around. Admittedly the pub was busy, but it would've been impossible for the two of them to miss one another. She was sitting by the entrance and facing the door. Unless there was a side door she didn't know about, she thought, craning her neck around – and Leah had come in that way. Still she could see no sign.

"Can't c u – where?"

"Bar."

Olivia looked over and while there were plenty of people standing by the bar, none of them looked anything remotely like her friend.

Confused, she sent another message. By now, her fingers hurt.

"Here? In Searson's?"

"Yes – can't see u either, very busy here. Meet u outside?"

"OK."

Although she was loathe to give up her table, she dutifully went outside to wait for Leah. She stood casually against the wall of the buzzy pub, trying to assume a disinterested posture amongst a group of ostracised smokers gathered around the doorway.

The door opened and a guy in a business suit glanced briefly at her, then looked left and right as if waiting on someone too.

Where the hell was Leah?

She stole a quick glance at the man, now deftly tapping on his phone. Then her own device beeped again.

"Outside now – where r u?"

Blast it. She *definitely* had the wrong place, because wherever Leah was, it wasn't here.

Better just call her, she thought, hitting the dial key. She didn't know why she hadn't thought about doing so in the first place. Besides her snail-like speed, this was the main reason she hated texting – there was so much bloody ambiguity.

But as soon as she'd dialled Leah's number, she heard another phone ring somewhere else.

"Hello?" Olivia heard the business guy utter, and her blood ran cold when she realised that she was listening to his voice not just nearby, but also through the tinny earpiece of her own phone.

"I JUST DON'T UNDERSTAND IT," she said, reddening when realisation dawned on them both. "I was supposed to meet my friend here – to celebrate – she passed her driving test you see and –" She was aware that she was babbling but she couldn't help it.

Mortifying ...

But the guy in the suit was smiling – in fact, not just smiling but laughing, a big hearty laugh that would normally make Olivia chuckle too, except she was so embarrassed.

"I thought I was meeting my business partner," he said. "I had just clinched a deal and we were supposed to be celebrating too but, in my excitement I must have punched in the wrong number. My old phone was stolen so all my pre-programmed contacts are ..." He trailed off, laughing again.

"Oh," Olivia exclaimed, understanding. "You sent a message to me by mistake and I automatically assumed it was my friend and ..." She reddened again. *Oh god* ... "I'm so sorry, I should have made sure but –"

"No, *I'm* sorry," said the man, his grey-blue eyes twinkling. "I would normally call but he had some kind of family event on today and I knew his wife wouldn't appreciate the interruption, so I sent a text. I should have known there was something up when he – or should I say *you* – suggested going for a drink."

"Oh dear."

"I'm Matt by the way," he said, extending a hand.

"Olivia," she replied, taking in his open friendly face, and deciding that he reminded her a little of Kate's husband Michael, but better-looking.

"Nice to meet you." He chuckled. "And here we both were, thinking we were out for a great night." He looked sidelong at her, and for reasons she couldn't quite fathom, Olivia almost hoped he would suggest they go back in for a drink anyway. He was lovely.

"Ah I suppose it's a good thing after all," he said, his mind elsewhere. "For once I'll have a clear head when I take my son to football practice in the morning."

Olivia smiled. "Ellie, my daughter, plays football too – well, the four-year-old version of it. She loves it."

"Adam's the same age," Matt replied. "Good to get them into sport early, isn't it?"

She nodded, and then self-consciously repositioned her bag on her shoulder as if to move away.

"Can I give you a lift anywhere?" he asked. "Or I should say, do you want to share a taxi? I left the car back at the office."

"No, it's fine – I'll just nip home on the train," she said. It would only be a short walk from here to Lansdowne Road station and a forty-minute train ride back to Lakeview from there. "Nice to meet you, Matt and sorry again for ... well, for the confusion."

"You too," he said with a friendly grin, before heading off down the road, and leaving Olivia feeling something akin to disappointment as she walked away in the opposite direction.

SEVEN

A few days later, having just about got over her embarrassing 'blind date', followed by a right telling-off from her mother, Olivia got a phone call from Leah.

"Have you seen this?" her friend cried in disbelief. "Please tell me you got one too."

Olivia laughed, knowing exactly what she was referring to. "Yes, it came in the post this morning."

"I cannot believe she is doing this. I mean, she made enough fuss about being pregnant but honestly, have you ever heard of anyone having a '*Mother-in-Waiting* party? Where does she *get* these notions? Why not just call it a bloody baby shower like everyone else?"

Olivia giggled. She had thought the very same thing upon opening the post and finding that she had been invited to their old college friend Amanda Clarke's latest soiree.

Andrew and his girlfriend had defied the critics (namely Kate) and had stayed together throughout university and beyond. They'd married the previous year, and in true Amanda-style she had gone all out with her wedding preparations for her Big Day.

Now another, even bigger day was imminent.

"Well, you know Amanda, any excuse for a party."

"Any excuse to show off, you mean," Leah said wryly. "And it's not all that long since she went overboard with that wedding. Poor Andrew must be doing his nut."

"Ah, don't be nasty."

"You think *I'm* bad – what will Kate say once she hears about this? I spoke to her the other day and she's still in shock after the pomp of the Clarke wedding, so goodness knows what she'll make of this." Leah said.

Kate, now also married and pregnant with her first, had spent the entire day open-mouthed in astonishment at Amanda and Andrew's wedding. Leah had spent the day proclaiming that silver service and personalised dinner plates were all very well and good, but what was the point if you 'couldn't feel the love'?

She and Andrew had remained in close contact all the time Leah had been away on her apprenticeship. Amanda had always been a little jealous of their friendship, probably a little threatened by it, but she need never have worried.

Living in Lakeview, Olivia didn't see much of the newlyweds, but she felt much the same way about Amanda as she had throughout college and took her attention-seeking with a pinch of salt. But because she was Andrew's girlfriend she had always made the effort for his sake. She'd particularly disliked the way Amanda had always been a bit superior and dismissive of Robin though.

A faint sadness stirred inside as she thought of her old friend who had moved to the States not long after graduation. It had been ages since they'd heard from Robin – or at least it had been ages since *she* had heard from her.

"I still can't believe Amanda invited *us* though," Leah said now. "I mean I could understand the wedding because, she was always great for showing off but –"

"Yes, but you're still quite close with them, aren't you?"

"With Andrew, maybe. But, Olivia, you remember what she was like in college, that last summer especially."

"Ah, we were all young and foolish back then." She paused slightly, remembering. "Didn't we make that stupid promise? That summer reunion pact?" Her stomach twisted when she thought about it now. Kate had been right about tempting fate.

"I know." Leah was quiet, probably thinking the same as she – that even though most had stayed in touch, fate had intervened in their grand plans for meet-up. "Kate was right – we were a bit naive."

"I suppose it felt like a nice idea at the time," Olivia said, shaking her head at the memory.

"So, are we going to this party or what?" Leah asked, changing the subject. "Actually, she's given me a bit of a brainwave. Do you think I should think seriously about a new range of chocolates specifically for Mothers-in-Waiting?"

"It's an idea." Olivia laughed, feeling a familiar pride in Leah's achievements. Her gift-chocolate business was doing so well, and having tasted some of her friend's more recent concoctions, Olivia could see why. She'd always been a terrific cook, but no one was more surprised than Leah when she had gone abroad to perfect her pastry-chef skills and returned as a trained chocolatier. "Are things still as busy as ever?"

"Yes, but it's calmed down a little since Mother's Day, thank feck."

"You'll have to think about taking on more staff. You'll work yourself into the ground otherwise."

"I wish I could afford to – but I'll have to do a bit better before I can think about taking on some poor misfortunate I can boss around."

"Like you do Josh, you mean?"

"Exactly." She laughed. "Better let you go, I want to catch Robin before she heads off for work. It should be around sevenish in New York at the moment, shouldn't it? I'm dying to find out how things are going with this boyfriend of hers."

"She's with someone?" Olivia probed, stung that she knew so little about Robin's life now. "An American guy?"

"No. All those handsome, loaded New Yorkers, and Robin had to go and find herself a paddy from the Wesht," she joked. "I'll tell her you were asking for her, will I?"

"Do – and tell her to give me a call sometime. Be lovely to catch up."

It was hurtful really, Olivia thought, going into her living room and slumping down on her sofa. Especially since she and Robin had been so close throughout university and firm friends right from their rather ... eventful first meeting.

OLIVIA AND PETER had been grabbing a quick coffee at the cafeteria in the UCD Arts Building when she'd noticed an alarming sight at the table right behind theirs.

Her first thought was that the girl must be choking on food, judging by her dangerously red complexion and the fact that she was struggling for breath. Yet at the same time she was groping for something beneath the table, but in her panicked state was unable to get to it. The girl was on her own, and no one other than Olivia seemed to have noticed that something was wrong.

Very wrong.

"Peter, look," she cried, getting up from her seat. "Are you OK?" she asked the girl feeling stupid, as it was pretty obvious she was far from OK. But then she realised that she wasn't choking – in fact, the girl seemed to be having some kind of ... seizure.

Before she knew it, Peter cleared a space behind them and swiftly placed the girl in the recovery position on the floor. At this stage, people had begun to gather and stare and soon was clear that lying her on her side was making little if any difference, and she was still desperate for breath.

"Call an ambulance or something," Olivia called out to one of the counter staff, standing shell-shocked along with everyone else – the students and staff of the café unused to such drama.

"Damn," Peter looked around wildly, trying to discover the root of the problem. He grabbed her wrist. "Her pulse is going ten to the dozen. Quick, check her handbag, see if there's an asthma inhaler or something in there."

Spying the bag under the table, Olivia realised that this must have been what she was trying to reach earlier. Moving as quickly as she could and trying to control her own rising panic, she emptied the bag's contents onto the table. Hairbrush, wallet, make-up, a pen and notebook, some lip balm, lots of old bus tickets … but nothing resembling an inhaler.

"Peter, there's nothing here," she cried, panicked. On the floor the girl was still struggling.

"There has to be something," Peter grunted, panicked too. He stood up and started frantically checking through the contents, going through her books, as if there might be something written down. Then he paused suddenly. "Damn."

"What, what is it?" Olivia demanded and frowned as Peter's gaze rested now on the remains of the girl's lunch – a barely-touched chicken bap. "Food poisoning?" she offered hurriedly.

"A reaction, I think," Peter was again urgently searching through the girl's things.

"Reaction? To what?"

"Not sure yet, but this should help," he said, immediately seizing what she had earlier dismissed as an oversized ink pen.

Lying on her side on the floor, her eyes wide, the girl was now gesturing furiously, pointing at her leg.

And then, before Olivia could take in what was happening, Peter had broken open the packaging and was back on the ground alongside her. He shook the syringe and squirted a little liquid out in a way that she had seen millions of times on TV.

Then he sat the girl up and carefully placed the syringe in her hand, helping her guide it towards her calf. Then, and Olivia didn't know how he did this but somehow – under the girl's panicked direction – Peter began to crudely administer the shot.

After what seemed like an age, the girl stopped shaking and within a few minutes, her colour had returned to normal.

Panic over.

"What was it?" Olivia asked Peter later, once the ambulance arrived from nearby St Vincent's, and the girl was safely loaded into it.

Still shaken from the drama of it all, the two had forgone the remaining afternoon's lectures and had stayed in the cafeteria. "In the syringe?"

"Adrenaline," Peter stated flatly. "She was allergic to something in that sandwich. Had a serious reaction and began to go into shock – anaphylactic shock, the paramedic said."

"Anaphylactic shock from an ordinary chicken bap?" Olivia couldn't believe that something so innocuous could have such an effect.

"They reckon that if she hadn't got the shot in time, she would go into a coma," Peter shrugged. "Maybe even died."

"Wow," Olivia said, her eyes widening. She put down her coffee cup and lovingly squeezed her boyfriend's arm. "You're a proper hero."

EIGHT

A week later, the girl was waiting for Olivia outside one of her lectures.

"Hi there," she said, recognising her immediately. "How are you feeling?"

"Fine, thanks to you and um ..." the other girl glanced around, as if expecting to see Peter.

She seemed so shy, Olivia thought.

"Oh, it was all down to Peter," she said easily. "I hadn't a clue what to do. I'm just glad you're OK."

The girl smiled, as if unsure what to say.

Olivia looked at her watch. "Listen, I don't have another lecture till two – do you have time for a coffee?" When the girl looked startled, she grimaced. "Oh, sorry – can you drink coffee?"

Her nervous expression finally broke into a smile, and she fell into step beside Olivia.

"No, I can drink coffee – it's just a few things I have to be careful with."

"Really? Like what?" She was fascinated. Imagine having to live your life not knowing whether something you eat could kill you. How did she manage? "Oh, I'm Olivia, by the way," she said, realising that she didn't yet know the girl's name.

"Robin." She smiled softly. "And I suppose I just wanted to thank you and your friend for helping me the other day. If you hadn't found my Epipen ..." She trailed off as they reached the cafeteria.

"So, what can I get you?" Olivia asked as they stood at the counter. "Tea, coffee ... and oh, good, they have those chocolate brownies back in again – want one?"

Robin looked uncomfortable. "Sorry, chocolate is a big no-no," she said, apologetically. "Anything with traces of nuts in it is a big no-no."

The poor thing, Olivia thought, trying to imagine not being able to eat *chocolate* of all things. No wonder she was so shy – she was probably used to being made feel like the odd one out.

"Probably better off," she said with a grimace, putting the brownie back on the shelf and, in an attempt to relax Robin a little added, "No wonder you're so slim."

"Not by choice, unfortunately." She gave a little laugh, and Olivia delighted in the small achievement.

They took a table near the window where they could look out at the comings and goings in the Arts Building.

"Gosh, really how do you do it?" Olivia chatted. "I can't imagine not being able to eat chocolate."

"You don't miss what you've never had I suppose. You can get special nut-free stuff, but I'm not that bothered."

"So how does that adrenaline thingy work then?"

"The shot takes you out of an attack. It's easy enough to use normally, but I was so far gone the other day that I needed help. It's a lifeline."

"A lifeline," Olivia repeated. "So, you really could have died?"

"I was heading for unconsciousness, definitely. After that, who knows?" She shook her head. "It's been a while. I thought I'd learned to control it. But I think it's the kind of thing you can never fully control – you just have to live with it."

"I can't even imagine what it must be like. Like every day could be ... well, you just never know. Sorry," Olivia muttered, shaking her head, "I don't mean to sound morbid."

"I get you," Robin said, laughing now, "but it's been a part of my life forever, so I don't know what it's like to be 'normal'. You do learn to live with it. It's harder on parents – my mother had a really terrible time with me. I don't think she had a day's peace once I started school." Then she grimaced slightly. "Sorry, I've just remembered I hardly know you and I'm already boring the face off you."

"Not at all," Olivia said smiling. "I think it's fascinating, and Peter will be dying to hear every detail. He's a Med student so ... Tell you what – why don't you pop over for dinner later?" Then she paused. "Now I'm a very plain cook, so I could make anything you like ..."

Robin laughed. "I'd love to, but I don't want to put you out. Cook what you like and I'll just bring a snack."

Olivia didn't push it.

"Great, and I know Peter would love nothing better to meet the girl whose life he saved. "

NINE

"I have a surprise for you," Ben said, his eyes mischievous as he led Robin along Lexington.

"What kind of surprise?" Knowing him, he most likely wanted to go and do something tacky and touristy, she thought fondly.

The two had met shortly after he moved to Manhattan, and in the very early days, Ben was like a child in a sweetshop, eager to experience all that this magnificent city had to offer.

Robin was a million miles away from being jaded – in New York she didn't think it could happen – but at that stage having lived in the city for a couple of years, she'd already done most of the touristy things.

At the time she hadn't intended on meeting anyone. Still feeling the effects of a particularly disastrous fling, the very last thing on her mind was meeting someone else, least of all another Irishman and certainly not at a New York society wedding.

Robin's close friend and workmate was marrying her high-school boyfriend, a lovely, gentle – and loaded – New Yorker. She was thrilled when she discovered that they planned to hold their wedding in the Plaza Hotel. If there was one place in New York that held special memories for Robin, it was the Plaza.

Many years before, on her very first visit to the city, she and her American cousin Fiona had sneaked into the foyer while the doorman was helping one of the hotel guests out of a limo.

Robin still remembered her absolute awe at stepping inside the luxurious hotel for the very first time. *Home Alone* 2 was one of her favourite Christmas movies and as this particular visit occurred over the holidays, it seemed as though she was reliving parts of the film herself. Earlier that day, she and Fiona had fed squirrels in Central Park, gasped in appreciation at the toys in FAO Schwartz, admired the skating rink at the Rockefeller Centre and then, to complete the most memorable Christmas Eve she had ever experienced, stood open-mouthed in wonder at the twinkling tree in the Plaza foyer.

The hotel's famous crystal chandelier almost paled in comparison to the magical, fairytale-like spruce standing majestically beneath it. Right there, staring at the tree's sparkling decorations, Robin's love affair with New York truly began – which was why the Plaza was one of her favourite spots.

And on Anna and Burton's wedding day, the hotel didn't disappoint. She had decided to wear an understated but sexy Robert Cavalli mini-dress for the occasion, and in such sumptuous surroundings, felt almost justified in blowing most of the previous month's wages on a delicate wisp of jade-coloured silk.

Her lack of funds for groceries as a result of her splurge had done no harm in helping her fit into it either, she thought wryly. She hoped that as one of Anna's pauper friends, she would be able to hold her own in the fashion stakes alongside Burton's megabucks relations.

Making an impression was of the utmost importance in Manhattan, but never more so than at a society wedding.

And speaking of impressions, she thought as she sat down, a cute guy with the warm chocolate-brown eyes sitting across from her at the table was definitely making one on her. He was sitting alongside Robin's date Gary, another work colleague and had caught her eye on several occasions already.

Despite herself, and unused to such obvious flirtation – especially in this town – she had to smile.

Just then, Gary looked across at her. "Hey, you two might know each other. Ireland's a small town, isn't it?"

"Sure, we're probably related," the other man said, in an exaggerated 'oirish' accent. "Begorrah, you look terrible like my cousin Eileen Dooley, so you do." With this, he gave her an almost imperceptible wink.

Robin's eyes widened in mock-surprise. "Not Eileen Dooley from Letterkenny?" she gasped. "Sure I'm only her second cousin twice removed."

"Go 'way out of that," he replied laying it on thick. "Jaysus, 'tis a terrible small world all the same, so it is."

"Wow." Gary sat back, impressed. "It *is* a small world. I've never travelled further than New Jersey but you Irish get everywhere, don't you?"

Robin and her 'cousin' exchanged an impish smile.

"Hey, why don't I let you two catch up," her workmate said, sensing that he would have little to contribute to the conversation between two long-lost Irish relations.

"Aye."

As Gary moved away, and Robin raised an eyebrow. "I think 'aye' might be Scottish..." she intoned amusedly.

"Scottish, Irish – it all sounds the same to the Yanks." He shrugged and Robin couldn't help but wonder if those Tom Cruise teeth were natural. There was also a very good chance that his deep brown eyes might simply be the result of a good pair of contact lenses. The only snag was, she'd noticed earlier that he kept tugging at his collar, a sure sign he wasn't comfortable with wearing a suit.

"What?" he asked then, his eyes twinkling.

"Sorry?" she replied, a little unnerved.

"You were making some kind of judgment, weren't you?"

"About what?" She was naturally cagey, and as she'd been told many times before, difficult to read.

"About me."

"What? What makes you think that?"

He smiled broadly. "You were, weren't you?"

"Was not."

"Were too," he shot back and she couldn't help but smile back.

"Tell me what you were thinking," he asked, sitting forward and resting his chin on his hand.

"I was ..." Robin thought quickly, "I was just wondering how you know the happy couple."

"Don't know them at all," he said, glancing towards the head table. "One of their folks is a shareholder in my boss's company. He couldn't make it so we went along in his stead."

"Oh." Who was *we*? she wondered.

"What about you?"

"Anna's a work friend." She followed his gaze towards the top table where the bride was beaming from ear to ear.

"Seems a bit cracked to me," he said. "Spending good money on all these fancy ice sculptures that'll end up as plain H_2O in a few hours."

Robin smiled. "I haven't heard that one in ages."

"Heard what?"

"That expression 'cracked'. I have a friend back home – Leah – she used to say it all the time." With an uncharacteristic bout of homesickness, she wondered what her friend was doing now, what everyone was doing now. She really should call her for a catchup.

"You know – you seem to spend an awful lot of time daydreaming."

"What?"

"I've spent the last ten minutes trying to chat you up and you keep looking dreamily into the distance."

"You're trying to chat me up?"

"Well, why else do you think I begged your man to swap places with me?"

"What man?"

"The one sitting over at that table with my workmates. He seems to be having a right old time."

She looked at him. "You're telling me that you switched the seating plan?"

"Yep."

"But ... what made you think I was fair game?" She demanded. "I mean, what if I was here with a boyfriend, or a partner or – "

"Didn't matter," he said, with an indolent shake of his head.

"What do you mean – it didn't matter?" she repeated, stunned at the size of his ego. Yes, he was attractive but ... "You can't go around assuming that every woman you like the look of is willing and available to fall at your feet at a quick flash of that smile – that's just so – so arrogant."

"You like my smile? Cool."

"I really don't know who the hell you think you are," she continued irritated now. Good-looking guys were all the same weren't they – so full of themselves and cocksure that they could pick any girl up at the drop of a hat. "But if you think you can just –"

"Ah, I'm sorry, let me introduce myself," he said cutting her off. "My name's Ben McKenna. I'm new in the city and assuming I play my cards right, I intend to be the guy you'll want to spend the rest of your life with."

TEN

Thinking back on it now as she followed Ben down Lexington Avenue in the sunshine, Robin couldn't help but smile.

Worse, he had thought it was such a killer line.

"What? What did I say?" he asked afterwards when Robin had recovered from laughing.

"What made-for-TV movie did you get that from?"

"Hey, that came right from the heart," he said, looking hurt as her shoulders continued to heave with laughter. "Was it really that bad?"

"Absolutely brutal."

But the fact that he'd genuinely assumed it to be a romantic overture had been one of the most endearing things about him. He had such a childlike, almost naïve, sense of wonder about everything, that it was as though Robin was living her earlier days in Manhattan all over again.

For the first few weeks of their relationship, they behaved like tourists and did everything from carriage rides in Central Park, trips across the river on the Staten Island Ferry, theatres on Broadway, shopping on Fifth Avenue, and Ben's favourite – viewing the city from the top of the Empire State Building.

But for Robin, there was sadly nothing that could ever beat the view from atop the Twin Towers. That day on the ESB with Ben, looking out at the panoramic view of the island below, her gaze drifted across towards Battery Park and she felt once again the gaping void the destruction of the Towers had left deep in the hearts of everyone living in the city.

She'd been on her way to work that fateful day, and like so many others working in the financial district, had been deeply affected by the tragedy – and possibly more so by the fact that she was still alive.

Immediately afterwards, she began to question whether or not she had done anything worthwhile with her life, and in this regard found herself sorely lacking. Yes, she'd been doing well in her career, had learned to live successfully with a life-threatening allergy, and had lots of friends. But her New York friends weren't the same as the ones she had left behind.

Feeling particularly lonely at one stage not long after the tragedy, Robin half contemplated leaving Manhattan and heading back home to Dublin. Yet, she knew in her heart of hearts that she wasn't ready yet, if ever, to do that.

No, her life was in New York and now that she had Ben, the city was home.

Now he was practically dragging her along the path on the way to – from what she could make out – Grand Central terminal.

"Seriously, where are we going?" she asked, struggling to keep up with him in this heat.

"I told you – it's a surprise."

She knew better than to ask more questions, especially when he was in a mood like this. Her interest was very definitely piqued though, when they entered the cavernous train station and Ben headed immediately towards the ticket office beneath the clock.

"We're going on a train – at rush hour?" she said puzzled, trying to grab the ticket off him.

"Oh, no, you don't." Ben put the tickets in his trousers pocket, hiding them away from view.

Minutes later, the two headed down to one of the platforms, where a virtually fully boarded train awaited departure.

"Ben, why are we going to Bronxville?" she asked seizing a free seat in one of the carriages.

He winked at her. "Just wait and see."

Fifteen or so minutes passed after the train moved away from the station, and as Robin silently watched Uptown Manhattan rush past them, she thought she could guess what he was up to. Bronxville was a charming area located some fifteen miles north of Midtown, and she knew Ben wasn't planning on going there today simply for a guided tour.

"You've been house-hunting again, haven't you?" she challenged him.

Ben smiled boyishly. "OK, I admit, I couldn't resist it. But this one is just perfect for us – just half an hour's train ride from Grand Central, a nice area and it's even got a garden and a study – a small one, mind you, but –"

"But you know I don't want to move. I love where we are now. What is so important about having a house? We don't need one – we've already got a loft that anyone would kill for, so why –?"

"Just take a look at it first before you say anything, OK?"

She could sense his irritation but wondered why on earth he kept doing this when he knew how much it bothered her.

"OK." She didn't have the energy to argue. She would humour him – again – by going through the motions of taking a look at this house, with its lovely garden and its perfect study and all the rest. Then she would do as she always did and tell him that the place they had was perfect and why would they want to move all the way out to the suburbs?

The latest object of Ben's affection was a spacious single-family home on a corner site with an attractive wooden porch all the way across the front.

It had obviously been very well looked after, the two bedrooms were spacious and nicely decorated and the tiny garden that Ben had been so enthusiastic about was admittedly a welcoming oasis of calm, something that was difficult to find in New York at the best of times.

Despite herself, Robin began to imagine the two of them sitting on that porch or in the garden on hot summer days, relaxing in the warm evening sun after another frantic day in the city heat.

For once, she could understand why he was so keen to get out of Manhattan, away from the noise, honking horns and hectic lifestyle. Yet the buzz, constant stream of activity, the traffic, the smells... the fact that the city was so full of life was what Robin loved about it.

Still, she mused, looking around the attractive, contemporary and – compared to their apartment – spacious house, she could picture herself living here.

The village itself was idyllic – a lovely spot nicely nestled alongside the Bronx river, full of towering lush trees and charming, stately Tudor, Victorian and Colonial houses. Despite herself, she had to admit that this might be one of Ben's better ideas.

"So what do you think?" he asked, although Robin could tell by his expression that he knew she was impressed.

"It's not bad," she said, giving nothing away.

"You like it – I knew it."

"I said it's not bad."

"Not bad? Robin, it's perfect for us. You saw inside – there's nothing to be done to it. The studio would be perfect for any work I bring home –" he nudged her, "so no more giving out about leaving my drawings all over the place. And look," he indicated out the window, "how could you *not* want to live in a house with a garden like that?"

"I know, but our place ..."

"You and I both know that we can't stay there forever. We're getting older now and although we're not exactly geriatric it would be nice to put down roots somewhere – especially since you've made it quite clear that you're not prepared to do that back home."

He was right. Goodness knows she had gone on enough about how her life was here and that she couldn't see herself ever wanting to move back to Ireland. And while buying a house was one thing, buying one with Ben was a different kettle of fish altogether.

She looked at him, her thoughts going a mile a minute. "I do like the house, it's just... I'm not sure ..."

"What aren't you sure about, Robin? What are you afraid of?"

"I don't know ..."

"Is it me – us? Are you not sure how you feel about us?"

"That's not it. You know I love you. It's just – "

"Just what? Just that you're still thinking about that gobshite, isn't it..."

"*What?*"

"Are you worried the same thing will happen again? Because I'm telling you that it won't. I won't ever let you down nor hurt you either."

He looked at her, his dark eyes honest and open and in her heart, Robin knew he was right. She did love him and she knew that he wouldn't hurt her. The problem was that she had the power to hurt *him*. He might love her now but if he were to ever find out –

"Hey we've been together a while now, and I think it's time we took things to the next level," Ben said, interrupting her thoughts. "We love one another, we're committed and already living together, so why not take the plunge and get a place of our own?"

"I suppose ..." She knew it wasn't fair to keep him hanging and yes, she truly did love him as much as ... well, as much she could love anyone.

Maybe he was right. Maybe she should just make the commitment, get the mortgage and buy the place.

"OK," she said, feeling a burst of adrenaline – for once, not from a syringe – but a natural high. Conflicting emotions rushed through her all at once, but she tried to concentrate on the positive. "Let's do it. Let's get a place of our own – let's buy this house."

Ben's eyes widened. "Are you sure?" he asked, a huge grin on his face. "Are you positive?"

"I'm absolutely positive," she repeated before she could change her mind.

Ben was already tapping numbers into his phone. "I'd better tell the realtor we'll take it, otherwise a place like this will be snapped up in no time."

But later on, the way back on the train listening to his excited chatter, she couldn't help having second thoughts.

She'd just made a decision to commit herself to this man for a long time – a very long time. And although she loved Ben dearly, Robin wondered how on earth she was going to tell him that buying a house together was the closest thing to full commitment she could ever give him.

Anything beyond that wasn't an option.

ELEVEN

Olivia was late, unbelievably late. She was on duty at the rescue centre in little under an hour, she still had to drop Ellie off at her grandmother's and it seemed as though the world was conspiring against her.

Her daughter wasn't any help either. She had picked today of all days to be contrary and was at that very moment standing in the hallway in a pair of pyjama bottoms.

"Don't want to go to Grannie's," she said sulkily. "Don't want to go with you – want to stay here on mine own."

"Honey, you know you can't stay here on your own without Mommy. Anyway, don't you want to see Granny? She'll be very disappointed – she might cry."

"Grannies don't cry, silly," she giggled and Olivia thought that if Ellie's humour lifted that easily she might just get away. At the best of times, her daughter was as stubborn as a mule and if she didn't want to go, then she bloody well didn't want to go.

Sometimes she was so like Peter it hurt.

"She would cry," Olivia insisted, "and she'd cry even more if she saw you wearing your pyjamas instead of those nice jeans she bought you. The ones she got for your birthday with the pink flowers on them?" She crossed her fingers behind her back and then exhaled a sigh of relief when Ellie turned and started up the stairs – hopefully willing to change.

Ten minutes later, they were finally ready to leave. But the gods definitely weren't with her today, Olivia thought, furiously searching for her car keys. Blast and damn it, she cursed inwardly as she opened cupboards and drawers, lifted newspapers and magazines until finally she spied the elusive keys sticking out from under a pile of newly dried washing.

"OK, let's go," she said, buttoning Ellie's jacket and heading outside.

Then her face fell. A Land Rover, likely belonging to someone visiting next door had partly blocked her entrance. In fairness there was just enough room for her to reverse out, but she would have to be painstakingly careful. Great, more time lost...

She settled Ellie in her car seat and proceeded to inch her way past the other car's tailgate. It was a bit nerve-wracking though because she was reversing blind out onto the road. She couldn't take any chances either with Ellie in the back.

Olivia's was the last in the row of semi-detached houses on Cherrywood Green and her gateway was right at the corner of the main entrance, which any cars entering tended to take very quickly. She prayed that at this hour of the morning, things would be a bit quieter.

Beep! Beep!

Olivia jumped. So much for it being quiet, she thought, moving the car forward and craning her neck behind to try and see what was happening. Some drivers just wouldn't give an inch, would they? And because she couldn't see a thing over that monstrous Land Rover, she was *never* going to get out of here.

She was just about to release the handbrake and try again when in her wing-mirror, she saw someone who appeared to be waving her on. Well, thank goodness for that, she thought – must be the Land Rover owner. But why the hell didn't the guy just move the bloody thing?

Soon thanks to her saviour and much to her relief, she was safely out on the road. She looked across and was about to wave her thanks and move off when surprised recognition dawned – and not just for Olivia. The man, the 'text guy' as Leah laughingly called him, looked equally surprised to see her.

"Oh! Hello again," she said, winding down her window as he approached.

"Hello again, yourself," he said his dark eyes as warm and lively as she remembered. "You live here too?"

Too? Surely he couldn't be one of her neighbours? She would have noticed if someone that cute had been living in the vicinity and if she hadn't, then Maeve McGrath from down the road certainly would have. Her gossipy sixty-odd-year-old neighbour had a radar for spotting attractive, male neighbours suitable for 'misfortunate and manless' Olivia.

He must have just moved in.

"Yes, this is my house, and if it weren't for that tank," she added wryly, "I'd be out and gone already."

"I was on my way back from the shop and I saw you struggling, so I said I'd give a hand. I had no idea it was you though," he grinned. "Hey, speaking of which – did your friend pass her driving test that time?"

Olivia shook her head ruefully. "No, poor Leah. She had a terrible time actually, so there would have been no celebrations after all."

"That's a pity. But, you'll be pleased to know that I've been extra careful since. No more making arrangements with strangers."

"Me too." Olivia blushed slightly at the memory.

"That was mad, wasn't it?" he said, shaking his head. "Two eejits sitting in a pub waiting for one another and neither of us had

a clue." He laughed. "And your face when I answered the phone –
an absolute picture!"

Olivia laughed too. "For a second there I thought I had been
set up by one of those hidden camera shows or something."

"Mommy, I want to see Granny!" Ellie wailed. Strapped into
her car seat which she hated, she was getting impatient.

Matt peered in, having spotted her for the first time. "Hello
there," he said easily. "What's your name? Oh, don't tell me," he
added before she could answer. "I bet it's something like Barbie,
'cos you have lovely blonde hair – just like Barbie."

Ellie giggled. "I'm not Barbie," she said delighted. "I'm Ellie."

"Pleased to meet you, Ellie." Matt reached in to shake her
hand and Olivia nearly fell off the seat when Ellie offered her own
in return. Olivia had had one or two dates since Peter, but none of
them had gone any further than just that – a date. Probably
because Ellie caused such a ruckus and behaved like the child
from hell she thought wryly.

But Matt was obviously well used to and very comfortable
with children, and then Olivia remembered him mentioning
before that he had a young son.

"Matt, breakfast!" a woman called faintly from the doorway of
a house across the green and confirmed Olivia's slightly deflating
conclusion that, of course, Matt was taken. No wonder Maeve's
radar hadn't detected him – there was no point.

But if he lived across the green, he hadn't been there that long,
otherwise, she would surely have noticed him before now. Obviously one of many 'blow-ins', she thought using the Lakeview
locals' slang.

Matt turned towards his wife and put a hand up as if to signal
he was on his way. Then he turned back and grimaced. "Better
go," he said. "Catherine can be dangerous with a frying pan."

Olivia smiled at him. "Thanks again for helping us out."

"No problem." He stood back as she went to move away. "Nice seeing you again,"

"You too," she said, moving away from the kerb.

"Bye, Barb– I mean, Ellie!" Matt gave her a little wink and, thrilled Ellie waved happily back.

Casting a glance at Matt's departing figure in her rear-view mirror, Olivia couldn't help thinking that it was a very rare man indeed who could put a beaming smile on the faces of both Gallagher women.

TWELVE

Across the green, Catherine stood at the doorway and watched Matt fawning all over some woman.

Who the hell was *she*? she wondered, her stomach plummeting as she began to feel an all-too-familiar niggle of suspicion.

She couldn't believe it when she'd looked out the window and had seen him leaning casually against some strange woman's car, chatting and joking as if he'd known her forever.

How *did* he know her though? He couldn't have got to know the locals already, could he?

She knew he loved going to that coffee shop - Ella's café downtown - whereas Catherine wasn't too crazy about it, since everyone seemed way too friendly and interested in your business.

Was it just like Dublin, where Matt seemed to be on friendly terms with everyone in the apartment building – including the brunette who lived down the hall?

Catherine didn't like this at all. She'd thought that moving away from the city to this quiet little town would be ideal. Ideal for helping Matt to focus less on work and more on Adam and family life – the important things.

The last thing Catherine needed was the love of her life focusing on smiley attractive women living across the road.

THIRTEEN

The following lunchtime at Olivia's invitation, Leah called over with an armful of Sunday papers and a rumbling tummy.

Josh was working Sundays at the DIY store he managed, and Olivia was glad of the opportunity to get Leah on her own. Although she often invited her to Lakeview, this time she had a particular motive – she desperately wanted to confide in someone about Matt.

"And what are you going to do about him?" Leah wanted to know and Olivia glared at her. "What? You're the one going around with the glazed look in your eyes..."

She blushed. "I just can't stop thinking about him. He just has this lovely way about him and he's so friendly –"

"But he's taken," Leah interjected. "He might be lovely, he might be friendly and Ellie might have warmed to him, but he's taken."

"I know." She sighed. "It's just typical, isn't it? The only man who has made my heart beat faster in years and he has to be married."

It was true. Olivia couldn't remember the last time she had even looked at a man with anything other than passing interest.

The few she'd been out with recently hadn't appealed to her all that much – she'd gone out with them more for the sake of moving on than anything else.

But Matt was different and Olivia suspected that it wasn't just one side-sided. She remembered the way his eyes lit up when he recognised her in the car. And how he had said 'See you again sometime' before she drove away. There was meaning there, definitely. He wasn't just being nice to her – he liked her too.

When she mentioned this to Leah, she wrinkled her nose. "If that's the case, he doesn't sound like such a nice guy to me. Chatting up and flirting with other women – would you like to be married to someone like that?"

"It wasn't like that," Olivia insisted, although she supposed her friend was right. "He just seemed nice, that's all."

"This *really* isn't like you."

"What?"

"Going all gooey-eyed over some bald, ageing, married Lothario."

"I told you – Matt is *not* a Lothario and he's definitely not ageing – late thirties, I'd say? And he's not bald either."

"Which means he probably hasn't been married long enough to use the old 'my wife doesn't understand me' line."

"Leah, he hasn't used any line," Olivia's heart sank. She'd been out of the game too long to even recognise any such line.

Anyway, Matt hadn't exactly said anything remotely like that, had he? He had just been friendly because he recognised her and was probably taken aback that they lived in the same area – end of story.

"Oh I suppose you're right – I am being stupid," she admitted. "The man is just being nice because he feels sorry for me and desperate, lonely idiot that I am, I immediately want to jump on him."

"Is he *that* good-looking?"

She imagined Matt's sparkling eyes and open, laughing face. "Yes," she said, dreamily, "he is." Then she burst out laughing.

"Oh, dear – you have it bad then."

AFTER LUNCH, they decided to have coffee in the living-room.

"So Andrew's in good spirits?" Olivia asked, putting a plate of chocolate marshmallows on a tray before remembering that Leah, who was surrounded by handmade chocolate daily, would have no interest in high-sugar mass-market chocmallows.

"Mmm I love these," Leah leaned against the work-top while waiting for the kettle to boil, "but I'm stuffed after all that lunch."

Olivia wondered how on earth someone who never seemed to stop eating and was surrounded by such temptation every hour of the day could manage to stay so slim. Not that Leah was stick-thin, but she had a nice figure, and could still get away with wearing a white T-shirt with skinny jeans, unlike Olivia who these days looked as though she was wearing an inflatable swimming aid around her middle.

"Yep, he was in flying form," Leah answered. She had met up with Andrew the previous night for a drink and as was so often the case 'one' had turned into a lot more. "We had a great old natter – and he was asking for you."

"Was he?" Olivia was pleased. She and Andrew had always got on well, although they were never particularly close. She remembered him phoning her once or twice after Peter and although she was sure it was just a polite duty call, she appreciated the gesture.

Some of their so-called social circle had all but ignored her afterwards, which had been deeply hurtful.

Back then, Leah had been abroad, Robin in New York, and she and Kate had kept in fleeting contact but by then both had their own lives.

It was only when Leah returned that the three had become friendly again. She was somehow the heart of the group, the one that kept them connected even after all these years. Olivia supposed it was different too, because she and Peter had been so close back in college that no one else had ever really got a look-in.

"So what does he make of Amanda's party?" she asked with a slight grin. She and Leah hadn't quite made up their minds as to whether they were going to attend that little soiree, but as neither of them were expectant mummies – nor likely to be, Olivia thought wryly – it was unlikely.

"Taking it all in his stride, as usual," Leah answered. "Oh, she overdoes the helpless kitten act, but you know Andrew, he doesn't take the blindest bit of notice."

"Is he still so easy-going?" It was hard to believe that Andrew had done so well for himself. Unfortunately, a knee injury had prematurely ended his hopes of becoming a professional rugby player. But his computer studies had served him well and he was one of the few who had actually made any money out of the dot-com boom.

A tech entrepreneur in that he had a great business idea plus the wherewithal to follow it through, rather than just a fancy website and catchy buzzword. Andrew had come up with break-through web-based business-to-business software and like all the best ideas, his was simple and easy to operate and he had little problems in raising venture capital for it.

He also showed great vision and sold the company for a small fortune just before the tech bubble burst. Since then he'd invested his money in commercial property tax-incentives across the city, earning him a comfortable living with little effort.

Which is exactly how Andrew Clarke liked it. Now it seemed he was quite happy to just sit back and enjoy life. Which was nice work if you could get it, Olivia thought.

"So what else is new with him?"

Leah grimaced guiltily. "I'm not too sure. We were so out of it I can't remember much to be honest. He kept buying rounds of tequila, which is why I was so twisted last night."

"Oh dear," Olivia smiled, trying to remember the last time she had been 'out of it', "that bad?"

"I must have been because Josh barely spoke to me before he left for work today. Apparently, I nearly woke up the entire street coming home last night. I can barely remember getting back. Andrew was worse."

"Oh dear," Olivia said again, thinking she sounded like her mother. Leah's exploits were beginning to make her feel ancient and there was only a year between them.

"I'd say Amanda wasn't too impressed with Andrew either." Then she put her head in her hands. "Oh crap, I've just remembered!"

"What?"

"Oh, I'm such an eejit. I starting shooting my mouth off about work, about how it was impossible to qualify for a business grant, and all sorts of rubbish like that." She paused. "And then Andrew ..." She trailed off, shaking her head in embarrassment.

"Andrew what?"

"He offered to help me out. Well, no, knowing me I *asked* him to help me out. And we had this long conversation about him putting money into the business and I told him all about my dream of opening a shop and plans for world domination."

"You didn't?" Olivia laughed.

"Oh I hope he didn't think I was serious. He's probably sick to the teeth of people looking for a leg-up."

"Don't be silly. Andrew's your friend – he knows it was only the drink talking. Anyway, if the two of you were as bad as one another, then chances are he won't remember either."

"I hope not. I'd hate him to think I was being a leech."

"He won't think that. Anyway, if I were you, I'd start worrying about what you're going to say to that poor boyfriend of yours for staying out most of the night with some other guy."

Leah cringed. "I know. I told Josh we were going out for one or two. Then I arrive in at all hours of the morning twisted."

Olivia couldn't help but giggle. "How does he put up with you?"

"I don't know, and at the same time I don't know what I'd do without him either." Her voice grew serious. "You know, I never thought I'd see myself settling down, particularly not with someone like him."

"What do you mean?"

"Well, I don't know. I just thought I'd spend the rest of my life chasing after the same troublemakers that I did throughout college. The unattainable ones, the dangerous ones, not the normal, down-to-earth nice ones, like Josh."

Not to mention good-looking, Olivia thought, picturing her friend's extraordinarily attractive boyfriend. "Yes, but you guys are a partnership – you've both brought something to the relationship. He's lucky to have you too, Leah. Not every girl would be as understanding."

"I know." Leah's face clouded slightly and she turned her attention to making the coffee.

She put the two mugs on the tray with the chocolate marshmallows and followed Olivia into the living-room, where Ellie sat playing with her toys in the corner.

"Which house did you say that guy lived in?" she asked, setting down the tray.

Olivia went over to the window. "I'm not sure. It's either the one with the green door ..." she pointed to one of the redbrick semis across the green, "or that one with the hanging basket."

Although she'd lived in Lakeview for some time, she had kept herself to herself and knew only a handful of her neighbours. Maeve McGrath had a lovely daughter-in-law Liz, who ran a kennel service just outside the town and possibly due to their shared interest in animals, was probably the closest thing she had to a friend there.

Cherrywood Green was a quiet, mature little mews and a lot of the residents were older and settled with grown-up families. They liked their privacy and generally didn't interfere with one another – which was exactly why Olivia liked living there.

Leah's gaze followed in the direction she was pointing and as she did, the green door opened and Matt stepped outside.

"That's him!" Olivia exclaimed, jumping out of sight and feeling immediately foolish.

"Hmm," Leah continued peering out the window. "Not much of a Lothario, I suppose – no gold medallions and as far as I can tell from here, he does seem to have all his own hair."

"Leah!"

"What? I'm just telling you what I think. Now, he's getting into – oh, nice car – worth a few quid."

Olivia stole a look as Matt steered his Volvo out onto the road and around the other side of the green.

"He's not bad, though hard to tell from here, really," Leah continued a running commentary. "I wonder why the wife wasn't with him? Judging by the get-up, he looked like he was going off somewhere nice – Sunday lunch perhaps?"

Olivia didn't answer. She was too busy thinking how handsome Matt looked in his dark suit.

"Ah – there's someone else coming out now," Leah said, beckoning. "Must be the wife."

"We shouldn't be doing this – we're like a pair of children spying on people." Olivia was trying to stay sensible although she had to admit she was interested in getting a look at Matt's wife – very interested.

"Don't be stupid – this is better than *Coronation Street* – here, take a look. She's got the kid with her too."

"What's she like?" Olivia looked over, expecting to see a stunning blonde with a perfect body and an equally perfect face and heart plummeting, realised that the woman coming out of Matt's house fit the bill exactly.

The son looked about the same age as Ellie and was cute, dressed all in denim and running way ahead of this mother to chase after something in the air – a butterfly.

They had definitely just moved into the area, as Olivia was certain she had never seen either before.

"I wonder why they've not gone with him though?" Leah moved away from the window. She sat down on Olivia's sofa and began spooning sugar into her coffee. "He must be one of those workaholic types – off into the office on a Sunday or something."

"I doubt it." Matt didn't come across as a workaholic type. He came across as someone energetic and fun, someone who enjoyed life.

But then again, what did Olivia know? She'd met him – what, twice? Hardly a proper meeting either time. How could she possibly make any assumptions as to what type he was?

Feeling strangely deflated she joined Leah on the sofa and picked up one of the newspapers, hoping to take her mind off the image of gorgeous Matt's equally gorgeous wife innocently out for a walk with her son on a Sunday afternoon – completely unaware that some slattern across the road had taken a fancy to her husband.

All of a sudden, Olivia felt ashamed of herself. Matt Sheridan was *not* interested in her and certainly had not been flirting with her. He was simply a decent, happily married family man, who was reasonably chatty to strangers and silly women who had problems reversing out of driveways.

So there was no point in wasting her time thinking about him any longer – no point at all.

FOURTEEN

But trying to forget about Matt wasn't proving easy.

The following Thursday evening it was lashing rain and, having discovered she'd run out of milk, Olivia made a quick dash to the shop around the corner, leaving Ellie waiting in the car.

It would take forever to get her organised to go out in this weather and she'd only be a minute or two at the most. She was chatting pleasantly to Molly the shop's proprietor, when Matt walked in.

"We must stop meeting like this," he chuckled, shaking his wet head out of its hood and flashing her a broad smile, instantly turning Olivia's insides to mush.

Calm down she thought, berating herself for getting carried away simply by the sight of a decent-looking guy. If she heard any of her friends were behaving like this around a married man she would murder them.

Although having thoughts about carrying on wasn't the same as *actually* carrying on, but still …

"Hello," she said easily, praying that the heat in her cheeks wasn't blatantly obvious – but either way she knew that the shop-keeper's keen eyes were taking in everything.

Molly Brogan was a lovely woman, but there was something about Irish women in small-town corner shops that ensured they had access to an information network better than most government agencies.

Her daughter Trish worked at the local newspaper, *The Lakeview News*, so it seemed a certain level of 'inquisitiveness' ran in the family.

Molly was a chatterbox who seemed to know everything, and like most women Olivia knew at that age – except for her own mother – was constantly offering her introductions to Mrs Murphy's son or Bill Harrington's nephew, or whoever she thought might be suitable for the "misfortunate young single mother".

So Olivia tried her very best not to let her true feelings be known, especially where Matt was concerned. And for all Olivia knew, Molly might already know Mrs Sheridan, who she was certain wouldn't be at all pleased to hear that the neighbours were making eyes at her husband in the corner shop.

But judging from Molly's apparent interest, and blatant appreciation of Matt's good looks, she herself was as yet unaware of the Lakeview newcomers.

"So, how are you?" he asked, paying for his newspaper. "Did you get to where you wanted to the other day?"

"Yes," she answered and wondered why it was that the mere presence of Matt Sheridan made her monosyllabic. "Yes, I mean – thank you for helping us out – it was very good of you."

"No problem. How's Ellie?" he asked and Olivia marvelled at how friendly and easy he was when her own insides seemed to be melting. "A dotey little thing," he said, nodding towards Molly to include her in the conversation. Once again Olivia couldn't help thinking how lucky his wife was to have ended up with such a charming, friendly – oh, sod it – *yummy* husband.

"Lovely just like her mother," Molly said, with a slight smile and a definite meaning in her tone.

Matt laughed. "You're right about that," he said, studying her closely and in that moment she knew that she wasn't mistaken. It *hadn't* been wishful thinking, he *did* seem keen on her, and as much as she knew how wrong it was, Olivia couldn't help feeling warmed by the thought of it. It had been ages since she'd felt like this.

Sod's Law.

She laughed in what she hoped was a carefree manner. *Beep! Beep!* The sound of a car horn from outside brought her back to reality.

"Better go," Olivia gasped. "Ellie's in the car on her own and she could be up to all sorts." She snatched up the milk from the counter and smiling a quick goodbye at them both, hurried out of the store.

"You forgot your change," Molly went to the door and called after her, but it was too late. Olivia's car was already halfway down the road.

"Poor thing," the shopkeeper shook her head sadly and went back behind the counter. "Having to bring up that child on her own."

"On her own?" Matt murmured offhandedly, before picking up his own change and putting it in his pocket.

"Yes, and an absolute shame it is too," Molly continued, obviously bursting to fill him in. "The husband died suddenly while she was pregnant with the little one," she informed him, leaning forward conspiratorially. "Just took a turn and dropped dead one day after coming home from a hard day's work, apparently." She sighed dramatically. "Isn't it terrible the way the young people are under so much pressure these days with work and big mortgages and everything? It's the stress that does it if you ask me. And him a radiologist, practically a doctor himself – but that didn't save him."

She sighed dramatically. "She moved here not long afterwards. It's not easy bringing up a child on your own, but I'll tell you one thing, father or no father, you won't find a better-behaved young one than Ellie Gallagher and that's no easy claim these days. A lovely little thing, so she is."

"She is indeed," Matt replied.

"But it's an awful shame," Molly rambled on. "Such a young couple and married only a short while when tragedy struck. God love her, it was a terrible thing to happen to anyone but especially to someone so young."

Matt nodded. "I'd better be going," he said, putting his newspaper under his arm and heading for the door. "Thanks again," he smiled at a visibly disappointed Molly.

But despite his curiosity, Matt was unwilling to partake in idle chit-chat about Olivia, a woman he hardly knew, yet who'd occupied his thoughts since he'd first laid eyes on her.

FIFTEEN

Robin and Ben met his sister and her husband for dinner in a trendy restaurant on the Upper East Side – Brian spending a rare few consecutive days at home.

Robin adored Sarah, and while lately she and Ben had been making more of an effort to visit her and little Kirsty in New Jersey, they didn't socialise enough together.

Now she studied the menu the waiter had given them with habitual caution.

"So, how's Kirsty?" Ben asked, and instantly his sister tensed.

"Don't mention the war," Brian grunted, rolling his eyes as he set down his menu. "It was hard enough persuading Sarah to come out tonight as it was. For some reason, she seems to think that the child will spontaneously combust if she's not around."

"Brian, don't start, please," his wife whispered, embarrassed. "I'm just a bit worried after that last stay in hospital," she added by way of explanation. "The baby-sitter is new enough. She doesn't really know how to handle Kirsty if anything –"

"Seems no one knows how to handle Kirsty, other than her mother of course," Brian interjected dryly.

Just then, the waiter arrived to take their order, and Robin felt sorry for Sarah. It was obvious he felt she was being unrealistically overprotective of Kirsty's asthma, yet she couldn't be blamed for worrying.

"I get it. It's a big responsibility, isn't it?" she said warmly. "Hard to rely on someone else to know what to do if something happens."

Sarah nodded gratefully. "It is – and to be honest, I'm not just worried about Kirsty. As she gets older she's learning that she needs to take her inhaler, but it's not fair to the babysitter. She knows she's asthmatic but still ..."

"Still we can't wrap the child in bloody cotton wool," Brian said. "Honestly, the more you fuss over her, the worse she gets!" He looked at Ben and Robin, exasperated. "It's not good to molly-coddle a kid like that."

Robin and Ben exchanged awkward glances. The way Brian spoke about her, you'd swear that Kirsty was just some trouble-some 'kid' instead of his own chronically asthmatic daughter. But Brian was away with work most of the time, so didn't understand the worry and stress poor Sarah had to endure.

"I'm sure the baby-sitter will manage just fine," Ben soothed.

Sarah nodded, red-faced and embarrassed at her husband's lack of etiquette and, Robin suspected, hurt by his lack of under-standing. Her own father had been the same.

"I suppose," Sarah bit her lip. "I feel guilty leaving her though – it's so humid this summer and the pollen count is –"

"Oh, for goodness' sake, will you give it a rest? The kid will be fine, which is more than I can say for myself. This is my first weekend at home in ages – we're supposed to be out for a relaxing dinner, and already you're giving me heartburn."

For a long moment, an awkward silence descended on the table until waiter returned with their first course and Brian turned to Ben. "So," he asked, purposefully changing the subject, "how's business?"

"Good, very busy actually," Ben answered, equally eager to change the subject, more so, Robin thought, to take the spotlight off poor Sarah.

She didn't know how she put up with such an ignorant oaf for a husband. "She'll be fine," she mouthed, giving Sarah an encouraging smile, before taking another sip of her wine.

The others had begun making inroads into their starters but as she was unfamiliar with this particular restaurant, Robin had declined to order one herself.

She glanced at Sarah's green salad and the others' deep-fried shrimp, and while everything seemed innocuous it was just too much of a chance to take. She had taken chances based on doubtful assurances before, and while she lived to tell the tale, Robin knew too well that it just wasn't worth it. Anyway, she didn't want to ruin the meal for everyone else by throwing caution to the winds, and particularly not for Ben, who, if the worst came to the worst, would have to administer her adrenaline.

"Aren't you having anything?" Brian asked her then. "Oh, I just remembered, you're another one of these faddy dieters, aren't you?" He shook his head. "You should hear some of the crap the girls at the office come out with – if they're not on Atkins, they're in some 'Zone'," he made quotation marks with his fingers, "or else they've talked themselves into believing they've got some kind of wheat or dairy intolerance..." He laughed derisively. "But seriously Robin, you don't need to lose weight – you look great."

At this Ben put down his menu and gave his brother-in-law a look that could cut him in two.

"Brian!" Sarah gasped, mortified.

But there was no point in getting upset about it. Brian was just an idiot who couldn't help putting his foot in it.

"A load of baloney, as far as I can tell," he went on. "When we were kids there was no such thing as nut allergies and pollen allergies, and goodness knows what else these drug corporations are dreaming up these days. You do know that that's all it is, don't you, Robin? Big Pharma's brainwashing, preying on people like you and Sarah. They get us all worked up about our health and our kids, so we go and dutifully pay them lots of money for drugs that help ease our worries and conscience." His point made, Brian went back to the rest of his shrimp.

Things had been tense all evening, but it seemed that this was the last straw for Sarah.

"Brian!" she whispered harshly, her voice a mixture of embarrassment and outrage. "How dare you paint Robin as some kind of raving hypochondriac. What do *you* know about worry and conscience, when you spend the whole time off on your bloody road trips? When was the last time you had to rush Kirsty to hospital after an asthma attack? When was the last time you had to listen to her struggle for breath and wonder if her little lungs were going to give out?" Tears shone in her eyes. "And then you have the cheek to sit here and accuse *me* of being overprotective? Of course I'm being over-protective, you asshole because I need to make up for both of us." With that, she stood up and grabbed her handbag.

"Well, so much for a pleasant evening." For once, Brian looked flustered – obviously, Robin thought, unused to his wife standing up to him like that. Good for her.

Although, catching sight of Ben's hard stare as his sister and brother-in-law exited the room, Robin knew that doing Brian good was the furthest thing from her boyfriend's mind just then.

"HE'S SUCH A PRAT," Ben said when they returned to their apartment later that evening. "Lecturing you like that – who the hell does he think he is?"

They left the restaurant soon after, the thought of dinner no longer quite so appealing. Instead, they had picked up a pizza from a reliable place near home.

"It wasn't so much that – it was the way he lectured Sarah that annoyed me," Robin answered, taking a huge bite out of her pizza. "Honestly, you'd wonder why the likes of Brian ended up having children at all – he's never there for Kirsty and she adores him."

Ben fiddled with a strand of her hair. "She adores you too, you know," he said, "and wouldn't you wonder why the likes of you and me don't have children, when it's obvious you'd be a terrific mother?"

Robin moved his hand away. "Don't, Ben."

"Don't what?"

"Don't start this again."

"I can't understand why you're so against having children when you're a natural with them. Kirsty adores you, *all* kids adore you and despite what you say, I know you love them too."

Robin shook her head. Wasn't it enough for him that she had agreed to settle down and buy a house together?

"Do you have any idea what it would be like trying to bring up a child with my allergy?" she muttered. "Bad enough as it is – like tonight when I can't go to a restaurant, or even eat at a friend's house without a fuss."

"There are no guarantees that it'd be passed on –"

She had tried to explain this many times before but he just wouldn't listen. "There is *every* chance. It's hereditary, and because mine is so severe there's a nine out of ten chance that it would be passed on."

"But what about that ten per cent? Don't you think that having a child of our own would be worth taking that chance? Why let this ruin your chances of becoming a mother? As you said yourself, it takes over so much of your life, so why let it extend to this?"

"Ben, it's very easy to say that now, but look how Kirsty's

asthma has put Sarah and Brian's relationship and their marriage under severe pressure."

"That's because Brian is an insensitive prat who doesn't realise –"

"It's not that, of course he realises. He realises but he doesn't *understand*." She shook her head. "It was the very same with my parents. My mother had a terrible time with me and, as you know, was fiercely protective. My dad, although he knew that my allergy was serious, still thought that Mum was overly cautious and hysterical even."

"I know all this already," Ben said, "and that your dad wasn't cautious enough."

When she was six years old, her father had taken her on a trip to Tramore Strand one summer. After a pleasant day in glorious sunshine with Tom helping her build sandcastles and teaching her to swim, Robin was ravenous. Her dad had innocently bought them chips from a roadside van. Robin had taken a single bite and within minutes started going into anaphylactic shock. Luckily, her dad had remembered to take adrenaline with them, but left it in the car. In the time that it took for him to go back and find it, his daughter had almost died.

"Mum went crazy. Understandably she blamed him, and it eventually drove them apart." It was something that Robin had always felt guilty about, even though her mother assured her it wasn't her fault.

Now she turned to look at Ben. "No matter what you might think now, that of course you'd protect the child and make sure that nothing ever happened, you'd always feel as though you're sitting on a time-bomb. It changes your routine, your relationship – your whole life."

"I'm not being funny, but surely any parent could say the same thing? Children will change your life, no matter what. There's always the chance they could run out in front of a speeding car, or drown or whatever..." He trailed off, exasperated. "I think you're imagining the worst-case scenario and after what you've been through yourself as a child, I can completely understand that. But I don't think you should deny yourself or me the chance to become parents simply because of hard work. It's hard work anyway. And like I said, there's always the chance that the condition isn't inherited isn't there?" He caught her hand and looked her in the eye. "Isn't there?"

Robin sighed and looked away, wishing Ben would understand that it was still way too much of a chance to take.

SIXTEEN

Leah was sitting in her workshop going through a supplier catalogue when the phone rang.

"Hey," Andrew's cheerful tones came on the other end, "how's the head?"

"Oh, you're a bad influence, Andrew Clarke,"she exclaimed. "Josh is barely talking to me."

"I'm surprised he's still with you, considering. Anyway, I was in the same boat – Amanda was livid that I stayed out so late."

"What time was it?"

"It must have been four or five by the time I got in. I can't believe they stayed serving that long."

"Well, why wouldn't they, when you put your gold card behind the bar and kept buying rounds for everyone?"

"Ah feck it, don't tell me I was in flash-git mode, was I? That was your fault for making me out to be some hotshot businessman."

"But you are," Leah teased him, knowing Andrew did tend to lay it on thick but only when he was drunk. Anyway, why not? He was a hotshot so why shouldn't he show off a little?

"Give it up. So I can't talk long but I'm meeting with the

accountant soon about what we talked about that night. Can you give me some sort of idea of how much you need?"

"What?" Leah's heart stopped. "Andrew, I was only joking – please don't think that I was begging ..." She trailed off, mortified.

"What are you on about, you eejit? Wasn't it my idea in the first place? Anyway, I made some enquiries about a premises this morning and –"

"What?" Leah squealed. "A premises – what for?"

"For the shop, of course. Hey I know we had a few that night, but don't tell me you've forgotten the entire conversation..."

"But I thought it was just a joke, I didn't seriously expect you to –"

"Look, you have the basis of a very good business, but to go further you need to expand. You said yourself that your stuff would fly out the door if you had a retail premises. Well, that's what we're going to do."

"Andrew, I just couldn't take –"

"You're not taking anything from me – I expect a good return on my investment. I know a good business when I see it, Leah, and I trust you to make a go of it too. Even though you lot think I'm just a jammy sod who got lucky a few years ago, I *do* know what I'm talking about. Anyway, I'd rather put my faith in you than some fresh-faced business graduate that doesn't have a clue about the real world. And if you're willing to take me on as a business partner, a silent partner, mind – I don't want to step on any toes – then I think we can make a real go of this."

Leah was speechless.

"Well, are you going to get me some figures or what?"

"I'm just ... I'm just amazed by all of this. What'll Amanda think?"

"I've invested in a couple of ventures over the years you know – you're not the first one."

"Oh, I know that – I didn't mean ..." It was weird – all of a sudden Leah felt as though she was talking to her boss, not her crazy old college friend who could drink her under the table and used to let her cry on his shoulder whenever her latest squeeze dumped her.

As if sensing her thoughts, Andrew spoke softly, "What I mean is that I make the business decisions. Nine times out of ten Amanda doesn't know what I do with my money and, to be honest, she doesn't want to know. As long as there's enough in the joint account or on the credit card to keep her stocked with clothes and shoes, that's all she cares about."

"Are you absolutely sure though?" Leah was feeling a curious mixture of fear and adrenaline. With Andrew on board, there was no limit to what she could do. She could take on staff, and spend more time on her recipes without having to worry about accounts and suppliers. And an outlet – an actual store – wow!

"Of course I'm sure. Look, I get it was a drunken conversation, so I can understand that you might find it a little weird but Leah, I promise, once I put up the money, there'll be no interference from me. It's still your baby and I trust you completely. If you've any doubts in that regard, don't, 'cos I don't want anything to do with it – unless you'd prefer that I did, in which case I'd have to withdraw the offer as I just don't have the time – "

"No, no – that would be perfect! I mean, that's exactly how I'd prefer it too. I'm just finding it so hard to get my head around it but, wow, I haven't even said thank you. Andrew, thank you, thank you, thank you!"

"You're welcome. Now, do you think you could stop thanking me for a second and get your ass down to Blackrock and have a look at the place I have in mind?"

"Blackrock? You don't mean Blackrock, Dublin, do you?" Leah knew that in that bijou upmarket village, her produce would literally fly out the door.

"No, I mean Blackrock, feckin' Cavan, where else? I'm

meeting with the estate agent about another place at two, and then I was hoping we could pop over there for a look – what do you think?"

"What do I think?" Leah repeated, exhilarated. "I'll be there with bells on!"

SEVENTEEN

"Seems a bit sudden?" was Josh's dour response when later Leah told him the good news. "I mean, you haven't seen this guy since his wedding and all of a sudden he wants to make a huge investment in your business?"

"He's a good friend," Leah said, her spirits dampened by his less-than-enthusiastic reaction. "We've both been very busy with our own lives, you know how it is, but always stayed close. And if Andrew Clarke has enough faith in my talent to invest his money, well, I think I have a right to be pleased about it." She knew she was sounding petulant but she didn't care. Sometimes, Josh got a little bit funny about Leah's career, probably because he had always worked for his father, who ran a popular chain of DIY stores.

Josh hated working there and was always looking for any excuse to get out of it, yet the pay was good and the hours were flexible and having done nothing more than an Arts degree in college, he wasn't qualified to do much else.

"So what's he planning then?"

"*He* isn't planning anything, it's entirely up to me. But we went out this afternoon to have a look at the premises he had in mind for the shop and oh, it's just perfect! Blackrock, can you believe it?"

Kate certainly couldn't earlier when over the phone Leah had told her about Andrew's offer.

"Blackrock is just perfect, such a busy little spot, and upmarket too, ideal for Elysium."

One of the most desirable places to live on Dublin's Southside, the affluent and discerning inhabitants of the village and surrounding areas would be the ideal clientele for her. It would be a terrific start and she couldn't contain her excitement at the prospect.

"So what happens now?" Josh asked her. "Are you going to go for this place or what?"

"Well, Andrew is hammering things out with the estate agent about the lease, but based on the figures we went through this afternoon, we should be well able to manage things. I'll need to take another look at range, see how I'm going to manage fridge displays and all that, so I'm going to take a pop into town tomorrow to check out some of what will soon be my competitors." She hugged Josh delightedly. "Can you imagine me, with my very own store? Honestly, Josh, I knew I was doing OK with supplying trade, but retail will just take the business to a completely different level."

"I know it will, congratulations." He returned her hug, half-heartedly.

Leah knew it was hard for him knowing that she would be working a lot more than usual to get the shop set up, but the way Andrew was driving forward, it shouldn't take much longer than a few weeks before they were open for business.

Yes, she would have to work like a demon between now and then to satisfy existing suppliers and come up with new stock for the outlet, but at least things were moving forward.

If Leah had her way, the business would get to the stage where maybe Josh wouldn't need to work with his dad any more, and she would be able to support both of them – well, not *she* – she knew Josh wouldn't like the sound of that – but the business certainly would.

Her margins were terrific as it was, and once she started selling direct to the public there would be no stopping her. Yes, she would have to sacrifice a lot of her home and social life to get there, but wasn't that what all business people had to do to be successful?

Then when everything had settled down and the business was more or less running itself, she and Josh could slow down and take things easy, maybe go on a nice holiday to the Caribbean or even go and visit Robin in New York or something. Josh would get used to it – it might be weird at first but he *would* get used to it.

He'd have to, wouldn't he?

EIGHTEEN

It was the night of Amanda's famous party, and Leah was just about ready to climb the walls.

The fact that Andrew was investing in Elysium meant that she had to speedily rethink her decision not to attend, as it would appear very rude not to. Thankfully Olivia had come along to give her some moral support. Which at that moment in time Leah badly needed.

Amanda seemed to have invited all her new-mummy friends, and if Leah didn't know better she could have sworn that the girl had also raided the nearest maternity ward, there were so many heavily pregnant women in attendance.

She was trying her level best to ignore the sight of them sitting on the sofa, gazing at and lovingly rubbing their expanding bellies. The room had been decorated with baby balloons, and *Mother & Baby* and *Your Pregnancy* magazines were strewn all over the coffee table. Although there wasn't a child in sight, Leah could almost smell the baby powder.

As usual, Amanda had gone way over the top, but judging by her apparent glee at falling pregnant in the first place, this wasn't surprising.

Leah recalled the strange phone call she'd received from the girl a few weeks earlier. She and Amanda weren't close so to say it was a surprise to hear from her was a complete understatement.

"Leah – hi, I'm so glad I got you at home!" she shrieked.

"Why, what's wrong?" She hadn't been able to tell by her high-pitched tone whether the girl was excited or upset. With Amanda, it was always hard to tell.

"Well, I have some amazing news!"

"Oh?" Leah waited for the impending announcement that Brown Thomas had had a last-minute 'day only' sale and that Amanda had secured an impossibly gorgeous Jill Sander dress for one of her fancy dinner parties, or something similar.

"I'm pregnant!" Amanda announced breathlessly. "Now, I know what you're thinking – and it *is* a bit of a surprise, seeing as me and Andrew have only been trying for a few months or so – but still, it's happened!"

Leah gulped, images of Amanda and Andrew 'trying' coming unbidden into her mind. Ugh, what a horrible expression – why couldn't people say something less graphic like 'hoping to have a baby' or something?

"Oh," she said, then quickly added, "great news – congratulations." Inwardly though, she couldn't help feeling slightly deflated.

Not another one.

"Thanks, Leah, imagine me – pregnant! It's hard to believe, isn't it? I can hardly get used to it myself, especially when I've just found out. We're supposed to keep it a secret and not tell anyone until the twelve weeks are up, but I just can't wait – I'm five weeks and want to tell the world!"

"Five weeks," Leah repeated, taken aback. That *was* a little early to be shouting about it. "So, how are you feeling? Have you been sick, or anything?" she asked.

"Oh, Leah, you wouldn't believe it." As if to demonstrate,

Amanda's tone all of a sudden sounded like that of a frail old lady. "It's been just awful – I'm so tired all the time and weak as a kitten. And then, each morning I'm like Mount Etna, throwing up over and over again. It's simply *dread*ful."

"You poor thing." At this, the slight envy Leah had been feeling ended quickly. She could only imagine what morning sickness must be like.

"But, you know me – easygoing as anything. I'll just take it all in my stride."

She couldn't help but smile. Amanda was probably one of the least easygoing people you could meet. Always quick to take offence, she would start an argument with anyone who looked at her sideways.

She and Kate had always been at loggerheads throughout college, no-nonsense Kate having little time for Amanda's childishness and Amanda, in turn, calling Kate 'a humourless cow'.

Leah idly wondered what a heavily expectant Kate would make of her news.

"Well look, I've tons of people to phone, but obviously I wanted to tell you personally – before word gets out." She put it so dramatically that, despite herself, Leah had visions of shrieking newspaper headlines proclaiming Amanda's condition to the world. "So, I'd better go – I still have a whole list of people to get through!"

"No problem. Pass on my congratulations to Andrew. I take it you two will be breaking out the champagne?"

"Oh, no celebrating for me," Amanda said, piously. "From now on, I'll have to be *very* careful – no alcohol."

"You can have a glass, surely?" Leah said surprised. At only five weeks, was a total ban on alcohol absolutely necessary?

"Oh, no," Amanda was adamant. "Anyway, Andrew wouldn't allow it – he's treating me like a china doll as it is! Honestly, Leah, you should see the way he looks at me, as though I'm the most fragile and precious thing in the world!"

And don't you just love that, Leah thought, rather uncharitably. Amanda adored being the centre of attention and of course, this meant that Andrew was undoubtedly waiting on her hand and foot. No doubt she'd milk the role of delicate mother-to-be to for all it was worth.

Lucky old her.

"Well, tell him congrats from me, won't you?"

"I will. Oh, be sure to tell Josh the news?" Amanda added.

"Of course – he'll be delighted," Leah said, ringing off and thinking privately that pregnancies and children were so far down her boyfriend's agenda, it wouldn't register with him if Amanda was having a litter of kittens.

Now, someone with a very similar agenda, one of her party guests, in fact, was droning in Leah's ear, the woman's nasal tone piercing her brain. "Being a mother changes your life in ways you couldn't *possibly* imagine."

"Oh, it changes you *completely*, Grainne." Another guest joined them, and Leah was sandwiched in between the two. Having nothing to contribute, she silently beseeched Olivia, who was standing at the other end of the room for assistance, but in vain. Her friend was deep in conversation with someone else.

The woman called Grainne had strolled in earlier dressed to the nines in designer gear, accompanied by a put-upon nanny, and Leah immediately decided that, even if this woman had ever *seen* a nappy in her lifetime, she would almost certainly not know what to do with it.

"Don't you find that you look at life completely different these days?" she went on.

"Absolutely," Amanda, her blonde hair styled to perfection, drifted towards the group to join the conversation. Stuck in the middle of all this, Leah felt decidedly uncomfortable. "Sometimes I feel as though I didn't know what life was really all about until I discovered this new one growing inside of me." Dressed in over-the-top designer maternity wear, Amanda pushed out her non-existent tummy and bestowed a beatific smile at Leah, who smiled politely back.

Grainne nodded gravely. "The thing is, you really don't understand true suffering until you've experienced childbirth," she declared, and Leah noticed Amanda's dreamily serene expression deflate slightly at this. "Nor, until then, can you truly understand what it is to be a woman."

"What?" Leah asked, her hackles rising slightly at this. "But what about other achievements in life – your degree, your career, your relationships?"

"All those things become superficial once you have a child," Grainne spoke as if motherhood had helped her achieve some form of Zen state. She and Amanda exchanged patronising smiles. "You'll understand when you have one of your own."

Leah's heart skipped a beat. "And what makes you think I *will* have one of my own?"

At this, it was as if all conversation in the room halted, and everyone turned to look at them. Out of the corner of her eye, Leah saw Olivia approach and then felt a protective hand on her arm.

"Oh Leah, I had no idea ..." To her credit, Amanda looked perturbed.

Grainne shook her head and assumed a sombre expression. "You must think we're very insensitive."

Insensitive? Idiotic, more like.

"It's grand," Leah said, relaxing a little, "but sometimes I *do* find it difficult – "

"You know," Grainne went on as if Leah hadn't spoken. "I sometimes wonder if there's something in the air these days – something *literally* in the air from those nuclear power plants or something – because so many of my friends are having similar problems." The other women nodded in agreement.

"Problems?"

"Well, you know what she means ..." Amanda actually looked embarrassed.

"Fertility problems," Grainne finished.

"Leah," Olivia began, "let's just –"

"No," Leah shrugged her off, blood rushing to her face as she faced Grainne. "I'd like to know why Ms Earth Mummy here seems to think that I have a fertility problem."

Grainne frowned. "Well, you said you couldn't have children, I just assumed –"

"You assumed wrong. And I didn't say I *couldn't* have children – I just choose not to."

"Oh." The shocked disbelief on the other woman's face was a picture.

Leah sighed inwardly. *Same reaction, every time.*

"But, but why? I mean ... why not?" Grainne blustered.

"Why should I?"

"But – but why would you *not* want them?" Amanda said, looking at her as if she had gained another head. "I mean it's only natural, isn't it?"

Leah's heart tightened and for a moment, she couldn't think of a reply.

NINETEEN

"You know that shit gets to me," Leah raged later, when she and Olivia had left Amanda's and were back at her apartment eating a fish and chip takeaway.

"Look, they're just pampered biddies, that's all," Olivia said softly. "Between the nanny and the housekeeper, they all have plenty of time on their hands to sit back and think about the 'psychology' of motherhood. I'm willing to bet that Grainne one has never had to clean up after a sick child, or been kept awake all night with a screaming baby. It's a warped view of motherhood, a rose-tinted Hollywood version, and I can tell you from experience that it's nothing like that."

Leah shook her head. "I just hate being made to feel like I'm a leper, that's all."

Olivia was silent for a moment. "You shouldn't let them upset you," she said. "You and I both know that what they're saying about motherhood being all sweetness and light is utter crap. I love Ellie to bits, but most of the time I'd be lucky if I actually got any time to ponder over how 'wondrous'," she made quote-mark signs with her fingers, "the whole experience is. As it is, I'm torn between one minute wanting to hug her to bits, and the next wanting to shake her to bits." She laughed. "You know all this anyway, and you shouldn't be letting Amanda's stupid cronies get to you."

"I know, but I've been hearing a lot of this lately, and it's driving me mad. People always assume that Josh and I are childless either because we're waiting to have them in the future, or we can't have them at all. They can't bloody accept that we are child-free by choice. And the problem is, I always seem to end up having to defend myself – as if I've committed some kind of crime or something." She shook her head. "Why is choosing not to have them such a taboo, Olivia? Open the papers and all you see is people talking about how childcare is too expensive, and how much strain and pressure they're under trying to raise them. Yet when some of us decide *not* to put ourselves through it, they call us self-obsessed and heartless."

Olivia nodded, but for a long moment, an uncomfortable silence hung between them.

"It's just so bloody frustrating. As women, we're supposed to have all these choices and stupidly, it seems – I thought we were free to make them. Yet, when I'm honest about *my* choice not to have kids, I'm made feel as though I've done something wrong." She shook her head. "And to be honest, what with Kate's pregnancy and now Amanda's, I seem to be feeling it even more."

"I'd imagine it is frustrating ..."

Again there was a strained silence, until eventually, her heart beating quickly, Leah looked at Olivia. "Do you mind if I ask you something?"

"Of course not."

In truth, Leah felt guilty about it, and was loath to push it, being very aware that reawakening memories could be very hard. Still, and especially after tonight, she needed to ask.

"What *is* it like?" she asked her. "What was it like in the early days – the really early days, when you knew nothing about babies, nothing about looking after them or feeding them or all that?" She watched Olivia closely for a reaction. "Was it anything like you'd imagined?"

Olivia gave a wry smile. "I'm probably the wrong person to ask."

"Sorry, I really don't want to reopen old wounds but – "

She waved her away. "It's fine. It's just - obviously, with Ellie, I wasn't myself at the time. I was still grieving, so I think I went through it all on complete autopilot. I had to decide whether I would fall to pieces over losing my husband, or be there for our daughter. Course, I had a lot of help from my mum."

Leah remembered how devastated her friend had been after the funeral, and how Olivia's mother had thrown herself into caring for her daughter and then a few months later, her new granddaughter.

Olivia had come through all the heartbreak eventually, but Leah knew she was today a completely different person to the one she had been back at university. Back then, Olivia had been a planner, and a perfectionist and everything from study time to nights out needed to be organised and planned down to the very last detail. Peter had been the same – hardworking, diligent and equally fastidious – so the two of them as a couple had been so perfectly matched it was incredible.

Thinking back now, Leah suspected that this very fact might have been part of the reason for their short break-up that last summer.

She knew that Olivia had struggled after graduation, the lack of routine and structure that suited her so well in college life having completely upended her in the 'real world'.

Trying to make sense of what she wanted to do with her life, and unsure of all the plans she had so carefully laid, Olivia panicked, and out of the blue finished with poor Peter.

Leah had been in Paris at the time, and couldn't believe it

when she heard that the 'golden couple' had broken up, yet she suspected that it wouldn't last long.

She was right. After a short while, the two were back together and, if anything, their time apart galvanised them into action. Peter proposed, they made plans for their wedding and bought their first house and from then on it seemed there was no stopping them.

But tragically, as Olivia had eventually discovered, there were some plans that couldn't be fine-tuned to the last detail, some things that just couldn't be controlled.

"Earth to Leah," her friend teased, and she smiled, realising she had spent the last few minutes deep in thought. "Look, don't worry – you shouldn't feel as though you have to justify your decisions to anyone."

"I suppose, I'm worse. In fairness, I should just let them think what they like, or that I *do* have problems. But yet, I don't see why I should have to. I respect any woman's choice to have a child, so why can't they do the same for me?"

Olivia looked sideways at her. "What's brought all this about? Are you and Josh OK?"

She sighed and shook her head. "Granted we haven't seen all that much of one another lately, what with work being so busy, and he's not all that excited about all the hours I'm putting in to get the shop going." She rolled her eyes. "Still, we'll be fine."

"You should take it easy. Work isn't the be-all and end-all, you know."

"Nah, things will be fine, he knows what I'm like – and once we get the shop opened and I take on some staff, things will settle down. It's just ..." She took a deep breath.

"What?"

"It's not ... it's not just tonight that's got to me. It's *all* this talk of pregnancy and motherhood, with Kate too. I don't mind admitting that lately I feel a bit ... weird. I'm not quite sure how to handle it." She looked embarrassed.

"Weird?"

"Well, for a start, I worry that I'm not giving Kate enough support. We've always been close, and I suppose I'm afraid that our friendship will suffer because we can't share all this pregnancy stuff."

Olivia nodded. "In college, you were the one who wanted children, Kate insisted she didn't, and then she went off and did it anyway." She laughed, seeing Leah's expression. "You know what I mean – Kate was probably the last one of us you could picture as a mum. Besides Amanda – who of course is just being Amanda – looking for attention, and getting lots and lots of it."

Leah rolled her eyes. "I know."

"But hey it hasn't happened to *us*, has it? I've been a mum for years and you and I are still close as ever - despite living in different places even."

"But that was different. I was away for your pregnancy and most of Ellie's early days. Other than sending her presents on her birthday and hearing about it all on the phone, you couldn't really say I was involved."

"But you don't have to be involved. You can still be a good friend, you still *are* a good friend."

Leah nodded and looked away, although she still wasn't quite sure how to get her feelings across without sounding silly. "It's just ... oh, I know you're going to think I'm crazy, and after all this time, it's not as though I can do anything about it but –"

"But?" Olivia waited patiently for her to continue.

Leah grimaced. "At Amanda's tonight, I don't think it was just the comments that bothered me."

"Go on."

"I mean, the talk about how motherhood 'completes' you drives me up the wall of course. But then, there's the basic pregnancy stuff that Kate is excited about, and I can't join in. I feel like such an idiot when I try to because obviously I haven't a clue what I'm talking about and then ..." She paused and looked directly at Olivia. "I suppose it might be getting to me a little now that I won't be able to join in – ever."

Olivia reached for her hand and squeezed it. "I wondered if it might be that, but I didn't want to say anything. You've always been so ... decisive about it."

"I'm ... I think I'm a little jealous, actually," Leah blurted. There, she had finally admitted it. She saw Olivia give her an encouraging smile. "I swore that it wouldn't matter. After all, my business is my baby as such, and I have other fish to fry. So, it didn't matter – not at the time – but now, when it seems that I'm the only one of the old gang not settling down and having babies, I'm not so sure. I think that's what made me so tetchy tonight. I'm feeling ... left out."

"Hey, I can completely understand that. You were bound to feel that way at some stage and now with Kate, one of your closest friends, going down that road, plus being forced into a roomful of blissfully pregnant women tonight, it's inevitable that you'd question things. But having doubts about your own decisions doesn't necessarily mean that they're wrong. You had to make some tough choices and it's only natural that sometimes you'd question them. I'm sure Josh, in his quiet moments – if he has them, that is – would possibly question them too."

"It's a little too late for that now though, isn't it?" Leah said sadly.

Olivia squeezed her hand again. "I suppose so."

TWENTY

Despite her friend's protestations that the decision not to have kids didn't bother her, Olivia had always wondered.

She wondered if someday the time might come when Leah would regret her decision, and the fact that she had to choose.

She remembered how, when Josh and Leah started going out first; Josh had blown them all away and seemed almost too good to be true. They'd all got on like a house on fire and he adored Leah. Yet, only a few months into their almost fairytale relationship, Josh had dropped the bombshell.

Leah hadn't been in a serious relationship for some time, so it wasn't as if the subject was foremost in her mind, but one evening Josh took her out to dinner and told her that he loved her very much, that he could easily see himself spending the rest of his life with her, but that he didn't – *couldn't* – ever see himself wanting children.

Leah had laughed at the time, thinking he was joking, wondering why on earth he had even begun such a stupid conversation. She'd recited it word for word to Olivia afterwards.

"I've had some ... problems in other relationships," he'd said.

"And I just wanted to come clean and let you know exactly how I feel about it before we go any further."

By his face, Leah had known that this was no joke: Josh was deadly serious. His face was solemn, his clear blue eyes thoughtful as he tried to explain his feelings.

"It's something I've known for a long time – something I've always known, actually. I like babies and kids and I love my nephews and my little niece, but I also know for certain that I don't want a kid of my own."

"But how can you possibly decide that at this stage? You never know, you might feel differently in a few years' time."

Josh shook his head. "I'm not getting at you in particular, but why do people always assume that you don't know your own feelings about something like this – that you might change your mind? From as young as seventeen we're all expected to make decisions as to what university we'll go to, or what career we'd like. If you can be trusted to make a life-affecting decision like that at such a young age, then why not this?"

"Yes, but that's completely different, you could easily change your mind and –"

"Leah, I won't," Josh took her hand and looked deep into her eyes. "I've had plenty conversations like this with various women over years." He smiled when Leah raised an eyebrow. "I know how that sounds too. But this is the reason. I care about you a lot, I think we could have a future together, so I think it's only fair that you should know everything about me so that you can make an informed decision."

"Decision?"

"Yes. Because if you keep going out with me, thinking that maybe my feelings will change, then you'll be kidding yourself from the word go, so there's little point in our going any further with this. I won't change my mind, believe me."

Leah breathed deeply. "You're really serious, aren't you?" she asked. "But why?"

He shrugged. "I don't think there is a reason as such. Cowardice could be one of them. Another is the fact that I enjoy my life and I enjoy my lifestyle. I've never had any great desire to repopulate the universe. I don't buy into the fact that's it something we all 'have to do'."

"And what about your parents – your own upbringing?" Josh's dad had worked hard at building up his business and as a result, he now owned one of the most successful DIY chains in the country. Leah knew that the two didn't exactly see eye to eye at the best of times, but still that didn't give Josh enough justification to never want a child of his own.

"OK I hate this psychology stuff, and I suppose if you think deeply enough about it, you could say that all of this stems from my background. You know I'm adopted, and that me and my adoptive dad don't have a terrific relationship. But, Leah, I honestly don't think that's it, I don't think that I'm trying not to repeat the 'sins of the fathers' or anything else like that. I'm just making a lifestyle choice, in the same way that some people become vegetarian. Surely I'm entitled to do that without having to justify it?"

"Well, I don't know if it's quite the same as vegetarianism," Leah said with a grin, "but I suppose you are entitled to make your own choices."

"Exactly."

Josh said nothing more for a moment and Leah thought about what he had said earlier.

"So, some of your previous relationships haven't gone well as a result of this?" she asked.

Josh gave a wry smile. "That's putting it mildly. My last girl-friend Sharon, knew about my feelings on this right from the beginning. So, she accepted it from the outset but I suppose much like yourself, she thought that maybe over time I'd change my mind." His eyes fixed on Leah's. "But I didn't and I haven't, and I can't see myself changing my mind – not over time, not now, not ever. I'm certain of that."

"I see."

"So what I'm asking you to do is go away for a while and think about it. Think seriously about whether or not it is enough for you just to have me in your life, or whether you want something more."

"That's not an easy decision to make, though. I mean, I don't know where we're going. I care about you too, but we haven't been together all that long and ..." She trailed off.

"I know that. But I'm mad about you, Leah, more than I've been about anyone in a long, long, time. We have a great laugh together, we like the same things, you're strong, independent, you know your own mind, you don't take shit from anyone ..."

She laughed. "Glad you realise it!"

He reached for her hand across the table. "Seriously though, this is important. If I had some sort of medical issue or something I would have to tell you straight away. This isn't a medical problem – as far as I'm concerned it isn't a problem at all – but it is something that will affect you and your future. If you're the kind of person that can live with that, well and good, but if you find you can't, well ... I wouldn't like to hold you back."

"So what happened, the last time, with that girl? Did she try and change your mind?"

"Not exactly. For the most part, Sharon accepted it and we were fine for a long time. Towards the end though, occasionally I would spot her looking lovingly at a cute child in the street, or she'd been watching some sentimental TV show about childless couples or something and then I could almost read what was going through her mind. We were together nearly three years when she decided she couldn't take it any more. It was as though she hadn't really thought about it when we got together first – after all, we were very young, but then when one of her friends had a baby and she realised she couldn't ever have one of her own –"

"She realised she couldn't make that sacrifice," Leah finished. Josh nodded and she took a drink from her glass.

"So you'll have a think about it then?" he asked. "A good think about it too – don't be afraid to get another point of view or discuss it with your friends or anything like that. Don't worry about breaking my confidence, Leah, because as far as I'm concerned I've nothing to hide, and I stand by my decision."

She nodded. "OK, thanks for being honest with me. And I promise that if I choose to go along with your decision, I'll be faithful to it. I *won't* change my mind. If I decide to respect your choice, then it'll be my choice too."

But looking at Leah now, confused and upset once again after having to justify that choice to others, Olivia wondered if her friend's words to Josh still held.

TWENTY-ONE

The following weekend was hot and sticky and Robin cursed the fact that the air-conditioning unit really picked its moments to give up and stop working.

She wasn't long home from work, the summer heat was putting her in bad form, and she debated whether to make dinner or just phone Luigi's for a pizza.

There was little point in cooking for herself when yet again Ben was working late. Last week and the week before, if he wasn't working late in the evenings, he was spending extra time at the office doing the American equivalent of a 'nixer' in the office.

Robin thought he was taking a chance, as the management of Grafix Solutions would not be impressed to learn that a senior staff member was using company equipment and resources outside of normal working hours.

But Ben was determined to complete whatever project he was working on, irrespective of Robin's warnings, or indeed complaints. They had been a bit cagey around one another since 'that' conversation.

Since then, things had been a bit tense, and Ben had said nothing more about looking for another house. The one they'd gone to see in Bronxville had been snapped up before they'd even had a chance to bid on it. Lately, he was being decidedly cool with her and as he was normally so happy and carefree, Robin didn't know what to make of it.

To make it worse, they'd visited Sarah and Kirsty in New Jersey the previous weekend and while Robin was playing with Kirsty in the living room and telling her silly made-up stories, she overheard Sarah commenting to Ben in the other room about what a wonderful mum she would make. Ben had said nothing and quickly changed the subject.

Now, her head snapped up as she heard the phone ring. It had to be Ben, on his way home and asking if she wanted him to bring anything for dinner. Robin raced to answer it.

But the caller wasn't Ben.

"Hey stranger!" Leah's sunny tones bounced down the line "How are you?"

"Leah –hi! What time is it over there?" A pointless question, Robin knew, but one she instinctively asked, just so she could picture her friend's surroundings and get an idea of what she might be doing.

"About eleven – Josh is out, and I'm here on the couch, stuffing my face with Pringles and watching a *Sex and the City* rerun, so obviously I thought of you and how I haven't been talking to you in about ...oh, I'd say it's nearly two months now. Did you get my message from before?"

Robin felt guilty. She did get Leah's message – weeks ago – but in truth had completely forgotten to call her back. "I'm sorry – things have been manic."

"I can only imagine," Leah said dryly. "All the shopping, and the movies, theatre and all that ..."

"Hey, it's not quite like the TV shows, you know," Robin laughed, "We actually do the odd day's work here too."

"Don't ruin all the glamour for me," Leah scolded. "But seriously, how are things? Are you and that fine Irishman still going strong? I've said it before, and I'll say it again, Robin Matthews – I really don't know how you manage it. Probably the only decent single man left in the country and you have to nab him."

"Ah, he wasn't in the country at the time," she chuckled. "And he's great – working late."

"Working late in *that* sense? That doesn't sound like Ben."

"No, working late in the *actual* sense," Robin said, feeling a bit foolish for allowing Leah to plant a previously unthought-of idea into her brain. Not that she would be malicious, but now that Robin thought of it, what else would her friend say to something like that?

There wasn't a chance that Ben would ... was there? Robin shook her head, and resolved not to think about it.

"So how's everything with you?" she asked, changing the subject.

"Great, we're all fine. Did you get those photos I sent you of Andrew's wedding, by the way?"

"Yes, she looked amazing." Typically, Amanda looked every inch the radiant bride on the day and she and Andrew looked very happy together. Robin had been invited to the ceremony but she couldn't get the time off work. At least, that was her excuse. "You looked stunning too – and I loved Olivia's dress."

"Yeah, she's looking great, isn't she?"

"So are you?" Robin continued. "Josh is still as gorgeous as ever. How are things going with you two?"

"Fine."

Immediately, Robin sensed a slight hesitation in her voice. She knew, of course about Josh's kids thing and wondered if Leah was having second thoughts. Her friend had always insisted that she'd love a family but then had settled for having the man of her dreams instead. Josh seemed lovely and she hoped he and Leah were OK.

Weird, Robin thought, that she was going through a similar situation at the moment, although in her case she was being the reticent one.

But when Leah explained all about Andrew's involvement in her business, and that Josh seemed a bit put out about that, and the fact that she would have to work around the clock to get the store open, Robin realised she'd been wrong.

"So, do you the rest of you see much of one another these days, what with Kate pregnant and Olivia busy with her little girl ..." she trailed off, wondering if the others were still as close as they had been throughout college.

She was no longer part of that 'gang', no longer a paid-up member of the close-knit group after that last summer together. Leah kept her updated but Robin now felt very much detached from them all.

They were once as close as a group of friends could be, but now over time, distance and circumstance, the once-formidable strength of the friendship had been irrevocably fractured.

"Oh, I can't believe I almost forgot to tell you," Leah cried then, and Robin could almost picture her large dark eyes widening in anticipation.

"What?"

"You won't believe it, but Amanda is bloody pregnant too."

"Wow! Is she thrilled?"

"Well, of course, she is," Leah replied. "Sure, won't all the attention be on her and you know our Amanda – she'll only be too happy to lap it up." She giggled. "You should see her, Robin – she's so funny. Barely a few months gone and she's walking around, supporting her back and waddling away like she's carrying a sack of potatoes. I'm telling you, she'll milk this for all it's worth."

Robin burst out laughing, recalling how little patience Leah had for Amanda's theatrics. She could imagine Amanda doing just that too, not to mention bending the ear off everyone she knew about how 'dreadfully wearying' it was being pregnant.

Despite her airs and graces, or even more so because of them, Amanda's antics could be hilarious. Robin could afford to be more gracious about how the girl had treated her in college, now that she was thousands of miles away.

"Tell her I said congratulations," she said. "And say hello to Kate." She paused slightly before adding, "And tell Olivia I was asking for her too, of course."

"Don't you have her number? I'm sure she'd love to hear from you."

"Oh, I'm sure I have," Robin said quickly. "I must give her a bell sometime."

"Do. She often asks about you and I know she'd love to hear how you're getting on."

Robin bit her lip. "You should come over sometime," she said, trying to keep her voice light. "Here I mean. You'd really enjoy the city and I haven't seen you in so long –"

"But when are you coming back here?" countered Leah. "It's been years now. I know your parents have visited, but don't you miss home at all? Don't you miss *us*? We hardly know what's going on with you these days."

"There's nothing much going on at all," Robin said, laughing nervously. "I'm sure your own life is a lot more interesting. As I said, Ben and I are working hard at the moment, and that's about it."

"Just try and keep in touch more often, OK? You might not miss us, but we miss you, me in particular."

Robin was touched. "Thanks. And believe me, I do miss you, but I have a life here now and this is my home."

"You don't think you'll ever move back then?" Leah asked, faintly shocked at the thought that there was even a chance she might not want to.

"Certainly not at the moment, anyway. Then she added, hoping to lighten the tone, "Besides, I'm up to my eyes in credit-card debt."

"I'm not surprised – with all that temptation!" Leah sounded decidedly envious. "Listen, now that I think of it, will you try and get a copy of the new Godiva catalogue for me? I need to keep an eye on what the competition are doing!"

"No problem," Robin answered. "I'll get right on it, but better you go, this call will be costing you a fortune."

"It is, but not to worry, you're worth it. Speak to you soon!"

Leah rang off and Robin replaced the receiver, guilty and a little sad, but at the same time relieved that Leah seemed to have forgotten her earlier enquires about when she would next be returning home.

As far as she was concerned, it wouldn't be any time soon.

If ever.

TWENTY-TWO

"Mornin' you."

Ben planted a light kiss on Robin's forehead, waking her. After Leah's call the night before, she'd had a couple of glasses of wine and had stayed up late watching crap TV. She couldn't remember going to bed or hearing Ben come in. He couldn't have been working that late on a Friday night, surely?

Recalling her conversation with Leah, her stomach gave a nervous flip.

"Morning to you back," she replied before adding tentatively, "What time did you get in last night?"

He swung his legs out of bed. "Not sure, sometime after one, I think. You were flat out on the sofa. I had to carry you in."

"Was I?" Robin couldn't focus properly - she was too busy worrying about what was keeping Ben out until one o'clock in the morning on a weeknight. "Did you go out for a drink after or something?"

"No way – I was shattered." There was little sign of a lie or evasiveness in either his tone or expression. "I thought I'd never get it done in time, but luckily I did."

"Well, whoever he or *she* is, I hope they're happy," Robin

couldn't keep the petulance out of her tone, "because I've hardly seen you this last week."

"Oh, I think she'll be happy," he said, cheerily. "In fact, I think she'll be over the moon when she gets a load of this."

Typical she thought, Ben was completely oblivious to subtlety – no, just completely oblivious full stop.

Here she was trying to let him know that she was teed off about all these mysterious late nights, and there he was letting it go right over his head.

She tried a different tack. "What was so important that kept you in the office every night this week then?" she asked, yawning as she pulled a sweater and some jog pants out of the wardrobe.

"Come here and I'll show you," he said, his expression mischievous, and Robin suspected that whatever dumb presentation or corporate brochure it might be, she had better pretend to be impressed.

But when he led her into the living-room and pointed out a slim booklet lying on the coffee table, she didn't have to pretend. "Oh, my goodness – it's amazing!" she said, studying Ben's computer-aided illustrations.

Kirsty had recently suffered another severe bout of hay fever, and while visiting her, Robin had picked up the beanie toy and made up a silly little story about an alligator that also suffered from hayfever.

The character 'Atchoo' was a big, strong and very adventurous alligator, but he was always running into trouble as a result of his allergies. The moral of the story was that Atchoo could have lots more adventures if he looked after himself and took his medicine when he was supposed to.

Kirsty was fascinated by the tale and made her tell it over and over again that afternoon. Upon their return from Sarah's, Robin had written down the story so that she wouldn't forget it between then and the next time she saw her.

But Ben had since 'stolen' her scribbled notes for the story, come up with some cute graphics and reproduced the entire story from beginning to end in attractive child-friendly font, along with accompanying cartoon illustrations.

"Cool, huh?" he said proudly leafing through the pages of *Atchoo the Alligator*. "It's a great story and Sarah was raving about it so I thought, why not give Kirsty something she can keep, something to remind her of Atchoo's adventures? It might convince her that it's OK to take her inhaler in school."

It's ... incredible," Robin said putting a hand to her mouth as her eyes wandered through the story, marvelling at the amount of work he had put into the graphics. "This is what you've been working on all week?"

"I knew we'd be going up there again this weekend so ..." He shrugged as if it was no big deal, but by his beaming smile, she knew he was delighted by her reaction.

"Kirsty is just going to love this..." she cried, awed by this thoughtfulness. What a wonderfully thoughtful and considerate gesture.

Again, Robin wondered what on earth she had done to deserve such a kind, loving, man like Ben McKenna.

THEY WENT to visit Kirsty that same day, and as expected, the little girl adored her personalised copy of *Atchoo the Alligator*.

"Who knew I had such a talented brother?" Sarah was equally thrilled, and hopeful that Atchoo's experiences and the instructions in the book would help Kirsty feel more at ease.

"Hey, I can't take all the credit – it's Robin's story."

"Can I show it to the girls in school, Mom?" the little girl asked.

"I dunno, hon, Uncle Ben and Auntie Robin worked very hard on your storybook. It might get ruined in school."

"It's not a problem," Ben said easily. "The paper quality isn't the best so it probably will get wrecked. In any case I've got the file, so I can always print out another copy." He stroked Kirsty's dark curls. "You can show it to your class if you like, kiddo."

"Yay!" she cried happily.

Robin had to smile at Ben's so easily adopted Americanisms. She'd picked up a few expressions herself over the years, but compared to her, Ben had only been here a wet week. He was worse than people who went to London for a weekend and then came back asking for 'arf a laager, mate'.

"Just be careful you don't get sacked for using company equipment though," Sarah said, her face worried as the thought struck her.

"For printing out a teeny insignificant booklet like that? Not a chance."

BUT BY THE FOLLOWING WEEKEND, Ben had to print many more copies of *Atchoo the Alligator*.

Robin had been at work one-day mid-week when she got a call from Sarah.

"Hi, what's up?" she asked, feeling slightly concerned. Sarah usually called only if something was wrong. "How's Kirsty?"

"She's great," she said cheerfully. "She's been using her inhaler properly ever since you and Ben gave her that little book."

"Great."

"But the thing is, well, you know she brought it to school with her?"

"Yes?" Robin suspected now that she knew the real reason for the call. The flimsy copy of *Atchoo* had already come apart.

"Well, Kirsty must have shown it to one of her teachers, because this morning I got a call from the principal asking where they could pick up a copy."

"What?" Robin instinctively checked the date on her computer screen to reassure herself that it wasn't April 1st.

"I'm serious. I explained the situation, and she wants to know how to go about getting more copies. She asked if you wouldn't mind giving her a call."

"She's looking for more printouts?"

"I think so. She thought it was a genius idea. Can I give you her number?"

"Sure," Robin was intrigued and also a little bit proud. When Sarah had finished reciting the number, she rang off, and immediately called Kirsty's school.

The principal was very friendly. "Robin, hi, thanks so much for calling. I understand you're responsible for that neat little storybook Kirsty brought to school last week."

"Yes, well, I wrote the story, at least."

"Are you a children's writer by profession?"

Robin burst out laughing. "Gosh no – I work in finance."

"Well, you certainly have a way of getting through to kids, especially kids like Kirsty."

"She's been having such a tough time of it with her asthma lately. I just thought it might help."

"She's not the only one having problems sadly. That's why I think this is such a great idea. Do you know I have at least three other children in Kirsty's grade alone suffering from allergies? Not to mention kids in other grades." She sighed. "Anyway, I asked if I could bring it along to our most recent parent/teacher meeting. When I showed it to the parents of other kids with asthma, they went crazy for it."

"They did?"

"Yes, they all wanted one. So, that's why I called Sarah trying to find out which bookstore stocked it, so I could tell the parents where to get it. But then she told me that it wasn't in bookstores, and that it was just something you guys had done all by yourselves."

Robin smiled. It was brilliant to think that something she and Ben had done might be helpful to other kids with asthma.

"Leave it with me. I'll talk to Ben and see if he can get a few more for you."

"The school is only too happy to pay you, of course."

"Oh no, that won't be necessary," Robin was embarrassed.

"Believe me," the principal informed her, "if this little book can help parents and teachers educate on how to control their asthma, it's worth it."

"No, please. We'd be delighted to help. I'm sure it won't be a problem but I'll check with Ben and give you a call in a few days – OK?"

"That would be great, thank you."

The principal rang off and, as she hung up the phone, Robin couldn't help but smile.

Ben would get a right kick out of this one.

TWENTY-THREE

Leah jumped when the phone rang.

She had been run off her feet all day trying to get a huge batch of product out to an important customer and had been so immersed in her work that she had almost forgotten where she was.

The chocolates needed to be ready for collection the following morning, and with the way things were going, Leah thought, her face flushed from exertion, she'd be here till all hours trying to get it done.

The order had come in only that afternoon, but Bags n' Bows were one of her best customers and she had no intention of letting them down.

Still, at that very moment, surrounded by ribbon and tulle, she sorely regretted her decision to advertise her gift boxes as 'hand-wrapped'. Why couldn't she do generic boxes and be done with it? Still she knew that much of her custom derived directly from the fact that her chocolate boxes looked so appealing.

Now Leah cursed inwardly as, partially wrapped box in one hand and ribbon in the other, she reached for the handset. "Hey, what time will you be home?" Josh asked cheerfully.

"I'm not sure – I'm really up to my eyes here," she answered.

"Do you need a hand?" he asked and Leah bristled. Of course she needed a hand but there was no point in Josh coming all the way over here to 'help'.

He had tried that before, and all he had succeeded in doing was to annoy Leah and slow her down.

Not to mention the time he packed twelve full cases of chocolates, which Leah had first thought was terrific until she realised that he had failed to include the protective bubble-wrap which kept the boxes from hitting against one another.

Everything had been squashed and completely ruined in transit, and the customer had been livid. Leah had spent almost a full day trying to calm the customer down, and the rest of the *week* replacing the order.

"I'll be fine, Josh, thanks, but I can't talk – there's way too much to do here."

"Are you sure you don't want me to come over? I could bring a takeaway. It seems like I haven't seen you in days."

"Well, that's because I've been so busy." The shop would be fitted out and ready within a few weeks, and she was working flat out to get everything ready.

"But you're always busy, Lee. I know things are a bit up in the air at the moment, but who goes in to work on a Sunday?"

"Josh, it's not as though I could get anyone else to do it ..." Yes, she had gone back to the workshop last Sunday, so she could get a head-start on the following week's stock. If there was work to be done, then it had to be done, end of story.

"It could have waited. You need time for yourself too, you know – and us."

Great, the last thing she needed was a bloody guilt trip.

Of course, she was working hard. Wasn't she trying to get everything ready for the shop, while at the same time trying to keep the day-to-day stuff running?

Why couldn't he understand that this was a crucial time for her, and that she just didn't have the luxury of running home because he was bored and had no one to play with?

"Josh, I'm sorry but I just don't have time for this," she said.

"It's half-seven in the evening. You've been in there since six this morning. You're killing yourself!"

Damn ...Leah thought, checking her watch. It couldn't be that late surely? Which meant that she would be home a lot later if she didn't get off the phone.

"Josh, I have to go, OK? Get whatever you want for dinner, I'll grab something on the way home."

"But what time will you be –"

"I'll be home when I'm home, OK?" Then Leah felt like a heel when there was silence at the other end. "Look, I'm sorry, I don't mean to be short. But you have no idea how much there is to do between now and the opening. Look I promise this weekend we'll do something, OK?" *Just get off the phone and let me go back to work.*

"OK?" she repeated, when Josh didn't answer.

"Yeah, OK, see you later then."

Still holding the chocolate box in one hand, Leah hung up and returned to her work desk. Of course she was working hard – with all that was happening at the moment, what else did Josh expect?

Andrew had put a lot of faith in her by investing all that money in her business and Leah was determined not to let him down.

"HE'S JUST BEING SO childish about it."

A few days later, she tried to explain her annoyance to Olivia.

"From day one, he made it quite clear that he doesn't agree with Andrew's investment," she told her friend. "He doesn't agree with Andrew full stop. To be honest, I'm finding it a bit of a strain.

I mean, here I am, working my ass off to get everything ready for the opening, and all Josh does is spend the whole time moaning about Andrew and what he has to gain, and why doesn't he share some of the work."

"And do you think Andrew should?" Olivia asked. She knew that Leah was desperately looking forward to getting the store up and running, but also worried that her friend was doing way too much on her own.

"No, of course not. I don't want Andrew involved, he doesn't want to get involved. That's the only reason I agreed to do this in the first place. The business is mine and Andrew is simply a silent partner. Josh can't understand that. As much as he seems to dislike Andrew, he still thinks that he should help out more."

"Well, maybe he does have a point. What about giving Alan some of the load?" Leah had recently taken on a part-time assistant, a shy quiet young man called Alan who went about his work diligently, eager to learn all he could from his boss.

"Alan is just an assistant – he doesn't have the know-how when it comes to running a business."

"Well, maybe he might surprise you. You should give him a chance – that's what you're paying him for, surely?"

"It would take way too long to train him," Leah said, dismissing the idea. "There's no point in doing that at this stage anyway. I'll get it done quicker by myself."

Olivia knew that sometimes Leah found it difficult to let go of the business she had built from the ground up, and found it hard to assign control to anyone else.

But now, looking at Leah's tired and gaunt face and the determined look in her eye, she was concerned that with this new store, her friend might well be taking on way too much. Josh had every right to be concerned.

"Try not to worry about the opening date too much. Surely a week or so won't make much of a difference?"

Leah sighed. "I don't suppose it will, but at the same time this is the date that Andrew and I agreed. I don't want to let him down."

"I'm sure he wouldn't mind one way or the other. Didn't he say that it's yours to run whatever way you choose?"

"You're starting to sound like Josh."

"And like me, Josh doesn't want you running yourself into the ground over this. I can't say I've had any experience with building an empire, but I know the Romans slept sometimes too."

Leah laughed. "It'll be grand. Josh is just teed off because I don't spend much time with him in front of the TV any more."

"You are making some time for yourselves surely?"

"It's difficult." She shrugged. "I'm at the workshop as often as I can, so now he's started to do some more shifts at Homecare. You know Josh – he's one of those people who hates being on his own."

Olivia refilled her coffee mug. "Still, you really should try and take down the tempo a bit, head off for a dirty weekend away or something."

Leah laughed. "At the moment, there aren't enough hours in the day, let alone time away at weekends. Things will get better once the business opens. Josh just has to bear with me for a while, that's all." She looked at her watch. "Anyway, I'd better let you get to work yourself. Do you want me to drop Ellie over to Eva's for you?"

Olivia was due in at twelve and usually dropped Ellie off beforehand. "Um, no thanks, we've loads of time," she said, keenly aware of Leah's driving limitations.

"Grand – so I suppose the next time I see you will be at the launch party?"

"Try to take it easy in the meantime, won't you? I'm sure it's tough for Josh too."

"Don't worry, we'll be fine," Leah assured her.

As she closed the door behind her friend, Olivia hoped that they would be.

Then again, she thought, going upstairs to get Ellie ready to go to her granny's, she was probably just being silly worrying.

Leah and Josh had been through tougher times and hadn't they come out of it all just fine?

TWENTY-FOUR

Across the green, through her front window, Catherine watched *that* woman bundle her child into the car.

So pathetic the way she kept making big eyes at Matt, fawning all over him whenever they happened to bump into one another.

Which Catherine mused rather worriedly, seemed to be happening a lot lately. Only the other day when Matt should have been tucking into the gorgeous beef stew she had spent all afternoon preparing, she had again caught the two chatting easily at the woman's front gate.

She'd have to put a stop to that – and quickly. She didn't want Matt getting too friendly with the neighbours, especially unattached female neighbours.

They'd had that issue before and if it weren't for darling little Adam she would have been none the wiser. No, there was no letting him out of her sight this time. She and Matt had been through far too much together to have it all ruined by some slattern living across the way.

Didn't the woman have any shame? Catherine shook her head in disgust as she watched her drive away.

Laughing and flirting with him in full view of the green and all the while knowing that he had a family – a young son! Catherine had a very good mind to go over there and give the silly cow a piece of her mind. But Matt would go mad if she did that. He flew off the handle altogether the last time. No, she would simply bide her time and if Matt showed any sign of slipping well then she would *have* to do something.

Her hands shook as she went into the kitchen and opened the cupboard. Why did he do this, she thought, taking out the ironing board. Why was she not enough for him?

Did she not look as good, if not better than that witch from across the road?

Catherine had got one really good look one day passing in the car. She and her little girl were out in their front garden and yes, her eyes were a wide, deep blue and she was very striking.

But there was no glamour, no character – and she was a couple of stone overweight too.

Catherine ran a self-conscious hand over her own flat stomach and tiny waist. Surely all those hours at the gym, not to mention the hours at the hairdresser touching up her highlights counted for something?

But a lot of the time, Matt didn't even notice her hair or her slim figure or her salon tan. No, he was too busy organising his next business venture or fussing over Adam. If it weren't for Adam, Catherine wondered if he would bother with her at all. If it weren't for Adam, he might be long gone - off into the arms of some plump, dullard.

She wrinkled up her nose. *Her* name was Olivia, apparently. Matt had mentioned that one day after Catherine had once again interrupted one of their little 'chats'.

"She's lovely," he'd said. "Very friendly but a little bit shy too, I think. And her little daughter is just so cute – the resemblance is amazing actually."

Every word had cut Catherine to the quick and immediately

she hated Olivia – Olivia with her cute daughter and her big blue eyes and her bright smile. Olivia, who was obviously single and desperate for a man – any man, to brighten up her boring domestic routine.

Catherine knew all about boring and domestic routines – sometimes she wondered why on earth she'd ever given up her full-time job and agreed to spend all day doing housework and looking after Adam.

But she didn't have to think too long about the answer. She did it to support Matt since they both knew it wouldn't do for Adam to be looked after by a stranger, or fed yellow-pack fish fingers for dinner.

So, despite how bored she sometimes felt, Catherine was still glad she decided to do it. Though at times like this, she wondered if Matt appreciated the sacrifice she'd made. He'd given her a lot of support certainly, and the move away from Dublin had been his suggestion – and mostly paid for by his wages – but still, it was hard not to feel frustrated.

She sighed. At times she wondered why on earth she bothered. It wasn't as though she had any shortage of attention – she was always getting wolf-whistles and admiring glances when she was out and about.

She knew she was attractive; had worked hard to ensure she *stayed* attractive, and it was satisfying to find that she still had the power to make men go weak at the knees. She smiled as a thought entered her mind. Like that *very* attractive guy she'd noticed checking her out the week before at the café. A sexy George Clooney lookalike - Conor was his name - they had got chatting and he owned a graphic design company based in the village.

Well, she decided, thoughts of Matt's 'friendship' with their unglamorous neighbour propelling her into action, maybe she might just take a trip down to the Heartbreak Café and do some more flirting.

What's sauce for the goose is sauce for the gander, she decided going upstairs to choose an eye-catching and suitably flirtatious outfit, something that would make Mr Graphic Design pay even closer attention.

Twenty minutes later, Catherine stood in front of the mirror and assessed her over-the-top but unmistakably sexy appearance. Matt was away this weekend, so this was the ideal opportunity to put her plan into action.

She smiled. By the time she was finished, neighbourly relations would be the last thing on Matt Sheridan's mind.

TWENTY-FIVE

The following morning, Olivia was sitting in her kitchen nursing a mug of hot coffee and wishing that the caffeine-jolt would hurry up and do its job.

She hated early mornings, and there was nothing she'd like more than to go back to bed and curl up under the warm duvet.

But there was little chance of that today. She'd brought home a few hours worth of paperwork from the centre yesterday, and although the work wasn't terribly urgent, she wanted to get a good head start on it before Ellie got up. It wasn't practical to be going through patient files when her daughter was around – dangerous because her attention needed to be elsewhere, and difficult because Ellie in true toddler fashion made the very most of it. Olivia had learned in the early days that when Ellie was quiet, it was usually because she was up to no good.

She went into the living room, sat down by the window at the sideboard that doubled as a desk and switched on her laptop, wishing that she had done the sensible thing and let it warm up while she was getting breakfast.

The computer, which Olivia was convinced was running on the crudest operating system imaginable – probably based on Bill

Gates original Windows doodling – took forever to get going. She gazed unseeingly out the window while she waited, her eyes tired and watering.

She wasn't sure how long she had been sitting there when a small movement across the green caught her eye. Oh, it was someone coming out of the Sheridan house again, she thought, guiltily averting her eyes.

Anyone would think it was her *intention* to spy on the new family, and what if Matt himself noticed her light on across the way and Olivia sitting at the window gawping? She went to move out of sight, giving a glance to ensure that she hadn't been seen.

Olivia's mouth opened wide. This time she didn't – *couldn't* – look away. There was Matt's wife, barely dressed in a satin bustier affair that wouldn't look out of place in an issue of *FHM*. Wrapped around some guy – a tall, blonde, *young*er guy that definitely wasn't Matt! What was she up to?

Well, it was pretty obvious what she was up to, Olivia thought, seeing the woman pull her beau closer for another kiss.

But why? Why would any woman who was lucky enough to have a loving, devoted husband and gorgeous child – the perfect family – recklessly put it all in jeopardy for a fling?

Then Olivia berated herself. Who was she to judge? What did she know about that woman and her family? Who knows what goes on behind closed doors – isn't that what her mother always said?

She was a fool to presume; for all she knew Matt and his wife might have a terrible relationship and lover-boy, whoever he was, was her only means of happiness.

But still, what would he think when he realised she was having an affair – and worse, flaunting herself and her fancy man all around the neighbourhood?

Although it was hardly flaunting, Olivia mused, trying to calm herself. It wasn't as though the woman expected the elderly neighbours of Cherrytree Green to be spying on her at that hour of the morning. Still, it was brazen enough all the same.

She heard a car drive away, and when she looked back at the house the wife had gone back inside.

Where was Matt? His car was in the driveway – surely she wouldn't have been carrying on while he was asleep in another room, would she?

"Oh, for goodness' sake, it's none of your bloody business either way," Olivia muttered out loud, striding purposefully towards the kitchen for a fresh caffeine fix. But this time it wasn't to wake her up; this time it was to calm her down.

What should she do? She and Matt were neighbours after all – friends to some degree – should she say something?

Of course not - it wasn't her place, she didn't know him *that* well, and she couldn't exactly admit that she had been spying on his house and knew all about his wife and their son and so-called perfect life.

She couldn't do it, she *wouldn't* do it, and it was absolutely none of her business. She would not be the one to tell Matt anything about his family that he might not know.

Olivia would *not* be the one responsible for breaking up a family because of her own selfishness.

Not this time.

TWENTY-SIX

A few days later, Matt walked towards Olivia's, little Adam by his side. "Hello there."

She was outside, pulling weeds and vainly trying to make the garden look at least half as presentable as that of the green-fingered couple next door.

"Hello, yourself. Doing a bit in the garden, I see?"

"For my sins," Olivia groaned, removing her gloves and throwing a sideways glance at the garden next door. "Just trying to keep the place up to standard."

"Good for you – I've always hated gardening and luckily my place doesn't need it." She didn't have a chance to examine the state of his own garden across the way before he came through the gate and introduced his son. "This is Adam, by the way. Adam, say hello to Olivia."

The little boy looked up at her with watchful eyes but said nothing.

"Hi, Adam, nice to meet you," she said offering her hand, remembering how Ellie had responded to Matt when he introduced himself properly to her like that. Obviously, little Adam didn't feel the same way.

"Want Mummy." Adam squealed, turning away and ignoring her.

"Sorry about that. He can be a little bit wary of strangers."

"That's OK – Ellie can be the same," she said hoping to make him feel better and trying to ignore the fact that the boy didn't look remotely like his dad. Matt had dark hair and was lightly tanned whereas Adam was very fair, with a smattering of freckles across his cheeks, and his not-so-friendly manner suggesting to Olivia that his mum's genes were the dominant ones.

Then horrified, a thought came unbidden into her mind. Maybe Adam wasn't even Matt's child. Maybe the wife had been carrying on behind his back for years and poor Matt knew nothing about it. She put her gloves back on and tried to shake the horrible thought from her mind, then got down on her knees and quickly resumed her weeding.

"Er ... do you have something against those kinds of flowers?" Matt asked, looking curiously at her.

Following his gaze, Olivia looked down and realised she had been taking her frustrations with Matt's errant wife out on her poor Busy Lizzies, the one flower that returned year after year, despite her failings as a gardener.

"I can't believe I just did that. Sorry, I was miles away."

"Well, maybe we can still save them," he said, in the manner of one of those hunky doctors on *ER* and inwardly, she swooned. "Adam, stay there, while Daddy helps Olivia, OK?"

With that he got down on his knees alongside her, and began replanting what was left, the hint of an amused smile crossing his lips.

Just then, Olivia realised that Matt must think her an awful ditz. The first time, there was that confusion at the bar, the next she was having problems reversing her car out of the driveway, then ran out of the shop that time without her change. And *now* for no apparent reason, she was merrily pulling up perfectly decent flowers in her front garden.

"It's fine, really," she protested, cheeks red with mortification at the fact that once again, the mere presence of this man had turned her into a demented idiot. Wait until she told Leah about this – she would kill herself laughing.

At the thought of her friend's reaction, and the ludicrous situation in which she once again found herself, Olivia too couldn't help but giggle.

"What? What's so funny?"

"I'm sorry," she said, trying to stifle a laugh. "I know you already think I'm an idiot, and I'm certainly living up to it now."

"An idiot? How so?" Now Matt was smiling too.

"It's just –" She didn't care how it sounded, she just knew she had to come clean, otherwise every time she saw him, things would just keep getting worse. "It's just every time we meet, I seem to end up doing something stupid. I'm not sure why that is, but I can assure you that I'm not like this all the time. I'm not really any good around men ... since my husband ..." Then she floundered, horrified. "Not that I consider you a man in *that* sense, I mean, I know you're married and everything, so please don't think that ... it's just ..." Oh she was making a mess of this, she thought, heart pounding. So much for coming clean and trying to save face.

"I'm sorry," she said eventually. "It's just, I suspect you think that I'm a complete ditz and really I'm not, but for some reason, you seem to have that effect on me ... I mean ... " She trailed off then, realising that she was just digging herself in deeper with every word. She was never going to able to explain it properly, and especially not now, not when Matt's truly mesmerising grey eyes were that close, his gaze steadily fixed on her face. Trying to decide whether or not she should be committed, Olivia thought, deflated.

"I'm really sorry if you thought that, but –"

"Matt!" Thrilled to see him, Ellie bounded out the front door, cutting off whatever he was about to say and, thankfully, sparing Olivia's embarrassment too.

What *had* he been about to say? She didn't know but, by the apologetic look on his face, it could only have been some kind of brush-off. Perhaps he thought she was coming on to him.

"Hey, Ellie." Matt stood up and seeing her daughter race into his outstretched arms, Olivia's embarrassment was swiftly replaced by panic. This was crazy. Her daughter had clearly fallen for him as much as she had. And he was *married*, for goodness' sake.

"Hey, Adam, come say hello to Ellie," Now Matt was introducing the two children and the earlier sullen Adam seemed much more receptive.

Great, that was the last thing she needed, Ellie becoming friendly with Matt's young son and having to be brought to his house for playdates and birthday parties and the like.

Much better to just cut all contact now, for her own, and indeed Ellie's sake. But to think that his brazen wife across the road was quite happy to carry on with one of the locals, and here was Matt resisting Olivia's stupid attempt at explaining her feelings, putting his wife and child first without a moment's hesitation.

Yet that was why she liked him so much, wasn't it? He was such a warm charming guy – a little like Peter used to be.

"*Matt.*" Hearing a voice from across the green, they all turned around to see Matt's wife standing in the doorway, waving in his direction.

"Better go," he said.

"Aw can't Adam stay and play?" Ellie asked, looking almost as disappointed as Olivia felt. Adam looked hopefully up at his dad.

"Some other time, sorry." He smiled warmly at Ellie before

hoisting Adam up onto his shoulders. "Adam, say goodbye to Ellie and Olivia, OK?"

"Bye, Ellie, bye 'Liva," This time he gave a broad smile, and only then could Olivia see the resemblance, right down to the tiny gap between his two front teeth.

"Bye Adam, see you soon," she said, still mortified about her earlier ramblings, and unable to look in Matt's direction, let alone look him in the eye.

"See you soon." This time his tone was devoid of its characteristic warmth and, with Adam hoisted high on his shoulders, he went back across the green; Olivia and Ellie staring silently at his retreat.

TWENTY-SEVEN

"Careful what you wish for - you just might get it," Leah's grandmother used to say. Well, Leah did get it: she had a growing business, her first retail outlet – and Amanda bloody Clarke.

Stupidly, she hadn't seen that coming. She was just so thrilled at the scope Andrew's investment would give that she hadn't even considered that Amanda might be interested too.

As the opening of the store drew nearer, Amanda had been spending lots and lots of time there and had begun to get on Leah's nerves.

Only last week she had 'popped in for a look' but by the end of the visit had tried to commandeer control of the shop's layout. At the time, Leah had been so preoccupied with getting things ready that she had just assumed Amanda was showing a friendly interest.

But she had also insisted that the decor Leah had chosen was "all wrong for the store's image". The company logo was cream with gold calligraphy lettering, something Amanda decided looked dated. With all the work she was doing to get the store set up, Leah had little time to tinker with her logo. But she held her tongue, simply because she hadn't the time nor the inclination to get into an argument over something trivial. Not to mention the fact that Amanda and Andrew were, in effect her landlords. So Leah had said nothing, assuming that once Amanda found something else to occupy her she would soon get bored with the new store and leave her and Alan alone to get on with the day-to-day running of the business.

And in fairness, Amanda's social connections might be a bit of bonus.

She'd insisted on having an official launch party and "a chocolate-tasting evening" for Elysium and suggested they issue invites to some of Blackrock's most prominent business-people and some local media.

Leah suspected that most of the attendees would probably be more interested in a possible interview with hotshot entrepreneur Andrew Clarke than in supporting her new store. Notwithstanding, the exposure would be terrific, and hopefully it would give the shop a timely boost. Then, after all the celebrations and excitement, it would be down to the tough task of growing turnover and making the business work, something Leah hoped she'd be doing on her own.

Still, she couldn't get away from the fact Andrew had made all of this possible, and as much as she'd like to, she couldn't very well turn around and tell Amanda to butt out. She had made a deal with the devil or more aptly, the devil's husband.

She sat down at the kitchen table and went through the invite list for the official launch party. She knew most RSVPs were largely ignored or forgotten about – by her own friends anyway – and most of the old gang would be going.

It was such a pity that Robin wouldn't be around, but she had missed lots of reunions over the years.

She sighed, remembering their college days. That last summer they were all together seemed like a lifetime ago. Back then they had nothing to worry about other than men, the occasional exam and whether they had enough money for a decent night out any given weekend.

How had things changed so much in just a few years? Robin had moved away, Olivia a grieving single mother, Kate was pregnant and ...

Speaking of Kate, she really should give her friend a buzz. She hadn't spoken to her in a few weeks, and was eager to find out if she and Michael would be coming to the launch party, especially as it would be happening so close to Kate's due date.

"Hello, stranger," she said when Kate answered. "How are you feeling?"

"Hello, yourself!" her friend replied, obviously pleased to hear from her. At this, Leah felt a little guilty. It was ages since they'd spoken, what with all the running around. It seemed Leah had had little time for anyone lately.

They chatted for a little while about this and that, Leah's new store and Amanda's unwanted interest.

"You should tell her where to go. The last thing you need is her under your feet all day. Anyway, I can't see her being much good to you in her 'condition'."

Now eight months pregnant, Kate had only recently – and rather reluctantly – taken maternity leave from the city-centre advertising firm in which she worked. As with everything in life, her friend had taken pregnancy in her stride.

"I don't think she even has to do any housework over in that mansion of hers," Kate continued. "I mean, what about all these expectant women who go out and work in the fields, with one baby on their backs and another one on the way? I doubt anyone runs around after them, mopping brows and feeding them grapes on a chaise longue."

Leah giggled, enjoying this gossipy diversion. "Well, she did tell me she couldn't drink anything other than purified water until after the baby's born, and that it's only fair she gives up red meat, dairy products and potatoes too."

"What? You're joking."

"That's what she told me."

Kate exhaled sharply. "Honestly, if I didn't know better, I'd swear Amanda Clarke believes she's the next Virgin Mary – although the virgin part might be a problem," she added tittering.

"Ah give her a break. She's just getting used to the idea. I expect most are the same in the early days." No point in including Kate in that category; she had treated her pregnancy in the same no-nonsense way she did everything else.

Kate was unmoved. "If she's like this while pregnant, what'll she be like once she has the little sprog? You know how some mothers become about their little darlings."

"So, do you think you and Michael will be able to come to the launch party?" Leah asked, changing the subject.

"Of course we're coming. I wouldn't miss it for the world." Kate enthused. "Not when I finally have an opportunity to show off my toned bod in a leather catsuit."

Leah laughed. It would be just like a heavily pregnant Kate to turn up in something like that. She didn't give a damn. And she would undoubtedly still look great.

"How's Olivia? Is she going? I'm really looking forward to seeing her too. Feels like ages."

"I know - with the way I've been carrying on, I'm lucky to have any friends left. But yes Olivia's coming."

"And Robin?" Kate asked, her tone changing slightly. "Did you invite her?"

"Sure she couldn't possibly come all the way for something like this, Kate. You know how it is."

"She could if she really wanted to," Kate replied, unmoved. "Although, if she couldn't be bothered coming home for the funeral that time ..."

"She had her reasons, you know that. But I can't imagine she'd want to come back for this either," Leah said, breaking the terse silence that followed. "Her life is in New York now."

"Still. The two of you were such good friends, and this is a big deal for you. I think she should make the effort."

But Leah knew better. What were the chances of Robin flying all the way back for her small gathering?

Little or none, she decided glumly, thinking it would be a very long time before their old friend returned to Ireland again.

If ever.

TWENTY-EIGHT

Olivia stood back and stared in awe at the newly decorated facade of Leah's chocolate store.

It was the evening of the official launch party and Elysium Chocolate was truly living up to its name. From the outside, the place looked like one of those old-style jewellery stores and Leah's confections were little jewels in themselves, Olivia thought, running her eyes across the gorgeous glass-fronted displays.

Kate was already inside.

"You look fantastic!" Olivia said embracing her old friend warmly. "Not much longer to go?"

"Thanks, I know I look like the side of a bus," Kate replied wryly. "Still, I'm determined to make the most of tonight. It won't be long before I'm chained at home to the bottle warmer."

She sat down alongside Olivia, and the two chatted easily until Leah joined them with plates of food.

Dressed in a simple black shift, she looked great, her dark eyes lively and shining with pleasure. She soon had to leave in order to circulate among the guests and they saw her strike up an animated conversation with someone who was either a client or shortly about to become one.

Josh, by contrast, seemed sullen. He'd greeted Olivia briefly upon arrival but since then sat quietly on his own in another corner of the room.

No doubt he and Leah were both very tired, the strain of working all hours to get the shop going obviously taking its toll on them. Hopefully, things would improve soon. She and Josh were so well-suited that Olivia would hate to see them break up. Still, it could happen to the best of them, as she herself knew well.

She remembered how she and Peter used to argue immediately before their big break-up after graduation. As though the two of them purposely engineered these arguments to bring some form of drive or energy to the relationship. At that stage, they had been together so long they had been in something of a rut. But when finally things did come to a head, and they spent some time apart after which Peter proposed, they hadn't looked back.

Olivia wondered idly if it would take an upheaval like the one she and Peter had experienced to get Josh moving on a proposal.

She shook her head, thinking that she was beginning to sound like her own mother. Get moving on a proposal indeed! There was Leah, an extremely talented, independent, successful woman celebrating her success with her friends, and the only thing Olivia could think about was that Josh hadn't proposed.

She was definitely turning into an old biddy, she thought, trying to push the recent spying incident on Matt Sheridan's wife out of her mind.

Just then, Amanda floated across the room, looking healthy, tanned and – as Kate had pointed out earlier – designer-clad.

"But how can you tell the clothes are designer?" Olivia had asked. "I mean without physically lifting her skirt and getting a look at the tag?"

"I have an eye for these things," her friend said, stifling a grin. "Well, I don't actually but whatever it is, it's expensive and I don't think the likes of Amanda Clarke – pregnant or otherwise – would be seen dead in anything other than haute couture."

Amanda did look great though, Olivia thought, and pregnancy obviously suited her. Her blonde hair tumbled in long layers around her shoulders, Claudia Schiffer style. The dress was deep crimson red and with Amanda's tanned skin and highlighted locks the effect was doubly striking.

And the shoes! Like nothing Olivia had ever seen before. They were almost too gorgeous, too elegant to be used for walking. If anything, they should be sitting in a glass case in some fashion museum somewhere. She wondered if they were designer too – if so they had to be Prada or Fendi or that guy the fashionistas loved, the one with the name that sounded like a cross between an Irishman and a toy train, Jimmy something ...

"Guys, how *are* you?" Amanda trilled, and as she embraced her Olivia caught the scent of expensive (probably designer too) perfume. "I'm so delighted you two could come along."

Olivia smiled a dutiful smile. '*I'm* so delighted ...?' Wasn't this Leah's party?

"Sooo sorry I haven't had a chance to say hello until now," Amanda continued in that weird faintly out-of-breath tone that she affected. Olivia knew that this drove Kate up the wall, and at that precise moment she could understand why. "This is exactly what it was like at my wedding, remember? Everywhere I went people were pulling out of me trying to chat – but tonight it's all because of this." She caressed her stomach softly and laughed, enjoying all the attention immensely.

"I heard. Congratulations." Kate plastered a smile onto her face.

Olivia bristled. Yes, it was only natural for her to be excited about her news, but tonight was Leah's night.

"Did you two get something to eat?" Amanda asked them,

evidently a little put out that they didn't seem as enthused as everyone else seemed to be about her 'condition'.

"I'm fine, Leah got us something earlier," she said, indicating the empty plates on the table.

"Oh she's been great at keeping everyone happy," Amanda gushed. "I just don't know what we'd do without her,"

"Without her? This is Leah's launch party, isn't it?" Kate said aloud the words that had been right on the tip of Olivia's tongue.

"Well, of course – of course it is. I just meant that she's so good with people, you know? Of course, she's worked in retail for most of her life, so she knows how to deal with the *general public*." She might as well have just been honest and came right out and said 'riff-raff'. "Whereas I can't deal with all these strangers wanting a piece of me, all because I happen to be married to Andrew Clarke."

With that she beamed regally, and Olivia could see Kate physically struggling to hold her tongue.

"Anyhow," she said, sitting down alongside Kate and patting her hand, "where's Michael tonight? And more importantly, how have you *been*?" she asked dramatically.

"Michael's on his way, he had to work late," Kate replied shortly, knowing well that Amanda couldn't give a damn where her husband was, she just wanted another male to fawn over. "And me? I'm grand – besides the burning cystitis, crippling piles and constant farting." At this Amanda visibly balked and Olivia had to bite down on her lip to keep from laughing. Kate had never been one to airbrush reality. Amanda should know better than to expect Kate to join her in gushing new-mommy sentiment.

For once, Amanda was lost for words. "Oh, there's Grainne Fingleton, I'd better go and say hello." With that, she quickly made her exit.

Olivia and Kate looked at one another and burst out laughing.

"You wicked woman," Olivia said. "You've just ruined the dream."

"Oh, come on, she was asking for it," Kate took another sip of her mineral water.

Right then Leah approached, a glass of champagne in her hand. "Do you think it's going OK?" she asked hesitantly, looking around the room "I can't believe there's so many people here. Lots of Amanda and Andrew's friends, mind you but ..."

"Well, whoever they are, they seem to be enjoying themselves – and the chocolates." Kate looked across the room to where a couple were making serious inroads on a selection of truffles. "You should be very proud of yourself, lady."

"At the moment, I'm too bloody nervous to be proud," Leah confessed, sitting down at their table. "But it is going well, isn't it? Amanda's great at organising these things – I wouldn't have known what to do."

"So, is Amanda going to be permanently involved in this, or is she just helping you get started?" Olivia asked carefully.

Leah grimaced. "To be perfectly honest, I'm not quite sure. She pretty much organised this – you know how she is, always loves to be in the middle of everything. I think it's a bit of a novelty for her at the moment so ..." She trailed off and shrugged her shoulders. "Put it this way, I think me and my little chocolate store will be way down on her list of priorities once tonight is over."

Olivia wasn't so sure about that, not after the way Amanda had been so condescending earlier, but she said nothing. No point in saying anything to Leah tonight, not on one of the biggest nights of her life.

"I still can't believe that you and Andrew are in business together," Kate said, shaking her head in wonder. "He was so lazy in college – he was the last person I'd have said would end up a successful businessman. It's weird the way things work out, isn't it?"

"Andrew was always a dote," Olivia smiled.

"Shame about the wife," Kate added sardonically.

"Ah stop that, Amanda's not that bad. You just have to know how to handle her, that's all."

"Mmm," Kate wasn't convinced.

Just then, a smile broke across Leah's face, and Olivia followed her gaze to see the gorgeous Josh approach.

"Hey you two," he said, smiling at Olivia and Kate. "Enjoying the night?"

"It's a great night," Kate said, beaming unashamedly.

One night over a few drinks, she had admitted to Leah that Josh was the only man alive that could tempt her to cheat on Michael. Olivia knew exactly what she meant. Josh was so attractive it was unreal. Deep blue watchful eyes, shiny tousled hair, a jaw-line made for snowboarding, and a tanned athletic body ... he was most women's idea of perfection.

"You'd run away with him," her mother would say, and did when she met Josh for the first time at Olivia's one night, keeping him talking in a corner for most of the evening.

"Have you taken anything video clips yet?" he asked Leah.

"No, I'd forgotten all about it. I suppose I'd better get some footage of the party oh – and outside too. We have to get photos and video of the shopfront and all the balloons," She leapt up out of her seat.

Josh was soothing. "Relax, hon, I'll do it, you just stay there and enjoy yourself."

"Would you mind? I left the camcorder out back it should be underneath my jacket –"

"It's fine, I'll find it," he interjected with a grin and turned to the others. "Andrew Clarke doesn't know what he's letting himself in for. This one would forget her head if it wasn't screwed on."

Leah feigned outrage but Olivia could see she was trying not to smile. Things had obviously improved between those two, and whatever rough patch she had thought they were experiencing must have been overcome. Good.

"If you keep on like that you'll find yourself out on your ear one of these days," Leah said. "Now stop annoying me and go and get some footage before people start leaving."

"OK, OK, I'm going," he said, and with a final cheeky wink at Olivia and Kate – one that left them panting in his wake – off he went.

"Don't end up taking too much rubbish," Leah called after him. "Short clips of something are better than long clips of nothing." But Josh was already out of earshot. She turned to the others and shook her head. "He's a disaster with that camera. It's a terrible pity we don't have one of those new-fangled LCD ones, then he might have some idea of the rubbish he's actually filming."

"I'll say it before and I'll say it again: Leah Reid, you are one lucky wagon," Kate said, shaking her head. "What I wouldn't do …"

"Hey, honey."

Kate froze instantly when, as if from nowhere, Michael appeared and put a protective arm around her shoulders. "Congratulations, Leah, great party." He took a sip of champagne. "What were you saying, just then, love?" he asked his wife. "What wouldn't you do?"

The three women looked at one another and promptly burst out laughing.

TWENTY-NINE

Robin wasn't sure she had heard right.

"Are you serious?" she asked, wondering if the oppressive humidity was making her imagine things. There she was, sitting in an eighteenth-floor office on Park Avenue with a view over Central Park most New Yorkers would kill for, and the scary woman sitting across from her had said that their little booklet was "a brainwave, a money-spinner, a work of genius".

"But – but it's not even a book!" Robin interjected, stopping the other woman's enthusiastic rant. "I mean it was just a thought – just a joke, really."

This was all too surreal for words.

It had been weeks since she had provided Kirsty's school with extra copies of *Atchoo the Alligator*, but since then, the school principal had been phoning them regularly to pass on compliments and thanks from some of the children's parents.

"The story's message is getting through," the principal told her. "These parents have been tearing their hair out for years trying to empower their kids, and this book is working. They'll be forever grateful."

One particularly grateful mother had come in the form of

Janine Johnston, an employee of Bubblegum Press, a small New York children's publisher with offices on Park Avenue. Immediately recognising the book's potential, and the fact that it had an immediate effect on her young asthmatic son, Janine arranged a meeting with the company's Acquisitions Editor. By the end of following week, Robin discovered that – without ever once having thought about it – she was to become a published author.

"It'll be huge," Marla, the publishing director had enthused, after informing Robin of her plans over the telephone. "The story is simple, and accessible, and if we get a good illustrator on board, we could make a real killing here."

"So you don't want to use the same graphics?" Robin asked, wondering how Ben would feel about all this. It was his book, after all, his idea and his hard work that had made the book what it was.

But as it turned out, Ben couldn't care less. "I just downloaded the stuff from some clip-art site," he said. "It's your story and if they want to bring in some hotshot illustrator to improve it even more, then all the better."

Now, listening to Marla outline her plans for publishing *Atchoo the Alligator*, Robin wondered if this was all a set-up, just another one of Ben's silly practical jokes.

"I've had to rearrange our list so as to get it out by the end of the year. So we can make a quick killing at Christmas before the rest get in on the act."

Robin looked at her blankly.

"The other publishers. Once the biggies get wind of this thing they'll be in like wildfire with one of their own."

"Oh."

"So to generate word of mouth we're going to heavily target schools, hospitals, support agencies, yada yada. Once we've got a buzz going, then we'll think about blitzing bookstores and ..."

Robin let most of Marla's plan of action go over her head. She still couldn't believe that they were offering to publish her little book. How was it possible? Surely, there were hundreds, if not thousands, of children's writers, *any* writers, more suitable for this than she? When she said as much to Marla, the publisher laughed.

"Robin, in this game, most of the time, the writing doesn't matter. It's the idea, honey, the *concept* – forget wizards in boring old boarding schools, this is the next big thing in children's publishing, I can feel it!"

"Well, you're the expert," Robin said, not quite sharing Marla's enthusiasm. *Atchoo* was a cute little story certainly, and Kirsty and her classmates seemed to love it but ...

"There's more," Marla said, leaning forward and interrupting her thoughts. "David and I had a meeting this morning," David was Bubblegum's MD, "and he wants to take it further, corner the market before the competition jumps on the bandwagon." She nodded sardonically out the window. "Once a trend starts on Park Avenue, it won't be long before every publisher on the avenue, and America, follows suit. Bubblegum is determined to keep ahead of the game."

The game? With all this talk of tactics and blitzing, Robin wondered whether publishing was actually some form of war. She wondered what else was coming.

"We want you to do some more," Marla said, "cover some more children's problems – things like say *Diabetes Deer*, or *Epilepsy Elephant* or *Asthma Ass*. A whole series." She laughed. "Hey, I dunno – you're the creative one here, but, Robin, do you know what percentage of American children suffer from one or other of those ailments I just mentioned? Take peanut allergies ..."

Robin opened her mouth to speak but Marla plunged on, explaining that the number of children with severe peanut allergies in the US had grown tenfold in a generation.

"It's the most common food allergy, and there's no cure and no means of prevention," she told Robin, who had given up trying to get a word in. "I read only yesterday somewhere that two and a half million Americans now are peanut allergic, and something like five percent of all children under age six. Several hundred thousand are at risk for life-threatening reactions – talk about a target market! We're sitting on a fortune here!"

Robin was in two minds. Yes, the thought of writing more stories that might help some of those children appealed to her enormously, but she hated the way the publisher made it all sound so predatory.

Still, she supposed, business was business, and if *she* didn't do it, then it wouldn't be long before they found someone who would. And this was too exciting an opportunity to turn down.

IT DIDN'T SURPRISE Robin when later over lunch, Marla informed her that before working in the always-dynamic publishing world, she had worked in the even faster-paced New York fashion industry.

"Now, about your advance," Marla began, "I think we're looking at twenty-five per book and so far we've come up with four ideas, so how about a hundred?" She looked at Robin for affirmation.

A hundred dollars for a couple of evenings' work? Robin was hardly listening. A story about an epileptic elephant had already began to form in her mind and –

"And then say six, seven per cent on royalties, plus seventy on any foreign rights, plus the initial hundred grand advance and ... oh, I don't know, sweetie I think you'd better get yourself an agent." The publisher drained her coffee mug with a flourish.

Robin sat rooted to the chair. Did Marla say ... did she really *mean* ... were they seriously offering her a hundred *thousand* dollars for these simple little stories? This was *definitely* one of Ben's elaborate jokes.

But Marla didn't look at all like she was joking. She was now looking distractedly at her Rolex, apparently eager to get this meeting over and done with so she could flit off to the next 'big thing' in publishing.

"So whaddya say, Robin?" Marla asked her impatiently. "Are you gonna come on board, or what?"

THIRTY

If Olivia wasn't careful, she was in grave danger of turning into a serial curtain-twitcher. But she just couldn't help it.

How could she *not* look when the house was right across the green and the front door was plainly visible from her desk and her couch? It was only natural that any movement outside the window – be it at Matt's house or elsewhere – would catch her eye, wasn't it?

"Olivia, when did you re-arrange the furniture?" her mother asked, her brow furrowing as she sank into her favourite armchair, which was usually in a nice spot in front of the telly but was now positioned back to the window – where the sofa used to be.

"Oh, I saw something similar on *Changing Rooms* and I just thought it might make the room a lot bigger."

"I don't think so, dear – in fact, I think it makes everything a lot more cluttered. Why on earth would you put the sofa facing the window like that? I know there's only the two of you but ..."

Olivia gritted her teeth. "I suppose you're right. I just wanted to try something different for a while, that's all."

Just then Ellie stormed through the doorway, Olivia's phone

clutched in her hand. "A message, Mummy!" she declared excitedly.

A waste of time, more like, Olivia thought. No doubt it was yet another of those messages that would tell her that she was the lucky winner of a million euro, but to claim her prize she would need to phone this number and stay on hold until she was old and grey. They were the only kind of text messages she got.

She reached for the handset, and her heart raced as she stared at the number displayed. There was no mistaking it – Olivia had it almost memorised by now. It was him. Matt had sent her a message.

"Is something wrong?" her mother enquired.

"No, nothing wrong," she replied, trying to keep her voice even. "Just one of those silly 'you've won a big prize' messages." She stood up, eager to read the message in privacy – whatever it might say. "I'm making a cuppa – want one?"

"But we just finished one – Olivia, what is the matter with you? You really are behaving very strangely."

"There's nothing wrong, Mum – I just fancy another cup, all right?"

Phone in hand, Olivia almost pranced into the kitchen. Her hands shook as she pressed *read* and almost as soon as she had, the thought struck her that Matt might once again have mistakenly sent her a message, perhaps another one destined for his business partner.

But then, her heart leapt as she read the words.

"Can I come over? Need to ask you something."

Olivia read and reread it at least five times. He wanted to come over? Damn, how was she going to get rid of her mother?

No, think about it, this *could* very well be a message to his business partner. She sent a tentative message back to him, which seemed to take her all of five minutes to type. *"Matt, Olivia here, did you mean to send this to me?"*

Now, that wasn't too bad, was it? She hadn't said yes or no, hadn't referred to the message at all really, and if it turned out that he had indeed sent it by mistake, well then she hadn't gone and made an eejit of herself by gleefully answering back and coming across like an eager beaver. Now all she had to do was wait.

It was as though an eternity passed until she got a reply.

"Yes. Yep, but sorry, can see why you thought that. Can I?" Then the phone beeped again. *"Please?"*

Olivia was grinning from ear to ear. She'd replied before she had time to think about it, her fingers dashing across the keys in an unusual display of text-dexterity. *"Give me twenty mins – c u soon."*

"Mum, I'm afraid I have to go out," she said, coming back into the living room and trying hard not to betray the fact that she was almost delirious with excitement.

"Oh?" Eva raised an eyebrow. "Anything serious?"

"No – it's just – no – one of the mums from Ellie's playgroup. Her daughter isn't well and she's asked if I'd do some shopping for her."

"Oh. Well, I'm in no rush home anyway – why don't you head over now and I'll look after Ellie while you're gone?"

"No ... I mean, the thing is, she really wants Ellie to come and visit her too, so I'm taking her with me."

"But it's almost her bedtime! And if this woman's child is ill, I don't think it would be a good idea to expose Ellie to ..." Seeing her daughter's expression, Eva gave up. "All right then, I'll have to come and see you some other time. It's a pity really, I was looking forward to a nice evening in together, just the three of us. I feel like I haven't seen you in ages."

Immediately, Olivia felt guilty. This wasn't right. She shouldn't be shooing her mother away so that she could make way for some man – a man that wasn't even a decent prospect. Her mother would be horrified if she thought that the one man Olivia had been able to think about romantically after Peter happened to be married to somebody else.

"Look, why don't I call over tomorrow morning?" she said to her mother. "Maybe we can head up to Dublin and do a bit of shopping or something. I'm sure Ellie would enjoy that."

"Yes, do that," her mother said, and with some relief Olivia saw that she was getting up to leave.

Hopefully, Matt wouldn't arrive before she left, otherwise, Eva would be very suspicious indeed.

But she needn't have worried. Matt arrived a good half hour after Eva left, and to Olivia's utter surprise presented her with a bunch of brightly coloured gerberas.

"What's this for?" she said, blushing, while glancing worriedly towards the house across the way. What was he doing bringing her flowers like this? Wasn't he being a bit obvious? Then her heart sank. Obviously, Matt had no intention of taking Olivia in his arms and asking her to consider a raging affair, not when he was so casually arriving on her doorstep with a big bunch of flowers in full view of the entire green.

"You'd better let me in or people will start talking," he said, his eyes twinkling with amusement. If Olivia didn't know better, she could have sworn he had read her thoughts just then.

"Oh, of course." She stood back to let him into the hall and, as she did, the unmistakable scent of Paco Rabanne XS aftershave assaulted her nostrils. In that instant, thousands of memories raced through her brain – it was the same brand Peter used to wear.

"So, where's Ellie?" he asked, looking around her living-room with interest. "Hey, nice room, although Catherine seems to think the sofa looks better against the window. I quite like it like this though."

"Ellie's in bed. So, would you like a drink or a cup of coffee or ...?" she asked him, feeling annoyed all of a sudden. If he wasn't here to persuade her into having an affair with him – and seeing how enticing he looked just then in a pair of dark Levis and a tightly fitting khaki T-shirt, he wouldn't have to do too much persuading – what the hell *was* he here for?

"A beer would be great if you have one," he answered, and to Olivia's amazement he jauntily followed her into the kitchen. She rummaged in the back of the fridge.

"I don't drink beer myself but there should be something here left over from our last barbecue. My friend Josh drinks Carlsberg so ..." She trailed off, sensing Matt's presence directly behind her and hoping that the cool of the fridge would help soothe her flushed cheeks. What was he doing here?

"Ah, there's still a few here," she said, locating some cans of beer. She closed the fridge door behind her and, without looking at him, offered him a beer.

"So, what is it that you wanted to ask?" she said, leaning against the kitchen worktop and trying to keep her voice light.

"Olivia, I think you and I both know something is going on here," Matt blurted out.

"I'm sorry?" was all she could say, but her insides leapt. She knew it. It wasn't her imagination after all – he *did* have feelings for her too.

Now he was moving towards her. "I don't really know how to say this, but I've never met a woman like you."

Olivia gulped, unable to believe what she was hearing.

"I haven't been able to look, to even *think* about another woman in the last few years, but with you – with you it's different."

Oh no, Olivia said silently. Don't do this. Don't ruin it with clichés about how your wife doesn't understand you, and how you think you married too young and all the rest of it. The feelings she was having for Matt – although wrong – were still very real and she did not want to feel as though she was in an episode of some pathetic soap opera. Had Leah been right about him after all? Was Matt just another faithless married man, eager to hop in the sack with any poor eejit who happened to be taken in by his charms?

"I don't know, it was weird, but after that first time, after that stupid text message thing, I just – I just couldn't stop thinking about you." He shook his head. "I know that sounds pathetic, but it's true. And then when I realised you lived in Lakeview I – "

"You thought, great – nice and handy to be able to just pop over for a bit of nookie when the wife's away? After all, if she's at it – why not you?" The words were out before Olivia could stop herself, and she barely noticed him shrink backwards, his expression shocked. For some reason, the way Matt – a *married* man – had expressed his interest so casually really annoyed her.

Even though she was interested in him too, she was disappointed. Somehow she'd thought more of him – expected more of him. And then, she knew she had no intention of having a seedy affair with this man. Whatever about Matt's own circumstances, or the problems he might be having in his marriage, she just wasn't going to do it; she wasn't going to be part of it. The love she and Peter had was much too important to be cheapened now by a seedy affair. Yes, she was attracted to Matt Sheridan, unbelievably so, but this wasn't right.

He was sitting at the kitchen table, his face white. "I don't know what you're talking about. I never said anything about having an affair ... while ... while my wife's away ..."

"What?" For a second, Olivia panicked. She hadn't misread the situation, had she? But what did he mean when he said –

"Olivia, my wife is dead," he stated flatly.

She stared at him, shocked.

"What are you talking about?" she said, her voice dropping to a whisper. "Didn't I see her before, calling you from across the green, about a phone call?"

Matt shook his head, and then he smiled slightly. "I suppose it could have looked that way but ... Olivia ..." He sat forward now, obviously understanding her earlier reaction. "Catherine is not my wife; she's Adam's caregiver, my wife's best friend. Natasha died two years ago in a car accident."

"What?" Now Olivia didn't know what to think. "You live with your childminder?"

Matt was smiling broadly now. "No, no, I don't live there at all. Adam and I have a place in Greystones. We spend a lot of time here – well because there isn't much space in an apartment for a child of his age to run around. I've been looking for a house, but work is so busy and ..."

Olivia's mind raced as she slumped into the chair across from him. "But – before, in the garden – Adam said he wanted his mummy ..."

He sighed. "His mum's still a part of his life, I've made sure of that. She died when he was two but yet he seems to remember her. Of course, the apartment is full of photographs and we watch a lot of home movies ..." His voice trailed off, his green eyes full of emotion. "I'm sorry, it's still hard sometimes."

"I can imagine."

"Better than most, I believe," Matt said gently. "The woman in the corner shop, she told me all about your ... situation."

"Did she now?"

"I'm sorry, I wasn't looking to pry or anything but –"

"It's fine," she said, waving a hand dismissively. "I know Molly has a bit of a mouth on her."

"So, I know what it's like – I know it isn't easy."

"No, it isn't." She didn't want to talk about this, not here, not now, not with him. "But I'm fine now, I'm over it."

"It isn't easy on your own. Parenting, I mean."

Olivia shook her head. "It was difficult in the early days,

certainly, but my friends and family were great – I don't know what I would have done without them."

"I don't know about you, but in a way, I think having Adam to worry about helped me a little. I couldn't be selfish; I couldn't retreat into myself because I had him to think about."

"I know what you mean." She looked away sadly.

"Listen," Matt said, standing up and moving towards her. "I didn't come here so that we could stir up painful memories of our respective spouses."

She nodded and was about to say something, but before she could open her mouth, he had taken her hand in his.

"As I was saying earlier, I've been on my own for over two years now, and in all that time I haven't even looked at another woman. Yet, since I first met you ..."

Olivia looked into his beautiful, earnest eyes and knew that this was something special. Everything she had wished for, had hoped for this last while was happening, and yet despite her exhilaration she felt – frightened.

But Matt seemed to understand. "I could be making a fool of myself here. Maybe I've been misreading the signs, maybe you don't feel like I think you feel. But, Olivia, I think you do, and with all you've been through – with all we've *both* been through – I think that you're also a little afraid. But that's perfectly normal because I feel that way too." With that, he reached upwards and tenderly tucked a tendril of hair behind her ear. "What do you think?"

That simple gesture, the faint touch on her skin, had at that moment the effect of removing all reason, all thought from Olivia's mind.

"I think," she said, putting her arms around Matt's neck and reaching forward for a much-longed-for kiss. "I think we might be on to something ...."

THIRTY-ONE

"I'm so pleased," Leah grinned. "He seems really, really nice."

The following Saturday, Leah drove down to Lakeview for lunch and Matt had been there when she arrived. She very quickly gave him the once-over, before deciding that he was perfect for Olivia.

All that week, Olivia had been walking on air and she couldn't keep the smile from her face. That first night, she and Matt had talked well into the night and it was almost dawn by the time he'd left the house.

From her doorway, she watched him sneak like a schoolboy back across the green to Catherine's house.

An odd scenario, that was for sure, she thought, closing the door behind her and heading upstairs, hoping for an hour or two's sleep before Ellie woke.

Matt had told her that he, Catherine, and his wife had known one another for years, having all grown up in the same area of Dublin together. Catherine wasn't married.

"She enjoys single life way too much," he said with a laugh. "But she's been great – great to me, great to Adam. I really don't know what I would have done without her. I suppose she's the only one who understands what it's like. She loved Tash as much as I did. She was a bridesmaid at our wedding, godmother at Adam's christening, you know the way."

"So she looks after Adam while you're at work?" Olivia asked.

"Yes, she's great with kids, really great."

"She must be," Olivia said, impressed. "By the way, I never asked, what is it exactly that you do? I remember that day after the text fiasco," she rolled her yes, "that day we first met, you had just clinched a major deal?"

"Ah yes, that must have been the Big One," he said, smiling at the memory.

"Big One?"

"Yeah, a new apartment complex – in Bulgaria this time. I'm a property consultant, an overseas property consultant. Not an estate agent as such, rather our agency finds investment property for Irish clients overseas. We used to do a lot of stuff in Spain and Portugal but the market's saturated now and there's no value to be had there any more. These days we concentrate only on emerging markets." He smiled. "The Bulgarian developer had just given us sole agency in Ireland, which was a huge boost and ...sorry, I'm probably boring you."

Olivia smiled. "Not at all. It's very interesting actually, although I always pictured you overseas property guys as small, heavy, and sporting a nice tangerine glow from all that time spent in the sun."

Now, Leah wrinkled her nose when Olivia told her this. "He seems nothing like those Costa del Dosh types."

"He's not. As you said yourself, he is really, really nice," Olivia beamed at her friend. Then she threw a short glance over her shoulder checking to see if Ellie was within earshot. "Although I still don't like saying too much in front of – "

"Mommy where's Matt gone?" Ellie piped up from behind.

She had run downstairs and was holding a still-wet colourful painting, the paint splattered all over her hands and cheeks.

"He had to go home," Olivia said, filling the kettle with water. "And he said to say goodbye, but he didn't want to interrupt you while you were painting."

"But I wanted to show him my picture," she cried mournfully.

Leah raised an eyebrow. "Matt seems *very* popular."

"Don't worry – he'll be back later," Olivia told her.

"Goodie! Is Adam coming too?"

"Yes, Adam's coming too. Now go and wash all that paint off your hands – we're having lunch soon, and then we'll go and put your picture on the grave, OK?"

"OK, Mommy," Ellie dutifully rushed back upstairs to the bathroom.

Leah sat down at the kitchen table. "She seems to have taken to Matt in a big way. And judging by that silly grin on your face, her mum seems to have taken to him in a big way too."

"He's great," Olivia said with a smile. "And yes, Ellie is crazy about him."

Leah paused slightly. "And have you told him ... about Peter and everything?"

Olivia's expression clouded. "Not everything. He's told me all about his wife and how she died, but I just can't bring myself to tell him my sorry stories."

Leah shook her head. "I suppose it's a bit early all the same. Still, Matt seems lovely and I hope you're not stalling because you still blame yourself. "

"Who else is responsible for the fact that Ellie doesn't have a father?" Olivia stood up and looked out the window and into the back garden, her eyes tired and sad.

Leah gritted her teeth. "Olivia, you're the best parent I know. You've done a fantastic job in raising Ellie without Peter and, unlike Matt, you don't have someone helping you out like he does with his friend Catherine – quite the opposite. Speaking of which, have you heard from Peter's folks lately?"

"Not for a little while, but in a way, I'm glad. It only confuses Ellie. She goes up to Galway for weekends and when she comes back it's all Daddy this and Daddy that. She doesn't really understand."

"Still as you said yourself, you can't pretend he never existed."

"I know that, but I'm the one that has to make all the excuses and explanations ..." Tears sprang to her eyes. "They've always blamed me too, you know."

"I'm sure that's not true."

"Still, they loved him and now he's gone."

Leah looked sideways at her. "I haven't seen you like this in a long time."

"I haven't *felt* like this in a long time, to be honest," Olivia replied sadly. "Am I doing the right thing?" she asked, panicking now, wondering if she was being silly thinking she could have a relationship with Matt.

"I think you're doing the right thing," Leah said, standing up and putting a comforting arm around her friend's shoulder. "And I also think it's time you moved on. What you had with Peter is long gone, Olivia, you know that, and you've suffered enough. Now, you have to make the most of what you do have, and look to the future."

Olivia thought about it, she had thought about it many times over. Leah was right; she *did* have to move on, and finally come to terms with the fact that Peter wasn't coming back.

THIRTY-TWO

Olivia was sure she was being watched.

It was a strange sensation really, and something she couldn't quite put her finger on, but she was almost positive of it. She'd felt it the other day when she and Ellie were heading out to visit Kate and her new baby at the hospital, and she'd had the really weird feeling that someone was watching her every move.

She didn't like it, not when the estate was normally so quiet, and people in the village generally left her alone. She gave a slight glance towards Catherine's house, suddenly feeling guilty and understanding what it must have felt like when she was peeping out her window at them.

"She'll be mad about you," Matt had enthused one evening when Olivia made cautious enquiries about Catherine.

"You two must be very close," Olivia ventured carefully, wondering why on earth an attractive young woman who by all accounts had the world at her feet had stepped into the role vacated by Matt's wife.

He seemed adamant that they were just childhood friends, and their relationship became galvanised even more by their bereavement. But Olivia couldn't help wondering if there was, or ever had been, anything else between them.

"She's great," Matt said, interrupting her thoughts. "She adores Adam, would do anything for him."

"And did you two ever ...?" She felt like a heel for even suggesting it when she saw his expression cloud over.

"She was Natasha's best friend."

"Of course." Olivia wasn't sure what that meant, but she suspected that he and Catherine had loved Natasha too much to betray her memory like that.

Still, she had to admit that she found it all very strange, and she wouldn't mind meeting this Catherine, who seemed to have sacrificed quite a lot of her own life to accommodate a simple friendship. Then, she all of a sudden remembered the young guy sneaking – well, in retrospect she had only *imagined* he was sneaking – out of Catherine's house that morning a while back. She was making too much of this – Catherine might be a very good-looking girl who was being supportive of her friend, but she obviously wasn't living like a nun either.

And of course, if she was such a good friend and as lovely and obliging as Matt was saying, then Olivia was sure that the two of them would get on like a house on fire.

CATHERINE WAS BANGING pots and pans around as if she was rehearsing for a kitchen-utensil recital. What was Matt playing at, inviting *her* over here for dinner?

How dare he flaunt the trollop in front of her. Was he toying with her now – was that it?

Well, he could go sing – Catherine wasn't going to lie down without a fight – not this time. After all those nights he'd spent crying on her shoulder, telling her that he loved her and didn't know what he would do without her, and then, at the first opportunity, he goes and takes up with some dizzy wagon from across the road.

She couldn't comprehend the hurt she'd felt when Matt didn't seem at all bothered that she was seeing a guy from the village.

"I'm so pleased for you," he'd said. "It's not easy to find someone these days." He went on to say that he had always been concerned that their close friendship might prevent Catherine from finding a partner, that their heavy involvement in one another's lives might be a stumbling block to her independence.

She couldn't believe it – it was as though he was *happy* she'd found someone, almost as though he was now free to go off pursuing other women – like dumpy Olivia.

How could she have got it so wrong? She'd been so sure that seeing her all dressed up and ready for a night out with some man, someone that wasn't him, would make him realise what he was missing.

But no he didn't seem at all bothered about it – in fact, he had collected Adam and without a care in the world had simply toddled off across the road to *her* house. Yes, Conor was a nice guy, very charming and very flashy with the cash, not to mention owned one of those gorgeous heritage cottages down by the lake, but really he had nothing on Matt.

How could he not see it? How could Matt not realise that they were perfect for one another – that she could give him all the love he needed and more?

She didn't presume to replace Natasha, she would *never* dream of that, but since Tash died she had dedicated her life to helping Matt cope with his grief, helping him and Adam to move on.

She'd even moved to this godforsaken hell-hole to lay the foundations for settling down to a quieter pace of life together away from Dublin.

Granted, this Olivia seemed to have a lot in common with him

– she had also lost her husband and was raising a child on her own.

Was this what attracted him? Was it the fact that he felt some kind of empathy for her situation?

Catherine didn't know. All she knew was that she was not going to let some desperate widow from across the road come between her and her happiness.

Olivia would soon find out that the course of her and Matt's apparent 'true love' was not going to run smoothly.

At all.

THIRTY-THREE

"Your house is gorgeous," Olivia gushed, looking around the living-room. "You have a much better grasp of interior design than I have, I can tell you."

She gave a weak laugh, feeling more nervous about meeting this woman than she cared to admit. She took another gulp from the glass of white wine Matt had put into her hand when she had first arrived, only then realising that, in her nervousness, she was drinking it too fast.

Matt had invited her to dinner at Catherine's, insisting that she loved every opportunity to show off her culinary skills.

Catherine's taste in clothes wasn't too bad either, she thought, feeling rather self-conscious in her plain attire of jeans and ordinary black woollen jumper compared to Catherine's colourful off-the-shoulder top and flirty leather skirt.

Judging by her slim figure and flawlessly applied makeup, she obviously looked after herself, and because of this Olivia couldn't quite put an age on her. Mid-thirties, maybe?

"Thanks," Catherine replied to her compliments, although there was little warmth in her tone.

She walked immediately into the kitchen and, although she hadn't been asked, Olivia followed, hoping that Matt would soon return from settling the kids. Catherine didn't seem to mind them playing in another room while the adults had dinner.

"Matt has been telling me all about you, and how great you are with Adam," Olivia ventured again.

Catherine continued busying herself with the dinner preparations as if she wasn't even there.

"To be perfectly honest, I do feel bad about you having to entertain tonight." Olivia knew she was babbling but still felt she had to fill the silence. "We could have gone out somewhere in the village to save you all the effort, but Matt insisted ..." She trailed off, wondering what was wrong. The way Matt went on, Olivia had thought that the woman wouldn't hear of them having dinner anywhere else.

"Not at all – I enjoy cooking for Matt," Catherine said, with a hint of a smile.

"Well, do you need any help at all?"

"I have everything under control, thanks." She continued opening cupboards and drawers, leaving Olivia standing in the middle of the kitchen like some kind of spare tool.

Again, she wondered what to say next, but luckily didn't have to for much longer as just then Matt reappeared.

"How's everything going? Anything I can do?"

Catherine exhaled deeply and wiped her brow with the back of her hand. "If you could finish setting the table, and look after the drinks, it would be a huge help," she said with a grateful sigh.

Great, Olivia thought, piqued that the woman had rejected her offer to help. Now, it looked as though *she* was some ingrate, expecting to be waited on hand and foot.

"I'll set the table if you like," she offered and Matt gave her a warm smile.

"No, no, you go and sit down," Catherine swatted her away like a fly. "Matt and I will take care of everything. Matt, why don't you fill up Olivia's glass for her? It's almost empty."

Olivia flushed mortified that Catherine had somehow managed to make her look like Lady Muck.

Soon after, dinner was served and the others joined her at the table.

"Is Adam OK?" Catherine asked, letting her long blonde hair fall loose from its clip and taking a dainty sip from her wineglass. She was gorgeous, Olivia thought, feeling downright dowdy sitting alongside her.

"He and Ellie are entranced by some DVD," Matt answered, his mouth full.

"Well, as long as they stay entranced until we've finished eating, I'll be happy," Olivia laughed, eager to relax the obvious tension.

Catherine frowned slightly. "Do you let Ellie watch television a lot then, Olivia?"

She tensed, immediately sensing that she had said the wrong thing. "No, of course not. I merely meant that it would be nice for us all to get to know one another and have a bit of a chat in peace."

"So, Ellie can be a bit disruptive ..." Catherine said, spooning cheesy potato gratin onto her plate.

"Well no, it's just – as I'm sure you know yourself, kids are kids..."

"We don't let Adam away with any nonsense do we, Matt?"

"Certainly not." Eyes wide, he shook his head. "Adam's generally very well-behaved, but he knows full well that he'd get a tap on the behind if he started acting up in front of either of us."

Olivia didn't know what to say. "Ellie knows that too of course, but you know when kids get together ..." She trailed off as she poured the dregs of the wine bottle into her glass. For a moment there was a strained silence, and then Matt stood up from the table and went to the fridge. *Great,* Olivia thought, mentally kicking herself for taking the last of the wine. *Now I look like a bloody lush.*

"I really can't understand why some parents feel it's wrong to give a child a smack if they step out of line," Catherine said, smiling appreciatively at Matt as he opened the bottle. "Although I suppose, in your case," she went on, "it must be difficult to find a balance, what with being on your own and all that."

"I'm sure I'm not the only parent who finds it difficult to find a balance, but of course, I have no problem at all with disciplining Ellie when she's bold. Having said that, I don't need to do it very often because she *is* a good kid and – "

"I suppose television is great for keeping her quiet all the same," Catherine interjected as if Ellie was only good because of this.

"Yes, she does watch quite a lot of telly, doesn't she?" Matt was helping himself to some of Catherine's immaculately prepared roast lamb.

"Not really – it's just the few times you've called – "

"I really feel exercise at a young age is so important for a child," Catherine interjected as if Olivia hadn't spoken. "I take Adam for a good walk in the park most days – time much better spent than sitting on his backside in front of the box. It's habit-forming and hopefully he'll grow up a much healthier child as a result."

Matt smiled. "She's an out-and-out gym bunny, aren't you?"

"I love a good stint at the gym and I know I'm certainly not going to stay a size eight by sitting on my ass watching *Eastenders.*" She laughed. "And at our age, we *have* to make the effort to look after ourselves, don't you think, Olivia?"

She tried to tell herself that this wasn't a pointed jibe at the fact that her size-eight days were truly long gone. Yet, her rounded figure never seemed to bother Matt before so ...

"Of course, but I get enough exercise running around after Ellie – not to mention all the housework and cleaning up after her." She rolled her eyes fondly.

"You're right, she *does* sound quite disruptive," Catherine said, shaking her head. "And if you don't nip it in the bud now, things will only get worse."

Just then Adam burst into the room, his face red and wet with tears. "Daddy, Ellie won't gimme back my Tweenie!"

Catherine stood up immediately. "Darling, come here," she said, opening her arms. For someone who was such an advocate of hard discipline, Olivia thought, she seemed all too eager to plamause the child.

She stood up too. "I'm sure Ellie will give you back your toy – where is she?"

Adam pointed towards the room down the hallway, and Olivia made her way to Adam's playroom.

Her eyes widened as she took in the mayhem. The floor was littered with toys – popular, expensive toys, the television blared noisily in the background, and poor Ellie was sitting in the corner crying her little heart out.

"He hit me on the head, Mommy," she wailed. "I wanted to play with the Tweenie and he hit me with a Tommy Truck!"

"Adam, come here, please," Matt called sternly down the hallway.

"Ellie, are you sure you two weren't just playing?" Olivia was only too well aware of how kids could exaggerate a situation to their own advantage when adults were involved, and she didn't want to get Adam in any trouble. Though a quick examination of Ellie's forehead revealed a red mark and a throbbing bump.

"Adam wouldn't do something like that unless he was provoked," she heard Catherine say from the doorway. "He's a very gentle child, and even at play school has never had any problems with the other children."

"It's fine, I'm sure they were just being kids."

"Maybe should take her to a specialist or something," Catherine went on. "She obviously has some anger issues."

Olivia tensed. "With all due respect," she said, glancing sideways at Matt for his reaction. "There are two of them in it and knowing kids of their age, I doubt either are completely blameless."

"You don't honestly believe that Adam hit her for no reason," said Catherine. She kissed Adam's temple. "Poor baby."

Olivia couldn't believe what she was hearing. And even worse, what she *wasn't* – from Matt. Catherine was being downright rude and unreasonable – wasn't he going to say anything? Not that Olivia would expect him to take sides, but she was doing her best to be sensible and objective about her child's involvement in this.

Matt shook his head uncertainly. "She must have done something ... Adam does seem very upset."

At this Olivia stood up, a tearful Ellie in her arms. "We don't know what's happened here, so there's little point in our fighting about it." She went to pass Catherine in the doorway. "Thanks for dinner, I'm sorry we didn't get a chance to finish it." She tried her best to sound cordial, but inwardly she was raging.

The other woman gave her a winning smile. "Some other time maybe, perhaps when Ellie has better reined in her behaviour."

"Olivia ..." Matt called after her. "I'll phone you tomorrow?" he said, following her to the front door.

"Sure."

"Bye, Matt, bye, Adam," Ellie said, waving tearfully over her mother's shoulder, upset that she and her new friend were fighting.

Olivia closed the gate behind her. "Come on, pet, we'll go home and have some of that nice ice cream Mummy got in the shops yesterday – what do you think?"

"Yay!"

Embarrassed by what had happened, and stung at the fact that Matt wasn't prepared to help defuse the situation, Olivia walked slowly back across the green.

So much for neighbourly relations.

THIRTY-FOUR

"She sounds like a right old wagon." Leah gave the house across the way one of her famous laser stares.

It was the following afternoon, and Olivia was telling her all about her not-so-cosy dinner.

"It was very strange," she said. It had hurt that Matt hadn't come to her defence. She could have understood it if Adam had been injured, but Ellie was the one with the sore forehead. "You should have heard the way they talked about how they discipline Adam, and how Catherine loves cooking for him. I was supposed to be there as Matt's guest but I felt like a complete outsider."

Leah wrinkled her nose. "Well, I don't think it's strange at all. In fact, I think it's pretty obvious that Catherine fancies him, has probably *always* fancied him, and now she doesn't like it that he's taken up with you. She's threatened by you."

"I don't think so. They've been friends for a long time – though Matt did say before that she could be a bit possessive. Anyway, if Catherine does fancy him, I don't know why he *isn't* with her. You saw her – she's gorgeous and she puts the like of me to shame with her slim figure and her glossy hair." Since comforting – no, *gorging* – herself last night with a big bowl of Ben

& Jerry's upon her return from Catherine's, Olivia had decided to go on a serious diet.

"Don't be silly – you look just as good as she does, and don't you dare think otherwise," Leah said. "Not every man thinks stick-insects are attractive, you know."

"Are you serious?"

"Well, if she's so gorgeous and wonderful and such a good cook, why *isn't* he with her then?"

"I don't know. But up until a couple of weeks ago I was sure they were married, and now I think I understand why." She bit her lip. "It's just typical, isn't it? The first guy to come along in years that I actually like, and now it seems as though it's over before it's even begun."

"Over? Why?"

Olivia explained how Matt had barely even tried to prevent her from leaving, and how she hadn't heard from him since.

And that was what hurt the most, Olivia thought. She had really believed that he was different, that there was something special between them, and she had been willing to give herself up to the possibility that they could have a future together. But after his behaviour last night, it was hard to see how.

"And I can't believe the nerve of the woman implying that you're a bad parent," Leah fumed. "If only she knew. I'm sure Matt will come to his senses and if he doesn't, then he wasn't worth it in the first place and –"

The sharp shrill of the doorbell cut off the remainder of her sentence, and Olivia jumped up to answer it.

Matt stood at the doorway, his face drawn.

"Can I come in?" he asked sheepishly.

"If you like," Olivia stepped back to let him pass. "Leah's here," she added and he visibly tensed.

Leah jumped up from the sofa. "I'd better get back – I'm going out on the town with Kate tonight." She picked up her bag and gave Matt a curt nod. "I'll talk to you later hon."

When the two of them were alone, Matt tentatively took one of Olivia's hands in his.

"I'm so sorry," he said, and almost instantly she melted. "You must have had a terrible impression of us."

Us? Olivia repeated silently. The way he was talking, you'd swear that Catherine and Adam were a package.

"It wasn't what I had expected, that was for sure."

"How's Ellie? I feel so bad. In fact, I was so shocked at Adam's behaviour that I couldn't think straight. The poor thing must have been in an awful state."

"She was upset, not so much about the bump, but more so about the fact that she and Adam were fighting."

Then he sat down and ran a hand through his hair. "Whatever I was saying before about discipline, I do think that sometimes I can be too soft on him. But he's all I have left now." He looked at her sadly. "You can understand that surely?"

"Of course I do," Olivia said, sitting down beside him. "And I understand too that kids will be kids. Parents shouldn't really take sides in these situations, Matt, not when they don't know the facts. Otherwise, we'd all end up at each others' throats, and what kind of example is that to be setting?"

"You're so understanding," he said, shaking his head. "I told Catherine that you'd understand but she was sure you'd tell me to go to hell."

"I don't think Catherine liked me very much," she said cautiously, not willing to add that the feeling was very definitely mutual.

Matt shook his head. "No, no, it's not like that all. I know she wasn't overly friendly last night but ... look, you have to understand that Catherine and I are very close - sometimes, to our detriment. I know she's started seeing some guy now and while I'm delighted – because I worry that with all she does for Adam and me that life is passing her by. I suppose I'm a bit protective of her in the same way a big brother would worry about his sister. Catherine is exactly the same with me, possibly more so because of Natasha. She knows what I've been through and she doesn't want me to get hurt."

Olivia considered this and decided that, yes, there was certainly a possibility that Catherine would be suspicious of her. A while ago, he didn't know Olivia from Adam (she groaned inwardly at the unintended pun) and then all of a sudden he was involved with her and her daughter.

It was only natural that a good friend would be concerned, wasn't it? Still, thinking back on Catherine's behaviour last night, she couldn't get past the sneaking suspicion that Leah was right. Maybe Catherine and Matt *were* unusually close, but wasn't it also possible that in the other woman Olivia could have a serious rival for his affections?

She hoped not, because she didn't think she could cope with something like that.

Not again.

THIRTY-FIVE

Leah turned into Kate's driveway a little bit faster than she realised and jerked to a stop right behind Michael's black BMW.

Whew ... Michael certainly wouldn't appreciate her slamming into *that* with her little Fiesta. And really, her car had more than enough dents on it already.

She mentally reminded herself to apply once more for her driving test now that she had a little bit more time on her hands. Although, she thought with a sigh, it would undoubtedly be another complete waste of time.

Only the other day, she'd been trying to manoeuvre out of a tight spot near the shop, and to reverse out, had no option but to scratch the paintwork of the jeep parked alongside her. Leah had left a note on the owner's windscreen, and later had endured a barrage of abuse, which she supposed was justified.

She'd have to pass her test soon, otherwise her insurance company would just flat out refuse to cover her and her now scratched and sorrowful-looking Fiesta. And that certainly wouldn't do.

Getting out of the car, and having to choose her steps extra carefully on Kate's cobble-lock driveway in her heels and clingy chiffon skirt, Leah approached the front door.

Unusually, the house looked unkempt from the outside: the flowers hung limply in their hanging baskets, and the front lawn looked as though it hadn't been touched in months.

And shock horror, Leah spotted greasy handprints on the sliding doors of the porch. She smiled to herself.

The arrival of her newborn had evidently affected Kate's normally fastidious housekeeping. Her friend was famous for her compulsive cleaning – a fact that used to annoy Leah no end when the two shared a flat together throughout university.

A harassed-looking Michael appeared in the doorway.

"Hello," She reached forward and greeted Kate's husband with a hug and a kiss on the cheek. She hadn't seen him in the few weeks since the baby was born, and with his unshaven jaw and the tired, ravaged look in his eyes, he looked equally as unkempt as the house.

"Hi, Leah," He returned her greeting with considerably less enthusiasm. "Kate was trying to call you ..." He trailed off and by his tone, Leah knew immediately that their planned girlie night out had hit a snag.

"Let me guess, she's still getting ready ..." Leah said with a conspiratorial smile. Despite her apparent devil-may-care attitude, Kate was as fastidious with her appearance as she was with her housekeeping, and she knew from experience that it could take her an age to get dolled up for a night out. Post-pregnancy, especially.

"It's not that," Michael replied wearily, directing her through to the living-room.

A wrecked-looking Kate was sitting on the couch with new baby Dylan in her arms. Leah had never seen her friend looking so dishevelled. She knew that babies could be disrupting, but because Kate was normally so calm and in control, Leah hadn't expected the chaotic sight that greeted her.

Apart from the baby essentials – nappies, creams and toys that were scattered all over – the room looked as though it hadn't been tidied in years. There were half-empty coffee cups on the floor around the sofa, glasses on the mantelpiece, empty takeaway cartons ... in all honesty, it looked to Leah like one of their old dingy student flats.

This was so out of character for Kate that she felt rather unsettled and instantly guilty. She hadn't seen her friend since that time in the hospital. Thinking that the new parents would need time to enjoy this much-wanted new baby, she had consciously kept out of Kate's hair – not to mention the fact that she too had been up to her eyes at work. She had made all the usual offers to help and 'call me if you need anything' platitudes, but thinking of it now she wondered if she shouldn't have insisted.

"Hey," she said, sitting down alongside her friend on the couch and forcing a smile so as not to betray her unease, "How are you?"

"OK," Kate whispered and immediately, seeming to take his mother's shifting attention as some form of rejection, Dylan screwed up his tiny face and cried – *roared* – even louder.

"Ssshh, ssshh, it's OK love, Mummy's here, Mummy's here," Kate soothed, holding him close and rubbing his back in a comforting gesture. "I'm sorry," she said wearily, "but I think we'll have to call off our night out."

Oh. Leah hadn't expected that. She thought that they'd be a bit late getting to the restaurant but ...

"Oh, dear, is he unwell?" she asked, realising. "Does he have ..." She racked her brain for the common baby-sickness that Ellie had when she was a baby. "Group or something? The poor little thing." She reached across and touched the baby in a sympathetic gesture.

"I don't know ... Michael?" Kate's eyes widened with alarm and she looked to her husband for assistance. "Could Leah be right? Could there be something wrong with him?"

"I'm sure there's nothing wrong with him." He gave Leah a look that conveyed blatant irritation, before continuing, "He's just tired, that's all."

"But what if there *is* something wrong with him?" Kate's tone hinged on hysterical. "How am I supposed to know? He can't tell me, can he? What if there is something wrong with him, and he needs to go to the hospital or –"

"Love, he's fine. Babies cry you know that. It's just that this particular one happens to cry more than most," he added, almost under his breath.

Leah began to feel more than a little uncomfortable and out of place in this family scene. She knew now that her hoped-for pleasant night out catching up with Kate, wasn't going to happen. She knew that newborns could be tough going, but Kate had said herself that she was dying to let her hair down.

"So ..." Michael continued, his tone more placating, "if you're not going out and Leah's staying on, I might head off to the local for one or two?"

"Sure, go ahead," Kate said with an absent nod, as Dylan's cries began to subside. "It's just ... couldn't possibly leave him like this you know?" She turned to Leah. "I'd just be worrying and worrying about him all night, and I wouldn't be able to enjoy it. You don't mind, do you?"

Michael didn't seem to mind leaving him, Leah thought uncharitably. Surely if the baby was that hard going, Kate needed a break too?

"Of course I don't mind," she said, trying to inject some enthu-siasm into her tone. This wasn't exactly how she'd envisaged her only night off in weeks but still ... "Look, why don't you and the baby just lie down for a quiet moment and I'll get out of your way."

She'd have to ring the restaurant and cancel, she thought, and she felt lousy about that because she'd had to beg for a table in the first place. If only Kate had rung earlier to let her know the situation, then she could have slung on a pair of tracksuit bottoms and brought a bottle of wine or something.

Although she thought guiltily, it was hardly fair to expect Kate to worry about putting Leah out. Well, if nothing else, she thought, removing her trench coat and hanging it over the banister in the hallway, she could give a hand with tidying up.

Kate's priority would now be the baby rather than cleaning the windows, but surely Michael could muck in that little bit more?

Evidently the new arrival caused more disruption than they'd imagined. She couldn't imagine it herself. In her and Josh's teeny apartment they could barely stretch to having visitors, let alone giving it all over to the chaos that evidently went hand in hand with a newborn.

Removing her shoes, which were already becoming uncomfortable not to mention completely out of place in this domestic situation, Leah went back into the living room to find Kate lying full stretch on the couch.

Seeing Leah about to speak, she put a finger over her lips in a silencing gesture, and indicated gently to Dylan's crib at the other end of the room.

She had finally succeeded in calming him then, Leah thought, freezing in mid-movement. At least she and Kate might get to do a bit of catching up then. Maybe her friend had a bottle of wine stashed somewhere and they could crack that open and have a good old giggle and relax a little. It was almost nine o'clock – Dylan would sleep for the rest of the night now, surely?

Kate swung her legs onto the ground and carefully – painstakingly – tiptoed to where Leah stood motionless in the doorway.

"You should go," she whispered faintly, while keeping one eye on the baby's crib. "He'll be fine now – I think I have him down until his next feed."

Leah was startled. "Go? I thought I'd stay on for a while, share a bottle of wine or something ..."

Kate motioned her to the other side of the door and out into the hallway.

"A bottle of *wine*?" she repeated, an edge to her voice. "What kind of a mother would I be to go off getting pissed with my baby son in the next room? What if he wakes up again and I'm too out of it to see to him properly?"

"I never said anything about getting pissed, Kate." Leah was taken aback at her tone. "I just thought it would be nice for you and me to relax a little since we're not going out – have a bit of a girlie night in, I suppose." She shrugged, unsure what to say.

"For heaven's sake Leah, there's more to life than going out and having silly conversations about nonsense," Kate whispered, but to Leah it sounded more like an impatient hiss.

Stung, she looked away.

"I'm sorry," Kate sighed, running a hand through her hair. "I'm just ... not up to it tonight."

"I wasn't suggesting anything like that." Leah tried not to betray her upset. "I just thought that with the way things are at the moment, you kicking back and relaxing a little might help."

"What? What do you mean 'the way things are at the moment', Leah?" Kate snapped again. "Do you think that just because Dylan was crying tonight that I'm not coping? That I'm not a good mother, is that it?"

"Of course not. Of course that's not what I meant. I wouldn't *dream* of suggesting anything like that." She looked up and seeing

Kate's hard expression, realised that whatever she said tonight would probably be the wrong thing.

All of a sudden, she felt terribly guilty. Poor Kate was worn-out and hassled, and most likely all she wanted was an early night while she had the chance.

Leah had been silly in suggesting anything else, and she shouldn't really blame her for getting frustrated. She would be frustrated too if she had been stuck all day and night with a screaming baby who couldn't settle, and then the first second she has to relax, her friend wants her attention.

No, Kate was right. She should leave her alone, and let her get some much-needed sleep.

"You're right," she said, resting a hand on her friend's arm and getting a weak smile in return. "You're tired, and I'm sure the last thing you need is visitors tonight. I'll go and leave you to it, and perhaps we can arrange another night when you feel up to it."

She winced, regretting her choice of words as soon as they were out, and Kate's expression instantly hardened.

"I'm not ill, you know," she said touchily. "I just happened to have a bad day with him today – he's usually fine."

"I know that." At this stage, Leah couldn't wait to leave. She picked up her coat from the banister. "Get some rest tonight and I'll give you a ring during the week, OK?"

Despite herself, Leah felt hurt. Of course she could appreciate her friend was tired and weary, but was it necessary to be so short with her? Her only intention tonight had been to help Kate relax, get her out of the house and back to the real world, albeit temporarily.

She was sure that her friend would appreciate that, that she would be grateful for a chance to escape the chaos for a bit.

But, obviously, Leah thought, as she got in the car and pulled out of Kate's driveway, she had got it badly wrong.

· · ·

"WHAT DO YOU THINK? Was I being selfish?" Leah asked Josh after he'd returned from yet another late shift.

"I wouldn't see it like that," he answered, taking a beer from the fridge. "Kate arranged with you in the first place – it's not as though you just arrived on her doorstep, dressed up to the nines and demanding to be entertained."

Leah bit her lip, recalling Kate's impatience at her suggestion that they stay in with a bottle of wine.

"It was the way she looked at me though – as if I was this shallow idiot."

"I wouldn't make too much of it, Lee – it's probably just a phase she's going through. How old is the kid now – three, four weeks? She's bound to be finding it hard going."

"I know, but I just thought she'd appreciate ... oh, I don't know ..." She followed him through to the living room, and then slunk down on the sofa beside him.

"And Michael snaked off to the local, huh?" he said, putting an arm around her. "Looks like fatherhood's getting too much for him already."

Leah had her own opinion on Michael snaking off and leaving Kate holding the baby, but she didn't say anything. She was still reeling from Kate's insinuation that she was shallow. Was she shallow? OK, so she knew nothing about motherhood and never would, but surely it couldn't be good for either Kate or her baby if she couldn't take time out for herself. Of course, if Dylan was ill, that would be a different story but the child wasn't sick, was he?

If anything, he was just being a baby. Although she wasn't around at the time, she remembered poor Olivia worrying incessantly about Ellie, and despite her friend's insistence that she was never going to be one of those mothers who picked up her baby at the first whimper, she wasn't exactly blasé about crying either.

That's what she'd do, Leah decided, she'd talk to Olivia. Maybe that would shed some light upon Kate's behaviour, and why she seemed rather obsessive about her role. Unfortunately, Leah couldn't understand what her friend was going through now and, she thought sadly, never would.

In the meantime, she thought, cuddling into Josh on the sofa, if Kate wasn't interested in catching up, then she and her boyfriend could certainly do a bit of catching up of their own.

THIRTY-SIX

Ben and Robin stood in their apartment, and looked at one another in awe. Robin picked up and flicked through the glossy pages of one of the proof copies she had just received from the publisher.

Atchoo the Allergic Alligator was now a beautifully illustrated picture book and completely different to the one they had jokingly put together a couple of months before. The basic story remained the same, though Robin had added a few more dramatic adventures before Atchoo finally learns to take his medicine properly, but she decided it was the illustrations that made the book so impressive.

Bubblegum Press planned to release all books in the series one after another so in the meantime, Robin had written another three in a similar vein, but featuring different animals with different medical conditions.

Hazel the Squirrel – a story about a squirrel with a nut allergy, and a subject obviously very close to Robin's heart, – *Dick the Diabetic Duck* and *Eleanor the Epileptic Elephant*.

Due to some very well-timed press releases, the *Atchoo* series was gaining a lot of advance publicity. A few weeks earlier,

Bubblegum had fallen over themselves in an attempt to issue a press release shortly after the US Health Department published alarmingly high statistics on children's allergies, and the part our disintegrating environment had to play.

Pre-publication copies of the books had already been distributed to local and governmental health departments, and also to key children's hospitals throughout the state. The response so far had been extremely positive, and the publishers were expecting considerable sales once the book was in stores. The major bookstores – Barnes and Noble and Borders – had initially dismissed the series as an aid for local health departments, but once Walmart decided to stock the series as a result of the media exposure, they tentatively began making enquiries too.

The first book *Atchoo the Alligator* was due for publication at Christmas, and the others thereafter.

"Seems I'm going to be busy," Robin said shaking her head in amazement.

She had met again with Bubblegum since, and Lucy, the head of PR, had informed her that upon publication they would be doing state, and possibly nationwide TV, radio and newspaper interviews.

Although the initial campaign would be focused primarily on *Atchoo*, the release of the other books should sustain interest and hopefully increase the series' profile and momentum. Could Robin make herself available for a couple of weeks around then?

So, she had booked her two weeks annual leave from Greene & Co, and instead of spending them on holiday in Florida as she and Ben had planned, she would be touring around New York State, visiting bookstores, radio stations and possibly school and health agencies.

It wouldn't be much of a holiday, but Robin didn't mind – in fact, she couldn't wait, and she still couldn't believe that this was actually happening, let alone happening so quickly. At Marla's insistence, she had found herself an agent, a lovely woman called Jessie who had negotiated her contract and (in Robin's opinion) her completely unwarranted advance – the first part of which was sitting in her bank account until she and Ben found a house.

Now, seeing her own words in print for the first time, Robin felt a shiver up her spine. "I think I could get used to this," she said, flopping back onto the sofa, book in hand.

"Well, you'll have to," Ben laughed. "There are still another three books to come."

"No, I mean I could get used to *this*," she said, pointing to the text. "To the writing. I love doing it, but yet I never once considered it before now. Imagine me – a children's writer?"

"But you've got talent, Robin," he said, sitting down alongside her. "I know you think the illustrations are impressive but they bought the story, they bought *your* story." He shook his head. "And it is a bloody good one ... charming and silly and playful and adults will *love* reading this to their kids. You've got it, Robin – whether you believe it or not, you've got it."

"I'd love to believe I do have 'it' – whatever that may be – but I don't see how. I don't know all that much about kids. Other than Kirsty."

"And you're so good with her, you're so good with kids in general." He shook his head. "You know it is such a shame that ..." Ben quickly trailed off when she flashed him a warning look. "OK, OK, let's not go there now, not at a time like this anyway." He picked up the book and began flicking through it one more time.

"'Let's not go there'," Robin teased, mimicking his accent.

"You brat," he laughed, tickling her. "Don't start going all high and mighty with me, just because you're now a published author!"

Robin giggled and then Ben sat up and once more studied her name on the front cover. "Wow, you're a published author!" he repeated, as if realising it for the first time. "This calls for a celebration, Robin Matthews, and I'm taking you out to dinner!"

Robin sat up and grinned. "Great, where will we go?" she asked, feeling both excited and nervous about the thoughts of eating out somewhere.

"Chinatown?" Ben suggested with a twinkle in his eye, and Robin threw a cushion at him. "No, seriously, remember that place we went for our anniversary – it was safe enough, wasn't it?"

"Safe but bland and way over-priced," Robin said, remembering.

"Well, as long as the champagne tastes good, I couldn't care less," he said, and Robin wanted to hug him. Poor Ben, it wasn't fair on him that he had to pick and choose where they ate, and at times like this, it really hit home how lucky she was.

"Champagne sounds great," she said, getting into the spirit of things. What did it matter about the food? They were celebrating!

"Why don't you go and get ready, and I'll sort a table," he said, shooing her into the bedroom.

As Robin picked out a suitable outfit for the swanky but safe restaurant, she thought again about her little book and wondered what they'd all make of it at home. She'd told her mother about the publication deal, but her mum, while pleased for her, didn't really understand, and seemed to think that Robin was printing out and publishing these books herself.

She was just glad that Peggy hadn't asked when she was coming home for a visit. Her mother was good like that and seemed to accept that Robin's life was in New York now. It was as though her mother was finally able to have a life of her own, now that she no longer had to worry about Robin.

She had always felt guilty about her parents' break-up, and although her mother had never blamed her, it was fairly obvious that Robin's allergy had been the problem.

Peggy and her dad were on speaking terms these days, but Tom was with someone else now, and there was little likelihood of them getting back together. Anyway, Robin suspected that her mother didn't care. After years of stressing and looking after a sickly child, she was now free to do as she pleased without worry.

Robin hadn't yet said anything about the book to Leah either. She wondered what she and the others – particularly Olivia – would think. Would they be pleased for her? They would definitely be surprised anyway, and she could almost imagine Amanda Clarke going apoplectic over the fact that Robin becoming a published author.

She really should tell Leah though. It was nice of her to send Robin and Ben an invite to her big launch night, but there was never any question of them going.

Leah understood of course, but at times like that, Robin wondered how long they would be able to keep up their friendship 'for old times' sake'.

She had moved on, moved away from it all, and while she occasionally missed having a solid, dependable friend like Olivia, or someone to go out and have a good giggle with like Leah, she knew that it was inevitable that they would lose touch.

Friendships, just like relationships, couldn't really survive long-distance. Robin was certain of that.

THIRTY-SEVEN

At the weekend, Olivia met Leah in the city for some shopping.

After weeks of ignoring her appearance, Leah had decided that her image needed serious sprucing up and to Olivia's amazement had taken a rare day off. Olivia for once was off duty too, since Ellie was visiting her grandparents in Galway.

Peter's parents tried to involve themselves in their grand-daughter's life as much as possible. But occasionally, his mother could be a bit interfering, and yesterday morning was one of those times.

"Who's this Matt, she keeps chattering about?" Teresa enquired.

"Matt?" Olivia repeated warily to her mother-in-law.

"Yes. It's all Matt this and Matt that, and Adam this and Adam that. I gather that Adam is a young friend of hers, but who is Matt?"

"Adam's father." Despite herself, Olivia reddened. It had been years, but still she felt guilty. She knew that Teresa would no doubt view it as a betrayal.

"And does Ellie see much of this Matt?" Teresa sniffed disapprovingly. "Do *you* see much of this Matt?"

Olivia had a good mind to tell Teresa to butt out and mind her own business, that she would see as much of Matt as she liked, but yet she hadn't the heart to.

"He's a neighbour - a very nice man and a good friend, that's all."

Teresa sighed. "Look, far be it from me to stick my nose in your business, but just be careful, won't you? You have to consider Ellie's welfare, and it wouldn't be good for her to have these come-a-day go-a-day men in her life."

Olivia gaped. As if she was seeing other men left, right and centre! Matt was the first, the only man she'd even *thought* about seeing seriously since Peter – how dare she? Again, she bit her tongue. There was no point in arguing over this. The woman had made her point and, as Ellie's grandmother, she did have a right to make it. But she had a bloody cheek all the same, considering.

This weekend though, she was just going to enjoy her free time, and not be worrying about Teresa or indeed Catherine.

"I just didn't know what to do or say," Leah's confused tones brought Olivia back to the present. In the meantime Kate had rung and apologised for letting Leah down.

"She said we'd definitely arrange it again soon, but, to be honest, I don't want to be the one to do the arranging, as I seem to pick my moments," Leah told Olivia. "But she says Dylan seems good now, which is great."

"Well, your birthday's coming up soon," Olivia reminded her. "So we'll all be getting together for that?"

Leah shook her head. "I don't know. I don't think I'd have the energy to organise a bash, especially since it's not all that long since the launch party. I might just have a quiet dinner some-where, just a few of us."

"Are you sure? Seems a bit dull compared to all that fuss you made for mine – and Kate's."

Olivia smiled to herself. Despite her reticence, Leah's

birthday might turn out to be a much bigger cause for celebration than she'd expected. She'd had a conversation with Josh recently one night at Leah's a little while after the launch party, which led her to suspect that he might be working up to a proposal. Normally jocular, he had been strangely serious, asking questions about Peter and their break-up back in college.

"You loved one another deeply, didn't you? You and Peter?" he asked, while Leah was out of earshot.

"Of course," Olivia said, a little taken aback at his directness.

"But Leah said that you had some problems, back before you two got engaged. Do you mind if I ask you what changed your mind?"

Olivia immediately deduced that he was trying to place his feelings about Leah in context. Some men were like that. For years, they could just go along in a relationship, never really questioning their feelings, never really wondering where the relationship was going.

"You mean, why did I change my mind about breaking up with him?"

Josh nodded.

"I just had a case of cold feet," she said shrugging. "The two of us had been together all throughout college, and as far as everyone else, including Peter, was concerned, we would be together for the long term. It's difficult to explain now, but I just felt a bit trapped, I suppose. So, I panicked, and one day I told him that I wasn't sure about us any more, that I wanted some time alone to get my head together."

"But it wasn't that simple," Josh stated.

Then Leah came into the kitchen and the conversation ended.

It was so obvious that he was going to propose – likely for her thirtieth birthday – but Olivia wasn't about to tell Leah that. She was so pleased for her.

"Wow, Olivia, you have it bad," Leah said, grinning and bringing her sharply back to the present.

"What?"

"When are we all going to meet Matt properly? That first time, I barely had a chance to talk to him before you bundled him off. Nervous I might work my charms on him, were you?"

Olivia laughed. Of course she wanted the others to get to know him, but she still wasn't sure. She wasn't sure whether or not she wanted to admit to herself – let alone the others – that she might have a future with him. She couldn't remember the last time she enjoyed herself so much, the last time she had laughed so much with any man other than Peter, the last time she had felt so happy. But, with the strange and disconcerting situation with Catherine, she thought grimly, it was difficult to know at this early stage if she and Matt had any future.

"Sometime soon," she said, and then added wickedly, "if Mammy Catherine allows it."

Leah laughed. "Don't mind her. She might be a good friend now, but Matt is a big boy and well able to make his own decisions."

"It's weird though. I'd swear the woman is spying on me. The other day, I called a plumber out to fix my washing machine, and later that evening Matt came over and oh-so-casually asked me if I'd had a visitor. I couldn't believe it. Catherine obviously must have been trying to suggest I was having it off with the plumber."

It *had* been really strange and rather worrying to think that Catherine was watching her every move. The tables were being well and truly turned, she thought with a grin, remembering her own curtain-twitching.

"Silly cow obviously has nothing better to be doing," Leah tut-tutted. "Next thing you know she'll have one of those surveillance cameras on you, probably trying to catch you and Matt doing the deed." She shook her head. "Nosy wagon."

"Speaking of cameras, I still have your camcorder. Josh left it in the boot of the car on the night of the party." Olivia was designated driver that night, and had driven the two home.

"Believe me, there's no rush," Leah drawled. "That footage might never seen the light of day. Apparently it's a big deal to get it all transferred onto disc, and I haven't a notion, so ..."

"Why not just pop the tape into one of those adaptors? I've got one at home. And we're finished here, aren't we? Fancy spending the night in Lakeview and we can watch it tonight? I want to give you back the camcorder anyway. I'd be afraid something might happen to it – Ellie might pick it up or –"

"Yeah, I love the idea of quiet night at yours. Perfect."

LATER BACK IN LAKEVIEW, Leah swung her legs beneath her and got comfortable on Olivia's couch.

"The party seems like so long ago already," she groaned, fiddling with the remote. "Back then when I was so innocent and thought that the business was mine and mine alone. I hadn't bargained for Amanda Clarke."

"It'll be funny. She was preening and practically drooling at the camera all night," Olivia said.

"Well as long as she wasn't drooling over the cameraman I don't mind," Leah laughed. She pressed *play* on the VCR remote control and watched excitedly as images from the party appeared onscreen. "Oh look, there's Kate. Wow, I'd almost forgotten she was still pregnant then. Doesn't she look great?"

Olivia had to agree that Kate did look great, much more like her old carefree self. It was disconcerting to hear from Leah that she was struggling lately.

"And look, there's bloody Amanda *again* – pretending that she doesn't know the camera is on her," Leah groaned. Then she let out a horrified squeal. "Aw, why didn't you tell me that dress made me look like a heifer?"

"What? You didn't look like a heifer, you looked gorgeous."

"Thank you for trying to make me feel better, but there is no disguising the fact that my backside looks like the back of a bus in that."

"Ah, probably the television, I think it could be set on widescreen or something," Olivia argued.

"Josh's camera work isn't too bad actually," Leah commented then. "He can be a bit zoom-happy sometimes. Oh look, he got some great shots out front – my goodness, I still can't believe that's my store – can you believe it, my very own store!"

Olivia smiled at her friend's almost childlike delight. She was thrilled it was all going so well for her. With all the work she'd done, not just now but throughout the years, Leah deserved every bit of her success.

Next the camera seemed to swerve sharply downwards towards the pavement, and for a few minutes all they could see were the tips of Josh's shoes.

"Just when I said he was doing so well ..." Leah groaned, as the camera seemed to focus on the ground and a pair of feet came into view.

"Nice shoes," Leah noted.

"Great, while he's chatting to guests, the tape's still running. No wonder it ran out so quickly. I wonder who he's talking to?" She picked up the remote and hit the volume control.

A flirtatious giggle ... a male laugh ... and instantly it was obvious that something was dangerously off kilter.

Josh's voice could clearly be heard. "... didn't know you were living around here these days."

"Didn't know you were a cameraman in your spare time either."

"Here, give me the remote," Olivia urged. "Fast-forward through that, there's nothing to see and – "

"Leave it." The words sounded like bullets.

"Leah, I really don't know if –"

"I said leave it."

Her heart pounding, Olivia sat back and said nothing.

Josh's voice again. "So how have you been?"

"Great and you?" Chirpily.

"OK."

"What's going on in there?"

Warily. "Leah's launch night – she's inside."

A smile in the woman's voice. "I see." The feet turned and pointed towards the store, and Olivia deduced whoever the woman was she was trying to get a peek inside. "So you two are still together then."

"Sharon ..."

"*Sharon?*" Leah repeated out loud, almost to herself.

"You know her?" Olivia asked, relieved.

"Yeah, I know her. Josh's ex."

"Oh."

Olivia stopped short, as Josh's voice again came through all-too-clearly.

" ... just one night. I never meant for it to –"

Leah's face paled, and she put a hand to her mouth.

Olivia's gaze stayed glued to the screen, horrified.

"Hey don't beat yourself up about it. Old times' sake and all that." A coquettish laugh.

"Oh god..." Leah intoned, her eyes wide and sorrowful.

"I'd better go back inside ..."

"No problem. Nice to see you again. And hey, don't worry, I'm not in the habit of wrecking other people's relationships. I'm a big girl."

Josh now sounded decidedly standoffish. "Right. Look, I'd better go. See you around."

Then sudden movement, as the camera swerved, and Josh seemed to walk back inside. Then they heard Kate's voice. "Josh over there – quickly. She's about to make her speech."

Then the screen went dark for a second until the camera cut this time to Leah, beaming delightedly at her boyfriend on her big night.

THIRTY-EIGHT

Leah's hands shook as she turned the key in the door to the apartment. She didn't think it was possible to feel such a mix of emotions all at once.

But as soon as she saw Josh dozing on the sofa, obviously not long back from work, one particular emotion came sharply into focus – betrayal.

Her legs felt like jelly. She didn't know how she was going to deal with this. She had watched a replay of the video three times, and each time things were even clearer. Josh had spent the night with his ex-girlfriend. There was no other explanation, despite Olivia's protestations.

"You can't just jump to conclusions – they could be talking about anything," her friend had said.

"Oh, come on, Olivia. 'Just one night?' 'For old times sake?' What else could they be talking about?"

"Go home and talk to Josh about it first– show him the tape, and see what he says. Whatever you do, don't accuse him straight out because you could have the complete wrong end of the stick."

"Olivia, I know as my friend that you're only trying to make me feel better, but we're not teenagers. There could only be one end of the bloody stick."

How could she have been so stupid? So naïve in thinking that she and Josh were back on track? It had been a bit rough while she was getting the shop set up because they rarely saw one another, but after the opening, it seemed like things were better than ever.

But that wasn't it, Leah saw now. It wasn't that things were getting back to normal – it was that Josh was feeling guilty.

Now there he was sprawled indolently on the couch, oblivious. For a brief second, Leah wished that she could go back in time and never have seen that video.

"Wake up!" she cried, throwing a cushion at him, adrenaline pumping through her veins as the anger slowly began to take over. On one hand, she wanted to keep throwing cushions at him all night, on another she wanted him to take her in his arms, give her a perfectly reasonable explanation, and they would both laugh at her silliness.

"Lee? What?" He sat up, eyes blinking in the bright light. "What time is it?"

Leah didn't answer, and a sudden calmness seemed to descend upon her as she crossed the room. She took the disc out of her handbag and put it into the machine.

"What's this? Oh, is it the launch party? Olivia finally gave back the video then. Is it any good?"

"Depends on how you look at it," Leah said flatly.

He looked at her and grimaced. "Ah no, don't tell me I messed it up again, did I? Aw I'm sorry – I probably had one two many – the focus might be all over the place."

"No, the focus is just fine, Josh. It's the sound that could have been little bit clearer, actually."

"You know what these things are like – with all that music in the background, and people chattering amongst themselves ..."

Amazing, Leah thought. He had absolutely no idea, no clue at all he'd been caught. Strange how you think you know someone so well and, once the mask had been removed, everything seemed to come sharply into focus.

"Hey, I think I'm doing all right so far," Josh said, smiling at the screen. "Why are you standing up? Come and sit down. I know you've seen this already, but I haven't ..."

He trailed off, following her gaze back to the TV screen, just as a pair of silver strappy shoes and red toenails came into view. For a few seconds he just stared at the footage and when Leah increased the volume, and he heard his voice come through loud and clear all the blood seemed to drain from his face.

"Lee –"

"Hush Josh, I'm trying to hear what you're saying. You know, you're right – it *is* almost impossible to make out what people are saying over the music and the crowd. So, how did Sharon enjoy the party? Funnily enough, I didn't see her there."

He looked at her then and despite Olivia's insistence that there might be any explanation, one look at his expression told her there was only one.

"I'm so sorry," Josh croaked.

At this, at hearing the admission so simply, so easily, a wave of emotion crashed over Leah, engulfing her in sorrow, disappointment, regret, anger.

I'm so sorry. In a way, she wished that he would try to deny it. But there was no denial. The facts were straightforward. Josh had cheated on her, plain and simple.

"It had nothing to do with you – with us," he was saying, his voice now a sharp contrast to his joviality earlier. "I love you – I still love you. You're the best thing that's ever –"

"Oh my God, I can't believe I'm even hearing this. *I'm* the most important thing? You *still love* me? What do you think this is – some poxy soap opera? How dare you admit to cheating on me and then have the cheek – the *gall* to say that it had nothing to do with me. Me – who agreed to love and stay with you, who put aside my own hopes and desire for a family because I thought I had found someone special. Someone I thought would be enough. How dare you turn around and tell me that it had nothing to do with me."

"But it's true! It was a stupid situation, a crazy drunken thing. I met Sharon one night in town and – "

Leah cut him off. "Stop it. I don't want to know." But she did, of course she did, yet at the same time, hearing how it happened would make it all the more real, and she didn't think she could handle that.

"I had no idea the tape was still running, I had no idea ..." He put his head in his hands.

"I see. So you would have been quite happy to keep it all a secret, happy to keep me in the dark."

"I wanted to tell you but – Lee, it was a mistake – a massive mistake."

"Yes, it certainly was."

"You and I were in a bit of a rut – you admitted that yourself. You were so wrapped up in getting the shop ready and we just weren't spending any time together any more. You were totally preoccupied – "

"Oh, I see. So poor little Josh wasn't getting the attention he wanted, the attention he deserved. So instead he decides to get it elsewhere – but not just anyone would do. Couldn't you have picked up some stranger from somewhere, Josh, if you wanted it that badly? Why did it have to be someone you knew, for goodness sake?"

And how dare he suggest that she was too preoccupied with the shop to give him the attention he deserved. What about the support *she* deserved? She'd been working her backside off trying to get this going – trying to get them the life they wanted. She knew Josh didn't want to spend the rest of his life under his father's thumb, and she had always thought that success in the shop meant that he could scale down a bit, and maybe start doing something for himself. Now, he had gone and ruined it all.

"Love, this is all my fault and I'm not blaming you at all. I suppose I'm just trying to let you know my state of mind at the time. You have to admit yourself that things weren't great between us."

"But that doesn't give you the right ..." She trailed off, shaking her head. Never in her wildest dreams had she imagined this. Somehow she had always thought too much of Josh, had believed him to be an infinitely decent person, which is why she didn't have to think too long about making the sacrifice of never having children with him. She thought she had found the elusive 'One' and, although things were never going to be exactly as she wanted them, she thought that she had enough. She loved Josh enough, was sure that he loved her too, and there was nothing or no one that could keep them apart.

"Why?" Leah asked now. "Was it really just because our sex life had dwindled? Or was it something more?" She couldn't quite believe that he would be so shallow as to throw away everything they had over sex.

Yes, things had gone downhill, but lately, she thought cringing, that had really begun to improve. Had he learnt a few new tricks from Sharon, she wondered, trying to banish unbidden thoughts of them together, what they might have been doing to one another, if Josh nibbled Sharon's ear in the same way that he nibbled hers, if his hands ran across ... Stop it, she warned herself. She would drive herself mad if she thought about it.

"It was a stupid, stupid mistake," Josh said, and Leah could see the beginnings of tears behind those dark eyes. "I know it sounds like a cliché, everything I say now is going to sound like a cliché, but, Leah, it's true. At the time, it had nothing to do with us – it was just sex, drunken pathetic sex, nothing more." He winced and ran a hand through his hair. "I knew I'd been an idiot and, believe me, I agonised about telling you for days – weeks – afterwards but things were finally coming together with the shop, and you were so happy. I knew it would ruin everything."

"What did I do to deserve such a thoughtful boyfriend?" Leah said coldly. "So, first of all, you went off with *her* because I wasn't paying you enough attention, and then you decided not tell me, because you were worried about my *feelings?*"

"Please believe me, I am so, so, sorry. The last thing I ever wanted to do was hurt you, Leah. I love you so much you wouldn't believe it."

He reached for her hand, and it took every ounce of strength she had to move away. She had never seen Josh cry, had never seen him so emotional. But as much as the sight moved her, she couldn't let such a tactic sway her.

"I know you probably won't believe me, but," he sat back on the couch, drained, "but I was going to propose to you on the night of the launch party. I had it all planned ..."

Stop it. Leah raged inwardly. *Don't do this – don't you dare do this to me.* Josh was as unconventional as they came, and as much as she loved him, Leah knew she could take nothing for granted. Now, hearing those words, her heart ached to the core.

"But when I went outside and met ... met her, well then, I just ... couldn't," Josh went on. "I couldn't in good conscience go in there and ask you to be my wife, ask you to spend the rest of your life with me. Because I knew then that I didn't deserve you, that I was a spineless, pathetic idiot who didn't know how lucky he was."

Leah finally sat down. She didn't know what to think or what to feel.

"I've blown it, Leah, I know that. I could sit here all night and try and think of a million different excuses, different reasons for why I did it. But there are none. I was an idiot and there's no getting away from it. I let you down, I let *us* down."

"Yes, you did," she whispered, and by then she was crying too.

"Look," He turned to her, his eyes sorrowful, "I won't insult you by trying to explain my way out of it. I made a mess of things, I know that. But you have to believe me when I say that I do love you. Yes, I know you're thinking I have a funny way of showing it, but I know in my heart that it's true. I don't think I can ever make you understand why I did it – I don't know if I understand it myself. But you mean the world to me, Leah, you always will. Our time together has been nothing short of amazing. You're my best friend."

"Josh, please ..." She couldn't listen to it any more. It was all so final. There was no going back from this. He had betrayed her in the worst way. She didn't know what she had expected. She supposed she thought he would beg for her forgiveness, ask her to try and understand, maybe even blame her a little?

In a strange way, she respected him for his honesty, his blatant regret for what had happened because it left her with her dignity intact. But she had lost her best friend, the love of her life, the person with whom she was so sure she would spend the rest of her life.

"I'm sorry," he said again, and before Leah could stop him, he reached across and placed a soft, salty kiss on her lips. "I love you, and you don't deserve this – I'm so sorry." With that, he stood up, and walked to the doorway. "I'll stay with Paddy tonight," he said with a haunted look in his eyes.

"Oh. Does he know about ...?"

"Of course not – no-one else knows. I wouldn't do that to you. I'll tell him I lost my keys or something ..." He knew she wouldn't want his friend knowing what had happened.

"OK." All of a sudden, she felt empty, bereft of all feeling for the situation, for Josh, everything.

"I'm so sorry," he whispered, before opening the door. "For everything."

Leah heard the apartment door close softly behind him.

"So am I," she whispered, warm tears coursing down her cheeks. "So am I."

THIRTY-NINE

Robin slowly opened her eyes, and groggily lifted her head off the pillow. The incessant shrill of the telephone had woken her out of her deep sleep, and was now piercing her throbbing brain. Which, she supposed, served her right for drinking so much last night. Who the hell could be ringing at this hour, she wondered, her eyes barely focusing on the digits on the alarm-clock. Ben's side of the bed was empty, so Robin deduced he must have already gone out for his morning jog. Catching sight of the time, she groaned. It was eight fifteen, and she was barely in the door after hitting the town in a major way last night with Anna and her other workmates.

"Robin, hey! Good morning!" She sat up as Marla's chirpy tones floated down the line, instantly waking her up. What on earth was her publisher doing ringing her at this hour? "Marla – hi. Is everything OK?"

"Everything's fine, just fine! Listen, can you come down for a meeting this morning? I couldn't get your agent on the line, so I haven't had the chance to tell her yet, but – this is such great news!"

"She's away," Robin said. "And what's great news?"

Still feeling very bleary, she could barely concentrate on the conversation.

"I really don't want to say too much on the phone," Marla said. "Just try and get your ass up here as soon as you can!"

With that Marla hung up and Robin was left staring at the phone in bewilderment as Ben came into the room.

"Good morning," he said mischievously. "*Someone* had a good night out last night." Then he noticed her bemused expression. "What's up?" he asked.

Robin rubbed her eyes. "It was the publishers – and to be honest, I'm not too sure what's up," she replied, dragging herself out of the bed, "but, knowing Marla, whatever it is, it'll be worth hearing."

AN HOUR OR SO LATER, Robin was wondering if she had actually woken up at all or whether lack of sleep had seriously affected her hearing. "Are you serious?"

"It's true," Marla said, her blue eyes shining. "We didn't want to tell you until we had the details worked out, but *Atchoo* will soon be appearing in French, Italian, Russian, German –"

"But it hasn't even gone on sale yet..." Robin blustered.

"Yes, but there's already a huge buzz and then now," she paused dramatically, and Robin knew instantly that there was more, "well, we didn't want to say anything until we knew for sure but," Marla took a deep breath, "Nickelodeon's come on board for TV!"

"What? The children's channel?"

"Yes, they want to do *Atchoo*." Marla beamed. "Yes! And we're going to make them pay a fortune for it. Gawd, this couldn't have happened at a better time. The book will be in the shops later this year and once news of this deal gets out, the trade will be hammering on our door!" She paced excitedly up and down the room. "Lucy's working on the publicity tour as we speak."

Just then, the aforementioned Lucy, Bubblegum's publicist, entered the room.

"Hi, Robin, great news," she said, hugging her enthusiastically.

Marla checked her watch impatiently. "I've got a ten thirty, so try and make it quick."

Lucy took a seat alongside Robin, and flicked through some papers.

"So, Robin, I think you'd better have a chat with your boss and see if he'll give you some more time off – "

"Ha!" Marla interjected. "If I get the big money I want from Nickelodeon, Robin, you might have more time off than you'll ever need."

"More time off? For what?"

"So at the moment, we're in the process of arranging some promotional appearances in Europe – they're going wild about your story, especially because of your own background with the allergy thing. Honestly we seem to have really tapped into a trend – everyone – American, French or German – knows, or has a child who suffers from some kind of allergy. The media are going crazy for it." She looked at her notes. "And they're going crazy for you in the UK because of the rights hype, and also probably because of the connection – you are Irish, aren't you?" she asked, when Robin's face dropped.

"Yes." Her heart thudded as she suspected what was coming. Oh, no, she couldn't do this. No way.

"We issued the press release earlier – and the media are going crazy over it, especially over the Nickelodeon interest. Phone's been ringing all day since. They really want a piece of you, Robin – school appearances, radio, TV, you name it. So we have to get you back home – and soon!"

Robin's stomach dropped. They couldn't – they *didn't* expect her to go to Ireland, did they?

"I'm telling you, from what I've been hearing, you'll be a bit of a national hero over there. I can already see the headlines: *Our very own JK* !"

Marla laughed when Robin eyes widened. "Hey, it's not quite Harry Potter, but by the time we're done here, who knows?"

Robin forced a smile.

"So, if you could have a chat with your boss, and let us know when you're available," Lucy said. "To begin with, we'll be concentrating mostly on the UK and there'll obviously be a major campaign in Ireland. Don't worry, we'll make sure you're reimbursed for your time," she added, when Robin looked sick to the stomach at the thought of it all, although not for the reasons her publisher suspected.

"We're really on a roll here, Robin," Marla enthused. "And with the way things are going, who knows where it will all end?"

FORTY

Olivia couldn't quite overcome a sense of nagging unease. There she was, forty-thousand feet in the air, sitting alongside the man she was almost certainly falling in love with, heading for a romantic weekend away, and still she couldn't relax.

She couldn't relax because it was the first time in four years she had left Ellie. Her daughter had gone to stay with Peter's family many times over the years without her, but this was the first time Olivia had actually left *her* behind.

And the worst part was with whom.

Her own parents were away this weekend, Peter's mother wasn't well, poor Leah had enough to contend with and she wouldn't dream of landing Ellie in on top of a still-hassled Kate.

Matt had suggested that she accompany him on a weekend work trip to the Black Sea Coast in the guise of romantic getaway.

"There'll be very little work involved, I promise," he said, when Olivia raised an eyebrow. "I'll just be going along for the ride. I might have to make one or two phone calls to the builder while I'm there, but other than that, I'm all yours."

He'd been so excited about it, so eager for them to spend some time alone together, that his enthusiasm was contagious. Olivia wanted to spend time with him too and – considering that she hadn't had a weekend away, not to mention a foreign holiday since her honeymoon – she was chomping at the bit for some sunshine.

Still, there was the small matter of a baby-sitter for Ellie.

"Catherine could take her - no problem. You'd be doing her a favour actually, she'd be brilliant company for Adam."

That first night at Catherine's still fresh in her mind, Olivia almost laughed out loud at the thought of it. Yes, Catherine had apologised and was being quite cordial lately, but still, she couldn't bring herself to trust the woman.

"Ellie doesn't really know her though," she said, trying not to betray her true feelings. Matt tended to be a bit touchy when it came to Catherine, still believing the sun shone out of her very pert backside.

"But she'd be with Adam, they'd have a ball. Please, Olivia, it's only for a couple of days."

"Couldn't we leave it until another weekend, maybe? At least until my parents or Peter's are available or – "

"But why – when Catherine's already agreed? I think it's very decent of her actually, and she's obviously trying to make amends."

Olivia bit her tongue. So she should be.

"Like I said before, I'll be too busy to get away soon – not to mention that we won't be able to get seats on the charter flights for love or money."

"Matt, I'd feel better if I knew Ellie would be looked after by someone she – "

"Of course she'll be looked after," Matt insisted, pulling her close to him. "Catherine really wants to do us the favour, and you know how well Ellie and Adam get on."

"That's true but – "

"It's only a couple of days, seventy-two hours at the most," he said, and Olivia noticed there was a touch of irritation in his tone. She sighed inwardly. To be fair, it *was* good of Catherine to offer, and by hesitating it looked as though she was being very ungrateful.

"Why don't we ask Ellie and see what she thinks?" she said, trying to sound brighter than she felt. Blast it, she should cop on and stop sounding like a fussy, overprotective mother. Ellie was four and well behaved. It was true that she adored Adam and would probably jump at the chance of going on her own 'weekend away' even if it was only across the green.

"Yay! Wanna go on my holidays!" Ellie skipped around the kitchen when she put it to her, and Olivia's heart sank.

"You'll have to stay in Catherine's house and you'll have to be very, very good," she warned, realising that there was no going back now. "As Mummy will be gone away with the keys, you can't come back here until I do – you know that, don't you?"

Ellie nodded, her eyes wide with excitement. "Can I play with Adam's toys, Mummy?" she asked, the thought of making lots of noise with Adam's *Bob the Builder* tools appealing to her enormously.

"You'll have to ask Adam first, hon," she said, and groaned inwardly at the arguments that Catherine would no doubt have to diffuse. "And you'll have to remember that Adam is being very good to let you stay with him, so you should let him play with your toys too."

"'K!" Ellie started to suck on her thumb, something Olivia noticed she did more often after her trips to Galway.

"Ellie don't do that, hon, it's a yucky habit," she scolded. Why her grandparents let her get away with it, Olivia didn't know, but it might have something to do with the fact that Peter had also sucked his thumb when younger, and perhaps they found it endearing. *And you certainly shouldn't do that in front of Catherine*, she mused suspecting that Catherine and her apparent obsession with discipline, would be scandalised.

Hours earlier, when they'd dropped Ellie off at the house before leaving for the airport; Catherine had behaved as though she and Olivia were old friends.

"Olivia, you look stunning in that outfit – it's really slimming on you. Matt, make sure you *do* show her around and don't be spending *all* your time in the hotel," she'd said laughing gaily. "Ellie, come inside, I've got some lovely new games for you and Adam in the playroom, and I've got a *very* special place for you to sleep." She ruffled Ellie's flyaway hair. Again, Olivia noticed that she really should get it trimmed, but her curls were just so cute and once they were gone, they were gone forever.

"I thought we might all go for a picnic by the lake tomorrow, what do you think?" Catherine continued. At this, the kids' eyes lit up and trance-like, they followed her down the hallway without a backward glance, almost like those children in the *Pied Piper* story, Olivia thought, feeling somewhat bereft.

"Now, are you two sure you won't have something to eat – or a cup of tea before you go?" Catherine went on, fussing over them all like a mother hen, her behaviour the complete opposite of before.

Matt refused, citing Friday afternoon traffic as an excuse, but Olivia caught his surreptitious wink.

"Olivia, try not to worry – Ellie will be fine." Catherine smiled sweetly. "I'm sure she won't even notice you're gone."

Olivia smiled just as sweetly back, but she didn't miss the barb. Oh why had she agreed to this?

But as the captain made his airport landing announcement for Burgas airport, she knew that it was way too late to change her mind, and pointless even thinking about it.

She was thousands of miles away, and although she certainly wouldn't be able to forget, she would have to try to put her beloved little Ellie to the back of her mind.

It was only a couple days. A couple of days with Catherine couldn't do any harm, could it?

FORTY-ONE

As soon as they began their taxi journey to the coast only fifteen minutes away from the airport, Olivia immediately understood why Matt was so in love with Bulgaria.

Somehow, she'd expected austere, ex-communist tower blocks and bleak, barren landscapes, but instead they were surrounded by lush pine forests and acres and acres of fertile vineyards.

The area reminded Olivia of a trip she and Peter had taken to Tuscany shortly after they were married, back when they had been able to get away at the drop of a hat. She shook her head. Lately she'd been thinking a lot about Peter. She supposed that since meeting someone new, it was inevitable that he should be in her thoughts, but she didn't want this to intrude on what should be a special time. This was all about Matt, not about Peter, and there was no point in raking up the past.

Matt had told her that the clear mountain air, mineral springs and mountainous pine forests in Bulgaria made it ideal for holidaymakers seeking something other than just a beach holiday.

"It's great for campers, hill-walkers and health-junkies," he said with a grin. "People are tired of the same old Spanish beach thing. This place has still got loads of rural charm."

"And what about when you've finished building all your apartment blocks?" she challenged, thinking that it would be a shame to blight this gorgeous scenery with high-rise apartment buildings like the Spanish Costas.

"It won't happen," Matt said, shaking his head defiantly. "They're big on planning regulations here because they're in a position to learn from mistakes elsewhere ..." He shrugged. "We wouldn't get involved in anything that would be detrimental to the area and subsequently, our clients."

"You really are a salesman," she grinned, giving him a gentle dig. "I suppose that's a popular line for your 'clients' too?"

"I might be a salesman but I'm certainly not a dishonest one," he countered. "We do a good job for people – they're investing not only a lot of money but a lot of trust in our experience and knowledge. I don't cheat people, Olivia."

"I wasn't implying that you did," she said, surprised at this vehemence at what was intended as a joking remark.

They were booked into a luxurious beach-front hotel, and Olivia hoped that the weekend would be spent lazily sunbathing around the pool, going out for relaxing meals in the evening and, hopefully, she thought with a grin, spending lots of time in bed together.

To her surprise, she didn't think of Peter once when she and Matt were together. It was a strange relief as Olivia had always assumed that when she finally took the huge step of making love with someone else, her husband would completely dominate her thoughts. But no, once her body took over, all memory of Peter was banished, at least for a little while, and she certainly wasn't going to let memories of the past affect this weekend.

The same couldn't be said regarding Ellie though. Olivia swore to herself that she wouldn't obsess over her; she swore that she wouldn't let any worries ruin the break. But it was hard not to, when as it turned out, Catherine didn't seem too bothered about interrupting them.

Olivia had called immediately upon arrival at the hotel to let Catherine know that they'd landed safely and to enquire about Ellie.

"Well, she had a right tantrum just after you left, but we calmed her down eventually," Catherine said breezily, and Olivia could literally feel the guilt stab at her heart.

Oh, no ...

"Was she upset about my leaving?"

Catherine sniffed. "Not really – more upset about the fact that she couldn't get her own way, I think. She and Adam were supposed to be taking turns on the swing this afternoon, but Missy wouldn't let Adam have a go at all."

"Really? That doesn't sound like Ellie."

"And then, she wouldn't eat her dinner. She seems rather fussy about her food actually. I presume you don't feed her take-aways *all* the time?"

Olivia winced. She and Ellie usually had a Chinese takeaway on Friday evenings – it was their little treat. She couldn't see Ellie getting upset over the fact that she wasn't getting it on that particular Friday though, could she?

"Of course not," she told Catherine. "She loves Chinese food normally ... "

"Really, Olivia, all those additives aren't good and Ellie's diet could certainly benefit from some fresh food. It seems she also brought some crisps and sweets in her overnight bag – said you told her she should share them with Adam. Perhaps *I* should have told you that junk food is banned in this house."

"Oh." Olivia didn't know how to answer this. She didn't let Ellie gorge on junk food but a little treat now and again wouldn't do any child any harm. And it would have been nice to share with Adam ...

"Anyway, I confiscated them. She roared for about an hour and a half but when she realised she wasn't going to get any attention from me, she copped onto herself."

Bloody hell, the nuns at school had nothing on you, Olivia wanted to say, but there was no point. Instead she tried a softly, softly approach.

"I'm sorry, I didn't realise. I hope she hasn't been too much trouble – "

"Well, she isn't the easiest child in the world, that's for sure, but what can you do?"

Olivia felt so guilty she could barely continue the conversation. A minute or so later, and after listening to a further bout of complaints about her daughter, she said goodbye.

Wow. Couldn't the woman wait until Olivia returned from her supposedly relaxing weekend 'break' before she started badmouthing her child? Couldn't she understand that Ellie didn't know or understand Catherine's 'rules', that she hadn't outlined anything of the sort when offering to take care of her? Before dropping her over, Olivia had phoned to ask if there was anything she should or shouldn't bring.

Catherine had simply told her to bring Ellie and not to 'be fussing'. So how could she say now that Ellie was being deliberately bold?

Blast Matt anyway for persuading her to leave Ellie for the weekend, blast Catherine for being such a cow!

Her cheeks burning with rage and her heart aching for her daughter, Olivia let herself into the hotel room.

Matt was unpacking his bag. "Well, how are they?" he asked.

She bit her lip. "Not so good. Apparently, Ellie is playing up."

He frowned. "Maybe it mightn't have been fair of me to rope Catherine into babysitting."

Olivia's head snapped up. "What? What do you mean 'rope' her into doing it? I thought she *offered* to take Ellie?"

Matt reddened.

"I don't believe this. You told me that Catherine was only too happy to take her. You told me that she would be offended if I didn't take up her 'very kind' offer. I can't believe you tricked me into leaving Ellie with someone who doesn't want her."

"Olivia, calm down – of course Catherine wants her – it just takes a bit of getting used to, that's all. And she would have had Adam anyway so –"

"But that's not the point. If Catherine's been landed with a baby-sitting job she really doesn't want, then chances are Ellie will have picked up on it. Children aren't stupid, you know."

"Olivia, it's hardly my fault she's a difficult child, is it?"

She was stunned. She couldn't believe this. "Matt, she barely knows that woman."

Hearing her words out loud, Olivia truly realised what she had done. She had left her precious little girl with a woman they barely knew, and one that neither liked all that much, just because she, selfish Olivia, wanted to get away for a saucy weekend with some man.

How could she? How could she have been so blind and so stupid to even consider such a thing? Just then, she wanted badly to get out of there, and fly home to her daughter, where she belonged.

"Look, I'm sorry, I didn't mean that like it sounded," Matt said, coming to her side. "I know was difficult for you leaving her and maybe I shouldn't have forced the issue. But Catherine is great with kids and, given time, I'm sure Ellie will be fine. They're just getting used to one another, that's all. Catherine will sort it out."

Saint Bloody Catherine! Although Catherine wasn't so saintly about leaving them in peace, was she? And the things she was saying about Ellie, well, to her it sounded as though she was deliberately trying to upset their weekend away by worrying her.

"It's not like Ellie to be throwing tantrums," she said.

"Look, kids play up sometimes, especially when there are other kids around – I'm sure that's all it is. Tell you what, why don't we go out for dinner now like we planned and I'll give Catherine a ring later to see how they're doing – OK?"

Olivia nodded reluctantly, but there was little else she could do at that stage.

They went for a delicious but ridiculously inexpensive meal on the seafront and, as she studied the menu, Olivia temporarily forgot about Ellie, while wondering how on earth the locals could possibly make any kind of profit charging prices like those.

"The cost of living is about one-fifth of that at home," Matt explained. "It's almost impossible to spend money here. That's why it's growing in popularity as a summer destination – there's real value to be had. As for the drinks, well, let's just say we could drink champagne here the entire weekend and it wouldn't break the bank." His eyes sparkled mischievously.

Olivia shook her head. "Not tonight, Matt," she said and sighed as she looked out to sea. It was a beautiful place – such a shame she couldn't relax and enjoy it properly.

Matt took the hint and seemed to accept her mind was elsewhere, and they said little else throughout the meal. Eventually, he suggested they head back to the hotel.

"I'll give Catherine a call then and see how they're getting on, OK?"

Olivia nodded. Maybe when he heard his childminder whinging down the phone he might understand her reticence to go partying.

Back in the hotel room, Matt dialled Catherine's number. "Catherine, hi – how's everything going?"

Olivia sat back on the bed and tried to decipher what the other woman might be saying but she couldn't hear anything other than a tinny squeal.

"Oh, no, I'm sure she didn't think that," Matt said, with a little laugh. "No, of course she was concerned but ... yes, yes, I'll let her know." He smiled and gave Olivia the thumbs-up. "Catherine, honestly, don't worry about it, you've enough to be thinking about ... no, no, of course I understand."

Olivia sat up. "What's going on?"

"No problem, I'll make sure I tell her. I'm glad they've calmed down now. Say hello to Adam for me in the morning. OK, talk to you soon ... we will, bye."

"What did she say?"

Matt scratched his head. "The kids are fine now, they've settled down nicely and they've just gone to bed."

"But what did she say about Ellie?"

"She was quite apologetic actually. Says she felt awful after your phone call and only afterwards it hit her how upsetting it could be for you. She's kicking herself now actually, and is really afraid she's ruined our break. Of course, I told her she was overreacting and that you were fine."

Olivia harrumphed. Catherine knew *exactly* what she was doing – what else would complaining about her daughter's behaviour do other than upset? And now she was trying to pretend to Matt that it had been unintentional? The calculating...

Matt sat down beside her on the bed. "Olivia, everything's fine. She said to tell you to relax and have a great time, that she's got everything under control back there." He reached across and stroked her cheek. "Does that make you feel better?"

"I suppose so." There was no point in having an argument with Matt about it, but it was fairly obvious to her that Catherine had an agenda. She didn't feel any better about leaving poor Ellie with her, but what could she do? She was here now.

"Good, because if that doesn't make you feel better, I'm sure there are other ways ..." he trailed a finger along Olivia's spine and, moving closer, kissed her softly on her lips.

"I'm sorry, Matt," she said, moving away from him. "I'm tired and at the moment, I can't think about anything other than Ellie."

"But she's fine," he said, wounded. "Why can't you accept that? Catherine said – "

"Catherine said too much as far as I'm concerned," Olivia picked up the romantic novel she'd been so happily engrossed in on the plane. "I'm sorry, but I can't do this now."

"Fine." Matt stood up and began to strip off while Olivia did her best to ignore him. Then he got into bed and, turning away from her, reached across and resolutely turned off his bedside lamp.

She sighed inwardly. If Catherine's antics had been a ploy to disrupt their romantic weekend away, then it was one that had worked very well indeed.

FORTY-TWO

She couldn't comprehend the relief she felt when touching down at Dublin airport.

The weekend had improved somewhat after that first night, and after a few more (not-so-upsetting) phone calls to Catherine, Olivia had no choice but to try and make the best of it.

Still, for the remainder of the stay, she and Matt had been awkward and uncomfortable with one another, and the so-called romantic break they'd expected hadn't materialised. She didn't quite know how she felt about this; in fact, she couldn't think about anything other than seeing Ellie.

"I'm sorry you didn't enjoy it," Matt said on the drive to Lakeview, "but I had no idea you'd find it so hard without Ellie."

"I had no idea, either, to be honest," she said sadly, "but since that first night, I couldn't stop thinking and worrying about her."

"Well, it won't be long until you see her now," he said, reaching across and patting her hand, "and I'm sure she can't wait to see you either."

"The same applies to you and Adam," she said, feeling almost as though a weight had been lifted from her shoulders, now she was back on Irish soil.

He shrugged. "He's used to my being away a lot."

"I suppose." Of course, she had forgotten that Matt too was used to being away from his son, whereas this was the first time she and Ellie had been apart. It definitely wasn't an experience she wanted to repeat anytime soon.

Finally they reached Cherrytree Green, and Olivia almost bolted out of the car and up the path.

"Ah, here's the lovebirds!" Catherine was all smiles as she greeted them at the door. "Did you have a good time?"

"We had a lovely time," Olivia smiled back, unwilling to let the cow know that she had got her way. "But it's nice to be back all the same."

"The kids are out playing in the back garden, not a bother on them. Honestly, Olivia, since that first night, Ellie's a different child. I think once she knew she'd overstepped the mark she learnt her lesson."

Olivia followed her through to the kitchen and out the back door where she could hear children's laughter float through the air. The sound of Ellie's carefree giggle was instantly a balm to her soul.

"Like I said, it's really not like Ellie to be so difficult," she said, stepping out into the garden. "I'd imagine she was just getting used to –" She broke off when at the sound of her mother's voice, Ellie turned and raced towards her, arms outstretched. Olivia's heart lifted. "Hi, darling, I really missed ... *oh my goodness*."

Getting a proper look at Ellie, Olivia stood back stunned. She could hardly believe her eyes.

"What on earth did you do?" she shrieked accusingly at Catherine. Ellie's gorgeous curls had been cut away, and her daughter was now – unbelievably – sporting a blunt fringe!

Catherine looked right back at her, all innocence. "After after what happened that first night, I didn't really want to say anything on the phone ..." She trailed off and glanced at Matt. "You did say she was really upset."

"How dare you?" Olivia couldn't comprehend how angry she felt at that moment. "How *dare* you go and cut my daughter's hair without my permission ... what the *hell* were you thinking?"

"Olivia, calm down," Matt began.

"What? I hope for your sake, Matt, that you didn't know about this, because if you did ... "

Catherine bit her lip. "Maybe I should have said something, but I didn't want to upset you – "

"Of course you should have said something! You should have asked for my permission, and if you had, you would know that I would never, *ever* cut her hair that way!"

Ellie looked upset. "I'm sorry, Mommy, I didn't mean it," she said, and her bottom lip began to tremble.

Olivia lifted her up and kissed her gently on the temple. "It's OK, honey, it wasn't your fault."

"Well, that's the thing ..." Catherine began, and was Olivia imagining it, or did she say this with a hint of a satisfied smile? "Ellie brought some chewing gum with her and –"

"What? She did *not* bring chewing gum with her, she isn't allowed chewing gum – she knows that."

Ellie had by now buried her face in her mother's chest, so she couldn't see her expression.

Catherine put a hand on her hip. "Well, she must have got it from somewhere because she came in on Saturday and it was all stuck to her hair. It was everywhere." She looked at Matt exasperated. "I combed and combed it but there was no way I could have got it out. In the end I had no choice but to cut it out – there was nothing else I could have done." At this, her eyes sparkled with tears – *feigned* tears. Olivia was convinced of it.

"It's OK, I'm sure you did your best," Matt said, putting a hand on her arm.

"But why didn't you tell me?" Olivia said. "Why didn't you phone and *ask* me if it was OK to cut it out, if it was OK to cut her lovely hair in this – this grotesque style!" She didn't want to say too much in front of Ellie but she was pretty sure her daughter had no idea what 'grotesque' meant.

"Honestly, I thought and thought about it, but in the end I decided that there was no point in upsetting you again so I just went and did what I thought was best. You didn't see how bad it was, Olivia. The hairdresser said she'd never seen anything like it. In fairness, I don't know how she managed to save so much of her hair." At this Catherine burst out crying. "I really didn't know what to do!"

"Oh, Catherine, don't." Matt put a comforting arm around her shoulders and Olivia felt like throwing something at him. Could he not see what a terrible thing she'd done? She had no right to make that decision, no right to do something like that without consulting Olivia about it. It would take ages for Ellie's hair to recover, despite the so-called best efforts of the concerned hairdresser.

"Olivia, surely you can understand the position she was in," Matt said. "What was the point of telling you over the phone? What would you have done?"

"I would have got the first plane home, that's what I would have done. But if I were looking after someone else's child I wouldn't take it upon myself to make such a decision. Her hair is ruined, for goodness' sake."

"Can we go home now, Mummy?" Ellie pleaded.

Catherine pointed inside. "Her things are in the hallway," she sniffed tearfully.

"Fine."

Without a word of goodbye to either of them, Olivia turned and walked inside. "Yes, we're going home," she answered her daughter, who hugged her even tighter. "Back home where we should be."

FORTY-THREE

Leah was horrified. "You really should have asked me," she said when the following day Olivia and the newly coiffed Ellie visited her at the shop. "I would have been delighted to look after her, you know that."

"I'm sorry I didn't now, but I didn't want to put you on the spot – you've enough on your plate at the moment." In all the years they'd known one another, she had never seen her friend look so lost, so deflated.

She kicked herself once again for agreeing to go away with Matt when by rights she should have been around for Leah. "By the looks of things, you're still very busy here too." The shop was packed to the gills and Olivia almost had to fight her way through the crowds to get to the kitchen out back. Amanda was out front, flitting around like a butterfly on one wing and Olivia suspected – spying her casually flicking through a newspaper when there was a queue a mile long – about as much use.

Leah gave a rare smile, the first one Olivia had seen since the split with Josh. "I know, it's great, isn't it? But seriously, you should have asked me to take her. Alan and Amanda could have looked after things here and I certainly could have done with the diversion. I wouldn't have cut her hair without asking either – not like that anyway," she added archly.

Ellie was out of earshot and incredibly, Olivia thought, seemed to be enjoying all the attention her new hairstyle was getting. Eva had been equally horrified and the previous evening Olivia had to physically stop her mother from marching across the green to "tell that madam exactly what I think of her."

"But tell me, what happened afterwards?" Leah asked. "What did Matt say?"

Olivia shrugged. "We went straight home, obviously. He called over afterwards and, to be honest, he didn't say much other than to reiterate that Catherine had done what she thought was best, and didn't want to upset me by telling me blah, blah, blah." She rolled her eyes. "The weekend was a disaster, Leah. Bulgaria was wonderful but I was so stressed about Ellie being with that – that *witch*, that I just couldn't relax and enjoy it." She explained how Catherine had – purposefully, she was sure of it – tried to upset her by insinuating that Ellie was being a nightmare.

"I find that very hard to believe." Leah gazed lovingly at the little girl, who was staring fascinated at the huge blocks of chocolate that had been delivered earlier that day. They lay there like lumps of rock waiting for a talented sculptor to begin work.

"Well, I did too, and, as it turned out, it was *Adam* that was causing problems, not Ellie."

"Oh?"

"Ellie knew I was upset about her hair, and she told me that when Catherine took them for a day out at the lake, Adam picked up a dirty piece of chewing gum from one of the benches and put it in his mouth."

That wasn't the worst bit, Olivia thought. Back home, Catherine had instantly presumed it was Ellie who had somehow 'sneaked in' the gum. But as it turned out, it had been Adam who, when finished chewing the dirt and grime, had taken it out of his mouth and begun playing with it.

"Adam gave me the bold bubblegum, Mummy," Ellie'd said, troubled that once again she'd been betrayed by her new friend. "An' it got caught in my curls."

Leah shook her head. "And the silly cow never even thought to wonder if it could be Adam."

"Nope. He can do no wrong as far as she's concerned. Don't get me wrong – he's a nice kid but he's very spoiled, and personally, I think he's crying out for his dad's attention. Matt's away a lot, and it's Catherine who looks after him most of the time."

"A regular little family, aren't they?" Leah said sarcastically. "That whole thing with her is odd if you ask me."

"You know, I think you might have been right about her having some kind of crush on him," Olivia said, admitting it out loud. "But what should I do? Things are shaky enough between me and Matt as it is, and we've only been together a little while. He can't see any wrong in what she's doing, and he won't hear a word said against her."

"And how do you feel about it all? I mean, despite all this business with Catherine, do you think he's worth pursuing?"

"To be honest, I don't know where I stand with him, let alone how I feel. We tiptoed around one another at the weekend – it was hardly the love-in that we'd planned." Olivia chuckled, although it wasn't at all funny. "So, have you spoken to Josh since?" she asked, tentatively changing the subject and instantly a shadow crossed her friend's pretty face.

"I'm seeing him tomorrow," Leah admitted, almost shyly, as if she was being weak. "He's phoned every day since, but it's been hard ..." She trailed off, a catch in her voice.

"I know it is." Olivia touched her gently on the arm. "Still, I think you're doing the right thing by meeting him. You two still have some things to talk about, I'm sure."

"Yeah, mostly about how he should take the rest of his stuff and get out of my life for good," Leah said vehemently, but Olivia could see the sorrow in her eyes. "Just go and meet him and keep an open mind about what he has to say."

"I suppose." Leah didn't look at all enamoured of the prospect. "I might need a shoulder to cry on afterwards though."

Olivia grimaced. "We're invited to Kate's tomorrow night though, aren't we?"

Leah rolled her eyes. "I'd forgotten about that."

"Does she know about you and Josh?"

"No, I didn't want to say anything, because let's face it, she'd probably want to hunt Josh down and kill him."

Olivia nodded. As they both knew only too well, Kate was fiercely unforgiving about any wrongdoings towards her friends.

"I hope she's in the mood for vino this time though." Leah raised a tiny grin. "Something tells me I'll need to drown my sorrows."

"Well, look, there's no point in you driving then. Why don't I call to you beforehand and we'll go together. Mum's taking Ellie, and from what I can make out, is determined to do a patch-up job on her hair." She grimaced. "Not sure it's such a good idea but what can I do? It has to be better than – "

"Girls, girls!" Just then Amanda burst through the door and cut short the remainder of Olivia's sentence. Typically dramatic, she was flushed and seemed to be waving a newspaper over her head. "You have just *got* to read this!"

"Let me guess," Leah drawled. "BTs are having a mid-season sale?"

Amanda shook her head impatiently, as she flicked through the pages. "Nope, even better. It's last Saturday's paper actually, and I would have missed it only ...oh, where has it gone?"

"What is it?" Olivia asked, and then she and Leah gawped in unison as they caught sight of Robin staring back at them from the

Weekend Lifestyle section of the *Independent,* the headline over-head proclaiming: *Nuts about Robin – Irishwoman Takes US Publishing World by Storm.*

"Publishing world ...what?" Olivia asked, looking at the others. "I didn't know Robin had written anything."

"Neither did I," Leah said, and by her tone, Olivia knew she was a little hurt. She and Robin normally shared everything and Olivia knew that her friend had told Robin about her and Josh's recent split.

"According to the paper she's being paid a fortune for writing these dinky little picture books," Amanda said. "Aren't they always saying that you should write about what you know and, by the looks of things," she added, eyes widening, "Robin's making a nice little career for herself by doing exactly that."

"You don't mean ...?" Olivia's sentence trailed off as she scanned the article. As she tried to read the words, she felt as though a firework had just gone off in her stomach. Robin writing stories about ...

Leah, who'd since read the article from beginning to end, looked up from the newspaper.

"She has," she confirmed, astonishment written all over her face. "Robin's written a book about allergies – children's allergies – and now it's being made into a cartoon or a TV series."

Olivia looked at her in disbelief. "You're not serious."

"I know!" Amanda cried. "Believe me, Robin was the *last* one I'd have expected to do something like that." She put a hand on her hip. "I'm a bit annoyed, to be honest – I had hoped to try my hand at one of those baby manuals. But seems freaky old Robin has beaten me to it. Lucky cow, I bet she'll get to go on TV and everything."

"That's not all," Leah said. "It says here she'll be doing a promotional tour shortly. I can't *believe* she kept quiet about that. I'm always asking her when she's coming home."

Olivia said nothing. She was still coming to terms with the fact that Robin had written not just a book – but a book for children. With allergies.

"So, she's finally coming home, then," Amanda said. She shook her head wistfully. "Finally all the old gang together again." At this, Leah nudged her. "Besides Peter of course, sorry, Olivia," she added hurriedly, but Olivia didn't even notice.

She was too busy wondering what would happen when her old friend returned home, and when their paths crossed – as Olivia was certain they would – what would they have to say to one another?

FORTY-FOUR

Catherine rarely frequented the corner shop, preferring to get a full grocery shop in the larger supermarket on the outskirts of town, but today she had an ulterior motive.

In the few times she'd been in there since moving to Lakeview, mostly popping in for milk or after a day out with Adam, she'd realised that the shop's proprietor was a bit of a gossip and hoped that today the woman would be in fine fettle.

To her delight, the small shop was empty and the shopkeeper Molly gave her a friendly wave. "Warm outside today, isn't it?" she said, rolling her eyes and fanning her face.

Catherine gave her a winning smile. "It certainly is. I'm painting my dining room at the moment, but it's hard to keep going in this heat."

Molly leaned forward, her eyes shining with interest. "Oh, are you living locally?"

"Yes, Cherrywood Green. It doesn't need a lot of work, but still you have to make it your own."

"Of course, you bought Eileen Kavanagh's place, didn't you?" She made a half-hearted sign of the cross. "God rest her, she was a lovely woman."

"So I believe."

"Yes, I thought I'd seen you in here before. You moved in just before Easter, wasn't it?"

Wow, you don't miss a trick, do you? Catherine thought.

All the better.

She nodded. "It's a lovely place and very quiet, but at the same time, it can be hard to get to know people."

"Oh, I wouldn't worry too much about that, pet. Given time you'll know everyone, although in fairness most of them keep themselves to themselves up there on the Green. They're all a lot older than you too, of course – I can't see stuffy old bridge parties being your thing." She laughed gaily before adding as an afterthought. "So, you're there on your own then?"

"Single white female, that's me," Catherine agreed, with a self-effacing grin.

"Ah, I can understand then why you might find it lonely. No man on the scene at all?"

"Unfortunately, no. So that's why I'd like to get to know a few more people around here."

"Well, you know me now," the older woman laughed and extended a hand. "Although we haven't been properly introduced. I'm Molly Cronin."

"Catherine Duffy," she said, shaking Molly's hand with enthusiasm. "Although, now that I think of it," she added as if just remembering, "I do know one of my neighbours, although not very well really. Olivia Gallagher?"

"Of course. Wasn't I one of the first people Olivia met when she moved into the area? She's a dote, so she is. And I suppose she was a bit like yourself – you know, a single woman, no husband or boyfriend to look after her."

Catherine held her breath and waited for her to continue.

Molly shook her head sadly and then lowered her voice

slightly. "Poor thing, in my opinion, she deserves a nice romance, so she does."

"I don't know her all that well - she's a little bit shy and I didn't want to pry - but I believe she lost her husband ...?" She let the sentence trail off in the hope that Molly would take the bait.

The older woman looked pained. "Yes, it was a terrible thing, a terrible tragedy altogether. She often pops downtown with the little one to buy flowers for the grave, and it would break your heart seeing the two of them head off – Ellie with her little pictures and everything ..." She trailed off, a sorrowful expression on her face.

"A tragedy?"

"Yes." Molly went on to fill Catherine in on the situation with added gusto. "Oh, it happened before she moved to Cherrywood Green, and Olivia doesn't say much about it, but reading between the lines ..."

"Between the lines?" Catherine made a mental effort to stop behaving like a demented parrot.

Molly leaned forward and gave a glance towards the back of the shop, apparently not wanting to be overheard, but unable to resist passing on the rest.

"Apparently, she had some part in what happened to her husband. He had a turn and she wasn't there to help him. You do know she used to be a vet? But had to give it all up when the child was born. I think she does a bit now and again though for the Animal Centre up around Enniskerry."

"You said he had a turn? Like a heart attack?"

"Supposedly – and him only a young man. Isn't it terrible? But according to Maeve McGrath one who lives a few doors down from her – and who if you ask me is an awful motor mouth –" she added disapprovingly, "Olivia was cut up with guilt about it because she wasn't there to help him."

"But how was it her fault?"

"It happened at home, not above in the green mind, they were living in Dublin at the time, but anyway, the way I heard it, that day she was supposed to be home early, but she was called out on some emergency, and she was late back. If she'd been back a bit earlier she might have been in time to help him."

Catherine was thinking out loud. "But he could have had a heart attack at any time."

"That's what I thought, but sure, who knows how people deal with these things? Obviously, the poor crature felt she should have been there and, if she was, then she might have saved him, and all the rest of it. It's a very big if, but if that's how she feels, then God love her, that's how she feels." Molly blessed herself again.

Catherine nodded absently.

"And of course, wasn't it ten times worse because hadn't she only just found out that they were going to have a baby? They'd been trying for years, seemingly," she added authoritatively.

"How awful," Catherine murmured, although her mind was elsewhere. "You say the neighbour told you all this?"

Molly reddened. "Well, no, not all of it ... I mean, I know Olivia well of course, but some things you don't ask straight out. No, Maeve let slip a few things, and a lot of it I figured out for myself."

"Oh." So it was just tittle-tattle, gossip, Catherine realised.

Still, she'd shed some light on the situation. And oh, wouldn't Matt just love to try and help Olivia through that? Be her saviour and knight in shining armour.

"The poor thing," She plastered a compassionate smile on her face. "Now I understand why she can be so shy and mysterious sometimes."

"Yes, she can be like that. Now, you won't tell her about our little chat, will you?" she said, backtracking slightly. "I'd hate Olivia to think I was talking about her behind her back. She's a lovely girl and a good customer and normally I wouldn't say a word but ..."

"My lips are sealed," Catherine soothed. "And sure, you only told me because you know I'm keen to make friends, isn't that it?"

"That's exactly it," Molly agreed. "And if you two are going to be friends, it was only fair to fill you in on Olivia's background, just so you wouldn't put your foot in it or anything. I think you two might be just what the other needs actually – you both could go out hunting for men together."

"Maybe," Catherine said with a smile, before adding, "Of course, I'd hate for Olivia to think *I* was – "

"Don't worry about that, sure if she asks, I'll let on I hardly know you," Molly said with a maternal smile. "Although now you're a bit more settled in Lakeview, I do hope we'll see a lot more of you from now on."

Oh, you'll see plenty of me, don't worry, Catherine thought to herself, as she smiled and said goodbye to mouthy Molly. *I'm not going anywhere...*

FORTY-FIVE

Leah had agreed to meet Josh on neutral ground – in a café near the apartment – and it was amazing, she thought, how calmly and maturely she was managing their break-up.

There was no going back, she had told him, no second chances. He hadn't said much, but she had been shocked upon seeing him. His eyes were bloodshot, his face pale and he looked as though he hadn't slept in weeks.

Somehow, the calm, mature, adult way they were dealing with the situation made things much harder. In some ways, she longed to have a screaming match with him and hoped he would act like the typical cheating scumbag by begging for her forgiveness and swearing that he would never do it again.

But Josh didn't do that. He seemed to calmly accept that their relationship was over and kept telling her that he would go along with whatever she wanted to do.

"Whatever makes you happy," he said, and Leah thought mournfully that it would be a long time before anything made her happy again.

In the meantime, she had thrown herself into work at the

shop, experimenting with different flavours, textures and producing way more fresh chocolate than could be sold.

She wasn't particularly looking forward to this get-together at Kate's house tonight though. The invitation had been issued ages ago, and much as she needed to get away from her own company and her own thoughts, she wasn't sure that it would do her any good.

But when Leah and Olivia reached the house that evening, Kate seemed in flying form.

"Dylan's fast asleep," she said gleefully upon their arrival and, despite her own heavy heart, she was gladdened to see her friend looking much better.

This time she was fully dressed, although clearly, she wasn't yet back to herself, the shapeless tracksuit hanging off her rakish frame. By contrast, and to make herself feel better, Leah's hair was freshly styled, and she was wearing a bright multi-coloured Pucci-style top over blue jeans. Blast it, she'd thought, she might as well look as though she was coping.

"Come through," Kate said, leading them through to the kitchen, which was normally spotless and uncluttered, had now been taken over completely by baby-related appliances and paraphernalia. Babygros were drying on the radiator, stacks of Milupa lined against the wall, a whole vat of Johnson's baby powder on the countertop, and enough nappies to cover every baby born in Ireland for the next twenty years. Who'd have thought babies needed so much? Leah thought eyes widening, as she tried to take it all in.

"Now, I thought I'd get Dylan down much earlier," she twittered, "and I completely underestimated how long it would take to get dinner organised. So, if you two don't mind, do you think we could order Thai or Chinese or something?"

"Fine by me," Leah said easily and took a seat at the table alongside Olivia.

"Me too."

"Great. Now where did I put that menu – although at this stage Michael and I know it almost off by heart and ..." She stopped, only then sensing the atmosphere. "What's wrong?"

"Josh and I have broken up," Leah said, as calmly as she could muster. "I just wanted to let you know, and I don't want my problems to get you all down. I came here tonight to try and forget about it – so Kate, don't look like that."

"But – but, when did this happen? More to the point *what* happened?" Kate spluttered, sitting down alongside her. "No, hold on – don't tell me anything yet – I'll open a bottle first."

As Kate rummaged in the fridge, Olivia gave Leah's hand a reassuring squeeze. She didn't want to have to relive the whole scenario, but it was clear she didn't have much of a choice.

"The stupid ...!" Kate exclaimed, when Leah explained about the tape. "How could he?"

Leah didn't need anyone to rant and rave about Josh's betrayal: she was still trying her best to make sense of all of this, was trying to come to terms with how, if he loved her, he could still cheat on her.

Whereas could only ever see things in black and white – for her, grey just didn't exist.

"Everyone has moments of madness and can do things they wouldn't normally dream of doing. Some people aren't as strong as you are, Kate."

"There's something else," Leah said, refusing to look at them. "He told me that the night of the launch party, he was planning to propose." She paused, trying to blink back the tears. It was this admission that had got to her the most. "But once he met up with her he ..."

"Changed his mind?" Kate cut in and, seeing how much her remark stung, softened her tone. "Look, I'm sorry – I'm not trying to hurt you. But even you have to admit that it was a bit convenient of him to mention this when he was looking for forgiveness."

"That's where you're wrong. Josh never once asked me for forgiveness, he never once tried to explain his guilt away. All he asked was that I understand that he loves me and that he made a big mistake. He seemed to accept that he had messed things up and he didn't ask me to take him back."

People did make mistakes, didn't they? And didn't some couples go on after infidelity? Didn't they work even harder as a result? Didn't they forgive and forget?

Olivia nodded. "At the end of the day, you're the one that knows him best. You said before that you feel like you know him inside out. Do you believe that he is genuinely sorry for what has happened? Do you believe him when he says that he loves you, that he's always loved you and that he simply made a mistake? Do you think you can forgive and forget?"

Leah was silent for a moment. Those were the questions she'd been asking herself and she knew in her heart of hearts that her answer was of utmost importance.

"Do you think you can forgive him?" Olivia asked again.

It took Leah an age to speak.

"I don't know ... I ... think so," she answered hoarsely.

"Oh, come on!" Kate put her head in her hands in blatant disbelief. "Olivia's hardly the best person to be giving advice, is she?"

"Despite what you might think," Olivia said, her tone measured and calm, "I have no problems with forgiveness – in fact, I think it's good for the soul. Leah's entitled to ask my opinion and I'm entitled to give it."

Kate sniffed. "You two are unbelievable. Is there anything you *wouldn't* forgive, Olivia? Speaking of which, I see our old buddy is finally returning to the fold too, fresh from making money out of other people's problems. Typical, wouldn't you say? Here's an idea, Leah, why don't you ask *Robin* how to deal with this? I'm sure she'd only be too delighted to give you advice – before turning around and stabbing you in the back."

Leah shook her head sadly. "I thought that motherhood might soften you up a bit, Kate, but no, you're the same unforgiving, bitch you've always been."

"What? I've only ever tried to stick up for you two ..."

Kate just couldn't comprehend that sometimes people made mistakes, that it was inevitable, human nature, a simple fact of life. "We're not in college any more, and things are bad enough without your judgmental attitude."

"What? I can't believe you two sometimes! How long are you going to keep defending her, forgiving her ..."

"She was thousands of miles away," Olivia interjected calmly. "It would have been impossible – "

"It's not impossible to come home to promote her crappy book though, is it? And yet she wouldn't dream of coming home for a funeral."

"That was all a long time ago," Olivia said calmly, "and *I've* forgotten all about it – *I've* let it go, so why can't you?"

"Because I just can't!" Kate cried, and Leah was taken aback by how vehemently she felt – still. "So much for our friendship - our grand summer reunion."

"Don't you think that maybe Robin's suffered too?" Leah asked. "When was the last time you spoke to her? Five, six years?"

"I have nothing to say to her, not now, not ever and certainly not when she comes over here on her 'rub our noses in it' tour."

"Kate, that's crazy," Olivia said, laying a soothing hand on her arm. "There's no point. Robin is Robin and," she shrugged, "I'm sure she has her own regrets. It's in the past. And we have to let it go."

Still, Leah wondered then, as she listened to her friend trying to persuade Kate to forgive and forget, would Olivia – the strongest and most magnanimous person she had ever known – be so willing to do the same once she came face to face with Robin again?

FORTY-SIX

It had been seven long years since she'd seen the place, and still, Robin didn't miss it.

Too many bad memories, she supposed, looking tentatively around the arrivals area of Dublin airport. Too many painful reminders of everything that had gone wrong in her life since university, and not enough positives to balance things out.

Still, it would have been nice to have had the time to go home to Waterford this weekend but because this would be a very short stay, her mum was travelling up on the train to visit her.

Having obtained the obligatory shin-bashing from the golf club brigade at the carousel, which really helped her mood, Robin eventually claimed her luggage and made her way through customs. She paused slightly before coming through to the arrivals area. Would she recognise anyone? Worse – would anyone recognise *her*? Oh, come off it, she admonished herself. Who do you think you are – Madonna? Of course, no one would recognise her – no one knew she was here yet even.

Now, sitting in a taxi and heading towards her city-centre hotel, Robin thought back to the last summer in Dublin before graduation. Back before she and her friends went out into the big bad world, and everything went a little crazy.

They had all been so confident, so cheerful so *optimistic*. They all knew where they were going, and what they wanted to do, and despite their petty little differences, were so sure that they would honour their reunion plans, so certain that the friendship would stay the same forever.

Didn't any of them Robin thought, feeling a curious mixture of sadness and regret as they drove along O'Connell Street, realise how naïve they had been?

LATER THAT EVENING Leah was discussing something with Alan, when, outside the store, she caught sight of what had to be an apparition.

The features were the same, and the hair was the same but a little longer, but this girl was way too stylish and way too confident to be the same.

"Oh my gosh!" she cried, racing outside. "It's really you, isn't it?"

Robin smiled nervously. "Hi, I was going to phone, but I didn't have the number and I wasn't sure ..." She trailed off, as Leah reached forward and engulfed her in a huge hug.

"I can't believe you're actually here!" Tears sprang to her eyes. She had known Robin was coming home of course, but at the same time, it didn't seem real. After all these years, after all this time ... she couldn't comprehend how great it was to see her again.

"I know, it's strange for me too. The city's changed quite a bit since I was last here." Robin raised an eyebrow. "What's with that big flagpole on O'Connell Street?"

Leah laughed. "Not quite the Chrysler building, is it?"

"No, not quite," Robin grinned.

"When did you get in? Where are you staying? Are you here

for long and ...oh, for goodness' sake, listen to me rabbiting on. Come inside, I have to stay and work late this evening, unfortunately, otherwise we could go for a drink. Don't worry," she added, when Robin looked slightly wary, "there's nothing dangerous in there. The chocolates are all behind glass or boxed up. Everything else is safely locked away out back."

"I'm sorry, I didn't mean –"

"Don't be silly. It's fine. I'm in discussion at the moment with my suppliers about introducing some nut-free and diabetic chocolate. It's amazing, years ago you were the only allergy sufferer I knew – these days I'm getting non-stop enquiries."

Robin smiled. "We're a pain in the butt, aren't we?"

"Not at all." Leah led the way through the shop, proud to show off her little empire to this new, stylish and mature Robin. As it was teatime there was a lull in custom, so they could at least have a bit of an uninterrupted chat.

"I'm impressed," Robin said, checking out Leah's elaborate displays. "These look good enough to make me want to take a chance."

"Ah, I wouldn't recommend it," Leah grimaced, before adding wickedly, "Then again, if you want to die happy ..."

The two girls laughed.

"So where are you staying?"

Robin smiled, as if a little embarrassed. "They put me up in the Westin. It's fabulous – way too good for me. Irish hotels have come a long way since I left, I can tell you."

"Well, you're hot property now – a famous author and all that."

"I'm not a famous author. To be honest, I'm not even an author. I just got lucky and happened to be in the right place at the right time, that's all."

"That's hardly true. You were always good at stringing words together, Robin. In college, you were always the one with the interesting theories and subject matter. Professor Hughes was mad about you."

"Perhaps." Robin wasn't convinced, and then Leah realised that her friend hadn't changed that much after all – she was still the same reticent and insecure Robin she'd always been. This was strangely comforting.

"So, what about you?" Robin asked. "Are you and Josh still – "

Leah's face clouded. "Yes, but I don't want thoughts of that idiot to bring me down. Things are bad enough as it – hey," she broke off, remembering. "I was cheesed off earlier because Kate cried off from my birthday dinner and – "

"Don't worry, I hadn't forgotten. It's just with this jet lag I'm not sure what day I have. Happy Birthday."

"But you'll come out tomorrow night to celebrate, won't you?" Leah asked.

Robin paused. "I suppose so." But she looked a little worried.

"Don't worry, it won't be a big bash or anything - just dinner and a few drinks. Problem is, I've booked Thai so –"

"Oh, don't worry honestly. It's your birthday after all."

"You don't seriously think it matters to me where we eat, do you? I haven't seen you for so long. And with all your success, this is as much a celebration for you as it is for me." She reached under the countertop for the telephone directory. "Now, I'll just make some enquiries and see what we can get."

"Are you sure? I feel awful – it's your night and now you have to go and rearrange things for me."

"I said don't be silly," Leah said, tucking the handset under her chin as she dialled. "You'd do the same for me."

After a few failed attempts, she finally located a different restaurant, a nice place near the seafront in Dun Laoghaire, which would be a bit of a trek for Robin but handier for Olivia.

"So what are your plans for the weekend?" Leah asked. "I'm

taking the day off tomorrow so if you want to do some shopping or anything ..."

"Well, Mum's coming up to visit at some stage and I'm doing – I think it's called TV3 –" she looked at Leah for confirmation, "on morning Monday at eight." She groaned. "But tomorrow, I only have a couple of newspaper interviews before lunch and after that I'm free."

"Great! Let me know what time and I'll pop in and meet you at the hotel." She hugged Robin once more, thrilled to see her again. "The Westin, eh?" she laughed. "Haven't you come a long way."

FORTY-SEVEN

On her return to the hotel, Robin sat in the taxi deep in thought. She stared out the window, hardly seeing the places and landmarks of this city that had once been so familiar to her.

Should she do it? she wondered. Should she go while she was here – while she had the chance?

But what if she bumped into Olivia? Although that was highly unlikely. But there was always the possibility that someone else could notice her and then mention something to Olivia, so should she –

Oh, for goodness' sake, Robin, admonished herself, after seven years in Manhattan you'd think you'd know better. This is Dublin, not a tiny little village.

Feeling a sudden burst of nervous energy, Robin sat forward. It was now or never and she had to do it. She would never forgive herself otherwise.

"I'm sorry, I've changed my mind. Can you take me out to Shankill instead, please?"

The taxi driver looked at her as though she was mad. "Love, it's late-night shopping and we're on the outskirts of town – it'll take us a good forty minutes to get all the way out there."

"I know and I'm sorry," Robin replied, "but I need to go back."

"Your money, pet." He shrugged and went to do a U-turn.

She said nothing more for the rest of the journey, as she tried to convince herself she was doing the right thing. Then, about thirty-five minutes later, they reached the turn-off.

The taxi driver tapped his steering wheel to the beat of the music on the radio, not having any idea that he was echoing the quick tempo of Robin's heart.

"So whereabouts will I drop you, love?" he asked when they entered the village.

Her heart fluttered as though it was struggling to keep beating. "Shanganagh, please," she replied, her voice heavy with emotion, "Shanganagh Cemetery."

FORTY-EIGHT

"Hello, Robin." Olivia's voice was calm and neutral as she approached the restaurant table. She reached across to hug her old friend. "It's great to see you again."

"Good to see you too." Robin half-stood up from her chair and returned the brief embrace. The greeting was warm but, still, she wasn't sure what to think or how to behave. Her friend had aged, as had the rest of them, but as always Olivia possessed an air of calm serenity which somehow never seemed to falter.

Not even now.

"Matt, you know Leah of course, and this is another friend, Robin," Olivia said by way of introduction. "We were all in college together and Robin's just back from New York. Remember, I told you about the children's book she wrote?"

"Hey, Leah, Happy Birthday." Matt waved a greeting. "Pleased to meet you, Robin, and congratulations on your book. New York's a great city, have you lived there long?"

"Seven years," she told him.

"And do you get home much? Although I don't know why you'd want to," he added amiably. "Dublin's great, but the Big Apple is in a different league I think."

"Well, this is actually my first time home since," she replied, trying not to make eye contact with Olivia.

"Oh." Matt couldn't hide his surprise. "Well, living in a great place like that, I suppose I can't blame you."

"Doesn't she look fantastic, Olivia?" Leah gushed, already tipsy on the wine she was drinking. She'd had a few drinks before they went out, and had already knocked back two champagne cocktails before the others arrived. Robin suspected her friend was out to get well and truly blotto tonight.

"She certainly does," Olivia answered. "I love your dress, Robin, and you've kept your figure too. Now, if I wore something like that I'd look like Ten Tonne Tessie." She laughed gaily, but to Robin there was something forced about it.

"Thanks, you look great too."

"I think you and I both know that dieting was never my forte. I still have the old ice cream weakness," she added conspiratorially.

"Don't be silly, you look amazing," Matt said, looking up from his menu.

"Love must be blind then," Olivia rolled her eyes.

"Women," Matt said, exasperated. "Remind me again why I agreed to come along tonight."

All of a sudden Robin wished she *hadn't* come. Olivia was being way too nice to her and behaving as if she didn't have a care in the world.

Well, maybe she didn't. She was a bit taken aback at how easy and comfortable she and this guy seemed to be with one another. She supposed she was so used to seeing Olivia with Peter that it seemed sort of strange. Then again, why shouldn't Olivia move on?

Thinking of her last-minute visit to the graveyard yesterday, she shivered, ashamed. After all Olivia had been through, she deserved to be happy.

"So, things are going well in New York?" Olivia asked then.

"Great news about your book, although I must admit it was a bit of a surprise. I didn't know you were writing."

Robin was embarrassed now. It felt as though she'd let her down somehow. "It's all a little bit out of the blue for me too," she said. "I have a niece, well, she's not exactly my niece, she's Ben's niece but she's asthmatic and –"

"Ben'ssh her cute boyfriend," Leah interjected, her voice slightly slurred.

Olivia looked at Leah. "Slow down a bit there, you – we haven't even started eating yet," she admonished teasingly.

"It's my birthday, I'm single and I'll get pisshed if I want to," Leah laughed, her tone giddy.

Matt topped up his wineglass. "And if you can't have a few to celebrate reaching the big 3-0, sure when can you?"

"Cheers, Matt!" Leah clinked glasses with him, pleased she had a drinking partner in crime. She waylaid a waiter passing their table. "Three more Bellinis here please."

"I'm almost sorry I'm driving," Olivia said, grinning at Robin. "We're obviously in for a wild night."

She smiled back uncomfortably. Another cocktail sounded good because at that moment, she wasn't sure how to continue this one-to-one conversation with Olivia. She wished Leah would get involved a bit more, but her friend was too busy knocking back cocktails and chattering with Matt.

Just then, the waiter came to take their order and as usual, Robin stiffened, dreading the drawn-out exchange to come and the usual accompanying frustrated looks.

"Hi," she said, when he stood beside her, her complexion reddening slightly as she rattled off her usual spiel. "I'd just like to let you know that I suffer from a severe peanut allergy, and I'll need to ask you a couple of questions about this menu. If I eat something with peanuts in it, I might die."

To her amazement, the waiter smiled back. "That's no problem, madam, my youngest suffers from the same thing. I know how careful you have to be."

"Thank you," Robin couldn't comprehend the relief she felt. As the waiter went through the menu with her, she saw Matt watching her with interest.

"Must be tough," he said when the waiter had left the table. "Not everyone is so accommodating, I'd imagine."

Robin nodded. "That was rare. I don't blame them, but it's hard when you're made feel like an over-hysterical fusspot. People just don't realise, that's all."

Olivia smiled tightly. "It's probably much easier in New York too. I'm sure they're better geared up."

Again, Robin wished she wouldn't be so ... *nice* to her. She almost wished she'd be frosty, uncommunicative, anything but the understanding, sympathetic Olivia she'd always been. "It is when you know where to go. But, there are always risks." She turned to Leah, eager to change the subject. "Are you OK there? You've downed most of that wine by yourself."

"Why shouldssn't I?" Leah slurred, her eyes glazed. "When issh my birthday?"

Olivia caught Matt's eye. "Tell you what," she said to Leah, "why don't we just have water with the meal and then later we'll have some champagne."

Sensing now that her drinking was a little bit more than just celebratory, he swiftly removed the bottle of wine and hid it under the table. Robin was worried too. Leah was getting way too drunk way too fast.

"Where'sh the wine gone?"

"Don't worry, he'll be back with more later," Olivia soothed. "Oh, look, here's our starters."

Leah took a huge gulp of the water, and the table was quiet while they ate.

Robin took tiny bites, the discomfort of the reunion with

Olivia making her lose her appetite. She would have to say something, but not here, not now.

The conversation became a little stilted and awkward once the introductions and attempts at catching up were out of the way. Matt kept up some chit-chat during the main course, which lightened the tone a little, but Robin was finding it very hard to relax and even harder to find things to talk about.

She wasn't sure whether she should enquire about Olivia's daughter as she had never met the child, and hadn't exactly been supportive when she was born. She decided instead to concentrate on safer ground. "So how's Kate getting on?" she asked. "Does motherhood suit her?"

"Kate thinks you're a bitssh, Robin," Leah blurted drunkenly. "But I think she's a bitssh, so there."

Matt looked visibly uncomfortable, and Olivia looked as though she wanted the ground to open up and swallow her. "Leah, don't be silly," she said. "I know you're upset that Kate couldn't come tonight but –"

"She wassh alwayssh horrible to you, Robin, wasshn't she?" Leah went on as though Olivia hadn't even spoken. "She was a bitssh to you, when we all knew it wasshn't your fault."

"Leah, it's OK," Robin demurred, "Oh, look, here's the waiter – let's order dessert."

Leah shook her head exaggeratedly. "I told her it wasshn't your fault but she didn't believe me." All of a sudden, she looked distraught. She reached across and grabbed Olivia tightly by the hand. Then she reached for Robin. "You two are my bessht friends, my bessht friends, I want you to know that."

Matt stood up, evidently deciding it might be a good idea to give them some time alone. "I just remembered I have to phone Frank," he said, taking out his device and waving it in front of the others as if to demonstrate.

"That'ssh OK, Matt, that'ssh fine, you're my bessht friend, too," Leah giggled at his retreat.

Olivia caught Robin's eye. "Forget about dessert, I think it's time we got you home, pet," she said.

Leah's eyes widened. "Home? Will Josh be there?"

"I'll take her back in a taxi if you like," Robin offered after Olivia hurriedly paid the bill and the three of them joined Matt outside.

"It's OK, I'm driving anyway," she replied. "Can I give you a lift back to the hotel?"

"No, that's fine, you guys go ahead – I can get a taxi."

"Don't be silly," Matt piped up. "Sure, it could take you forever to get one, and once we've got Leah settled, it'll only take us a few minutes to drop you into town."

If Olivia was annoyed that he'd persisted, she didn't show it.

"I'll be fine."

Olivia spoke quietly. "Robin, it's no problem, although it might be a while before we get Leah sorted. She's very drunk and I don't particularly want to leave her on her own."

"I could stay with her," Robin suggested. As tomorrow was Sunday, her time was her own, and the next item on her publicity itinerary wasn't until Monday. "I could keep an eye on her, make sure she doesn't get sick or anything."

"That mightn't be a bad idea," Matt said. "At least then you wouldn't have to worry about her."

She nodded. "OK, let's get her to the car."

Sitting in the backseat alongside Robin, Leah wouldn't stay still. Nor, to Robin's discomfort, would she stay quiet. It was as if once the air hit her, she got another – giddier – lease on life.

"You know, I knew you two would be friendssh again, I just knew it! Thissh has been the best birthday ever – we're *all* friendssh again now – and don't worry about Kate, I'll deal with Kate – she'll come round. She just thought you were being mean to Olivia, but *I* knew you weren't being horrible, Robin. I undersshtood why you didn't come, and so did Olivia, didn't you? We knew that you jussht –"

"How's the shop going, Leah?" Matt asked.

"Fine, thanks very mussh for asking. You should come in and visit me soon – I'll give you a free chocolate."

"I'd like that – do you have any Turkish delights?"

"No, but I'll do some sshpecially for you, if you like." She giggled and whispered to Robin. "He'ssh very nice, isn't he, Robin? Nicer than bloody Josh anyway, and do you know sshomething? I think he's nicer than Peter too. There, I said it! "

"Oh, is one of these yours, Leah?" Robin asked, as Olivia slowed and turned into the entrance of an apartment block, hoping and praying that Leah would stop chattering.

"Yep, that's mine, sshee that one up there? Josh didn't care, but I wanted one with a balcony." She sniffed, and suddenly her mood changed. "I have the balcony all to myself now." She turned to Robin. "Why did he do it, Robin? I gave up ssho much for him – I told him it didn't matter that he didn't want shhildren – if he didn't want them, well then, that was fine, but then he goes and sshleeps with someone else. Why, Robin?"

"I don't know, honey." She knew that poor Matt was mortified. She was mortified for him and equally for Olivia – and indeed for Leah.

Olivia stopped the car and, having rummaged through Leah's bag got the keys to her apartment and let them in. She went on ahead to open the door and, as best he could, Matt helped Robin support poor drunken Leah as they made their way up the steps to her apartment. He gave her an embarrassed smile. "The poor crature – I'm sure she'll suffer in the morning."

"She certainly will," Robin agreed, relieved that they'd finally reached home. She followed Olivia through to her friend's bedroom. The two were silent as they helped her undress, Leah mumbling all the time. "I knew we'd all be friendssh again."

When she was safely tucked up in the bed, the two joined Matt in the living room.

"Is she asleep?" he asked, his face concerned, but also, luckily, a little amused.

Olivia nodded. "I think she'll be OK now." She turned to Robin. "Will the couch be OK for you? I think she has some spare blankets in the hotpress –"

"I'll be fine – I'll find them," she interjected. "It's late, and you two need to get home. I'll keep an eye on her, I promise."

Robin walked them both to the door, unable to understand why she felt so sad and desperate to say something. But it wasn't sadness, she decided, trying to read Olivia's expression as she lost her nerve and said nothing other than goodbye. It was guilt.

"So are you staying long ...?" Olivia ventured cautiously.

"No, I'm off to the UK on Tuesday, so I don't know if I – "

"I see. Well, the very best of luck with everything. I'll be sure to pick up a copy of your book for Ellie."

"Thank you."

Matt gave her a quick kiss on the cheek. "Good night, Robin – it was great meeting you. Good luck with the book and sure, we might see you again sometime?"

"Bye, Matt, thanks."

Closing the door softly behind them, Robin could now understand why Olivia was involved with him.

He was similar to Ben in a way – kind, considerate and loyal. They were both very lucky, but the big difference was that Olivia deserved someone like that in her life; deserved someone who cared enough about her to appreciate her loyalty.

The fact that Robin, with all her faults, didn't deserve a man like that was obvious, and something that, tonight, Leah's babbling had brought home even more.

FORTY-NINE

Olivia was mostly silent on the way back to Lakeview in the car, her thoughts scattered as she kept going over the evening.

She'd handled it well, she thought. She'd been polite, friendly and gracious – even though she had felt uncomfortable throughout, and especially towards the end with all Leah's gibberish.

With Leah so drunk, they had no choice but to slip into their old roles. Poor thing, she would suffer tomorrow, in more ways than one.

She sighed inwardly. Seeing Robin tonight really brought it home to her that she'd have to let Matt into her confidence soon. It wasn't fair otherwise. They'd been getting on extremely well lately and, luckily, Catherine seemed to be staying out of the way.

"Are you OK?" Matt asked softly.

Olivia jumped. She'd almost forgotten he was there.

"Yes, I'm fine. I'm just thinking about Leah, that's all. I've never seen her like that, Matt, and it worries me. She's always been great at convincing everyone that she's coping, that she's getting on with it. Stupidly, I took that at face value, when I should have known that she was suffering." She shook her head. "I'm her best friend – how could I not have known?"

"I don't know Leah very well, but she does strike me as the type of girl who values her independence. Yes, she's upset now and she's having a tough time of it, but that's only natural."

"I know, but I've never seen her so out of control."

"It was her birthday – a big occasion and the man she loves wasn't there to share it with her. I remember after Natasha died I went completely off the rails on what would have been our fifth wedding anniversary. I drank solidly the whole day long, trying to shut out the pain and the memories. It was a nightmare."

"I know." Olivia did know, but unfortunately, she never had the luxury of going off and getting blotto whenever a meaningful birthday or anniversary came around to mock and remind her of all that she had lost. She had Ellie to look after.

Still, looking at it from that point of view, it did explain why Leah seemed so out of it. Before this, her life was wonderful – she'd achieved her lifetime ambition, she had a man who loved her, and the promise of an exciting future.

Now, things were looking a whole lot different and, while her professional life was still on the up, her personal life was in tatters. Olivia felt for her and made a mental note to be there as much as she could for her over the next while since Kate didn't seem to be prepared to do the same thing. She knew Leah was suffering over that too. Since Kate had her baby, that friendship was slowly but surely slipping away.

Matt looked sideways at her. "Robin seems nice."

"She is," was all she said.

"There's a bit of history between you two then?" It was a statement rather than a question.

She shrugged, not wanting to get into it just then. "We were close in uni, but we lost touch when Robin moved to the States."

"So, tonight was your first time seeing one another in what – seven years? And you didn't keep in touch in the meantime?" Matt was amazed. "No wonder there was tension."

"Did you think there was?" Olivia was worried now. She thought she'd played it to perfection.

"Well, I thought she seemed a bit edgy, but I could have been imagining it." He seemed to pause intentionally, before adding "So Leah, in her own way, was hoping to be peacemaker then?"

"Peacemaker?"

"Well, I didn't understand most of her gibberish, but she kept repeating that stuff about you all being friends again and how this Kate thinks Robin's a 'bitssh'," he mimicked good-humouredly. Then his tone grew more serious. "It doesn't take a genius to work out that she wasn't there for you when Peter died." Matt shook his head. "That must have been tough. Or ..." he hesitated, "is there more than that to it? Did Robin–"

"*What?*" Olivia cried, then slammed down on the brakes and swerved as a car pulled out of a space on her left. She had all but hit it.

"He was indicating," said Matt mildly.

Olivia didn't answer. It was as though every muscle, every tendon in her body had all at once tensed to breaking point, and she felt as though a herd of horses had just trampled over her stomach.

Staring rigidly at the road ahead, her pulse still racing, she scrambled to sort out her thoughts. But how could she explain it all here – in the car, while she was supposed to be concentrating on driving? But she had to say something now, didn't she?

"Matt," she began. "I don't know how you... "

Just then his phone shrilled, and the remaining words died on Olivia's lips. He glanced at her apologetically, as he answered.

"Hey, Catherine."

Olivia exhaled loudly.

"Hi, yes, we're just on our way back – *what?* You're kidding..."

She glanced away from the road briefly, a question in her eyes.

Matt looked worried. "Well, did you call the doctor? What did he say? Good, well, look, I'll be back in say, fifteen minutes or so, OK? And try not to worry, I'm sure it'll be fine but ... Tell him I'm on my way, won't you? Right, right, see you soon."

"What's happened?" For a split second, Olivia wondered if she'd been wrong about Catherine coming to terms with their relationship, but by the anxious look on Matt's face, she knew the woman wasn't being dramatic just to try and ruin yet another night out.

His voice was fraught. "It's Adam, he has a fever and she thinks it might be meningitis."

"Oh, no." Olivia had a similar scare with Ellie one time and it was horrific. "Is there a rash? Did she try the glass test?"

"I don't know, it was hard to make out what she was saying, she sounded so distraught."

"I know it's impossible, but try not to worry – we'll be there soon." Instantly she increased the pressure on the accelerator. "Matt, it could well be something small."

"I know, I know, but I just want to be there now." He turned away and looked quickly out the window, but as he did, Olivia thought she saw the glistening of tears in his eyes. "I don't know what I'd do if I lost him too, Olivia," he said in a broken voice, and her heart went out to him. "I really don't know what I'd do."

She didn't know what to say. All she knew was that her own situation would have to take a backseat for a while.

Right then, there were far more important things to worry about.

FIFTY

Andrew Clarke sat in the arrivals area at Dublin airport, bored out of his tree. This had almost been as bad as the wait outside the delivery room last night.

Although at least he was outside, and not inside with all the screaming and thrashing around and stuff. He wasn't the kind of fella who could deal with all that sort of thing.

But Amanda had done well and apparently eighteen hours labour was a common enough thing. Andrew grimaced and once again thanked his lucky stars that he'd been born a man.

How did women do it? All that pushing and shoving and blood and goo – surely it wasn't natural? Surely, the human species had advanced far enough along the evolutionary chain to come up with some better way of reproduction than that sort of primal carry-on? Although, he thought, grinning to himself, the reproduction part being primal wasn't all that much of a problem, it was trying to get the finished product out that caused all the hassle.

But, after it all, he was now the proud father of a tiny little girl who as yet had no name. She'd arrived at 4 am that morning and Amanda was still dithering over names. He dreaded the final decision. Yesterday, before her waters broke, she'd been talking about naming the child, 'Manchester'.

"It's original and classy and the great thing is it would suit either a girl or a boy, wouldn't it?" she'd said, full of enthusiasm. All Andrew could think about was the hiding the child – male or female – would get all its life from football fans.

Amanda was thrilled it had turned out to be a girl though. She thought she was 'beautiful'. Andrew thought she was nice enough but, in all honesty, right after the birth she just looked like a small, shrivelled sausage with arms and legs.

He checked his watch. Hell, were Amanda's parents ever going to emerge? The eleven thirty Aer Lingus flight from London had landed a good half an hour ago and still there was no sign.

Amanda's mother was probably fussing over her luggage and no doubt redoing herself up to the nines in the Ladies'. Amanda's vanity was nothing compared to Mummy Langan's. Although, Andrew thought chuckling, these days the woman needed as much Polyfilla as she could get.

His stomach growled with the hunger, and he was just about to pop down to the Sandwich Bar near the bookshop, when a glut of passengers with Aer Lingus tags on their bags came through arrivals. There must have been some delay with the luggage then, Andrew thought, deciding that he'd better be here when Mummy and Daddy Langan did come through or there'd be Holy War.

He could always grab something on the way back to the hospital anyway. Luckily, he was one of those people who couldn't hear much when his jaws were moving, so he'd be spared the worst of Mummy L's annoying high-pitched rants about how the flight was delayed, and the luggage was lost, and how the air hostesses had some cheek because they didn't kiss her fat feckin' arse.

He began scanning the faces of the passengers, just in case his in-laws had changed at all since the last time he'd seen them, which in Andrew's opinion wasn't long enough ago. Just then, he stiffened as he thought he caught sight of a familiar face. It couldn't be, could it? Andrew blinked and looked again like they always did in the movies. He almost went to wave but then, he thought, no, he was wrong it couldn't possibly be ...it feckin *was*!

Should he go over and say hello and ... no, there was no time because here were the Langan's waving condescendingly and pointing to their bags. As if he was some thick hotel porter or something, Andrew thought, irritated, as he approached them.

"Hello there! Did you have a good flight?" he asked, kissing Mummy L on the cheek and almost retching at the whiff of her probably expensive, but definitely manky perfume.

"Don't talk to me," Amanda's mother waved a dismissive arm. "Don't talk to me about that flight. People just don't know a *thing* about customer service these days. Can you believe that they actually tried to charge me for a glass of Perrier? How tacky."

Andrew decided there was no point in asking if the two stingy feckers had anything to eat – no doubt Mummy would have gone apoplectic at the thoughts of paying five or six euro for a chicken sandwich. Good, that meant they'd have to get something on the way to the hospital. His stomach growled approvingly.

"Well, you're here now and you'll be glad to know that Amanda's doing fine and really looking forward to seeing you," he said, slightly annoyed that they hadn't even bothered to ask.

"Honestly the only thing I'll be glad to know is that the car is parked close by and ready to take us away from this poor excuse for a cowshed."

Andrew picked up the bags and followed them out to the carpark. He sighed deeply. It was going to be a long journey back to the hospital.

OLIVIA SAT IN HER KITCHEN, waiting impatiently for news of Adam. She hadn't heard a thing from Matt since he and

Catherine had gone to the hospital the night before, so she had no idea if Adam was still in danger.

She was reluctant to call – the phone would probably be switched off anyway if he were in the hospital – and she was even more reluctant to call Catherine at her house. She had phoned Crumlin Children's Hospital earlier that morning, but because she wasn't family they wouldn't give her any information about his condition.

At around midday, she got a call from Leah. The poor thing was dreadfully upset and embarrassed about her behaviour the night before. "I made such an idiot of myself," she wailed, mortified. "Matt must think I'm a lunatic."

"Don't be silly, of course he doesn't think that," Olivia said, and went on to explain that Leah's behaviour was the last thing on Matt's mind at the moment.

"Give him my best regards when you hear from him, won't you?" Leah said. "Oh, and while I think of it, I got a call from Andrew first thing. He's the reason I'm up out of bed, actually. Amanda had a baby girl early this morning."

"Oh, that's great news." Despite her own concerns, she felt pleased for Amanda.

"Yeah, apparently it wasn't pretty, and she threatened the midwife with litigation if she kept forcing her to push, but it all worked out in the end."

Olivia forced a smile at the image of princess-like Amanda going through hard labour. That would have been some sight. Then she thought of something.

"Is Robin still with you?" she asked, trying to sound casual.

"No, I made her go back to the hotel this morning. I felt awful about her having to sleep on my lumpy couch when she should have been in sumptuous luxury. She knew me and my hangover wouldn't be great company today, but I'm meeting her again before she heads off to London." She paused slightly, and Olivia knew what was coming. "Can you ever forgive me? I just wasn't thinking straight. I really didn't mean to drag everything up. It must have been hard enough for you as it was, seeing her again."

"Don't be silly – we were bound to come face to face at some stage," she replied, trying to keep her voice light. "Anyway, you should go back to bed and try and sleep that hangover off."

"I think I'll have to," Leah moaned. "At the moment I feel like my head is about to split in two. But let me know what happens with little Adam, will you? And try not to worry."

"I will – and I won't." She went to say something else but hesitated. "Talk to you soon."

"You too, bye."

Olivia hung up, realising that just then she'd been about to ask something else. Try as she might, she couldn't stop thinking about it, as she'd thought about it many times before.

After all these years, surely they had more to say to one another. Didn't Robin have any questions, didn't she wonder? Had it been that easy for her to shut it all out of her life?

Or was it that Robin simply didn't give a damn?

FIFTY-ONE

Robin sat in her hotel room, trying to decide what to do until her mum arrived that evening.

She had nothing on today, and there had been no point in staying any longer at Leah's. The poor thing was in bits, and not just with her hangover. She'd apologised over and over again, trying to convince Robin that Kate simply didn't know better and that she'd always been unnecessarily harsh on her.

Robin didn't care what Kate thought. But why was it so easy for Olivia to forgive her? Why had she always made excuses for her? Why hadn't she gone berserk when Robin had let her down? Many times over the years she had tried to imagine what she would have done in her situation. She didn't think she could forgive and go on as if nothing had happened, like Olivia had.

She had been so calm, so friendly last night at dinner that it was almost unreal.

Robin checked the time – it was just after one pm – just after eight New York time. She should catch Ben before he left for his morning jog. Ben religiously went for a jog every morning, even on Sundays.

"Hey. How's it all going over there?" His friendly voice

cheered her up instantly, but at the same time made her miss him even more.

"It's OK, a bit tiring. The journalists just ask the same questions over and over again. They don't really need to talk to me – all they need to do is copy everything directly from the press release."

"Get out of that – I'll bet you're loving all the attention," he laughed.

She raised a smile. "Well, I'll admit I did enjoy the first TV one, apart from the dreadful make-up."

"I hope you kept me a recording – I'm dying to find out if you come across like you have an American twang."

"No – that would be you," Robin teased him.

"So what else is going on over there? Did you get a chance to see your mum or your friends? What about Leah?"

"I'm meeting Mum this evening, and I was out with Leah last night for her birthday."

"Great – I'm glad you got the chance to meet up, although I hope you didn't bump into any old flames or anything?"

Robin smiled sadly. If only he knew.

"No."

Then she heard their apartment intercom ringing in the background.

"That's probably Dave. He's tagging along this morning. The poor guy is desperate to get rid of his love-handles."

"I'd better go too. I'm on the hotel phone, so I'm sure it's costing me a fortune."

"Bill it to the publishers," he said with a laugh. "Look, give me a call when you get to London. I wish I could have gone with you, Robin – I think I'm more excited about this than you are."

She smiled. "I'll be home soon and I promise I'll tell you all about it. In the meantime, you'd better let poor Dave in before those love-handles get any worse."

"OK, I'm going, I'm going. Love ya lots and tell your mum I said hello, OK? Bye." With that, Ben hung up.

Robin replaced the receiver feeling bereft. He seemed so far away and in all honesty she felt a bit lost.

She missed him desperately, much more than she'd expected. He really was the most important person in her life now, the only one who trusted her and loved her for what she was.

And yet she'd always been so unwilling to yield fully to that, to accept his love for her at face value. She supposed it was because she'd never been really able to convince herself that she was worth loving. After the mistakes she'd made, why should she deserve it?

Coming home had been hard, and although Robin had always known deep down that she'd have to do it eventually, visiting the graveyard the other day had been even harder. But still she had to do it.

She'd felt like an interloper standing there, reading the head-stone inscription. It was all so surreal. She noticed how well Olivia was taking care of the grave; it was obviously regularly attended, and she'd recently left some fresh flowers.

She saw too what must have been little Ellie's contribution of some childish paintings. At this, a lump came to Robin's throat as she realised that she really didn't belong there; she had no right to be there, just as she had no right to be at the funeral all those years ago.

Not a single day had gone by without a sense of aching regret, regret for not being there and regret for what had gone before. Kate thought she knew it all, but in fact she had no idea.

No idea how desperately difficult it was for Robin to come home and say goodbye to someone she too had loved, but never had any right to.

FIFTY-TWO

Catherine sat in her favourite spot by the front window, unable to concentrate on anything other than Matt and Adam at the hospital.

He'd sent her away earlier, telling her to go home and get some sleep.

But Catherine couldn't sleep, not when the most important people in her life were in trouble. She didn't know what she would do if anything happened to Adam. And she knew Matt wouldn't be able to cope with losing him either, after all he'd suffered after Natasha.

Catherine sighed. She'd been a fool to think that she could keep Matt all to herself. He didn't love her. He never had. He was in love with Olivia now, and there was nothing she could do to change that. And now, with all that had happened in the last twelve hours, she didn't know if she wanted to any more.

Matt didn't love her, at least not in the way she wanted him to. Take away the jealousy and she supposed Olivia was a nice enough woman, although she had nothing on Natasha. But Catherine knew that no one would ever replace Natasha in Matt's eyes – not Olivia, and certainly not her.

Maybe she should just let them get on with it and she should get on with her own life. She'd get over Matt, eventually – she had no other choice.

And Conor wasn't the worst either. What had started out as a little fling had gradually become something more, and only recently, Conor had said something about taking their relationship 'to the next level', whatever that meant.

He was crazy about her, and although she had convinced herself she was only using him to get to Matt, deep down she did enjoy his company. And in all honesty, he was a pretty decent prospect for a girl like her; he had more than a few quid in the bank, and a very nice house by the lake. So, Catherine decided, catching sight of a car rounding the corner at the entrance to the green, maybe she should just forget about Matt once and for all, and concentrate her energies on nabbing Conor before he went in search of someone else.

The car stopped outside Olivia's house and a tall, dark and – from what she could make out – attractive guy, got out. He paused outside the house for a moment, as if unsure whether or not he had the right place.

But no, Catherine decided, shifting her position to get a better view, it wasn't that, it was more like he was hesitating, pausing for breath.

Then, feeling more than a little silly, she shook her head. Her imagination really did run away with her sometimes. The poor guy was probably just another handyman, looking to price a job.

But by the look of utter dismay on Olivia's face when she opened the door, Catherine knew for sure that this guy was no handyman.

FIFTY-THREE

"What are you doing here?" she gasped, her face white with shock.

He looked nervously back, his features soft and his expression grave. "I wanted to see you. 'm sorry, I know I shouldn't but –" he ran a hand through his hair, through those locks that even now she ached to touch. "I ... I *needed* to see you."

Why now – today? When she was feeling terrible and even worse, she thought, *looking* terrible. Her hair was unwashed and still matted from the night before, and she knew she hadn't bothered removing her make-up. She'd barely dressed herself this morning – her mind had been completely elsewhere, and she just didn't have the energy.

"Can we talk? Please?"

He looked tired and drained, devoid of spirit. He looked ... vulnerable. And he was obviously suffering too. "Can I come in at least? Just for a minute or two, and I'll understand if you don't want to, but ..."

He looked into her eyes then, and her stomach leapt with the old familiar sense of longing. "I miss you so much, Leah."

She knew she shouldn't, she had to be strong, but it was so

hard. "We've been through this before. There's nothing more to say." Her voice sounded strange and alien, even to her.

"I know that, and I know you're probably still very angry with me, but ... I just can't explain how sorry I am." His voice was thick with emotion. "I made the biggest mistake of my life, I know that. But I also know that I love you."

"Josh, don't ..." She didn't want to hear this, yet at the same time she *did*. These last few weeks she could barely sleep or eat for thinking about it, for thinking about him, and how much she missed him too. And last night had been especially hard, which is why she'd ended up drinking so much. She'd hoped that getting really drunk would numb the pain and the emptiness she felt without him.

Still, no matter how much she loved him and missed him, Josh had done something unforgivable – Leah had to remember that. There was no going back.

Her mind firmly set, she decided that she'd listen to what he had to say, but that was it. Definitely.

Maybe ...

"Look, it's OK if you don't want to let me in. But I don't want to say what I have to say out here. This is between us, just the two of us."

Leah sighed. "Come in then," she said, going inside and expecting him to follow her.

Josh quietly closed the door behind him. "Happy Birthday, by the way," he said with a hesitant smile, taking in all her birthday cards on the mantelpiece.

"Thank you for the flowers." She indicated the lush bouquet on the coffee table. She'd been all at once annoyed and touched that he'd sent them, touched because he hadn't forgotten, and annoyed that he'd had the cheek.

"I wasn't sure ..."

The two of them sat at opposite ends of the room, Josh in 'his' armchair, and Leah curled up on the couch and under the blankets Robin had used only a few hours earlier. They served as some kind of comfort, some kind of barrier if necessary.

"Leah ..." Again, he ran a hand through his hair, as if unsure where to begin. "I don't really know where to start, so I suppose I'll just come right out and say it. I know I messed up big-time."

She said nothing, assuming that he expected her to agree, to move the conversation along. She wasn't doing him any favours.

"What I did – was one of the lowest moments in my life. I was disgusted with myself for letting you down, for letting myself down, for risking all that we had because I was feeling left out. That's exactly how I felt, Lee," he said, when she raised an eyebrow. "I felt left out of everything, thought that you didn't want me to share all the great things that were going on in your life." She opened her mouth to say something, but he stopped her. "Before you say anything, yes, I know it was stupid. It was stupid and immature and pathetic but it was the way I felt. I never liked Andrew Clarke, you know that."

"I do know that, but I could never understand why. Andrew never did anything to you. Actually, he likes you. He thinks you and I are well suited."

"Does he now?" Josh sniffed.

"Yes, he does," Leah heard her voice rise an octave, "and I'm not going over this again with you. Don't you dare try and tell me that you went back to your ex for a night of passion, just because you couldn't handle your own stupid jealousy."

"Lee, calm down, that wasn't it," he soothed. "In a way it *was* jealousy I suppose, but not the kind you think. With one flick of his expensive Mont Blanc pen, Clarke gave you everything you wanted. I couldn't do that. I'm just my dad's dogsbody, probably always will be, and as a result I felt threatened, useless, all the stupid things I never thought I'd feel. I felt it was *my* place to look after you, to support you in your dream. But he came along with his fat bloody chequebook and blew me out of the water."

"It wasn't like that. *I* approached Andrew for investment. Granted it was a stupid drunken conversation, which at the time I thought wouldn't amount to anything, but it did. And I'm grateful for that. You said yourself that Elysium is my dream. How could I have turned down that opportunity?"

"I never expected you to, but I also didn't expect you to be so gung-ho. You threw yourself into it without a second thought, and all of a sudden it was Andrew this and Andrew that. I felt ... threatened."

"Threatened? By an old friend who is, incidentally, married to another old friend."

"Like I said – it wasn't like that. I didn't think there was anything going on between you two, but I couldn't really express how I felt about it. You threw yourself into setting up the shop and didn't seem to want me involved in any of it. Instead of telling you how I felt, I just kept niggling you about the business being more important than I was. I know you began to resent me and probably not just for that."

"What do you mean?"

"Leah, I know you want a child of your own eventually. Despite what you said about my being enough for you. I know you were affected by Kate's pregnancy and, despite what you think, I understood how difficult it must have been seeing it all happen for her, all the time knowing that it might never happen for you.

"That's not fair. I made that decision long ago and it was *our* decision. Kate's pregnancy shook me a little, but that's because she's changed, not because I have."

"Well, with everything that was going on, I became confused. After a while, I began to wonder what you were doing with me. I couldn't help you with your business, I couldn't give you what you wanted. I was a total failure."

"Josh, I'm sorry, but this smacks of feeling sorry for yourself."

"I know it does. But the thing is, over the last few weeks, I've come to realise how stupid I've been, and how wrong I was to deny you that." He sat forward. "Leah, I know you probably can't even consider it at the moment, but if you could possibly think about having me back, then I'd like to have a baby."

She blinked. "What? Are you serious?"

"Yes, I know it would take a bit of getting used to, but I know you and I could make a go of it and – "

Never in a million years did she expect this from him, and despite the fact that Josh was now offering her everything she wanted, offering her the chance to start over, strangely, the idea just saddened her.

"Josh, you're delusional. You think that you can just waltz in here, tell me you're sorry for being unfaithful, but not to worry, sure a child of our own will make it all right. What planet are you on?"

"I know we'd have some work to do, but – "

"*Some* work? It's too late, there's no trust any more. And yes, maybe I did play a part in pushing you away and making you feel inadequate, but that doesn't mean that you had the right to jump into bed with the first available person."

"I know that, but Leah, surely we can work on it? I love you, doesn't that mean anything?"

"It didn't mean much when you were with her, did it?" she said in a broken voice. She turned away, willing away the tears that were threatening.

Josh moved across to sit beside her on the sofa. "I messed up – I know that, I knew it straight away. I wanted to tell you, but I knew you'd never forgive me and I didn't want you to think badly of me." He touched her hand. "I wish I could make you understand how sorry I am."

"That doesn't mean much now."

"Don't you think we could work through it, Lee?" he said, his voice soft and hopeful. "It would be a shame to throw away all that we have."

"If we don't have trust then we have nothing."

"But we can work on that, surely? I know it might be hard for you to believe me at the moment, but I know *I* can do it. I love you more than anyone – you're the best thing that's ever happened to me. You're my best friend, my life, all the usual clichés but they're clichés because they're true. I know I want to spend the rest of my life with you, even more now that I know what it's like to be without you. I'm willing to give it a go if you are." He smiled at Leah then, and amazingly uttered the very words she would have been elated to hear not all that long ago. "Let's settle down and buy a place of our own – let's get married and, yes, let's have kids. We could have a great life, Leah, I know we could. And I'm almost certain that we can get through this. People do, don't they? If they really love one another, then they can get through anything."

Her head spun. It was so tempting, so tempting just to throw her arms around him and agree that yes, they could do it, and yes, they could have a great life. He was telling her everything she so badly wanted to hear. But she knew in her heart and soul that she just couldn't forget what he'd done that easily.

She shook her head, and she could actually feel the tightness in her heart as she said the words.

"I'm sorry, Josh." She tried desperately to keep her voice even. "It's ... over."

"You don't really mean that."

"I do," she replied, trying to sound more determined that she felt. "And I'm sorry, but I think you should go."

"Please, just give me one more chance. I know we could make it work, I'm sure of it. Just one more chance."

"I can't – it's too late." Leah stood up and, legs shaking like jelly, moved across the room and opened the door. She stood back, appealing to him once more to leave. He stared at her, as if unable to believe that she was really serious. "Please," implored.

After a long moment, Josh acquiesced. "I'm sorry, Leah. Really I am."

"I know." She refused to meet his gaze, painfully aware that this really was the end. Every inch of her ached with sorrow. "Goodbye, Josh."

As much as she still loved him, and as tempting as it was to take him up on all he promised, she knew she just couldn't do it.

She couldn't handle his infidelity, the fact that he had broken her trust. She wasn't one of those people who could just pick up the pieces and move on. Wasn't strong enough to be one of those people who could forgive and forget.

She just wasn't Olivia.

FIFTY-FOUR

That afternoon, in order to take her mind off things, Olivia decided to tidy the garden shed.

It was a job that was way overdue, and one that she'd been putting off for ages. But as the house was spick and span, the ironing up to date and the shopping done, she couldn't think of anything else to do besides fret over the situation with Robin, and worry about Adam. Not to mention Matt's revelation in the car.

Ellie was at her mother's; Eva ensuring that Olivia should be free to travel to the hospital in Dublin should Matt need her. She had tried his phone a number of times since, but it was switched to messages. Despite what they said about no news being good news she didn't think it was appropriate in this case. Surely Matt would know she'd be on tenterhooks, wondering? At one stage, she'd been so desperate for something concrete, she'd almost called over to Catherine's. She was in the process of dumping some ancient paintbrushes and tins into a black refuse sack, when the doorbell rang.

Matt.

She raced back into the house, forgetting to remove her rubber gloves in her haste to get to the door – and hopefully put herself out of her misery once and for all. Oh she so hoped all would be well with Adam.

But when she opened the door, Olivia's world spun on a three-hundred-and-sixty degree axis.

"Hey," her visitor said with an uncertain smile.

She was so stunned it felt like a couple of hours before she could get the words out. "What – what are you doing here?" she whispered, dizzy with shock.

"I'm sorry, I know I should have called first. But my flight got in around lunchtime and I was anxious to get here so – "

"But what are you doing ... *here?*" she asked again. "What do you want?"

"What do I want? Olivia, surely it's obvious ... "

Somewhere nearby, she heard a car door slam.

"He's OK," Matt's relieved voice sounded over the air, followed by his footsteps up the path. "It wasn't meningitis at all, thank goodness – just some kind of reaction to ... oh, I'm sorry, excuse me ..." His voice trailed off as he approached and he looked at Olivia's other visitor and smiled apologetically. "Sorry to interrupt."

"That's wonderful news," She barely heard the sound of her own voice, so strong was the sound of her heartbeat thudding against her ribcage, so intense were the feelings of anxiety, confusion and – and out-and-out panic.

What on earth was she going to say now?

She saw that Matt was looking at them both unsurely, obviously waiting for an introduction, or even an explanation as to why she was acting so strangely.

She tried to clear her throat, and her mind and get a hold on her senses. How - knowing now that Matt had somehow got the wrong end of the stick – was she going to explain this?

Olivia willed her heart to slow down, willed her nerves to settle a little. She began to speak slowly, hoping to soften the blow. "This is Matt, a good friend," she said, her voice hoarse and her hands shaking as she made the introduction.

Then she turned and looked at a smiling Matt.

"And this is Peter – my husband."

FIFTY-FIVE

Matt visibly paled.

"What?" he demanded, staring at Olivia, his expression a mixture of shock and confusion, "What the hell ...?"

She scrambled to explain. "I'm sorry, I know you thought otherwise, but I only realised that last night when you said you thought he was –"

Peter addressed her as if Matt wasn't even there. "Obviously this is a bad time, so maybe I should – "

"Will somebody please explain what the *hell* is going on here?" Matt grunted. He glared at her. "I thought your husband was dead. You *told* me your husband was dead!"

Olivia floundered. She had never seen him so angry, but of course she could completely understand why. "Matt, I never told you that," she began, her words slow and deliberate, as if she were trying to explain something complicated to a child. Yet at the same time, her heartbeat was galloping. "I never told you *anything* like that. I know I haven't been exactly forthcoming about my past but I never, *ever* said – "

"Hold on a damn second. You *told* me you were a widow, that you'd brought Ellie up on your own, that you didn't know how you'd have coped without her. You didn't like to talk about it, you said – it was too painful. No wonder it was bloody painful – yer man was still around!"

Peter stepped forward. "Hey bud, watch your tone. I've no idea who you are but you've no right to talk to – "

"Peter, please," Olivia felt as though she'd landed on another planet.

What was Matt saying? She'd *never* told him that she was widowed or that Peter was dead – she'd barely said anything at all about him because it *was* too painful.

Where on earth had he got that idea? Granted he knew that she was married at least and that she and Ellie now lived on their own, but how could he have made that huge leap to the notion that Peter was dead?

She had definitely told him she was separated, hadn't she? Her head spun as she tried to remember various conversations they'd had about everything, tried to figure out how she might have somehow misled him.

But in her heart of hearts she knew she *hadn't*. Granted, she'd been evasive, but he must have come up with the assumption that she was widowed all by himself.

Still at that moment, she desperately wished that she hadn't been so reticent, so unwilling to let him into her confidence. Now it looked as though she'd deliberately misinformed him, although where he'd got the idea that she was a widow when she was to all intents and purposes more ... a single wife.

"Please come inside and let's talk about this. I don't know why you thought that, and I never, ever tried to mislead you." She ran a hand through her hair. What a nightmare. She should have explained all last night, but he was so upset after Catherine's phone call, she hadn't had the opportunity and ... oh what was she going to do?

Her thoughts and emotions were so confused just then that she couldn't think crooked, let alone straight.

She glanced at her husband and then back to Matt. "We've lived apart for years, but haven't yet divorced and ..." She trailed off then. "Is that why you're here?" she asked Peter, feeling an odd combination of relief and disappointment. "About a divorce?"

"I don't believe this ..." Matt was muttering as he marched back down the path. "I don't believe what I'm hearing, what I'm seeing. I thought you were special, Olivia, I thought you and I had something. But you're nothing but a liar."

"Hey, watch it," Peter called after his retreating back, but Matt was already in the driver's seat of the car. He started the Volvo and revved the engine ferociously before driving off.

Olivia watched him speed out the entrance to the main road. Strange she thought absently, that he didn't go straight to Catherine's.

"Olivia," Peter's voice brought her sharply back to the here and now. "can I come in? You and I need to talk."

She looked at his face then, one so familiar to her, it was as if they'd never been apart.

Then, with no clue as to what he wanted, Olivia stood back from the doorway and let her husband – the man whose return she'd dreamed about for five long years – into her house, and back into her life.

FIFTY-SIX

She stared into those expressive eyes she had once known and loved so well.

"I didn't plan for this to be so out of the blue, believe me," he began. "I was going to call first – I know I should have called first, but when I landed in Dublin airport this morning, I couldn't *not* come straight here."

"But what are you doing back in Ireland in the first place? Oh," she said, the realisation hitting her, "it's your mum, isn't it?"

She knew that Teresa had been unwell, but Olivia had never in her wildest dreams imagined that Peter would come all the way back from Australia just because his mother was feeling out of sorts.

"Didn't she tell you she's suffering from Parkinson's?" he asked, and instantly she felt like a heel.

"No, no, she never said a word." Olivia had noticed her slowing down of course, in the same way that her own parents were showing signs of getting on in years, but she had never once suspected that it could be anything serious.

So, Peter was home for Mummy then. Nothing to do with the

wife and child he'd so cruelly discarded. Then again, why did she think it would be any different?

"She's getting progressively worse and the treatment she's on doesn't seem to be having much of an effect." He studied her. "But I'd been thinking about contacting you for a while anyway, Olivia."

"Then why didn't you? Why turn up unannounced on my doorstep? For goodness sake, Peter, never mind me, but how did you think Ellie would react to you turning up out of the blue like this?"

"Do you ... do you really think she would know me?" he asked uncertainly.

"Of course she'd know you – she has photographs in her bedroom, and your parents show her pictures of you every time she visits. What they don't tell her is that her father was so angry with me that he decided to abandon *her*."

"That's not true – of course I care about her. But these last few years have been hard, Olivia. Distance was the only way I could get some clarity, you know that."

"And you had to go to the other end of the world - about as far as you could get," she said. "This is crazy, Peter."

"Is she here?" He looked nervously around the room, and his eyes rested on a framed photo of Ellie on the mantelpiece. It was a professional photograph Olivia had commissioned a few months back, on her fourth birthday. She was grinning happily at the camera, the gap in her teeth unmistakeable and adorable. Olivia followed his gaze and instantly folded her arms protectively across her chest.

"She's at my mum's," she replied shortly, offering up a relieved prayer that Ellie wasn't here when Peter arrived. "So four years and a few birthday and Christmas cards now and then, you think you're entitled to just pop in and see her – without so much as a phone call? How dare you, Peter?"

"I know, I'm sorry, but I just thought – "

"You thought you could waltz in here after abandoning her – abandoning *us* like you did."

"Hell, I didn't think I *would* come here, and certainly not so soon. I'm sorry but maybe I just wasn't thinking straight. I'm tired and jet-lagged and worried about Mum and ..." he trailed off. "Being back is a huge thing for me, Olivia – surely you can understand that."

She did understand, but still couldn't forgive the casual way he had just turned up on her doorstep. Then she thought of something. "How did you know where to find us? You sent the cards to your mother's and I never gave you this address, so how did you know how to get here?" Although, as soon as she'd asked, Olivia thought she knew the answer.

"Mum told me where you were, but she also told me to leave it for a while before getting in touch. She knew it wouldn't be easy for you, but at the same time, I think she knew I'd want to see you two eventually."

"And you thought *I'd* feel the same, I suppose?" Olivia was so angered by this she could hardly think straight. Who did the Gallaghers think they were, playing with her feelings?

Especially given all Teresa's snide remarks about Matt and her so-called 'concern' for Ellie's welfare. She was merely making sure that if Peter *did* decide to come home, he'd still have a ready-made family there waiting for him. "You thought *I'd* be sitting patiently at home, waiting for you to change your mind, to decide that you did love us after all – was it?"

The problem was – only a few months earlier, Olivia *had* been hoping the same thing. She'd been waiting for him to return, hoping that they might eventually be a family again.

But that was before, and now, try as she might, she couldn't concentrate properly on the sheer magnitude of his actually being here – in Lakeview. She was too concerned about Matt and the mess she had made of it all by being evasive, by trying to protect herself.

Peter sighed. "I'm sorry, you're right, this was a mistake, I should have called first, I should have at least told you – "

"Yes, you should."

He hesitated a little. "I know this probably isn't the right time but ... you're looking really well, Olivia. And it *is* good to see you." At this, he flashed his best Colgate smile, those teeth seeming even whiter against his Australian tan.

Amazingly, in all the years she'd known him, this was the first time that Olivia had seen through the compliment.

It was an attempt to control her, to get his own way, to soften her up a bit. She had always thought Peter was charming, had always thought she was lucky to find a husband who was so respectful and considerate not just to her, but to other women also.

Only now did it strike her that it was all a front and he was a weak, selfish cad. Absence didn't quite make the heart grow fonder – in this case, it made it insightful.

But, she thought, that wasn't the whole story, was it? Her feelings, or lack thereof for Peter now had more to do with Matt. She could come to terms with why Peter had abandoned her, but there was no excuse for his selfish rejection of Ellie.

All of a sudden, Olivia didn't care that Peter was back, or about what he did or didn't want.

"I'm sorry, but I can't talk about this now. Ellie will be home soon, and I don't want you here when she returns. I have a life of my own – *Ellie* and I have a life, one that you're not part of, that you haven't ever been part of. I know you had your reasons but, to be honest, I think I've done my penance. What you seemed to forget so easily was that it was agony for me too, yet I didn't have the luxury of taking off to 'get clarity'. I had a child to raise."

"I know." To his credit, Peter looked shamefaced.

"Yet, you didn't care about my suffering, did you? You just believed what you wanted to believe – that I had come home late because I didn't care about the consequences, that I should have been there." She shook her head, unwilling to relive the pain and the guilt all over again, especially in front of him. "But I just lost track of time ..." At this, her voice broke and she closed her eyes briefly, the pain almost too strong to bear.

"I know."

"And yet you couldn't see that, you kept insinuating that I had done it on purpose – as a kind of revenge or something. That was never, *ever* the case."

He nodded with heavy emotion. "I know, but there seemed no other way of getting my head around it. No matter what you say, there was always some resentment, Olivia – you admitted that yourself."

"Yes, but the resentment was entirely toward *you* – how did you not get that?"

For a long time husband and wife remained in silence, painful memories hanging heavily between them.

Eventually, Olivia shook her head. "Again, I'm sorry but I don't want to get into this now. Maybe we can arrange something later, but you can't just barge in like this. Matt, the man just now, he's very important to me and I have a lot to explain."

"I see." His hands in his pockets, Peter headed toward the door.

"No, you don't see," Olivia followed him out to the hallway. "You don't have a clue how hard these last few years have been for me and finally, when I get a chance at happiness, you turn up and ruin it."

"That was never my intention," he said, stepping out onto the front path. He turned back to look at her. "I never wanted to upset you, Olivia – I just wanted to see my daughter."

"Well, Teresa has my number. If you're still in Dublin, phone me later maybe – when I've had a chance to prepare Ellie," she added pointedly.

"I appreciate that and I would like to speak to you before I head up to Galway, if I could." Peter paused slightly as he turned to leave. "Look, I'm sorry for surprising you. I hope I didn't mess things up with you and that – that guy. I didn't mean to do that – I didn't even know you *were* with someone, I mean, Mum didn't say …" He trailed off, uncomfortable with the admission. "In fact, I'm with someone too."

"Good for you." Olivia suddenly realised she didn't care. She'd always suspected that he would have found someone else – after all, it was a long time – but now she decided she just didn't care about Peter, his new relationship, or even the fact that he'd finally come home. At that moment, all she cared about was Matt.

Maybe she *could* understand why he thought that Peter had died, but yet … Olivia's head thudded, her brain unable to cope with the enormity of all that was happening.

If only she'd told him everything right from the beginning. But she couldn't have done that. Not until she was absolutely sure that she could trust Matt enough to tell him the truth. The situation with Catherine complicated things too. She had to wait until she could be sure Matt would understand.

And mostly, that she wasn't to blame.

FIFTY-SEVEN

"Catherine, I really need your help,"

She was stony-faced. "I don't know where he is."

"His phone is switched off and he's not answering at home. Please, I really need to talk to him."

"I'm sure you do."

"It's very important."

"I'd imagine it is."

"Catherine, *please.*"

She sighed. "Look, I don't know what's going on between you two. All I know is that Matt is very annoyed. I presume it might have something to do with that man at your house a while ago?"

"My husband, yes."

Catherine's eyes widened. "Wow, no wonder he's upset."

Olivia didn't have the energy to explain; she needed to save that for Matt.

"I know he's here. Can you ask him to come out and talk to me, please?"

He must have gone elsewhere after leaving her house, as Olivia hadn't been able to reach him at his place, and then, some time after Peter left, she finally spotted his car outside Catherine's.

"I don't know if he'll want to talk to you. He certainly doesn't want to talk to me."

"Catherine ..." Both women turned towards the voice in the hallway. "It's OK. Come in, Olivia," Matt said quietly. "We might as well get this over and done with."

Catherine stood back to let her in, and the three stood silently in the hallway. Eventually the other woman spoke. "I'm heading back up to the hospital now anyway," she said, her voice low and gentler than Olivia had ever heard it.

She waited until the front door closed behind Catherine before speaking. "Matt, I don't know what to say."

"Neither do I."

He went into the front room, obviously expecting her to follow. Olivia obliged and sat nervously on the edge of Catherine's leather sofa, Matt sitting on an armchair nearby.

"It was only when you mentioned something about Peter's funeral last night that I realised you had the idea he was dead," she began, her voice slow and nervous. "And I was about to correct you when Catherine rang about Adam and – "

"But I've *always* thought that," he interjected, shaking his head. "The woman in the corner shop told me that you moved here after your husband died."

Olivia's eyes widened, surprised at this. "Molly actually *said* that?"

"Yes. I felt a bit uncomfortable about her telling me actually, as I didn't know you well at the time, and I hate those gossipy types."

But – but Molly didn't know anything, *nobody* in Lakeview knew anything – Olivia had made sure of that. It was the only way she could live in peace, knowing that she'd have none of the pitying smiles and sympathetic looks she'd had in their old estate.

She'd never said a word. How on earth had Molly come up with that scenario?

But then, Olivia realised that her insistence on maintaining her privacy had simply made her prime fodder for local gossip. Thinking of it now, she recalled her neighbour Maeve McGrath being quite intrusive in her questions when she'd bumped into her at the graveyard one day, although Olivia hadn't said much.

Maeve and Molly were bosom buddies, so between the two of them of course they'd taken two and two and come up with fifty.

She shook her head, unable to take it all in herself, never mind try and explain all to Matt. Granted she'd never been all that happy to call herself separated as she'd always hoped that someday Peter would return. But yet, she had no idea that all this time her neighbours thought she was a *widow*.

What a mess.

"I moved to Lakeview after Peter and I separated, not long after Ellie was born."

"But why did she think – "

"I'm not one hundred per cent sure myself actually, but it might have something to do with my visits to Shankill graveyard," she said, realising that this had to be the most likely scenario. "When they don't have all the pieces of a puzzle, some people like to try and make the most obvious parts fit." She sighed. "But I wasn't visiting Peter there."

A very long silence hung between them. Eventually, Matt spoke.

"Who – who *were* you visiting then?"

Olivia's eyes filled with tears and she tightly grasped her hands together. "Our son. Peter and I lost a toddler, Jake. His death was the reason we split up." Her voice began to shake.

Matt leant across and put a comforting hand on her knee. "I'm so sorry. I just assumed Ellie was your first."

Olivia took a deep breath before continuing. "She is, but she isn't – *wasn't* – Peter's first."

He waited for her to elaborate.

"Peter had a little ... summer fling many years ago, the year before we married actually. He and I had split up at the time."

"Oh."

"I'd initiated the break-up in the first place, and we only found out about the other girl's pregnancy once we'd made up and become engaged. I was devastated, naturally, but still madly in love with Peter and in the middle of making plans for our wedding." She paused, before continuing. "Eventually, I just resolved to get over it and get on with it." She shrugged. "And I agreed to take on the child as my own."

Matt was confused. "But what about the mother?"

Olivia shook her head. "She didn't want him. Peter discovered that she was going to have an abortion, but neither of us would stand for that. So we offered to adopt Jake – that was his name," she said, smiling, her eyes glistening with tears.

"And she agreed?"

"Like I said, she didn't really want a baby. It wasn't long after graduation and she wanted to go and do her own thing. I expect she felt guilty that Peter and I had got back together, and she didn't want to rock the boat, as such. She had no issue with letting us adopt."

"But she told him about the baby?"

"No, we heard about that from ... another source. But like I said, I couldn't blame Peter, I couldn't blame her, I could only blame myself. That summer, right after graduation, for some reason I panicked and told Peter that our relationship was stifling me.

I told him I didn't want to be with him any more. We had been together all throughout uni, and it seemed inevitable that we'd get married and be together forever. They used to call us the Golden Couple. But that last summer ... things changed. I felt smothered, tied down – it's hard to explain really. But after that time apart and a little space to determine how I really felt, I decided that I did want to be with him after all."

"But in the meantime, he was so upset that he shagged someone else? Doesn't sound so golden to me," Matt said sardonically.

"Perhaps," she said, "but it wasn't quite like that. They were friends and he'd been drinking and well, you know yourself. There was nothing between them, really." At least, that's what Olivia had always tried to convince herself – if she hadn't, she knew she wouldn't have been able to go ahead with the wedding, let alone the rest.

"So you took on the child. That must have been tough all the same."

She shrugged. "Once I'd made the decision that was it. And he was Peter's, so as far as I was concerned he was as good as mine. Still, he was a sickly child, and a challenge to look after sometimes. I think ... well, I *know* that Peter thought I resented him because he wasn't mine, but that was never the case – it was just that he needed a lot of watching and that could be tough going. We had one very tough year when he started going to a crèche – we were so fearful about entrusting him to strangers. The carers knew the situation of course and all went well for a while." Olivia paused, her face bleak, then continued with obvious difficulty. "Peter and I had a system going, whereby we kept in close contact to ensure one of us would always be there to pick him up in the evenings, whatever emergency might overtake either of us at work ..." She trailed off, the memory of it all so clear in her mind. "To this day, I still wonder why I went back to work at all, why I didn't just stay home and look after Jake full-time, but we felt that we could manage – stupidly *I* felt that we could manage. I thought it wouldn't be good to smother him, that interaction with other children was necessary for his development."

"OK, so the day he died, you were late collecting him from the crèche, is that it? Catherine mentioned something about you blaming yourself for ..."

"I wasn't just late, Matt – I completely forgot. I lost track of time ...we had an emergency, and it took a lot longer than expected, and in the middle of it all, I forgot to tell Peter I'd be late and ..." her voice shook. "When I realised the time, naturally I panicked. But for some reason, I couldn't get Peter on the phone, and no one in the crèche was answering ... So I just jumped in the car and to this day I don't know how I managed to drive home at all, because I knew. Deep down I just *knew* that something terrible had happened, and when I came back and saw the ambulance at our house ..." her words trailed off softly. "I swung by the crèche on the way, but everything was locked up, and they were all gone."

"So what happened? If you were both late, why didn't the crèche wait for you, or try to contact you?" Matt asked, frowning.

"One of the other mothers, Deirdre – she was a newcomer to the estate we were in – and she offered to take him home and keep an eye. The crèche would have normally phoned to ask, but there was a part-timer on that day who thought what the harm. So she let him off with the other mother, thinking she was doing us a favour. Like the neighbour too thought she was doing us a favour. She brought both kids back, and gave them both something to eat. But she didn't know about..." She stopped, unable to keep going, the pain of it all just too much.

"He choked on food...?" Matt supplied gently. "Olivia, something like that was an accident, it wasn't your fault."

"He didn't choke, Matt. He had a serious food allergy and needed medication, *specialist* medication that only someone with experience could administer. Poor Deirdre didn't know what to do – she rang her doctor but it was too late." Olivia looked at him. "My next door neighbour tried to ring me, but stupidly, I had forgotten to bring my phone, so instead she tried my mother. But by then, it was too late anyway." She paused again to steel herself. "Jake died because I wasn't there to collect him, Matt, and when it all went wrong, I wasn't there to help either."

Peter had been inconsolable, wanting to blame her, the crèche, poor Deirdre anyone. But ultimately Olivia knew it had been all her fault. She paused for a moment and Matt let her, giving her the chance to collect herself.

"Within a few minutes of eating the sandwich Deirdre gave him he went into shock and then into a coma. He died before the ambulance came."

"I'm so sorry, Olivia."

"Afterwards Peter blamed me, even more than I blamed myself. He accused me of being resentful towards Jake, and of the fact that he wasn't mine, that he was a reminder of what Peter had done. That wasn't the case – I loved him just as much as if he had been mine. It was terrifying living with the peanut allergy, but ..."

"Peanut allergy?" Matt repeated. "Like your friend Robin's from last night? I didn't realise it was so common. Before that I didn't know anyone else who had ..."

Olivia said nothing more – she just sat there, waiting as Matt's words trailed off as the realisation hit him.

"The mother, the friend Peter was with... oh."

She nodded, grateful for her own sake, that she didn't need to explain much more.

FIFTY-EIGHT

She'd never meant for it to happen, but it did.

She'd never meant to betray her friend, never meant to fall head over heels for Peter but she did. From the very first moment Robin laid eyes on him.

He'd known it too way back then, that night Olivia asked her round for dinner, not long after the episode in the cafeteria.

She remembered the way he watched her, the way he followed her with his eyes, and yet all the time continued to be nothing other than charming and gracious. How he made light of 'saving her life'.

"But you did, Peter," Olivia had insisted. "If you hadn't helped with that shot, she might have died."

"Ah, sure it's all in a day's work," he'd said, laughing it off, but still those watchful eyes were focused on her every movement. It was disconcerting, but strangely exciting too.

At least it was for a while, until Robin began spending more and more time with Olivia and her diverse group of friends, some of whom like Leah welcomed her into the fold like she'd been around forever, and others like Amanda, who viewed Robin's unobtrusive persona with suspicion. And she'd never been one hundred per cent sure how Kate felt about her.

Not to mention the fact that they all seemed to find her condition freakishly bewildering.

When they were all together, Peter's behaviour was even more disconcerting, as Robin watched him play devoted boyfriend to Olivia and often wondered if she'd been imagining it all. Feeling an absolute heel for even thinking for a second that her new friend's man was giving her the eye, Robin resolved to cop on to herself and stop imagining things.

But one night after a couple of drinks, Peter confirmed her suspicions. "You know there's something between us, don't you?" he'd said, slurring slightly. "Something special – a connection."

"I'm not sure what you're talking about," she said, precarious exhilaration stirring inside her.

But it was wrong, and she'd been naïve. In retrospect, she should have confided in Olivia, but she hadn't known her all that long, and Robin didn't want her to think badly of her boyfriend, or indeed of her.

Still, she couldn't help but be even more aware of Peter after that, disconcertingly aware. Worse, she really liked Olivia and had come to like her even more as time went on. Still, she was like a moth drawn to Peter's flame; she knew he could be dangerous, yet she couldn't resist moving closer.

Then that last summer the gang were all together, for some reason he and Olivia broke up, and Robin finally had a chance.

They had already begun to go their separate ways, Kate to an accountancy firm, Leah to France to continue her chef's training, Andrew to work on his new data-provider software, while Amanda, well ... she went to work on getting Andrew to propose.

But Robin made sure she was there for Peter. Although she tried to convince herself she was just being a friend, a shoulder to cry on, she knew deep down it was more than that. She was hoping that he would eventually realise that Olivia didn't need him, that he'd be better off without her, that there was someone else for him, right in front of his eyes.

When they finally started sleeping together, Robin felt she had no choice but to raise the thorny subject of Olivia.

"I'd hate her to find out from anyone else, or worse, horrified for her to think we were carrying on behind her back."

"She won't. But let's take wait a while before saying anything all the same."

Which is why it came as a major shock when, before she realised it, Olivia and Peter were back together and engaged.

Robin was devastated. By then she'd fallen heavily, believing their passionate nights were the start of something special - certain that by her own choice, Olivia was fully out of the picture.

She tried her best to smile and say all the right things when her friend proudly displayed her stunning engagement ring, and asked her opinion on wedding dresses. Ironically, she and Robin had become even closer by then, since Leah had gone abroad.

So she had to come to terms with what she'd thought was a blossoming relationship was nothing other than a stop-gap – something to keep Peter occupied until Olivia changed her mind.

And when later, Robin began throwing up in the mornings and feeling tired and listless at work, she realised that their fling was about to have devastating consequences – for everyone.

"You have to tell him," Leah tried to convince her over the phone from France, when Robin, wracked with fear and loneliness broke down and confided in her. "You can't do this alone."

"What else can I do? I've just started a job – a junior position with terrible pay and even worse prospects. How can I possibly bring a child up on my own? Olivia is bound to suspect something too – she knows I haven't been seeing anyone, and the timing is too obvious. Not to mention that I've been avoiding her since I found out they were back together."

It had all been so bleak, so desperate, that it seemed there was only one way out.

At college, she and Olivia had always signed up for pro-life demonstrations and rallies. It was easy to be idealistic or moralistic about 'choice' when it wasn't yours to make. Things seemed so much simpler in college, a cosy cocoon where you and your little student societies could all play at politics and at real life. But outside the walls of university - outside that structured framework of right and reason, it was all very different.

"You don't have to resort to that," Leah advised. "You should tell Peter – it's his responsibility too and I know he'd support you."

"But Olivia would hate me."

And Olivia did for a while, Robin knew that. Unbeknownst to her, and ostensibly for her own good, Leah approached Peter and let him know the truth.

All too soon, the newly reunited couple were there for Robin, and made it known in no uncertain terms they would support her.

The two, Olivia especially, had been wonderful and helped her through the remainder of her pregnancy. Which made Robin feel ever guiltier for messing up her own and her friend's life so spectacularly, but which also helped her with her next decision.

Once they had persuaded her to keep the baby, and not long before her due date, she knew exactly what she had to do.

"I don't want the baby, you know that," she said one day when she and Olivia were alone in her tiny bedsit. "I never wanted it." Her heart hammered guiltily as she lied. Of course she wanted the baby. Granted not in these circumstances, but still this little life inside her was precious – and hers.

"Don't say that, you're just nervous about the birth," Olivia said, dismissing her.

"I mean it," she persisted. "I don't want it. If you and Peter hadn't persuaded me to keep it ... I'm not a maternal person, you know that." Robin grasped at this and tried to convince herself that she really *wasn't* maternal, but with each passing day as she felt new life growing inside her, she came to love it more and more. It would be torture, but she knew she had caused enough misery.

And she also knew she had to try and make amends.

"You'll be grand," Olivia said, but every time Robin looked at her, she could see the sadness and betrayal reflected in her friend's eyes.

"I was thinking that maybe you and Peter might take it ...?" she went on, trying to make her voice sound casual, as if she was talking about a second-hand TV set, although once she'd uttered that simple remark, Robin felt as though she'd already lost a part of herself.

"What?"

"The baby. I was hoping that you two might take it? That's if you'd like to," she said, watching Olivia's face. "I know it's not ideal, but you've always said you'd love a big family." She tried to shrug off-handedly. "I know it's not be how you imagined but ... chances are I'll be giving the baby up anyway."

For a long moment, Olivia was silent. "Let me talk to Peter ..." she said.

And that was that. Decision made. Robin tried not to think too much about it after that, although inside her heart ached. She made herself imagine that it was Peter and Olivia's baby from then on in. And by rights it *should* be theirs. She had made a stupid mistake but at least this could be a way of making up for it somewhat.

So, by the time the baby was born a little prematurely, Robin had almost convinced herself that she didn't feel anything for the tiny little thing in the incubator, baby Jake Gallagher. Olivia had picked the name, at Robin's insistence.

When she returned from the maternity hospital – lonely and bereft – and found that a job she'd applied for before the summer was hers, and the New York-based firm would sponsor her visa, she resolved to move on altogether. She'd be better off away from Ireland, away from everyone and everything – away from all the trouble she'd caused.

And Olivia, Peter and little Jake would be much better off without her.

FIFTY-NINE

The following morning, Robin gave another interview about her children's books on breakfast television.

The bubbly blonde presenter was doing her best to relax her, but she just couldn't feel relaxed. The last few days had been torturous and she just didn't feel like gabbing on and promoting her stupid book.

It all seemed so shallow and inconsequential.

There hadn't been a single day in her life since giving him up that she hadn't thought of Jake, but especially after meeting Olivia the other night, Robin could think of little else, and the pain was all-consuming.

Now, she just wanted to go home, back to New York, to Ben and away from all the hurt and regret that being back in Ireland was causing.

The presenter asked her another question. "These stories won't just entertain, but will really help the children and the parents of allergy sufferers," she began. "Do you feel that your own experience helps you understand better than most the issue associated with such conditions?"

Robin sat forward, deciding she'd better just get it over and done with. "Yes, and it can be tough as an adult living with the condition, but at least I'm old enough to be able to take responsibility for myself." She paused. "I do know it's a lot harder for parents. The reason the book came about in the first place was because I saw how hard my partner's sister found it with her little girl, who suffers from asthma and hay fever. In a city like New York, especially in summertime, it's very difficult. And of course, she's now school-going age, so it's even more worrying for her mother."

"I can imagine," the presenter nodded sympathetically. "So the book did have an effect on this girl?"

"Yes, it did, but I think it had even more of an effect on her mother – but you have to remember this was all unintentional. I have no idea what it's like to look after a child with such a condition. I don't know how it must feel to exist permanently in a state of potential emergency." She stopped then, her heart thudding against her chest as she realised what she had just admitted. She did have no idea, no idea at all of what Sarah really had to go through.

Nor Olivia.

"So, your sister-in-law brought the book to the attention of the publishers?" The presenter glanced almost imperceptibly at Robin's left hand.

"No –" She went on to explain how she and Ben had provided their own crude booklets for the school, and that one of the parents worked on the production team for Bubblegum Press.

"And then Nickelodeon got in on the act. It's such an amazing story," the presenter was shaking her head in awe. "And you never even wanted to be a writer?"

"Not really. To be honest, I feel a little guilty about that. I'm sure there are thousands of people out there who could have done a better job on these books than I did."

"Yes, but you're the one who had the experience. You knew how to put the message across."

"Perhaps," Robin shrugged self-consciously.

"So, as a result of your series, hundreds, if not thousands of parents around the world could be helped. Congratulations, Robin. I'm sure every parent watching who has a child suffering from such a condition will be very grateful." The presenter smiled then, as if to wrap up the slot, but Robin shook her head.

"I don't know about that," she continued, her voice softer and less assured. "I had a friend ... a wonderful friend, who sacrificed a lot to look after a nut-allergic child like me. It didn't just affect her life, it affected her marriage."

"Oh, so more experiences to draw from then." The presenter tried to keep the tone light.

"The thing is," Robin went on, the reunion with Olivia, the visit to the graveyard, all of it, really hitting her, "I never really understood how much it had affected *her*. To be honest, I didn't want to understand."

And that was true, she admitted. She had been so intent on getting over her own pain, her own loss, that she hadn't really thought about what Olivia had sacrificed. Raising Jake wouldn't have been easy, plus the fact that he was a constant reminder of Peter and Robin's betrayal.

She looked away and her eyes shone with tears. "That's why I feel there should be more help for parents in general. People seem to think that keeping children away from the food in question is the answer. But it isn't. The family's entire way of life has to change and the pressure is enormous. I didn't really understand that."

She didn't want to understand it, she thought. She was too wrapped up in her own problems, in her own regrets.

"I see, well, thank you –" Again the presenter tried to wrap things up.

"But she's the most kind-hearted, unselfish person I've ever known, and I know she did her very best for that child."

"Did?"

Robin's head snapped up then, almost as if remembering where she was. "Yes," she said sadly. "My friend's son died actually." Robin's eyes sparkled under the bright studio lights, and just then the presenter realised that this bit wasn't on the press release.

"Oh, dear – I didn't know it could get that serious ..." Her gaze flickered fearfully to the production crew. Now she was concerned, not for Robin, but for the fact that this slot was running *way* over time.

But at this stage Robin was in full flow, as everything seemed to overwhelm her all at once, grief for Jake, for Peter and for the friendship that she had lost.

"But I think – I mean, I *know* my friend always blamed herself for that, and she shouldn't have. She was a fantastic mother and she did her best, more than her best for him. It was a tragedy, but one that was always possible until he learned to look after himself. But in the meantime, there was no one better than Ol – than my friend – to take care of him. No one could have done any better."

And that was true too. Despite the fact that Jake was lost to them both, Robin knew deep down that Olivia had done her best for that child, something that she herself could never claim.

"But you wish you could have helped more?" the presenter prompted.

She paused, unsure how to word this. "Yes, I should have helped more, and I hope she can forgive me for that."

The presenter nodded again. "I'm sure your friend is thrilled you decided to write a book about it."

"I'm not so sure about that," she answered sadly.

"Robin, thank you so much for sharing that with us, and thank you for coming on the show," she interjected while she had the chance. "Robin's first book is called *Atchoo the Allergic Alligator* and will be in bookshops next month." She turned to Robin. "Best of luck with it all."

"Thank you," she nodded uncomfortably.

With a winning smile, the reporter turned to face the camera. "Right, now we'll go over to the newsroom for an update and next up, our vet spot where we'll explain how *you* can best communicate with *your* pet!"

SIXTY

The telephone rang, and Leah put down her coffee mug and muted the TV.

"OMG, did you see that?" Kate gasped. "Who does that one think she is?"

Leah groaned. "Oh, give it a rest, will you?" she said, sick to the teeth of Kate's constant sniping and bad humour. "I thought she was very honest."

"What the hell would she know about it? 'There should be more support' indeed. She wasn't exactly that supportive of Olivia when Jake *died,* was she? No, she was too busy living it up in New York."

Leah shook her head "Kate, I'm sorry – you're my friend and I love you, but lately you've turned into an almighty pain in the arse."

Silence at the other end.

"What's with all the Robin-bashing? You weren't that close to Olivia back then either. What's it got to do with you?"

To her amazement, her friend began to cry. "I don't know!" she wailed. "I don't know what's wrong with me lately. I'm angry at Michael, at Dylan, at Robin, at everything! I'm sorry for not going out for your birthday – I know you probably hate me now, but I'm sorry."

"Oh, you silly goose," Leah couldn't help but smile. "I know you'll make it up to me."

Kate sniffed again. "I want you to be Dylan's godmother. Now it's OK if you say no because I know it might be hard and – "

"I'd love to." She was touched.

"Would you?"

"Yes, it would be an honour."

"Thanks." Another sniff. "I didn't know if you would want to after me being such a cow about Josh and everything. But you know it's only because I care about you and he was in the wrong ..."

"Kate, listen to yourself, seriously – you sound like a right moan."

"I do, don't I?"

"Yes!" Leah supposed she'd been unfair to her really, giving out about her not making an effort any more. It was pretty obvious that the root of Kate's suffering was baby blues.

And she had just the cure for that. "I have to go into the shop this morning, but I'll pop over later for lunch and a natter, OK?"

"OK," Kate sniffled, and Leah had to smile.

"And then afterwards, you get Dylan organised, and we'll go to the hospital and visit Amanda and the new arrival. Apparently, the planned slice and dice never happened," she added wickedly.

Almost instantly, the sniffling stopped. "What? You mean she Miss Too Posh to Push went through with it all – the old fashioned way?"

"Yep. Apparently her timing was all wrong, 'cos when she went in she was too far gone for the top down. Her waters had broken and the baby was coming. *And*, listen to this, Andrew said she was *also* too far gone to get the epidural too."

Poor Amanda.

"Oh my gosh, I can't miss this," Now she was sounding much more like the old Kate. "Don't you *dare* go to the hospital without me – I want to hear every gory detail."

"Are you sure you're feeling up to it?"

"Never better, now that I know she had to endure what I went through too."

With a slight grin at the thought of their visit, Leah replaced the receiver and began to get ready for work.

It was weird, she thought, driving towards the shop, but today she was feeling fantastic.

It was as though finally coming to terms with the fact that she and Josh weren't getting back together had been an epiphany for her.

Although then again, she thought with a smile, it could be that lovely feeling you get the day immediately after an almighty hangover.

Nevertheless, it was onwards and upwards from now on, she decided. No more feeling sorry for herself about Josh. No more feeling cheated just because her best friend didn't have as much time for her any more. Today was the first day of the rest of her life and all that.

Beeeep! Beeeep!

Leah slammed on the brakes as a huge Mercedes headed towards her from the right and she realised that she didn't actually *have* the right of way on the roundabout.

Yikes ... the rest of her life mightn't last all that long if she carried on driving like this, she thought, smiling her apology at the retreating motorist.

Well, to mark her newfound freedom, Leah decided there and then that she was going to learn to drive. Properly. For the first time in her life, she was going to take some lessons. Then she might at least have a hope of passing the blasted test.

And in the meantime she thought, turning onto Blackrock main street, and glancing adoringly at the her very own shop-front, she was going to enjoy being proprietor of the best chocolate emporium in Dublin.

SIXTY-ONE

"Robin? Hi, it's Olivia."

Sitting in her hotel room, Robin was lost for words. Oh no ... what did she want? Was she mad, annoyed, upset – what?

"I'll be in town today and was wondering, if you don't have anything else on, do you fancy meeting for a coffee?" Olivia asked pleasantly. "We didn't really get a chance to talk the other night."

Inwardly Robin was petrified. "I don't have anything else until tomorrow and I'd love to," she said, before she could change her mind.

"Great, would two o'clock suit? I'll meet you at your hotel if you like – it's the Westin, I think Leah said?"

"It is and, yes, that would be great."

"See you then."

Olivia rang off, leaving Robin feeling shocked and bewildered, not just at the call but at the reason for the impromptu invite.

AT TWO ON THE DOT, Olivia was standing at reception. "How are you?" she greeted. "I saw your interview this morning. I thought it was very interesting."

"You did?" For some reason, Robin hadn't considered that Olivia might be watching. She was so used to all the different TV networks back in the States that she thought it would be a blink-and-miss performance.

But of course, here there were only a few homegrown stations, and apparently only one did breakfast TV, so there was every chance Olivia would be watching. Crikey, did she say too much?

Robin knew she shouldn't have babbled on like that on live TV, but once she'd started she just couldn't stop and –

"So where would you like to go?" Olivia asked.

"We could head out if you like," Robin answered hesitantly. "But there is a beautiful tea room here."

"Why not? I'm sure it'll be better than fighting for a table in one of those postage-stamp cafes," she said, and Robin realised that this time the warmth wasn't forced. Something had changed about Olivia since Saturday, she was sure of it.

But when they were seated in the hotel's Atrium Lounge, and she found out what, Robin nearly spat out her tea.

"He did *what?*" she all but shrieked, forgetting that in the wide open space and the glass-domed roof, every word echoed right back through the room.

Olivia had just told her about Peter's visit. After she had spoken to Matt, she'd met with Peter locally about formally arranging their divorce.

"And are you OK about it?" Robin asked, feeling a little surreal talking to her so easily like this, almost as though all those years had never happened.

"Not great, but there's something else," she said, leaning forward. "You know I always blamed myself for ..." she paused slightly, "well for not taking better care with Jake, and not being there before he died."

"I've never understood that," Robin said. "And when Leah told me that you felt that way, so many times I wanted to pick up the phone ... But I didn't feel it was my place to say anything." Not to mention that it had taken her a very long time to come to terms with the terrible tragedy herself.

Olivia sighed. "I always wondered if maybe you blamed me a little bit too, if you thought that I didn't make enough of an effort. Peter used to accuse me of being resentful, but truly that was never the case - where Jake was concerned at least. I did my best. I know it wasn't enough but – "

"I never once thought that," Robin reassured her, although inwardly her heart ached. "I knew you'd take good care of him. There was nobody better."

"Peter didn't think so though. He was so angry and so accusatory." Her hands shook as she spooned sugar into the tea. "But I always believed that eventually he'd forgive me, and come to terms with it all. And that, when he did, he'd come back to me and Ellie and we'd be a family again." She shook her head. "I know it was stupid, but I'd forgiven him so much already, we'd been through so much and – sorry," she broke off then, remembering.

But Robin understood perfectly. Olivia *had* forgiven Peter a lot already - too much maybe.

"I thought it was only a matter of time, a couple of weeks perhaps. And when the weeks turned into months and the months turned into years ... well, you know how it is. Eventually I began to let go, tried to move on with my life. We moved to Lakeview to be closer to my parents and Ellie seemed happy enough getting birthday cards and the odd phone call every now and again. I also suspected he might have had somebody else at that stage, so I had no choice but to try and let go."

"And then of course, you met Matt."

"Yes," Olivia smiled. "Then I met Matt and I realised just what I'd been missing. Strangely, I began to notice all the things that were lacking in Peter. Matt's a great father and he's really good with Ellie. He's gentle, considerate and when I'm with him it's only me, you know? He isn't checking out the blonde at the bar, or the brunette with the nice legs like Peter used to. It's just me."

"I know exactly what you mean. In a way, that's what attracted me to Ben too. Peter was always so unpredictable whereas Ben is simple, uncomplicated, straightforward. From day one, I knew where I stood."

"But – does he know? About Jake?"

Robin flushed. "No. I haven't told him. It hasn't been necessary ... up to now. But he's so lovely and supportive I hope he'll understand ... when I do say something. He's not selfish like Peter was. Sorry, I know you probably don't need to hear that."

"Hey, I know better than anyone that Peter has hidden depths, and not just emotionally," Olivia said scathingly. "He's divorcing me because he and his Australian 'friend' plan on getting married. He told me the other night that he and this other woman were five years together."

Robin looked at her, suspecting that Olivia was waiting for a reaction. "I don't get it," she said.

"He's been seeing her for *five* years? Ellie's four. They worked at the hospital here before Oz – I think she was a nurse or something, and were obviously seeing one another when he and I were still together. Yesterday he finally admitted that, yes, he had been cheating on me." She paused for breath before continuing. "And on the day we lost Jake, Peter wasn't working late, Robin. He wasn't working at all ... he was away somewhere, screwing this other woman."

Robin almost dropped her cup into her lap. "*What?*"

"That's why he was so angry, so upset back then and I thought I understood his rage. But it wasn't me he was angry with – it was himself. Of course, he couldn't admit to it back then either. So after a while, the easiest thing to do was to take off with her and pretend that he'd left because he couldn't face me because he blamed me. But thinking back on it now, all the signs were there. He was always late, always tired and a little distant but stupidly, I just assumed he was working too hard." She smiled tightly. "I remember being worried about him actually, worried that all the late nights and stress at work were affecting his health. That day, the day I was ... late home, I'd been on at Peter to get himself seen to. Little did I know that he'd take me at my word," she finished sardonically.

Robin couldn't comprehend how she felt upon hearing this. How selfish could he be? How could Peter let everyone think that Olivia had been at fault? Hadn't he put her through enough?

Olivia smiled sadly. "In a strange way, it was a relief, a weight off my mind if you like. Now I know that it wasn't just my fault."

"But yet he let you think that."

"It was Peter's way of getting out of a difficult situation. Our marriage was under pressure as it was, there's no point in our pretending otherwise. Raising Jake was challenging, and I'm not saying that to get at you, I'm simply stating a fact."

Now, Robin ached with regret to think that her stupid attempt to make amends had been a terrible, fateful decision.

"I knew Peter was unhappy, but I loved him desperately, so I thought that if we had a child of our own it would be different," Olivia went on. "Yet, I think I knew in the back of my mind that we weren't going to make it." She gave a watery smile. "Then, when Jake died, I knew it was all over. I had no choice but to accept the blame for his death and for the fact that Peter was leaving me. What else could I have done?"

"But you were pregnant and grieving, and I just can't believe he let you think that for so long. How dare he?"

"Robin, you and I both know that Peter was never the upstanding guy he pretends to be. So then, immediately after the funeral, he told me he needed some time alone to get over it. And I never saw him again – until yesterday. "

Robin gulped slightly at the mention of the funeral. "I couldn't go," she whispered, her voice frail. "I toyed with it for a long time, but in the end, I thought it better that I didn't go. It wasn't my place."

Olivia laid a gentle hand on hers. "You would have been welcome, but I understood. I suspected it would've been impossible for you to endure."

Robin still couldn't grasp her friend's courage, her wonderful strength. Even then, at the height of her own grief, Olivia was still able to make allowances for her.

"I'd always thought you'd hate me for that."

"Of course it would've been difficult, having to pretend concern for me yet trying to hide your grief. And again, I worried that you too might blame me. After all, you trusted me to look after him, and look what happened."

Robin looked at her friend then, and hoped Olivia truly understood what she was trying to say. "All I've ever done is admire you, and I'll be forever grateful for what you did for me back then. I'm just so sorry that I didn't return the favour, that I wasn't there for you when you were struggling."

Olivia smiled, and her eyes twinkled. "I know, I found that out this morning – on TV of all places."

Robin grimaced, remembering. "The poor woman must have felt like a priest in the confession box. She didn't know where to look." And in a way, it *was* a confession, a release of all the confusion, guilt and regret that Robin had been feeling all these years.

The longer she stayed away she'd thought, the easier it would be. But she'd been wrong. There was so much she hadn't understood, so much she hadn't *wanted* to understand about Olivia's situation. She'd been too consumed with her own grief.

But here now sitting with her friend, Robin felt as though a huge weight had been lifted off her shoulders.

"Well, I'm glad you said something." Olivia paused as if she was unsure whether or not she should continue. "I can appreciate how tough it must have been giving him up, but at the same time I couldn't figure out why you didn't want to know about him?"

She wanted to know why Robin didn't seem interested in Jake, and what he was like, what her son, her baby was like. They'd never insisted that Robin stay out of his life; in fact, Olivia had been concerned that moving to America so soon after the birth was the wrong thing to do. She had been willing to share with Robin not only Jake but also the burden of coming to terms with giving him up. She was and had always been a true friend, yet Robin – to her own detriment she knew now – had knowingly abandoned that friendship.

"I did ... want to," she whispered. "Throughout this visit, I was desperate to ask ... about it. But yet, I couldn't deny that broaching it would be difficult for you. Plus you and I had grown so far apart that there never seemed to be a right time or place." She looked at her. "The other night, after dropping Leah home, I was sorely tempted to invite you to stay on too."

"Well, with the way Leah was that night, we might not have got a word in edgeways," she chuckled, lightening the mood.

"How is she about the Josh thing – really?" Robin asked. "I tried to talk to her about it the next morning, but she was very hungover."

"I think she'll be OK. You know Leah – she's tough and she'll push through it. And it might be good for her in the end. It wasn't fair of him to deny her the right to a family either."

Although it wasn't directed at her, the remark stung. Robin had been guilty of doing just that where Ben was concerned. She knew he was desperate to settle down and start a family and yet, she was denying him that because of her own reticence, her guilt at abandoning one.

He would be a wonderful father. Still, the root of Robin's problems was that she didn't know what kind of a mother *she'd* be. She'd already given up a child – who was to say she even deserved the chance to have another?

"And what about you?" Olivia asked then. "You've been with Ben a while now, haven't you?"

"Yes," Robin smiled once more at the thought of it. "He's great. I'm very lucky to have him – more than I realised."

"I'm pleased for you, Robin," Olivia said. "You didn't deserve to get mixed up with someone like Peter – neither of us did."

Robin looked at her, again in awe. Peter had done a terrible thing letting her take the blame all this time when he had been off with some other woman. Olivia had suffered a lot more than any of them, even more than Robin herself. She had been betrayed many times over and in the end, had wrongly been left carrying the guilt.

"He wasn't always that bad, and he loved you so very much."

Olivia shook her head sadly. "He loved the idea of me, I think. He got a hell of a shock when we split up because he didn't see it coming. He just liked the idea of his being in control, and when I pulled the plug he was blindsided."

"Maybe, but that never excused what *I* did."

"You just fell for the same things that I did, his smile, his charm, and that so-called little-boy-lost routine. Peter was always very skilled at making women fall for him." Olivia was looking at things a lot more clearly now. "I think I might have known it at the time too. It was easier to think that you two just had a drunken fling, but I don't think it was quite that simple."

Robin simply nodded. She didn't want to get into that with Olivia – it wasn't fair.

"Anyway," her friend sighed, "he's out of both of our lives now and, to be honest, I think we're the better for it." She grinned. "He can have his bloody divorce and good riddance! Although, in fairness, he was great with Jake."

There was silence for a long moment, as both women remained lost in their own thoughts and memories, neither knowing quite what to say next.

Then Olivia reached into her bag, took something out and laid it on her lap. She looked speculatively at Robin.

"I brought some photos – of Jake," she said carefully, and Robin's heart leapt with fear, anticipation, she wasn't quite sure what. "I was planning on sending you one on each birthday, but you were so insistent that you didn't want to look back ..."

Her stomach fluttered. "You were right – at the time, it would only have made things harder." She paused and stared at the small photo album. Then she smiled. "But I'd love to see them now." And she realised that she meant it.

"I hoped you would."

She duly laid the photo album on the table, while both scooted their chairs closer. Then the two old friends sat side by side as Olivia slowly turned the first page.

SIXTY-TWO

Amanda lay deathlike on the bed, looking tired and worn-out, although Leah could tell that her make-up had been carefully applied and her hair was freshly washed.

"Hello, Mummy Clarke," she said, and Amanda's eyes opened wide with delight when she saw her two visitors.

"Hi!" she said sitting up easily and then as if remembering, her face contorted into a grimace worthy of a day-time-soap actress. "Ah, sorry," she whispered frailly, "but I'm still sooo sore …."

"You poor thing," Kate soothed, but Leah could hear the sadistic pleasure in her tone. "So it wasn't as 'beautiful' an experience as you'd imagined?"

"There is nothing beautiful about any of it, as you well know," she said huffily. "I can't understand how they honestly think there's anything natural about all that huffing and puffing and pushing and oh, don't get me started…"

"You did it though, didn't you?" Leah looked in awe at the tiny pink bundle in the crib beside the bed. "And she's beautiful."

"Just like her mum, eh?" Andrew bellowed, entering the room.

He leaned over Amanda and gave her a delicate kiss on the forehead.

"Uh, stay away from me, you – it's all *your* fault I'm here in the first place," she groaned, looking thoroughly peeved. "And that's another thing," she said, addressing Kate as if by magic the two of them were now best friends, solidarity sisters. "*Why* do they let men in the delivery room with cameras? Honestly! Throughout the entire hellish experience, I didn't see Andrew for dust and then when it was all over and I'm lying in the bed looking like the Wreck of Hesperus with my hair matted to my forehead and my face drenched with sweat, he swans in with the camera."

Leah smiled weakly at the mention of a camera but realised that it didn't hurt her quite so much any more. She wasn't over Josh, but she was on her way and she knew she'd get through it.

"Just think, you'll be able to look back on that in years to come and little ... little ... hey, did you pick a name for her yet?"

Andrew and Amanda's eyes met and a secret smile passed between them. "Yes, we're going to call her Lulu," she confirmed.

"*Aww,*" Leah and Kate cried in unison.

"Sorry, we missed that – what are you calling her?" Olivia said from the doorway.

And to Leah's total amazement and delight, standing behind her was Robin.

"Come in, come in – hey!" Andrew grinned, surprised. "It's great to see you, stranger."

"Thanks," Robin smiled shyly around the room.

"Well, I must admit, I didn't expect *this* much attention," Amanda said, though Leah could tell she was delighted that so many of the old gang had come to visit. She looked around. "Me, Andrew, Leah, Kate, Olivia, Robin – it's a proper reunion."

"Like the reunion that never was?" Kate said sardonically. "I told you all at the time that it was a stupid idea ..."

Leah stood back and looked around at the faces of her friends; the ones she'd known all this time, the people she knew would help her get through any tough times ahead.

She and Kate had a great chat over lunch, and she knew now that her friend had been afraid to ask for help with Dylan because she worried Leah might feel obliged.

And find it difficult, given her own sacrifice.

Obviously, Robin and Olivia had sorted out a few things too, and now they looked relaxed and easy with one another. It was wonderful to behold.

Amanda had the new baby in her arms now, and she and Andrew were looking at their daughter and back to one another with such love and pride that Leah knew that motherhood – *parent*hood – was an experience she didn't want to miss, shouldn't have to sacrifice.

She smiled inwardly. Goodness knows who the misfortunate future father would be but ...

"My don't you have a lot of friends, Mammy Clarke." A nurse came in on her rounds and smiled at them all.

Amanda beamed. "Yes, I suppose I do," she said proudly.

"Well, give me that camera of yours," the nurse said to Andrew, "and I'll snap one of ye all."

"You don't mind?"

"Course not – these gatherings don't happen every day, and I know what it can be like. By the next time you lot get together it could be years."

They all duly gathered round the bed, and Leah realised that this *was* a reunion of sorts.

And although the old gang was missing the one that scattered them apart, they'd gained a brand new one who had somehow brought them together again. Today was a new chapter, a new beginning – for all of them.

Six happy faces looked into the camera and smiled.

The other just yawned.

EPILOGUE

Leah took a deep breath and tried to calm herself. This was easily the most terrifying experience of her life.

Worse than starting her business, worse than opening the shop, and even worse than breaking up with Josh.

She pulled into the kerb, trying her best not to drive up onto ... *oops*. Not a good start.

She turned off the ignition and glanced in her rear-view mirror. Where was the blasted driving instructor? He'd told her seven pm – it was now well after.

While she waited, she impatiently tapped the steering wheel and then switched on the radio. Whoever he was, he'd better not tell her that she couldn't have the radio on while driving. The music helped keep her mind off everything.

Then she realised suddenly that maybe that was why she *shouldn't* have the music on. It *did* take her mind off everything.

Only the other morning, she'd been on her way back from Lakeview, laughing at something the DJ was saying on air and what did she do? Completely miss the turn-off for home.

Not that she minded much, she thought with a smile. She and

Olivia had had a great catch-up, and it was wonderful to see her so happy, carefree and comfortable with Matt.

Peter was well and truly out of her life now. They had drawn up plans for their divorce, he had applied for full residency in Australia and Olivia and Ellie were finally free to move on.

In fact, all her friends seemed happier lately.

Back in the States, Robin and Ben had finally found their dream home and were making plans to move in. Her 'little book' had done well upon publication, and there were already high hopes for subsequent releases.

Leah suspected that an engagement might be on the cards for them soon too since upon her return to New York, Robin had told Ben everything about her past.

Amanda, much to everyone's surprise had taken to motherhood like a duck to water and incredibly, was now being a huge help to Kate!

Leah was so busy thinking about how well things had turned out for her friends that she almost didn't hear the sharp tapping at the driver's window. She looked up and saw what had to be the *cutest* driving instructor she had ever seen.

"Leah?"

"Yep," she answered, eyeing the guy unashamedly as he walked around and got into the passenger seat.

"Ian. Sorry I'm a little late," he said but she barely heard him. She was too busy trying not to stare. At those toned arm muscles, huge hands and that smile – jeez. Dare she say it; he was even cuter than Josh.

"So - your first lesson?"

Leah quickly stopped staring and resolved to concentrate on the task at hand.

"Proper lesson yes. To be honest, I'm a bit of a disaster," she blurted. "I've failed the test multiple times and although I try my best, I *know* I'm a terrible driver. So I just want to say that you have a big job ahead of you, because I will never *ever*, be able to pass the bloody thing." She couldn't resist a coquettish flick of her dark hair as she popped on her sunglasses.

"Don't be so defeatist," he said. "I've taught lots of different people over the years; some good, some bad and others downright terrifying." Leah groaned. She was definitely in the latter category. "But," Ian continued, and she tried her best not to stare at that undeniably sexy mouth, "I have my own little mantra about the test."

"What's that?" she asked, thinking that she didn't care a jot about the test but she couldn't wait to get going on the lessons – especially now.

Ian looked at her sideways and winked. "Never say never."

THE GETAWAY

EXCERPT

**Another unputdownable book club read from the
Irish Times #1 bestselling author.**

Careful what you wish for...

Three women routinely take the same coastal train service to
the city. All they have in common is that each is desperate for an
escape.

Newly-wed Dara would give anything to go back in time and
make a different choice. But she's married now and nothing can
change that. Can it?

Louise always wanted to be slim, pretty, and popular. So she
can't believe it when her luck seems to be changing. But is it all
too good to be true?

Widow Rosie has always tried her best to make her children
happy. Even though they're both grown adults, they seem to
expect more from her than ever.

But one summer morning, a shock incident on the train allows
each woman an opportunity to alter life's trajectory. Will they
have the courage to grasp it?

ONE

She couldn't miss this. And come hell or high water, she was *not* going to miss it.

But the rumbling was getting louder by the second, so despite her stilettos and pencil skirt she had no choice but to make a run for it. If she failed to make the train today she was in big trouble. Big. *Huge.*

She wasn't the only one running late this morning either she noted, seeing another harried commuter rush to the ticket booth. Tapping her travel pass, she scurried through the barrier and breathed a sigh of relief to see that the train was still at the platform.

Just in time.

Breathing heavily, she nipped inside the double doors seconds before they shut – nearly catching the hem of her trench in the process. But the person behind hadn't been fast enough, and as the train pulled off she felt bad for the unlucky straggler.

The coastal commuter service to Dublin was a busy route with usually only standing room in the carriages. Though today there was a precious seat a little way down that no one else seemed to have noticed.

She hurried to nab it, but as she pushed through the standing crowd her handbag slipped off her shoulder, falling awkwardly onto the ground.

Typical. She inelegantly bent down to try and pick it up – forward momentum plus the weight of the briefcase in her other hand, jerking her off balance.

"Here you go." A girl sitting nearest the aisle retrieved the bag, giving it a blatantly appreciative glance while handing it back. "Orla Kiely?"

"Yes it is, and thanks," she replied a little breathless. Sinking gratefully onto the seat, she put her briefcase on the floor and her prized handbag on her lap. The fashion label had since closed and thus these bags were rare as hen's teeth.

Dusting off her skirt, she shuffled exaggeratedly, trying to give a not-so-subtle hint to the guy beside her to move over. She'd noticed some extra padding on her ass lately, but his manspreading was ridiculous.

Catching the eye of an older lady sitting across the way, she flashed a conspiratorial smile. The woman was reading one of those fluffy romance novels and certainly didn't look to be on a work commute. Then again, she thought, catching sight of some guy in a tracksuit and briefcase pushing his way through the crowds, who knew what people might be up to?

Lucky thing, she thought eyeing the older woman's book and trying to remember the last time she had been able to lose herself in a cosy read.

Speaking of which . . . She reached for her briefcase and withdrew the documents for this morning's meeting. Cosy reading it wasn't.

Her idle musing was cut off by an overpowering, ear-splitting screech. *What the hell?* Heart leaping, she instinctively put her hands to her ears.

Then the carriage began to shudder, her body tensed and the

hairs on the back of her neck stood up. She looked wildly around, wondering if everyone else was experiencing the same thing.

Yes, the older woman across from her looked terrified, confused . . . everyone looked bewildered . . . and then there was an almighty roar, a sound so deafening it was unlike anything she'd ever witnessed.

Her heart hammered and her brain flooded with even more excruciating noise . . . then her seat jerked. . . and time slowed to a crawl. Until surreally, the entire carriage lifted and the vehicle seemed to be travelling in thin air.

But that couldn't possibly be, she reassured herself, before a tremendous force winched her out of her seat.

Trains couldn't fly. Could they?

TWO

The typically self-assured and flawlessly composed journalist was ragged and white-faced as she looked unseeingly into the camera. In her earpiece, she heard a voice from the news studio.

"Our correspondent, Clare Rogers is now live at the scene of this morning's tragedy. Clare, can you tell us anything concrete at this point?"

"Emergency services have just arrived at the location, so details are sketchy at this time." Clare's voice trembled as she spoke. "All I can confirm is that a train on the morning coastal commuter route to Dublin City has derailed and crashed at Sandymount Beach."

"Any indication as to what might have caused this horrific incident?" the news anchor prompted.

"Again we can't confirm any details at present. Rail Ireland will be making an official statement soon. But I spoke to some witnesses earlier – motorists stopped at the level crossing – who helped me reconstruct the scene. They saw or rather heard, the train braking from some distance, suggesting that the driver may have identified a problem with the signal. The locomotive derailed a few yards from the gates, careered across the tracks and crashed through a stone wall before ending up on the beach here behind us." Clare swallowed hard. "Luckily, there was no southbound train passing at the time," she added solemnly.

"So the driver tried to avoid crashing?"

"Again, we're just not sure. No doubt there will be a full investigation in time, but at the moment the emphasis is of course on the rescue effort."

"Signal failure, something that's unusual for our rail network, isn't it?" Richard went on – intent on getting to the bottom of the situation.

"Correct. Derailments are sadly more common for our neighbours in the UK, given that multiple rail companies operate there. The system is fine-tuned but signals can occasionally be confused. Which," she added, struggling to keep her voice even, "can lead to incidents like this."

"But we have only one rail carrier in Ireland, thus such mistakes are rare."

"Usually. But in recent months, Rail Ireland has been carrying out upgrades throughout the network. Although it is only speculation at this stage – and again, the company will issue a statement soon – it would appear that the signalling system on this particular crossing failed."

"Which would have serious implications for all involved," Richard finished.

"Very serious implications indeed," Clare agreed, her voice grim. "At this time of the morning, the train is packed with commuters, regular users of this busy city route, and – as I'm sure viewers can tell from our footage – there's likely a high incidence of serious injury and undoubtedly some fatality too."

"Thank you, Clare – we'll come back to you later for the Rail Ireland press conference."

Live footage of the wreck disappeared, and the feed cut back to the newsroom, where the anchor looked somberly into the camera.

"Our thoughts and prayers go out to any viewers at home with loved ones onboard the coastal service this morning. Stay tuned for further updates."

THREE

SIX MONTHS EARLIER

Rosie Mitchell waited patiently at the platform. The train was a little bit late this morning, she noted, checking her watch. Not that it mattered to her. A mid-sixties retiree, she was long past the morning rush.

Thank goodness for the train all the same, otherwise she'd be stuck. Her late husband Martin had always been the one to do the driving and often encouraged her to learn, but she never had any interest.

Luckily her home town of Lakeview was the first stop on the commuter route to Dublin. She and her family had lived for decades in the popular tourist village, centred around the broad oxbow lake from which it took its name. The fact that it had direct train access to the capital made it even more popular with visitors and relocating city families.

Rosie liked the train and enjoyed being able to sit back on the journey and admire the picturesque coastal view, gaze at the birds weaving in and out over the cliffs at Greystones, or stare in awe at the crystal clear waters of beautiful Killiney Bay.

Or if the day was cloudy and the scenery not so spectacular, she would read a book. Sometimes she'd be so stuck in the story that she didn't notice the hour or so journey.

So she wouldn't dream of getting a car. What was the point? The station was a short walk from her house, and with the service running multiple times a day, she had plenty of options. She could nip into the city whenever she fancied and her friend Sheila's new place was close to the rail line, as was her daughter Sophie's house.

For the moment anyway.

The train finally pulled in, and Rosie stood back, patiently waiting until the cluster of younger commuters were seated before she boarded. The upside of this was that she wouldn't get pushed and shoved. Since putting her back out in a badminton match a few months ago, her balance wasn't as sure as it used to be, and she liked to take her time. Course, the downside of waiting was that she was often left without a seat. But Rosie didn't mind. These people all had a hard slog ahead of them, whereas she didn't have a care in the world.

In fact, wasn't she the lucky one – a lady of leisure meeting with her daughter? She'd hate to have to face into work now like her fellow passengers. You could see the stress and strain in their expressions – all preoccupied with whatever awaited them. It was a shame really; the lengths people had to go to these days just to keep their heads above water.

It had been a lot different when she and Martin were starting out. Neither of them had to spend hours commuting and they were the better for it.

Her husband had worked in his father's gardening business in Lakeview since he was old enough to use a trowel, and Rosie had worked in the tourist office. They'd bought a house close to town so she could walk to work, while Martin went off in his van to wherever he happened to be working that day.

She smiled sadly as she thought of her beloved husband. There wasn't a day that she didn't think of him, or miss him, but she couldn't complain. They'd had a wonderful marriage, two healthy children, and in all their years together rarely a cross word had passed between them.

They'd both known that the day would come when she would be left on her own. High blood pressure was in Martin's family and when he suffered two near-fatal heart attacks in his latter years, it became clear that a simple change in lifestyle or medication wasn't going to save him. But it was lovely that he'd died doing what he loved, tending the roses out in the back garden – the evening sun just beginning to fade when Rosie found him.

Eighteen months ago she had buried the one great love of her life, having made him a promise that she would keep going, keep laughing and smiling and enjoying life, so that it wouldn't seem all that long until she saw him again. At times it was hard but Rosie was doing her best to keep that promise.

Anyway, she was very lucky. Her two adult children were happily married and with good jobs, David to a lovely Liverpool girl named Kelly (there was no sign of kids yet, and Rosie wouldn't dream of asking) and working as a builder in the UK.

Sophie and her husband Robert had toddler Claudia and good jobs too, but were still on the hunt for a house. That was another hardship for the younger generation. House prices in Dublin were obscene.

Today her daughter was taking Rosie to view a house she had her eye on.

"Mum, it's just ... perfect," she'd gushed on the phone the day before. "You've simply *got* to see it."

While she was delighted with her daughter's enthusiasm Rosie couldn't help feeling a little disappointed that Sophie would want to live so far away on the other side of the capital.

Still, it would be nice to see the three of them settled somewhere other than the city centre rental they were in now. There wasn't much space in an apartment, and with Claudia hitting the terrible twos, it couldn't be good for them all to live in what was basically one big room. With luck, this house Sophie wanted her to see today was a tidy semi-d like Rosie's own, with a small garden for Claudia to run around in.

The train emptied some of its passengers at the first city stop, and Rosie sank gratefully onto a recently-vacated seat.

Her back had been giving her a bit of trouble lately, and as much as she tried to tell herself otherwise, there was no denying that she was starting to feel the effects of advancing age.

Despite how energetic and cheerful she might want to feel, she *wasn't* getting any younger, was she? Rosie smiled. She definitely wasn't one of those glamorous granny types. With their coloured hair, perfect make-up and up-to-the-minute fashion, these women looked for all the world like they were still in the first flush of youth.

Sophie had injections into her face to keep the wrinkles at bay, which sounded horrific, but that wasn't Rosie's way. No, she was going to let her auburn hair go as grey as it liked, and her skin as wrinkly as it wanted – weren't these marks of a life lived? Getting older was nothing to be ashamed of and as much as you might like to, you couldn't outrun time.

But today Rosie wasn't running anywhere, she chuckled, getting off the train at Connolly Station and heading to the nearest bus stop. Shame that Sophie's car was in for a service today, otherwise her daughter could've collected her. Because today's train had been late, Rosie had missed the usual bus connection, but such was life.

She reached into her bag and took out the novel she was reading to pass the time.

The bus duly arrived, and forty or so minutes later, Rosie finally reached her daughter's apartment building.

She took extra care selecting the right buzzer, always afraid that she'd push the wrong one and wake up some poor misfortunate sleeping off night duty or something. Originally from County Clare, and despite living in Lakeview for all of her married life, she still couldn't shake off the 'small village inferiority complex' as her husband used to call it.

Rosie called it good manners and concern for a fellow human being, but outgoing and confident all his life, Martin didn't understand.

Nor it seemed, did Sophie.

"Mum, I'm just drying my hair – can you hold on for five minutes?" her daughter's voice blared tinnily through the speaker.

"No problem," Rosie replied agreeably, although the coastal chill was making her fingers numb.

"Hi!" It was a good ten minutes before Sophie appeared downstairs, dark hair sleek and shiny, and make-up beautifully applied. Her daughter always looked so stylish, and today she was dressed in a gorgeous fitted suit, something that even Rosie's inexperienced eye could see had cost an arm and a leg.

But it couldn't have cost that much because Sophie and Robert were mad saving for this house. Knowing her daughter's incredible talent for spotting a bargain, she had probably picked up the outfit for next to nothing.

"Sorry about keeping you waiting, but I think you were a little early – I said ten thirty, didn't I?"

Sophie could be a little bit scatty sometimes.

"No, the train was late actually – where's Claudia?" Rosie stepped into the hallway, eager to get out of this cold. Although it was supposed to be summer, the Irish seasons generally set their own agenda.

Sophie linked her mother's arm and steered her back outside. "With the childminder of course. I couldn't bring her with us – we'd have no peace with her wailing and whinging and *touching* everything."

"Oh." Rosie was disappointed. She had been looking forward

to spending time with her only granddaughter. "Maybe we could pick her up after?"

"Ah Tracy offered to take her for the day – she knows I need the break," Sophie answered dismissively. "And of course, she won't say no to the money either." Rosie nodded reluctantly as her daughter chattered on. "Oh, Mum, I am just *dying* for you to see this place – it is truly incredible!"

"I'm sure it is, pet, but don't get your hopes up too much either, OK? You know yourself there's a lot of competition out there and – "

"Mum, this is ours – I just know it is!"

As they ambled towards the residents' carpark, Rosie had to smile at her daughter's enthusiasm. She had been the very same as a youngster, always full of excitement and mischief.

The kids had been quite the handful growing up, and while Martin always insisted that Rosie spoiled and sheltered them too much, she was proud to say that they had both turned out well. 'A credit to them,' her own mother might have said, had she been alive today to see it.

"And I thought we might go for a nice lunch and a chat after – what do you think?"

Rosie was thrilled. A good old gossip with her daughter was long overdue. Although they spoke on the phone, she hadn't seen Sophie in a while, and she wanted to tell her all her news and she wouldn't mind confiding in someone about how her back was starting to give her a bit more trouble and . . .

She was startled when the flashy yellow sports car in front of them beeped noisily.

"What do you think?" Sophie grinned, proudly waving keys.

"Is this yours?" Rosie gasped in confusion. A brand new car? Despite herself, she couldn't help feeling a bit hurt. If her car was no longer giving trouble, why hadn't Sophie collected her from the station instead of having her wait twenty minutes in the cold and then another twenty on the bus? And how on earth would they get a child seat into that tiny thing?

"Yep," Sophie confirmed happily.

"But what about the old one? The one that was giving you trouble."

"I told you it was having a service because I wanted this to be a surprise." Sophie looked a bit crestfallen. "Don't you like it?"

"Of course I do." Now Rosie felt guilty. "It's lovely, pet – I can't wait to get a spin in it."

"Well, you won't have long to wait!" Her good humour restored, Sophie opened the driver-side door and sat princess-like at the steering wheel, while her mother eased herself into the passenger seat. She tilted the rear-view mirror and applied a fresh coat of lipstick. "Ready?" she asked, turning the key in the ignition.

Rosie's back ached from trying to manoeuvre herself into what amounted to little more than a biscuit tin. Sophie's swerving and quick lane-changing all the way to Malahide didn't help much.

About fifteen minutes later, they pulled onto a quiet tree-lined avenue.

Rosie was certain that behind all those expensive wrought-iron gates, intercoms and granite stonework were equally expensive houses – houses way beyond the reach of a part-time insurance clerk and her department store manager husband. There was a For Sale sign outside the one at the end, but surely they couldn't even *dream* of . . .

But Sophie slowed the car in front of the gates, rolled down the window and pushed the intercom button.

"Sophie Morris," she announced in a haughty voice that Rosie had never heard her use before.

"Love, surely you couldn't be thinking of buying a house like this? It must cost an absolute fortune."

"Well, in the scheme of things, it isn't that expensive," she replied airily. "Anyway, I just want you to take a look at it first and see what you think. We'll discuss the rest later."

The rest? What rest? Rosie wanted to ask.

But then it hit her. Just then she realised why Sophie was so eager to show her this house today, why her daughter had been so cheerful and attentive these last few weeks.

She had to give her credit, to be fair. Sophie had bided her time and had waited until well after her father's death before she once again raised The Question.

Now, she felt sad and more than a little used. She supposed she should have known better than to think that her daughter had brought her all the way out here just to get her opinion. Sophie didn't need an opinion – her mind was already made up.

And deep down Rosie knew that this time she probably *would* give in. In truth, she would have that first time too, only Martin wouldn't hear of it. Her husband had been dead set against the idea and that had been the end of the matter.

Until now.

As they approached the admittedly beautiful, but eyewateringly expensive house, Rosie sighed inwardly. Martin would not be happy with her – not happy at *all*.

END OF EXCERPT.

Continue reading THE GETAWAY, *out now.*

ABOUT THE AUTHOR

International #1 and USA Today bestselling author Melissa Hill lives in County Wicklow, Ireland.

Her page-turning emotional stories of family, friendship and romance have been translated into 25 different languages and are regular chart-toppers internationally.

A Reese Witherspoon x Hello Sunshine adaptation of her worldwide bestseller SOMETHING FROM TIFFANY'S is streaming now on Amazon Prime Video.

THE CHARM BRACELET aired in 2020 as a holiday movie, A Little Christmas Charm. A GIFT TO REMEMBER (and a sequel) was also adapted for screen by Crown Media, and multiple other titles by Melissa are currently in development for film and TV.

Visit her website at
www.melissahill.info
Or get in touch via social media below.

Made in the USA
Middletown, DE
30 June 2024